WHISPERED CURSES

PLAGUE AND MAGIC
BOOK 1

S.D. GREDELL

To my husband. My biggest supporter, my favorite person, and my forever.

PROLOGUE

In the middle of a sprawling forest, away from the rest of the world, lay the heart of Sylvan Reach. My home, though it had never really felt like one. A place where ancient trees loomed impossibly high overhead, the wind through their leaves seeming to croon mystical secrets to those who would listen hard enough. Their branches were like wizened fingers, just waiting to snatch up any passersby who dared tread too close. The air felt alive with magic in a way that you just didn't experience anywhere else in Aethralis. It made your skin tingle, your hair stand up on end.

My heart pounded as I walked hand-in-hand with my parents, sweat slicking my palms. The elders were always talking amongst themselves about how the village we came from had stood for thousands of years as a secret haven of greenery and mana, where the air was thick with the scent of blooming flowers and the trills of birds. And I supposed it was, but I just didn't see it the same way. It was beautiful, sure, but I didn't see it as this amazing place they made it out to be.

The Arcane Order, or the council of mages, had long held dominion here. I'd grown up hearing about how respected and revered we are while in classes, though I didn't know how true that is. Maybe if I got a good enough gift, everyone would give me some of the same respect, too. I could hope.

As my parents walked us through the forest, thoughts of my future tumbled through my head, each one coming faster as I grew more excited.

What would my gift be? Would it be useful? Would my parents finally be proud?

Maybe I would gain an affinity for fire and be able to become a forge master, able to bend the strongest metals to the will of my powerful flames. Or I could become a healer, fixing diseases and injuries. Maybe even able to fall into others' dreams like a Dreamweaver! The possibilities felt endless.

I released my father's hand and toyed with my hair as we continued our walk, the wavy strands of white flowing through my fingers like pale moonlight. My anticipation was becoming unbearable, my heart fluttering in my chest like a trapped bird. I'd thought of this moment for so, so long. And it was about to happen. I swallowed thickly.

"Are you ready, Lyra?" At my mother's words, my eyes snapped up to hers, breaking me out of my thoughts. She gave my hand a comforting squeeze, though there was a hint of worry in her honey-brown eyes. "I can't wait to see what gift you are blessed with." She had such a warm smile as she said it. Maybe I imagined the worry? All I knew was that I didn't want to disappoint her.

Wordlessly, I nodded, though my hands shook. I kept twisting my hair around and around my fingers. It was a nervous habit I'd had for as long as I could remember. We were approaching a circle of stones; the air crackled with charged magical energy. The hair on the back of my neck stood on end the closer we got to the line of stones. Despite the intensity of this place, our destination looked fairly ordinary, though animals avoided crossing the threshold, butterflies and birds carefully flitting around the circle. Absently, I wondered why, or what would happen if they crossed the circle. Would something happen to them?

My stomach churned, and those thoughts turned to ash, forgotten. Glancing between my parents, tears welled up in my eyes, though I refused to cry. I'd always felt so different from my parents. They looked ordinary. My mother had chestnut brown hair with warm brown eyes that always made me think of honey. And my father, tall but somewhat meek, with sandy blonde hair and green eyes. Both unassuming, fitting exactly where they should within the Order.

And then there was me, with my snowy white hair cascading in waves down my back and strange violet eyes. My skin was pale and smooth, so different from the bronzed skin of my family. Although my parents never for a second made me feel out of place, I had heard the whispers from the village elders.

They muttered about how I couldn't possibly be from our village, how they'd never seen a child born who looked like me.

Some even suggested I might not be fully human. Their words, though not meant for my ears, had always made me feel like an outsider in my own home. I knew my parents had probably heard worse, and I wanted to make them proud more than anything. It wasn't fair to them to have a child like me.

Shaking my head to dislodge those dark thoughts, I loosed a shaky breath. Before I could take a step, however, my father's hand shot out and grabbed my wrist, stilling me. He knelt in front of me and brushed away tears I didn't even realize had fallen.

"You got this, Lyr. I know it's scary because you don't know what your power will be, but I'm here. It's okay." Father's face was serious, but he gave me a wobbly smile. With a comforting embrace, he kissed my forehead and gave me a tight squeeze. I gave Father a small smile in return. Determination filled me and I turned back to the circle of stones.

I could do this. I *would* do this.

I could feel the magic humming beneath my skin as I stepped into the glade, just shy of being painful, its power almost overwhelming. The sunlight dappled through the canopy, casting comforting patterns that danced upon the forest floor in contrast to the pressure of the power contained here. I closed my eyes, taking in a deep breath of the sweet-scented air, and felt the energy dormant within me surge forth.

My body shimmered with light, and suddenly my bones were liquid fire, reshaping themselves with terrifying speed. One moment I was human, the next I stood on four paws, my senses overwhelmed by unfamiliar scents and sounds. Before I could even process the change, my form rippled again - bones hollowing, skin sprouting feathers, my vision sharpening until I could count the leaves on the furthest branches of the tallest trees.

Without thought, I was rapidly changing form, becoming an insect, to sprouting hooves, back to having wings and feathers. My heart beat erratically in my chest as I fought to control this power. My parents watched helplessly, their expressions masks of horror, unable to get me through this fight with my own magic.

I was panicking, spiraling, and I didn't know what to do.

Control. I needed control. Losing myself wasn't an option. I fought to still my body and my racing thoughts. My wings fell to the sides of my body and I took as deep of a breath as I could.

Become human. I repeated this in my mind, over and over, like a mantra.

I pictured myself in my mind's eye, concentrating heavily. Time passed. It could have been seconds, or days, for all I knew. I imagined the texture of my hair, the weight of my body, the feeling of my dress. My feathers began to dissolve into tendrils of ethereal light. Within moments, the luminescence coalesced back into the figure of a young girl. I had done it!

But the joy was short-lived. My parents stared in shock, their faces pale and stricken. Father's hand reached out to me before falling back to his side as though he was afraid to actually touch me. Mother's face crumpled, her eyes filling and tears spilling down her cheeks as she whispered, "Change back. Now." Her voice shook, causing fear to spike through me. "Lyra! Change back!"

I shrank away as Mother yelled. She never yelled at me. Confused and afraid, I looked down at my hands, turning them this way and that. I didn't look any different. My lower lip trembled as my eyes filled. "W-What do you mean? I did!"

My mother pulled a small mirror from her purse, holding it up to my face with quaking hands. I reached out and held her clammy fingers while looking into a face both foreign and familiar.

My hair was no longer white, but the same chestnut brown hair as on my mother's head. And the eyes looking back at me were no longer the amethyst that I'd grown up seeing, but my father's eyes, mossy green. It was the way I had always wanted to look. Like I fit in with my family.

The exhilaration of the transformation was replaced by an icy dread, adrenaline coursing through my veins. My chest tightened as my father took a step forward, his expression a mix of fear and anger, grabbing me by the shoulders and shaking me.

"This cannot be," he said, as his fingers dug into my pale flesh, bruising it. His eyes were wild, shock written across his face. "Transformation?"

"T-transformation?" I breathed, unbelieving.

Being able to shift into the form of an animal was one thing. Uncommon amongst mages across Aethralis, but not unheard of. However, true transformation magic didn't allow just for changing into animals. You could become other people, change things about yourself and your appearance without a second thought.

My heart sank. Centuries ago, the last mage with this power had infiltrated courts and kingdoms, sowing discord that erupted into devastating wars. Their actions led to the exile of mages to Sylvan Reach, forever tarnishing our reputation. Transformation magic became synonymous with darkness and ruin.

Seeing the fear and shame in my parents' eyes, pain lanced through my chest. I understood their dread all too well.

My mother knelt beside me, clasping my hands in a white-knuckled grip. Her fingers trembled where they gripped me. Mother swallowed hard, seeming to weigh her words. Her brows furrowed, her lips drawn tight as she looked at me. "You must hide this, Lyra. If the Order finds out, they will exile you, or worse. This magic is dangerous. We will tell the others that you are without a gift. Promise us."

Fat tears streamed down my face, the weight of my secret pressing down on me. With great effort, I looked back at the mirror and willed myself back to normal. My mother whispered over and over that she refused to think of me any differently, her presence warm at my back despite the chill settled over my body.

It took some minutes, but eventually dull white crept back through the brown tresses, flowing to the ends. My own violet eyes stared back at me, empty and dark.

I vowed to bury my abilities deep within, to let no one know the truth. The glade, once a place of promise and hope, now felt like a prison of isolation and uncertainty, suffocating me as I stood there with its oppressive power.

And yet...

Despite the fear, the shame, the contempt that I felt for this 'gift' I had been burdened with... it whispered to me.

And I wanted to listen.

CHAPTER 1

Fourteen years had passed since that day in the glade, but the memory still stung like a fresh wound just as much as it did when it happened. My face darkened as the shadows grew across the forest floor, a reminder of that night. The scent of oil and fire, the sounds of desperate, angry shouts, feeling my mother's tears hot against my skin as she gave me one last quick embrace before shoving me away. Now I stood on the edge of that same forest that had long ago felt like home more than anywhere else, even if the village within never did. I scoffed and turned away from those memories that stabbed at me like shards of glass. That was so long ago now. Dwelling on the past wouldn't change it, no matter how much I may wish otherwise.

Instead, I turned my gaze to the sky. The sun was lowering, painting the sky with burnt umber and tangerine, bleeding into the shadows of the forest like a fresh wound. The pack on my shoulders felt that much heavier being close to this place, but I ignored the weight digging into my flesh.

My fingers lightly traced the edges of my black cloak, which was lined with a delicate silver filigree. It was a gift from my mother that I had received the week before my exile. It felt soft beneath my touch, and I've done my best to maintain it over the years, though some parts had been obviously mended by someone with a less than steady hand. I tugged my hood up a little higher, ensuring that my hair and face were obscured. Now was not the time to be seen.

Once I had come of age, I did my best to hide my ability, shoving the magic down deep despite how much it hurt. This had made me even more of an outcast. Having no ability at all was almost unheard of, but I had to make them think that rather than risk being found out. Not that it mattered much in the end. I couldn't just let the power within me fester. It was like wearing clothes that were too tight. The mana just builds, until you feel you can't hold it in anymore. And the one time I tried to expel it safely, privately…

I angrily threw that line of thinking away and scanned the familiar paths, alert to any signs of the Arcane Order's watchful eyes. Though I had mastered the art of concealing my magic, the fear of discovery never truly left me.

The Arcane Order, or the Order for short, was an ancient and revered society, its origins lost to the mists of time. Comprised of the most skilled and knowledgeable of mages, they were the guardians of the mystical arts, ensuring that the delicate balance of magic in Sylvan Reach was maintained. The Order's influence extended far beyond their village, their reputation known throughout all the lands.

In the thousands of years since mage-kind had been segregated from the rest of Aethralis, the tensions had slackened enough to allow for the occasional troupe of mages to be found outside of Sylvan Reach. These wandering mages were also the responsibility of the Order, who would dispatch members to bring in any rogue magic-user found to be causing trouble, or who had made their way to places they shouldn't go.

My parents, Selene and Gregor were high-ranking members of the Order, as were most of my ancestors. The villagers looked at me with a mixture of awe and suspicion. I knew they hated me. They didn't do a good job of hiding it. Not that I could blame them. I didn't look like I fit in. I was an 'other', easy to revile. And when I slipped up and my powers were discovered, they tried to kill me without a second thought. With a pit growing in my stomach, I pushed the memory away, refusing to think about it any further. To be dragged back to that time.

Honestly, I hated being close to Sylvan Reach. It just reminded me of darker times. I pulled my cloak closer to my body and turned away with a heavy sigh, setting myself back on the path towards what would hopefully be a new life.

For days, the forest stretched endlessly alongside me as I made my way along a well-worn trail, branches reaching out like fingers as if to pull me back to Sylvan Reach. I brushed that eerie feeling aside as I made my way toward the village of Haleshade. The paths that normally would have been busy with travelers were instead eerily quiet. I'd not seen another person in at least a day, whereas usually I would see groups together making their way through from village to village. It was strange, but I attributed it to Haleshade being a smaller, out of the way place. Which is exactly why I chose it.

Though I was careful and seldom used my ability, rumor spread in Sylvan Reach that I had cursed magic. Eventually, the whispers and mutterings, the avoidance and fear became too much, and I was attacked at 16 years of age. I barely escaped with my life. I was incredibly lucky because they did not hold back despite my young age.

For the last ten years, I had wandered Aethralis on my own and I'd heard of this village in passing during those travels. Sounds like a quaint, unassuming village where others had started over. No one would look for you there. I hated to travel in this part of Aethralis, but if I had a hope of a new beginning, I felt it could be there. If I was lucky.

Leaves crunched underfoot as I trod along, breaking the stillness of the earth. I pulled my cloak tighter around me, fending off the chill as the wind whipped through the trees. My journey had been long and arduous, each step a reminder of the life I no longer lived, the person I no longer was.

As I emerged from the tree line, the village of Haleshade came into view—a quaint little cluster of modest cottages and thatched roofs nestled amidst the ancient forest. Smoke curled lazily from chimneys, blending with the mist that hung low through the streets. Unlike the last few villages I'd passed, this one showed some signs of life, which was comforting. The others had been almost unnervingly still, windows shuttered no matter the time of day, streets empty except for windblown leaves and dirt that wasn't cleared away. Here, the air was thick with the scent of wood smoke and grilled meats, a stark contrast to the pine and damp I'd grown accustomed to during my travels here.

I hesitated at the edge of the village. Mages outside of Sylvan Reach could often be regarded with much distrust, especially when traveling on their own. I had experienced it often myself, which is why they typically traveled in groups of at least three strong. Safety in numbers, I suppose, though I had never been afforded that opportunity.

The villagers moved about their daily lives, their faces a mixture of curiosity and suspicion as they glanced in my direction. I pulled my hood in tighter and willed my hair to change color.

A trickle of power escaped me as my tresses darkened to a rich mahogany. Using my magic felt like a hug from an old friend I never got to see, or taking a deep breath after nearly drowning. But I had to be careful. I couldn't get too used to that sensation, no matter how much it softened the ache of pushing my magic down deep all the time.

With a deep breath, I steeled myself for whatever may come in this village. Hopefully, it was less 'interesting' than the last one.

I shuddered as the memory flit across my mind. Some mages

from Sylvan Reach recognized me from my white hair and violet eyes. They turned the whole town against me before I could even introduce myself.

Never again, I thought, and have kept my hair and eyes hidden since.

However, before I could do the same magic to the amethyst of my eyes, a voice broke through the quiet hum of the village—a short, older woman with silver-gray hair twisted into a knot on the top of her head strode with authority towards me. My heart immediately sank. She wore a sky-blue dress with an ivory apron, the scent of baked goods wafting towards me as she stopped a few feet away on the packed dirt of the road.

"I've never seen you around here before." Her tone was immediately distrusting, her dark eyes looking me up and down. "My name is Nora. What can we do for you?"

I cleared my throat. "Lyra. I'm just wanting to settle down. I was hoping to stay here."

Her eyes narrowed. "Stay here," she repeated flatly. "A mage? What can you even do? What is your gift?" She crossed her narrow arms and planted her feet, somehow seeming larger despite her slight frame. I was used to these kinds of questions by now.

"I wasn't blessed." I let shame crawl into my voice, putting just a hint of a catch at the end.

Nora's brows rose. "Not blessed, hmm? So no magic at all? That's a pretty fancy cloak for a magicless mage." She gestured to my outfit to punctuate her words.

"My mother was one of the Order. My family was so

ashamed of me for not being blessed with magic that I thought it better to leave." I looked to the ground, doing my best to appear distraught. "I brought my mother's cloak so I wouldn't forget where I came from and so I could keep some part of her close."

Nora made a non-committal noise, and I looked up through my lashes to see that she was weighing my words. She glanced over her shoulder and barked out, "Hey, Griffin! Come over here."

My gaze snapped up to see a man approaching, his stride confident and purposeful. He moved like a predator, each step deliberate and near-silent, even on the cobblestone. He was tall and built with lean muscle, his tousled chestnut hair catching the fading sunlight. But it was his eyes that really drew my attention—golden as summer honey and just as warm, despite his wary expression. His presence somehow charged the air, almost like the moment before a thunder strike. My skin prickled and my magic to surged against its bonds within me, responding to something wild and untamed within him. I viciously shoved it down before it could surface, ignoring the pain it caused.

I wondered what he was. He didn't seem to be human like the rest of the villagers I'd seen thus far. There was just an aura about him that screamed 'other' and a subtle predatory grace to his movement that put me on edge. His clothes were simple and threadbare but well maintained, a testament to a life lived outside of any major cities or towns.

"Hey, Nora. Who's this?" he asked, stopping a few paces away from me. His tone was guarded, his gaze assessing my face, pausing when he saw the color of my eyes. As he continued to stare, a strange feeling curled in up in my belly that I couldn't quite place.

Nora shrugged. "A magicless mage, according to her. I don't quite know what to think of it. What do you think?"

White hot anger speared me while they talked as though I wasn't even here. Like I couldn't hear them. *What the hell is with these people?* I swallowed down my irritation and chose instead to stare daggers at the pebbles interspersed on the ground. I don't want to make a poor impression, given that I'm planning to live here.

I could feel the man, Griffin, looking at me with such intensity I felt as though my body would catch fire. I felt so exposed in a way I'd never felt before, like he was stripping away all of my layers I'd carefully built up to hide myself. It was very uncomfortable, and I shifted from foot to foot.

A pair of worn black boots stepped into view and a strong, calloused hand gripped my chin, lifting it. Up close, I could see a dusting of hair along his jaw, my eyes trailing up his face. I jerked my gaze from his lips to the warm honey of his gaze. I swallowed, my mouth suddenly dry. His voice was deep and rough when he asked, "What are you doing here?"

"Looking for a place to stay," I replied, jerking my chin from his grasp. I would not be bullied away from another village. There was an odd tension building in my body, adrenaline coursing through me, but I straightened my shoulders and lifted my chin. "I heard Haleshade welcomes outsiders." I took a step back despite myself.

He narrowed his eyes and cocked his head curiously, studying me. "What's your name?"

"Lyra," I answered, meeting his gaze head-on. "And yours?"

"I'm Griffin," he offered after a moment's hesitation. He had a lilt of an accent I couldn't place. Absently, I wondered where in Aethralis he was from. "I live near here."

"I had heard Haleshade is a place where people like me can find refuge. People with nowhere else to go," I repeated stiffly, irritation flaring.

The intense presence of this man felt suffocating. I glanced over at Nora, standing behind Griffin and just watching this exchange, a thinly veiled mask of interest over her face.

Griffin regarded me for a long moment, his expression unreadable. I held my breath, oddly captivated by the flecks of amber in his golden eyes. "Maybe it is. I'm just keeping an eye out for troublemakers. You never know what type of people may look for a place like this."

"I'm not looking for trouble," I insisted, my frustration bubbling to the surface. I was just so *tired*. My feet were blistered, my legs shaking with the effort of remaining standing right now. Arguing isn't what I'd hoped for immediately after arriving. Maybe a day or two down the road, but not *immediately*. I loosed a defeated-sounding sigh and shifted my pack on my shoulder. "Just want to find a place where I can start over."

He studied me a moment longer, his arms crossed while he seemed to consider something. Then he nodded curtly. "Fine. Nora, I'll take care of this one." He gestured towards me. "Follow me."

Without another word, Griffin turned and walked away, leaving me to follow in his wake. Nora gave me a wave I scrambled after him. "Good luck."

As we navigated the narrow dirt streets of Haleshade, unease crept its icy fingers along my spine, leaving beads of sweat. Griffin's distrust was palpable, his wariness a reflection of the villagers' apprehension toward outsiders like me. It would take time to earn their trust, to be accepted here. But I was determined to try. I was tired of running all over Aethralis to find somewhere that accepted me. I would *make* them accept me if I had to.

This place was far enough away from everything and quiet enough that I felt like I could have a real chance here, and at first glance, it looked like nearly all the villagers were human aside from Griffin, so that was a plus.

My eyes traced the small buildings as we passed, the scent of wood smoke, roasting meat and baking bread filling the air. Better than waste and rot like some of the other smaller villages I'd been to. That was another check to another box. It was clean and well-maintained.

A breeze caught the earthy, woodsy scent of the forest and some small, tense part of me eased. It smelled like home. Distantly, I heard children's laughter and a small smile curled my lips at the sound. I could definitely get used to this place.

We reached a modest cottage outside of the edge of the village—a small, sturdy structure with a thatched roof and smoke curling quaintly from the chimney. Griffin held open the door, gesturing for me to enter.

"You can stay here," he said gruffly. His tone was still hard as he said. "But don't think for a second that I trust you."

"If you don't trust me, why let me stay here?" I crossed my arms, already irritated. Traveling all this way just to be treated like trash, yet again. "There's got to be some kind of inn or something in Haleshade, right? Why can't I just stay there?"

Griffin frowned, his brows lowering. "If you're nearby, I can make sure you're not trying to do anything strange or dangerous for the other villagers here. As far as the inn goes, that's not a possibility for you. Mages especially have to earn trust around here and that's including for places of hospitality. Even ones that claim they have no magic." Despite his gruff words, he wasn't hostile. It was enough to make me wonder if there was more to his offer than simple suspicion. But why?

I couldn't fault his logic. If I were him, I would likely do the same. Keep your enemies closer and all that. Given the undercurrent of pure power that emanated from him and his intense presence, I didn't doubt that he could take care of anyone with wicked intentions.

Begrudgingly, I nodded, although I refused to thank him. As I stepped inside, the scent of leather and musk enveloped me, decidedly pleasant and uniquely masculine. I tried to ignore the way it made my pulse ramp up. The warmth of a real hearth and solid walls made my body ache with a bone-deep weariness I hadn't allowed myself to feel during my travels. I was ready to sleep for a month straight, even if it wasn't the most welcoming place I'd ever been.

But for now, it was a start—a chance to prove myself, and perhaps, to carve out a place where I could finally belong.

We entered a small living room and Griffin came in behind me, closing the door with a soft click. Various animal pelts adorned the wall, and the furniture looked handmade with expert craftsmanship. There was a stone hearth near the attached kitchen with dying flames that just barely stove off the chill from the changing weather. I was impressed despite myself. Maybe he was a woodworker? Artisan? It seemed like more than a simple hobby.

Sunlight filtered in through a large window, casting warm, comforting patterns on the wooden floor. There was another doorway opposite to us, a small hallway leading further into the cottage. It felt decidedly cozy, enveloping us in soft masculinity.

A surprisingly dainty table sat in the middle of the room, with two matching chairs on either side. It was ash gray and circular, with something around the edges and a knife laid in the center.

He definitely seems surprisingly crafty, I thought, placing my hand on the edge of the table and leaning in to look closer. They were gorgeous carvings of animals. Maybe a hunter? My eyes traced the pelts on the wall, the hunting knife on the table. The blade glinted with sunlight and looked as though it had been recently cleaned and polished. Definitely a hunter, I decided.

I turned to Griffin and asked, "I'm guessing this is your house?"

Griffin nodded, his amber eyes tracing the walls and furniture within. "Yes, I built this place myself," he replied, his voice gruff, but with a hint of pride. "You can stay here for now. Just remember, this village isn't like wherever you may have come from. I won't have a problem forcing you out if you start trouble."

His words were a reminder of the position I found myself in once again. Untrusted. A stranger in a place where gossip rules, and trust was hard-earned. I fought against the urge to scoff and nodded instead, already tired from my journey to get here.

"Yep, I got it," I murmured, glancing around the room once more. I slowly turned in a circle, then stopped. My eyes met his. The amber of his eyes seemed to glow from within, and I found myself unable to look away. Silence lapsed between us, a lingering tension hung in the air.

Griffin hesitated, his gaze lingering on mine for a moment longer before he turned away, busying himself with crouching to stoke the fire in the hearth, the cheery flames chasing away the chill. All the tension left the room, and I loosed a breath I didn't realize I was holding, tucking a loose curl behind my ear. The crackling of the wood filled the hush, casting flickering shadows across the room.

"So, where will I sleep?" I asked after another beat of silence, waving my hand vaguely around the room. There didn't seem to be a bed out here.

Griffin quickly stood, gesturing to the doorway I noticed earlier. "You'll stay back here."

I cautiously followed as he headed through the doorway, leading down a short hallway. There were three rooms at the end. A minuscule bathroom containing a toilet and a small curtained off area for bathing, along with a tiny washbasin, and two modest bedrooms across the hallway from each other.

He pointed to the door to the right of the bathroom, stating,

"This will be your room. I'll be across the hall, so don't think about doing anything funny."

I fought the urge to roll my eyes, and lost. "Despite what you may think of me, I have no nefarious plans, let me assure you."

His lip curled as though he was fighting a smile. I glanced at the room that would be mine, at least for the time being. I was going to be staying in a house with a man. My gaze slid to him briefly before I continued looking over what was to be my room. My heart fluttered, nervous energy filling me, before I tamped it down. I didn't need to be afraid of him. I was strong, too.

And he doesn't know what I can do, I thought sternly.

A narrow bed took up most of the floor space. It was simply decorated with a woolen blanket adorned with flowers, along with a chest of drawers at the foot of the bed. A ceramic vase sat there, full of wildflowers. The vibrancy of the colors was a stark contrast to the otherwise muted tones in the room.

Who was this room for? I wondered. I turned to look at the other bedroom, however Griffin blocked my view, closing the door.

"You don't need to worry about my room. It's nothing special," he grumbled.

"What do I need to do to repay your *kindness* in letting me stay here?" I asked bluntly. He didn't give me much of a choice, but it was at least some place to stay.

Griffin's golden eyes flickered with a mixture of surprise and something akin to amusement. He scratched the stubble on his chin thoughtfully before responding, his voice low and measured. I found my gaze drawn to the movement of his hand before looking away.

"Well, for starters, you could help with chores around here," he suggested, gesturing vaguely to the rustic surroundings. "Aid in keeping the place tidy, chopping firewood, things like that."

His eyes met mine as he murmured, "I'm not used to having company, so it'd be nice to have an extra hand." He dragged a hand across the back of his neck, looking as though he felt uncomfortable. There was a hint of vulnerability in his admission that caught me off guard.

He didn't seem the type to show weakness to others. I understood, since I was feeling the same. Frankly, I didn't want to stay here any longer than I needed to.

I nodded. "Fair enough. I can do that," I replied. His request was simple, at least.

He nodded back and lowered his hand, the corners of his mouth turning up in a faint smile. "Good. It's not much, but it'll keep you busy. As for food, you're on your own," he stated, turning back towards the living room. "There's a market in the village, and most folks trade for goods or hunt their own."

"That's fine," I said with a shrug, watching him move away. "I can take care of myself."

Griffin's voice carried from the other room. "I'm sure you can."

I dropped off my meager belongings atop the chest of drawers in the right-side bedroom. The few items I carried with me fit into a small satchel, and I would likely keep it that way. Who knows when I would have to leave, or how quickly? A faint floral scent tickled my nose as I lingered in that room. *My* room, at least for now. I inhaled deeply and steeled myself.

I meandered back out into the living area to find Griffin sitting at the table with a carving knife, whittling a small piece of wood, his gaze intense with concentration. He glanced up at me as I walked in.

Before I could even open my mouth, he said, "Look, I'm not one for small talk or idle chatter. If you need something, ask. Otherwise, we keep to ourselves. Understand?" His intense aura seemed to flare, filling the small room. It was suffocating. I took a small step back.

I felt my hackles rise and before I could stop myself, I blurted, "You don't have to be so rude."

A smirk curled Griffin's lip as though he enjoyed getting a rise out of me. That just irritated me further, and I huffed a breath. As much as I craved a sense of belonging, I knew I would be hard pressed to find it here. If I had to hide one of the biggest parts of myself, I may as well be alone. There was no way to truly belong if I couldn't be open in that way, but I would have to make do, I supposed.

My shoulders sagged despite myself. I may never truly be able to be myself. Never truly belong. But with time, maybe I could pretend here in this place. And who knows? After long enough, maybe I wouldn't even have to do that.

Griffin's deep gaze lingered for a moment longer before he stood and turned away, moving toward the small kitchen area. "Make yourself at home, then," he muttered over his shoulder, his voice already distant as he rummaged through the drawers, looking for something.

As I watched him, I couldn't help but feel a little curious and a lot pissed off. He's the one asking me to stay here, and he's acting like he's doing me a huge favor.

With another sigh, I glanced around the cabin, realizing that this place, for better or worse, was now my refuge. As I turned back towards my bedroom, I found myself unsettled by the thought of Griffin's presence just across the hall. I shook my head and went to take a nap. I made sure to push the drawers in front of the door before I fell asleep.

CHAPTER 2

The weeks had dragged on since I had first stepped foot into Griffin's cabin, and life had settled into a steady, if uneasy, rhythm. Meanwhile, the quiet hum of the village had become a familiar din in the background of my days, a stark contrast to the constant and isolating unease I had felt in Sylvan Reach.

Sweat traced a line down my back under my modest gray dress. Blistering heat from the sun bore down on my pale skin, turning it a soft pink. If I wasn't careful, I would end up with a sunburn in no time. The air was thick with humidity from a recent rain. I wiped my brow, looking up into the clear azure sky, the sun bright overhead.

I had started a burgeoning vegetable garden beside the cabin. Honestly, it wasn't much, but it was enough for me to live off of for now between the small hunts I'd been able to take in the forest nearby. The recent rainfall had been very helpful, as I hadn't had to water my plants in a few days, although the air was stifling once you stepped outside into the summer heat.

As I knelt in the dirt, tending to the budding plants and pulling weeds, a sense of peace drifted over me. The scent of the dirt, the feeling of it sifting through my fingers, and the satisfaction of being rewarded with my small harvest provided exactly what I needed.

Absently, my mind drifted to my mother's garden back in Sylvan Reach. It was always full of random plants and herbs. She would take the time to carefully explain the different uses for them she used in her healing magic and show the differences between plants that could help or hurt someone. We used to kneel side-by-side in the dirt together, pulling weeds or sowing seeds, watering the greenery. It was nice, one of the few quiet moments that we would have together when I was younger.

As I worked, I heard the crunch of gravel on the nearby path and the sound jolted me from my memories. Ezra, the young apprentice blacksmith, was hauling a cart of supplies towards the village square.

He was a younger guy, maybe late teens or early 20s, with shortly cropped red hair and ruddy skin covered with freckles. He wore a dirty, short-sleeved white shirt and a blacksmith's apron, a dark pair of jeans and heavy boots. His hazel eyes met mine, and his usually cheerful expression dimmed, replaced by wariness. Like most people I'd seen recently, he seemed especially drawn and tired, though I didn't know why. Was there something going on I didn't know about?

"Morning," I called out, trying my best to sound friendly.

Maybe I could get some answers.

"Uh, yeah. Morning," he mumbled, his gaze darting between me and the path ahead. He gripped the cart handle tighter and picked up his pace. As he approached, I saw that his normally ruddy face was pale and there was a sheen of sweat on his brow despite the breeze.

"Wait," I said, standing. "I was just wondering—,"

As I spoke, Ezra stumbled, losing his grip on the cart and almost falling. I reached out to steady him, but he jerked back as though afraid of being burned.

"Are you okay?" I asked hesitantly, wringing my hands as I fought the urge to help. Not that anyone around here wanted help from me, but I couldn't help but try.

"I'm fine, fine," he muttered, but his gaze was unfocused. "Just tired. Exhausted."

He swayed on his feet before continuing his way down the path, his expression strangely dreamlike. I sighed, turning back to my plants. It seemed no matter how hard I tried, no one around here wanted to give me a chance. I ripped out a weed more harshly than I needed to and threw it aside in frustration. I would not keep trying to help where I wasn't wanted.

This behavior was strange, though, even for Ezra. I'd have to ask Griffin about it later. Griffin and I existed in a state of uneasy cohabitation. We rarely spoke, each of us occupying our own spaces, the silence between us thick with tension. Though he was less overt about it, I knew he still didn't trust me. And I didn't trust him, either. I knew nothing about him, and I preferred to keep it that way. The less attached I became, the easier it would be if and when I inevitably had to leave. But I'd have to risk it. I needed answers.

He spent his days hunting or carving, his presence a constant reminder of my precarious situation in Haleshade. Despite his gruff exterior and the intense aura surrounding him, he hadn't shown me any ill will. Yet, I couldn't shake the feeling of unease that crept over me during our rare moments together. The silence was oppressive, neither of us sure of what to say to the other.

Honestly, I didn't understand Griffin. He exuded such a powerful presence that I'd expected him to be more domineering, to demand explanations or obedience. Instead, his restraint put me even more on edge. I couldn't fathom his motives for allowing me to stay, and that uncertainty gnawed at me.

I did my best to be unobtrusive, acutely aware that my continued presence here depended entirely on his whim. The thought of being so dependent on someone else's goodwill made my skin crawl and set my teeth on edge. For now, I had no choice but to endure it.

Before I knew it, the sun hung low in the sky, painting the sky with scarlet and burnt orange. Just a few more weeds to pull and I'd be done. However, as I dug in to unearth the roots of a stubborn weed, a sharp pain arced through my arm and I jerked my hand back, startled. Looking closer, there was a piece of glass buried in the dirt, and it had opened a deep gash on my palm. Blood quickly welled up, and I inhaled sharply. Of course, this had to happen.

I stood up, carefully wiping the earth from my hands while warmth dripped down my left hand. A hiss escaped me, the wound burning. I needed to clean this, or I'd get an infection. A hint of movement crossed the peripheral of my vision and I turned towards the treeline, noticing Griffin approaching from the forest. There were a couple of rabbits slung over his shoulder and a smear of dirt across his face. He acknowledged me with a nod, his expression as unreadable as ever.

"Back from the hunt," he said, jerking his chin towards the dangling rabbits, his voice breaking the silence. He glanced towards my plot. "How's the garden coming along?"

I fought the urge to respond with an attitude, but couldn't suppress a small eye roll. "It's growing well enough." I said shortly, tucking my injured hand behind my back. Was he trying to make casual conversation?

"Good," he replied, looking out over the neat rows of plants. "That'll be useful. Keeps you from relying too much on the market."

This was so awkward. I didn't know why he was choosing to talk to me like this. It was easier to just ignore each other's existence.

It reminded me of the first week we'd been cohabitating. After a few days of living with Griffin, the tension had become unbearable.

I had tried my luck at the village inn, hoping for a bit more independence to really spread my wings and make a place for myself here without relying on him any longer.

The innkeeper, a rotund man named Toran, eyed me

suspiciously as I approached the counter. "We don't have any rooms available," he said gruffly, before I could even open my mouth.

I frowned, turning around to view the clearly empty lobby area. "You don't look very busy—,"

"Listen," Toran interrupted, leaning in close enough for me to smell the sour scent of old tobacco on his breath. "We don't know you. Griffin might've vouched for you, but that doesn't mean we trust you. Mages aren't welcome here unless they've earned it."

My cheeks burned with humiliation and fury as I turned and fled, the innkeeper's words running on repeat in my mind. It seemed I was more trapped than I'd realized. Like it or not, this cabin with Griffin was all I had for now, unless I gave up and left. It was a sobering thought.

I snapped out of my reverie with a small jolt. Realizing Griffin was staring at me expectantly, awaiting a response, I gave a curt nod as a breeze rustled through the trees, carrying the scent of pine and earth. "I think I'm managing alright."

Griffin's gaze roamed over my face with a strange intensity, and then he dropped the rabbits, striding over quickly. Before I could move, he reached behind me and grabbed my left wrist, looking over my injury. I craned my neck up to look at him and scowled.

"What happened?" Griffin asked. Despite his usual gruffness, there was an underlying steel to his words that surprised me. "Did someone hurt you?"

I sputtered for a moment before saying, "No, there was a piece of glass in the dirt that got my hand. I just need to go clean it and bandage it. It will be fine." He held my wrist gently as he turned my hand this way and that. The warmth of his touch was intense, fever-hot and overwhelming. I gazed into his golden eyes, my stomach doing flips despite the pain. But he didn't look up, instead dropping my wrist to stride into the cabin.

Flabbergasted by his behavior, I stood there dumbly, unsure what was going on. But he returned moments later, carrying a plant with a silvery sheen, the leaves metallic. "Chew on this. It'll help with pain and can prevent infection."

At my confused look, he clarified, "This is called silvermint. My mother used to grow it back where I grew up." He had a distant look on his face before shaking his head, as though to clear the memories. He pressed the plant into my uninjured hand and headed back over to pick up the rabbits I'd already forgotten about.

This was the first time anyone had shown me any kindness in years. Tears pricked my eyes, and I bit my lip, willing them away. Griffin gazed at me with one of his usual unreadable expressions, adjusting the rabbits on his shoulder.

Recently, I noticed him looking at me more often, especially when he thought I wasn't paying attention. Stealing glances when I'm reading or out and about and we cross paths. It made my stomach do flips for a reason I couldn't place. I found myself sneaking looks too, taking in the angles of his jaw, the way his hair fell in waves across his forehead. But I refused to get close to anyone. It never ended well.

"I'll go clean a rabbit for supper. If you need help with anything, let me know," he said, gruff as ever. The moment was over, but definitely not forgotten. A warmth suffused me as I plucked a couple of leaves and brought them to my mouth, chewing on the bitter foliage. But it had nothing to do with the plant and instead with the man who brought it to me.

The warm, comforting aroma of roasting meat filled the air. Griffin was at the hearth, turning the spit and adding herbs from his collection. However I felt about Griffin, I had to admit he was an impressive cook.

I was surprised at how he managed to make even the simplest meals taste so good. It made me think he must have been alone to fend for himself for a while, or maybe his mother taught him how to cook? I'd have to ask him sometime, though I'm not sure if he'd answer.

Deciding to at least help with the meal, I washed and carefully bandaged my hand, the pain lessened to a dull ache from the silvermint. Then I took a small half-apron and tied it around my waist. I started a pot of water to boil and began chopping potatoes for a mash. After preparing enough for two, I unceremoniously dumped them into the pot of water with a pinch of salt.

This wasn't something I did often—the kitchen was kind of small, and Griffin was a large man. I felt dwarfed being so close to him. He had to be at least a head taller than me, and I wasn't short, either. A prickling sensation began at the base of my neck and I knew if I looked, I'd find a honey gaze burning into me. But I ignored it.

My body responded, though, against my will. A tightening in the pit of my stomach, my palms starting to sweat. A warm flush bloomed on my cheeks. However my traitorous body reacted, it meant no difference to me. Griffin and I weren't even *friends*. How could we become anything else? With a huff, I gathered the rest of the ingredients I would need for the mash. Milk, butter, a little cheese, maybe? Realizing I'd need some herbs, I glanced around at what was hanging nearby, but nothing was quite what I was looking for.

Opening cabinets, I finally found the herb I wanted. *Of course, it had to be on the highest shelf,* I thought with a scowl. Getting onto my tiptoes, my fingers brushed the leaves on the very bottom of the parsley that had already been dried and stored. I grunted with effort, stretching as far as I could, when I was enveloped in the scent of citrus and leather. Griffin's fingers brushed against mine as he effortlessly retrieved the bundle of herbs.

Heat radiated against my back and my breath caught. Griffin's voice rumbled through me, like molasses over gravel. "Parsley? That'll go well with the rabbit." He seemed to consider the leaves, but didn't move away from me, the warmth from his body searing me. My mouth dried and I turned halfway towards him, clearing my throat.

"Yeah. It's for the potatoes," I said pointedly, nodding towards the pot.

A rare smile curled Griffin's lips, making my heart flutter. What a pain in the ass. "Should be nice to share."

Retreating to my room, I gave myself a moment of respite from the intensity of Griffin's presence. I slowly let the color leech out of my hair. Although it was just a minor spell, maintaining it all the time was a real drain on my mana. This cabin, though small and unassuming, had become somewhat of a sanctuary. For the first time in years, I felt a glimmer of hope that I might carve out a place for myself. Maybe, in time, I could come to belong here in Haleshade. The thought was enough to bolster my spirits, and I soon returned to the kitchen to finish helping with the meal.

As the evening wore on, we ate our meal in silence, only broken by the clinking of silverware on plates. The longer I was around Griffin, I was getting more used to the strange intensity that he carried himself with, which was a relief. He was a frustrating, boarish man, but at least I didn't have my skin crawling under the pressure of his aura any longer. It was definitely strange, and I'd encountered nothing like it before.

My mind wandered as I chewed, since I didn't have to focus on conversation. I knew Griffin wasn't human. There was just something about the aura he had that felt contrary to anything I've felt from a regular human before, or even the Otherkind I'd encountered during my travels. Something that felt wild and barely contained, like a monsoon about to break. It was like the way people could feel that I was 'different' upon meeting me, without me even telling them. There was just something else there.

But, even after the weeks I'd spent here, I'd been given no hint of what it was, and Griffin didn't seem to jump at the chance to tell me either. Or much of anything, really, I thought with a snort.

It made me question a lot about him. What made him how he is? Why was he so leery of me, of other people? I couldn't help but wonder. In a way, it frustrated me. He demanded to know what seemed like my entire life story when I arrived, and yet he wouldn't give me the slightest shred of his past or what shaped him.

I looked up through my lashes at him to find his golden eyes already trained on my face. I glanced away and finished eating. As I cleaned up after the meal, I caught Griffin watching me from the corner of my eye.

When I turned to face him, he quickly averted his gaze, a faint color rising to his cheeks. My heart rate picked up in response, which I promptly ignored.

After dinner, we settled into our usual routine. Griffin took up his carving, and I found solace in a book I had borrowed from the village market. Once Griffin had realized that I enjoyed reading, a plush gray reading chair appeared near the window after I returned from the market one day with a large, wine-colored cushion adorning it.

It was one of my favorite places to laze about in the entire cottage. I begrudgingly thanked him for the chair, as I knew it had appeared there for me, given that he wasn't prone to reading books himself, but he just waved me off while rubbing the nape of his neck. He was awkward and stilted about it for the rest of the day, then refused to acknowledge its random appearance.

The simple, mundane tasks of our lives formed a comforting pattern, a stark contrast to the chaos of my past. As the sun sank ever lower, I lit a candle nearby to continue burying myself in the novel.

I always was a romantic, choosing love stories as my vice. I knew it would never happen to me, but at least I could pretend, right?

The hours passed, and while my nose was buried in my book, Griffin had already retired to his room. I felt the weight of exhaustion pulling at me, my eyes feeling gritty as sandpaper. Smothering a yawn with my hand, I shuffled back towards my bedroom. I'd forgotten to ask Griffin about Ezra's behavior, I realized. Needed to remember to do that.

Closing my bedroom door, I leaned against it with a sigh. My eyes slipped closed, and I felt the tingle of magic beneath my skin. I loosed a deep breath and opened my eyes, my gaze traveling to the mirror across the room. A gasp caught in my throat as my mother's face looked back at me. The details didn't seem quite right, but I couldn't really remember what she looked like anymore, I realized with a start. The honey of her eyes was missing their familiar warmth, and her skin seemed too smooth.

Did she have freckles? A scar? What could I have forgotten?

For just a moment, I felt like I was back in Sylvan Reach, a child just looking for my parents to protect and support me, and instead they watched as I was ousted from the village, fleeing for my life. I choked back a sob as the magic faded, leaving just me. As always…it was just me. I couldn't forget that. Slowly, I sank to the floor, silent sobs racking my shoulders.

CHAPTER 3

A couple of weeks had gone by and I decided it was time for a hunt. The sun had slipped down beyond the horizon and the sounds of night were creeping through the open windows of the cabin.

I checked to see if Griffin was in the living room, but the room was still and quiet, all the candles still unlit. Seems he was out. I didn't know where, he never told me. This was a perfect time for me to slip out and be back before he even knew I was gone.

The last rays of sunset painted Haleshade in shades of wine and shadow. Peering through the cabin's windows, I could see the village was settling down for the night—merchants were dragging carts home from the square, mothers were calling children inside and the few lamps down the paths were being lit. The village seemed quieter recently, almost as though everyone was especially tired and sluggish. Maybe it was the change in seasons?

I've been very careful about any hunting I've done since I

lived here. I had to use my transformation magic so that I could hunt as an animal, given that I wasn't adept at using a bow and arrows or other methods of catching game.

As far as Griffin was concerned, any meat I brought home purchased from the market in the square with money I had from selling my extra produce. I pulled my hair back and covered it with the hood of my cloak, stepping through the front door of the cabin and pulling it closed with a soft click. Then I started towards the edge of the forest, ensuring that no one was around to see me.

My boots crunched over fallen leaves as I approached the treeline. The boundary between village and wilderness was obvious here, with neat gardens giving way to immense undergrowth and massive trees. During the day, it wasn't as obvious, but at night, the forest loomed, ready to pull you in with whispers of freedom. As soon as I stepped over the threshold into the woods, the hush of the forest enveloped me. I closed my eyes and just listened to the croak of faraway toads, the burbling of the nearby river, the occasional rustle of branches.

There was something so soothing about being here, away from the hustle and bustle of the village. As I made my way further in, stepping over fallen branches and weaving my way through the foliage, I spied a small cluster of trees and changed direction to head there.

Once I reached the privacy of the grouping of trees, my mana surged, filling my body with such an intensity my skin ached, as though begging for me to shed it and take on a new form. I knelt down, placing my hands on the soft earth and digging my fingers in, then visualized the shape I wanted to take. A flare of magic sparked through me, a sensation I reveled in. It was so few and far between that I could flex my abilities. I had missed this. Within moments, my bones shifted, my muscles reformed, and a white wolf stood where I had been. I shook out my fur and took a few moments to adjust to my new senses.

The world exploded into vivid detail. Scents painted pictures that my human nose could never detect. Like a fox that had trotted through hours ago, mice nestled in their burrows in a rotting log, the rush of water in a burbling stream a quarter mile away. My ears swiveled, catching the barest whisper of an owl's wings overhead. But there was something else, too. A strange quiet, where normally I would expect to hear a symphony of sound from all the forest's creatures, instead it was a quieter din, almost as though they sensed something was off. It raised my hackles. But, as I waited, listening, I heard nothing else strange and decided to see what I could find to bring home.

Trotting through the brush, I reveled in the grass's feel beneath my paws. Every time I changed forms, it made me realize just how much I missed the freedom that came with being an animal. Or someone else, someone who wasn't Lyra. I shook my head, frustrated. Those thoughts didn't have a place here. Those were for human Lyra to deal with. Wolf Lyra had another goal in mind.

My hunt took me deep into the forest. The scent of game was faint but distinct in the crisp evening air. I moved silently through the underbrush, the softness of my paws making barely a sound as I followed the trail. My mind was razor sharp, focused on the hunt. I relished being in this form. Here in this forest, right now, I could be myself without fear of judgment or discovery. A version of me, at least.

As I skulked through the forest, I caught the scent of a herd of deer. I lowered my body, ears perked up, while I moved stealthily towards my prey. Adrenaline surged through me, every sense heightened, every movement precise. But just as I was about to pounce, an unfamiliar smell caught my attention—one that sent a shiver down my spine. It was musky, wild, and yet there was something different about it. Like no animal I'd met thus far in any forest I'd been through.

I froze, body low, while I looked around, trying to determine the source. The scent grew stronger, closer, and I realized with a start that I was not alone in this forest. There was another predator here, one that I instinctively knew was much more dangerous than I, even in this form.

Panic raised the fur on the back of my neck and I took off like a shot back in the way I'd come. *Run, danger!* My mind was racing faster than my legs could move. My paws pounded the ground, my muscles pumping. I heard a crash behind me as whatever I'd scented picked up the chase. Adrenaline burned along every nerve in my body and I was panting heavily, my lungs aflame. My eyes wildly darted around, looking for anywhere I could hide, any way I could escape whatever this was.

No random door or hidden path opened for me, so instead I forced my body to work harder, my ears pinned as I listened to the sounds of pursuit behind me. I dodged around trees and bushes, getting ever closer to the edge of the forest. To safety. I recognized my surroundings, a tree that had been burned by lightning and fell, a tree stump I'd sat on to read before. I was getting close to freedom.

Just as I was nearly to the edge of the forest, my paw caught a rogue tree root, causing me to do a complete flip and land sprawled on the hard ground, dirt kicking up from the force of the impact. All of my breath was knocked out of me and I wheezed, dizzy.

Slowly, another shape came into view, along with a low growl. My muscles tensed, my heart pounding in my chest as I tried to make sense of what I was seeing. A large, chocolate-furred wolf crept towards me, hackles risen. Its lips curled with a snarl as it took me in, a stranger in its territory.

This wolf was much larger than any other I'd ever seen, its presence commanding and powerful. I quickly staggered to my feet, and we stood there, locked in a silent standoff, each assessing the other. I refused to give any ground or show fear, instead locking eyes with my adversary. The wolf had amber eyes, glowing with fierce intelligence. I can't say why, but I had a feeling that this wasn't a regular animal.

The gigantic canine stepped forward, its movements fluid and controlled. My instincts screamed at me to run for my life, but I held my ground, surprisingly steady despite the fear currently threatening to choke me. The wolf's growl reverberated through the trees, and it circled me slowly, its eyes never leaving mine.

I kept my gaze steady, the fear falling away as my adrenaline surged. In this form, I was still powerful, still capable. I couldn't forget that or else I'd never be able to protect myself. The wolf stopped its circling, nose twitching as it caught my scent. It hesitated, something human flickering in its eyes. I refused to let my guard down, however, and kept a firm stance.

Its growl softened and slowly tapered away. It tilted its head slightly, as if puzzled. I watched as it took a deep inhale of my scent, and I wondered if I knew them. Or if they somehow knew me. The tension between us was palpable, a taut line that could snap at any moment.

Then, something changed. Its posture shifted, its hackles lowering slightly. It took a step back, the glow in its eyes dimming just a fraction. There was a flicker of recognition, a spark of understanding. Slowly, carefully, the wolf transformed.

The process was fascinating and more than a little unsettling to watch. Bones snapped and realigned, fur receded, and within moments, Griffin stood before me, his chest heaving from the pain and exertion of the shift. Our chase left him covered in a sheen of sweat and grime. His amber eyes were still intense as usual, but some unidentifiable emotion lingered there as well.

For a moment, we simply stared at each other, the moonlight highlighting every plane of his sweat-slicked skin. I'd never seen a member of the WereFolk Shift before, much less up close and personal like this. There was something raw about it, the way his body changed from one form to the next in a primal show of power. The Shift was painful, I'm sure, but there was also a macabre form of beauty in it, in the way his body reformed into the Griffin I knew and recognized. So this is what he had been hiding, a secret that mirrored my own.

I took a deep breath, the magic lightly shimmering around me in the dimness of our surroundings as I allowed myself to shift back into my human form. The transformation left me slightly woozy, but I steadied myself, brushing my dirty hands on my skirt.

Luckily, because of my ability, my clothes transformed with me. Griffin, however… I couldn't help but notice the way the moonlight played across the lean planes and musculature of his body. His naked body, I quickly realized. My cheeks burned as I quickly averted my gaze, a tingle flaring in my belly that I chose not to think about.

"I didn't expect you to have an ability like this," Griffin said, his voice gravelly after his shift back to human form. He shook out any remaining tension from his body and strode to a nearby tree, which held a cache of clothes for him that he quickly pulled on, covering his toned body with thin cotton breeches and a simple white shirt.

I nodded, feeling a strange kinship with him despite the wariness that still lingered. "I didn't expect you to be one of the WereFolk," I replied smoothly. "Although I suppose it makes sense, now that I think about it. I can't believe I didn't notice before." I felt dumb, frankly. But he wasn't aggressive and impulsive like most other WereFolk I had met along my travels. He was… different somehow, in a way I couldn't explain.

His eyes narrowed slightly as he crossed his powerful arms. "I thought you said you didn't have any magic. Is a wolf your only form?"

I shook my head slowly. "No. And I didn't tell anyone in the village because it's not safe for me."

Griffin thought on that for a moment and then sighed, running a hand through his hair and stretching to remove any remaining tension from his Shift. "We all have our secrets, I suppose," he murmured.

I nodded, the tension easing slightly. I couldn't believe that he was dropping it so easily. "Yes, we do."

There was a pause, then Griffin gestured to me and said, "So what's the deal with your hair? Is that some type of spell?"

My mouth opened and closed for a second as I remembered I had forgotten to change my hair back to a neutral brown. "About that. I look…different from the other members of the village I grew up in. I don't want to be recognized during my travels, so I usually try to keep it brown."

Griffin huffed a laugh. "I don't think we see many mages out here. And even if we did, you're a member of Haleshade now. They can't do anything to you. Not without going through me first."

As his words sank in, a flutter erupted in my stomach at the thought of just…being myself. Not hiding. Not worrying about others' thoughts about how I looked or what magic I held. But I knew that the latter, at least, was far off for now. The stories about the last person to hold my power went far beyond Sylvan Reach. The thought of the villagers looking at me with that fear and anger, pushing me out of Haleshade, too…

We stood there for a moment, the forest around us silent and watchful. There was a tentative understanding between us now, a fragile thread of connection.

Griffin's gaze softened ever so slightly, a rare, faint smile tugging at the corners of his mouth. "Well, no reason not to continue the hunt, right?"

I tentatively smiled back, shoving the dark thoughts away for later. At least, it wouldn't happen now. "Right."

Later, as we walked back to the cabin, our shoulders occasionally brushed. He carried a doe on the shoulder opposite to me, caught by the both of us. The silence between us was less awkward. I feel like I finally understood Griffin, at least the tiniest bit.

I noticed something off as we got closer to the cabin. It seemed… quieter than usual. I hadn't noticed it as much until now, walking with Griffin. There were no villagers ambling over to talk with him or rushing around to avoid me. There was a strange hush over everything.

I glanced at Griffin to see if he noticed, but he still had a faint smile tracing his lips and I decided to file away that thought for later. I was still new here, so who knows what I could be missing about the goings-on here? If he wasn't concerned, I wouldn't be.

Much later, someone banging on the front door of the cabin startled me awake. Adrenaline immediately surged and my body began trembling. I had no idea what time it was, but a quick glance out the window told me it was still very dark outside, stars winking in and out of view. The urgent pounding on the door continued, and I heard a faint voice.

"Griffin! Open the door, man!"

After a moment, I heard a groan from Griffin's room before

the sound of his door opening. His shadow passed underneath my door. What was going on?

Throwing the blankets off, I pulled myself out of bed, heart racing as I grabbed my cloak, willing my hair back to a russet tone. I couldn't imagine what would cause someone to come here in the middle of the night, but I was damn well going to find out. I crept to the door of my room, cracking it open to see Griffin's tall figure standing before the front door, his shoulders tight.

Just as I approached, Griffin opened the door and a man practically fell through the threshold, panting heavily. "Thank the gods."

Griffin caught the man before he fell and set him right again. As I slunk closer, I saw the man's eyes were wide with panic, his face pale and drawn under the moonlight. My breath hitched at his expression. I knew him. His name was Grant, and he was a produce monger who regularly made a stall in the village square. He looked more haggard than I'd ever seen him, his usually well-manicured outfit mussed and dirtied.

"Griffin," Grant wheezed, struggling to catch his breath and running his hand through his thinning salt-and-pepper hair. Sweat dripped off of his brow. "Something is happening in the village. We need your help."

Griffin's expression hardened, his jaw tightening as he pulled away from the doorjamb, standing up straight. "What is it? What's going on?"

"I don't know, but it's bad," Grant replied, his voice quaking. "It all started a few days ago, but it's getting worse. It's some kind of sickness and it seems like it's spreading. We don't know what to do. Louise... she's already overwhelmed. She's tried to help, but nothing is working."

Louise was Haleshade's singular healer. She was an expert at crafting potions and the like, although her magical ability wasn't anything to scoff at either. She could manipulate liquids, which was very helpful for removing impurities from the nearby river's water, ensuring that it was as pure as possible before use in her craft.

I stepped out from the hall, drawing Griffin's gaze. I pulled my cloak tighter around my night clothes while we shared a concerned look. He turned back to the merchant. "Alright, let me get dressed. I'll be there soon and we'll see what we can figure out."

Grant nodded gratefully before turning and scurrying back towards Louise's cottage near the central square of the village. Griffin slowly closed the door with a soft *snick* and turned to me, his face weary and his golden eyes dark with worry. He shook the tension from his shoulders and loosed a heavy sigh.

"I need to go help them," he said, his voice low but urgent. He had an unreadable expression as his eyes traced over my face. "You should stay here until I know what's going on."

Shaking my head, I turned back towards my room. "I want to help too. I can at least assist with gathering supplies or tending to the sick."

Griffin hesitated as though he wanted to force me to stay somehow, then released a heavy sigh, following me. "This isn't a good idea."

I stopped and pivoted on my heel to glower at him. At my

scowl, he sighed again. "Alright, but be careful. We don't know how this sickness spreads, and I don't want you to become ill."

As we hurriedly dressed, I couldn't help but notice how Griffin's concern seemed to extend beyond just the villagers. His eyes kept flickering to me, a worried crease between his brows. "Stay close to me," he murmured as we left, his hand briefly touching the small of my back. I chose to ignore how my pulse jumped at the contact. *It was just a surprise, that's all,* I thought angrily.

The warmth of his touch lingered long after he'd pulled away.

We stepped out into the cool night, the air thick with tension.

As we made our way to the village, we both glanced at each other as we noted the eerie silence. The streets of Haleshade, usually bustling with chatter and the sounds of life were now silent as a graveyard. A chill spread over me as I thought about what that could mean.

When we reached the center of the village, the sight was worse than I had expected. The children, normally so lively and loud, lay clinging to their mothers' skirts, while their mothers looked on blankly like empty shells, unaware of the sounds of cries and tears drenching the fabric of their clothes.

There were others, the baker and the weaver, who stood and swayed on unsteady legs, their eyes glassy and unfocused, their skin covered in a sheen of sweat. Some lay scattered across the ground, only the faint rise and fall of their chest revealing that they even still lived. It was heart-wrenching and eerie to witness.

The village healer, Louise, was a woman with tired, moss-green eyes and a determined expression. Her honey-blonde hair was pulled back into a messy bun on top of her head as moved among them, doing her best to provide comfort and care.

Griffin immediately stepped in to assist, his powerful presence bringing a semblance of order to the chaos. I scurried after him, my mind racing as I tried to recall any of the first aid my mother had taught me back in Sylvan Reach when I was younger. Louise glanced at us with a mix of relief and gratitude.

As we assisted her, I found myself hyper-aware of Griffin's presence. He moved through the crowd with quiet strength, his gentle hands tending to the sick with a care that belied his usual gruff demeanor. The determined set of his jaw and the intensity in his eyes as he worked painted a picture of a man I was only beginning to understand. Despite the dire situation, I couldn't help but feel a sense of admiration growing within me.

I noticed Griffin's jaw tighten when he had a moment to himself, his hands fisted. I cautiously approached him, surprised to hear the faint sound of grinding teeth.

"What's going on with you?" I asked, startling him.

"It's nothing. Just can't believe I didn't notice this sooner. I should have. I should have seen it. But I've been too distracted to see what was right in front of me." His voice was heavy with self-loathing and before I realized what I was doing, I placed a hand on his arm. The muscle jumped at my touch, but I didn't move.

"Grant said this just came on a couple of days ago. It seems to be a quiet illness. It's not like you go into every single person's house to check in on them. Cut yourself a break."

That unreadable expression was back, the amber in his eyes becoming warm like honey. I quickly pulled my hand away and cleared my throat. Before either of us could say anything else, Louise approached.

"Thank you for coming," she said, rubbing an antiseptic gel over her hands. Completely unaware of the awkward situation she'd interrupted, her voice was weary. "We've never seen anything like this before. I'm not sure what to do here. Nothing I've tried so far seems to make much of a difference as far as actually helping people to get over this. The most I can do is comfort them."

"We'll do what we can," Griffin replied, his tone firm. "Can you tell us anything about how this came about? Why are they like…this?" He waved a hand towards the almost catatonic people around us.

Louise sighed, scrubbing a hand over her face. "From my understanding, this isn't like a typical illness. There were several people who reported feeling some weakness. Maybe some fatigue. It seemed to affect more and more people day to day, but we attributed it to the hot weather. That's why there wasn't a mass alert out to the entire village. We just didn't think it was a problem." A second sigh. "But today, we saw the first instances of…whatever this is. People slowly losing the ability to speak, almost like they become locked into their mind." She gestured towards the square.

"I started researching and trying to see if I could find anything that would explain why a bit of lethargy and weakness could cause a catatonic state, but I couldn't find anything at all in any of my medical journals that describes symptoms like these. I know that you have a sort of—," her gaze slid to me before turning back to Griffin "—special type of magic, and wondered if you might have heard of something like this. That's why I sent Grant to come get you."

I realized Griffin must keep his shifting abilities under wraps. It made sense, I suppose. WereFolk have a poor reputation amongst humans as being violent and impulsive. Honestly, Griffin couldn't be more different from what I'd been led to believe as a child growing up in Sylvan Reach, hearing wild rumors of animal people with horrid tempers, destroying villages left and right, squabbling amongst themselves and constantly trying to conquer each other.

Regardless of how I felt about him, I had to admit that he was… kind, compassionate, and very protective of the humans living in Haleshade. I understood why he has kept me at arm's reach for so long. Humans were so delicate compared to the Otherkind. Otherkind is just a blanket term for any species that's not explicitly human. It was coined by humans thousands of years ago because I guess they just couldn't be bothered to learn the differences between species.

Aside from Louise and I, there were no Otherkind here besides Griffin. *It must have been lonely for him, being the only Shifter here*, I thought, then scowled. I shouldn't be feeling sorry for him. Almost against my will, my gaze was drawn to him. This was someone who understood what it meant to hide in plain sight, just like I did. How WereFolk were treated outside of their own packs, they were often feared and reviled as a violent menace, regardless of how they presented themselves.

It was no wonder that he kept everyone at a distance. No wonder he was so accepting when I didn't want to reveal my secret. The realization caused a warmth to bloom in my chest, which I quickly smothered. Getting too close to someone was dangerous, regardless of whether I could relate to their pain, and they to mine. With some effort, I tore my gaze away and refocused on the task at hand.

Griffin huffed and crossed his arms, corded with lean, powerful muscle. "I've never heard of anything like this, actually. This type of stuff didn't exist where I come from. We're pretty hardy, so we don't really need to worry."

Louise shifted on her feet, looking around at all the sick villagers, her face grim. "This is some type of wasting sickness. The villagers refuse to eat, drink, or react to their environment. It's going to kill them if we can't figure it out. The life within them is just being *drained*. We've already lost a few of the older villagers. And it's just going to keep spreading."

My heart skipped a beat as Louise's words registered in my brain. "We've already lost villagers? Grant said the sickness had just arrived here. When did this start?"

Louise's lips thinned in distaste, her jade eyes looking chipped from ice. "It's only been a couple of days, just like Grant said. I'm doing everything that I can. We need to figure it out, and fast."

The sight of a young woman trying desperately to help her father to drink from a glass, only for the water to dribble past his lips and down his chin caused my chest to tighten. She broke down sobbing, trying to mop up the spilled water. A nearby child was pulling at his mother's skirts to gain her attention, but she stood swaying, her gaze distant, frozen, lost to whatever gripped her mind and body in a vise. How long before they lost their parents?

How long before this illness turned on them, too?

If only I had the power to save these people. My magic surged beneath my skin, almost begging for release. But I knew it wouldn't help. With a shot of agony, I forced it back down into the pool deep within. *My power can't help anyone*, I thought sadly. It's nothing but a curse. But I had a thought. Maybe I *can* help somehow.

"I have a few of my own medical journals I brought with me to Haleshade. Let me go back to the cabin and see what I can find," I murmured, anxiety making my heart race. Of course. I had just gotten to Haleshade, and now this. Why was there always some kind of crisis? Some reason I had to leave? I heaved a sigh.

Turning on my heel, I started quickly making my way back to Griffin's cabin. There was a quiet exchange behind me and then Griffin was falling into step next to me. I had to find answers. I had to, no matter the cost.

CHAPTER 4

Griffin and I stood silently in the middle of the cabin, the air thick with tension. I could feel the weight of his gaze on me as I tried to steady my racing thoughts, my hands shaking. Adrenaline was coursing through my body at a breakneck pace, leaving me struggling to breathe. I didn't want to lose this place, too. Not now.

My gaze drifted from the book to the cabin—the worn, handmade furniture, the reading chair Griffin had gotten just for me, the feeling of familiarity that made it feel like *home*. There were memories that had been made in every corner of this room, good and bad. I didn't realize how much it meant to me until the threat of having it taken away really hit me. I swallowed thickly and strode further into the room.

"We need to find answers," Griffin said. "But I don't know where to start."

I grit my teeth as I bit out, "I'm going to do what I can. Give me some time."

I started going through the pile of books that had been stacked on the table near my reading chair. My fingers came to rest on a dark emerald tome with silver embossed letters in a foreign dialect. It wasn't spoken much outside of Sylvan Reach, but loosely translated to "Bits and Bobs in Medicine, fifth edition".

Despite the title, it was a very well reviewed journal of various medical maladies that could afflict various types of Otherkind, as well as humans. I stood, flipping through the pages until my feet ached and the sun started its descent. Griffin came and placed a gentle hand on my shoulder, startling me and breaking my concentration.

I sat the book down with a heavy *thud* and scrubbed my hand over my face with a sigh. My eyes felt gritty, and I was barely even retaining anything I read by this point. I pressed the heels of my palms against my eyes and tilted my head back.

"Are you having any luck?" he asked, surprisingly gently. "We may have to look elsewhere if you can't find anything."

"Does it look like I've found anything?" I snapped, then guilt immediately washed over me and I deflated. "I'm sorry. It's just… I don't want to leave this place, too." My voice cracked on the last word and I cleared my throat. "I just started getting used to it."

Understanding flashed in Griffin's eyes for a moment, but he wisely chose not to comment on it. How he looked at me then made something twist in my chest. He didn't demand any explanations that I wasn't able to give, didn't press for anything more. "Do you have any other ideas?"

An icy dread settled in my stomach. There was only one place that may hold the knowledge we needed, but it was a place I had sworn never to return to. Sylvan Reach. The thought of going back there, of facing the villagers who had cast me out and tried to kill me, filled me with fear. But the desperation in the eyes of the villagers of Haleshade were burned into my mind.

Taking a deep breath, I steeled myself as I came to a decision. I refused to let fear rule me when I felt I could help somehow. Nevertheless, I was tense as I turned to face Griffin. "We should go to Sylvan Reach."

He looked at me, surprise flickering across his face. "Sylvan Reach? Isn't that where the Arcane Order is based? Why there?"

I hesitated, then went with a partial truth. "Louise doesn't know what is causing this. It makes me think it could be a magical source rather than a known illness. The Arcane Order has knowledge about magical diseases, so if anyone can help us understand whatever this is, it's probably them."

He frowned, clearly sensing there was more to my words than what I was saying. "Are you sure? From what I've heard, they're not exactly welcoming to outsiders."

I nodded, trying to mask my fear with determination. "I know, but we don't have any other options. If we stay here with no answers, more people will die."

Griffin studied me for a moment, his eyes searching mine. Then he crossed his arms, his powerful aura overwhelming. "You stink of fear. What is going on? Is there something you're not telling me?"

His golden eyes searched mine, and I felt a strange flutter in my chest. His concern for my well-being was surprising and touching. I found myself drawn to the warmth in his gaze. Swallowing hard, my heart began pounding in my chest. "I just... I have a complicated history with Sylvan Reach. The villagers might not be friendly, especially to someone like me."

The thought of returning was terrifying, actually. If I was discovered, the Arcane Order wouldn't hesitate to end my life. A memory flashed in my mind—the sound of screams, the hiss of magical energy careening past my ear as they tried to strike me, the burning in my legs as I ran for my life. And yet, in a dark way, I understood. They felt they were protecting the mage race. We couldn't afford another incident like the last Transformation mage, even though it felt incredibly unfair that it had to be me.

His gaze softened with understanding and he reached a hand out, though he dropped it before touching me. I quashed the disappointment that flared. I did not have it in me to have childish little crushes. It only ended in heartache.

"Lyra, if it's too dangerous, we can find another way." He looked like he really believed that, too.

I shook my head with a huff, forcing myself to remain resolute. "No, we have to do this. The lives of the people here depend on it and I'd never forgive myself if more of them died because of my inaction." My hands balled into fists at my side.

Griffin nodded slowly, putting a hand in his pocket while the other dragged through his hair, leaving it a tousled mess. One of his few tells. He must not want to go there either. I couldn't help but wonder why. "Alright. We'll go. But we'll be careful. We'll stick together and get in and out as quickly as possible."

Despite the nervousness in his gesture, when I looked at his face, the determination in his golden eyes gave me a small measure of comfort. We wasted no time and immediately got to work packing our bags. Medical journals—but not too many, because I didn't want to be weighed down. Dried foods, so we wouldn't have to stop anywhere along the way, a change of clothes in case we had to flee quickly. It was almost mechanical for me, muscle memory from years without a place to call home. But this time was different. I had a purpose—I was choosing to walk into this, instead of running away from it. This time, I wasn't alone.

As we gathered everything that we would need for the trek to Sylvan Reach, unease gnawed at my insides. I'd have to tell Griffin about my powers. There's no way I could just walk in to Sylvan Reach without the other mages coming after me. I'd have to become someone else and sneak in to lessen any risk of discovery.

Griffin and I set out, the early morning light casting long shadows on the forest path. Each step took us closer to the place I had once called home and, with no small amount of luck, to the answers we so desperately needed. I ignored the rising nausea roiling through my stomach. I never thought I would go back. Not once in a million years. But for the sake of the villagers, for the chance to save their lives, I would push through.

With Griffin by my side, I desperately clung to a small spark of hope. Together, we would stop this sickness.

CHAPTER 5

The road to Sylvan Reach seemed to stretch out endlessly before us, winding through dense forest and open meadows under the vast expanse of the azure sky. Each step brought us closer to the place that detested and reviled me. Where the mages who lived there had tried to —

Shaking off that thought, I stole a glance at Griffin, his stride steady and purposeful beside me. His presence was surprisingly reassuring, yet my jaw was tight and my body wound like a spring. The sun was just starting to drop, casting a cascade of brilliant hues across the sky—fiery oranges, soft pinks, and deep purples blending together like the strokes of a masterful painting. Before long, it would be dark and I knew it was now or never.

"Griffin," I began hesitantly, my voice barely above a whisper. He turned to me, his gaze open and more trusting than I'd ever seen from him. I took a deep breath, gathering courage, knowing that with just a few words, he may want nothing to do with me, either.

Not that I could blame him, I thought bitterly.

"There's something I haven't told you," I admitted, my hands twisting nervously in the folds of my cloak, wringing the fabric. "About me, about who I really am. Why I didn't want to go to Sylvan Reach. Why I haven't talked about my magic before."

Griffin's dark brows furrowed slightly, his eyes searching mine. He didn't press me. Just waited, his face a mask of patience.

The words were catching in my throat. I swallowed hard, my anxiety mounting. How could I explain something that had ruined my life, that I had kept hidden from everyone, even myself? Years of deflections and lies bubbled up my throat, just waiting to be spilled. But I held my tongue. How could I trust him not to push me away, not to fear and hate me, too? Looking at him, there was a patience, an understanding there that I had so longed to see in someone else's eyes. My breath caught at the idea of Griffin turning away from me. He was the first real friend I'd ever had.

I paused and my body froze, the realization smacking me in the face. He was my *friend*. I'd never let myself get close to anyone before for exactly this reason—I didn't want the pain of rejection again. To feel like I belonged only to have that wrested away and to be completely alone again. It was easier not to be close to anyone to begin with.

But the fragile trust we had built on this journey demanded honesty.

"I—I have magic," I finally confessed, the words coming out in a rush. "I mean, of course I do. I'm a mage. You saw me change in the forest, but it's different—more than just that. It's a forbidden magic that was 'gifted' to me in the grove in Sylvanwood Forest. I didn't choose it, but I have it and there's nothing I can do about it."

If I stopped now, I'd never finish telling Griffin, so I plowed on without even stopping to take a breath. "In Sylvan Reach, they found out that I have this magic and I was almost killed to 'protect the Otherkind from another incident' like the age-old tales about the last person to have this power. I've hidden it my whole life. I feared what could happen if I were found out again." I just couldn't stop talking. The words kept tumbling out of my mouth in a frantic rush until there was nothing left.

Silence hung heavily between us, broken only by the soft shuffle of leaves underfoot and my own labored breathing as I caught my breath. Griffin's expression softened, a mixture of surprise and understanding dawning in his amber eyes. "Forbidden magic," he echoed quietly, more to himself than to me. "That explains a lot."

I nodded. My hair was a silvery curtain in my vision as I looked down at my feet, shifting my weight. "I didn't know how you would react," I admitted, my voice wavering. "It's dangerous, Griffin. The Order, they—they wouldn't hesitate to... to..."

Griffin placed a reassuring hand on my shoulder, his touch startling me. My gaze snapped up to his and for a moment, I swore I saw something warm behind his eyes. In a flash it was gone and I assured myself I'd imagined it. Still, I didn't move away. I was weak.

"I understand, Lyra," he murmured, his voice steady. "You've had to protect yourself, survive in a place that fears what it doesn't understand. You don't seem very scary to me. There's nothing to be afraid of, at least as far as I'm concerned."

I met his gaze, seeing understanding and empathy reflected at me. I didn't know how to feel. I'd never really thought about what it would be like to have someone accept me. A tension I didn't know I was holding loosened in my body and a trickle of relief flowed through me. How could I even respond to this?

"Thank you," I murmured, tears pricking my eyes. I refused to let them fall, balling my fists so tightly that my nails cut into my palms. The pain helped to calm me so I didn't break down. "For not turning away from me."

Griffin offered a faint smile, his gaze turning back to the road ahead. "We'll face whatever comes together," he assured me, his tone resolute. "We'll find answers in Sylvan Reach, and we'll protect our village from this plague."

I quickly wiped my eyes and squared my shoulders, walking once again on the path to Sylvan Reach. Every step felt lighter with Griffin beside me. It was a strange, new feeling. I had a genuine smile on my face for the first time I could remember. I slid a glance towards Griffin only to find him looking back at me, a faint smile on his lips. His expression caused an unexpected warmth low in my core and I bit the inside of my cheek, glancing away.

The path twisted and turned through the dense forest, the canopy of trees casting dappled shadows over us. Despite myself, I found myself speaking more freely with Griffin, our conversation weaving through memories of our childhoods, dreams for the future, and the challenges we faced ahead. I began stealing glances at Griffin as we walked. The way the dappled sunlight played across his features was mesmerizing, and I caught myself wondering what it would be like to trace the line of his jaw with my fingertips.

It was kind of awkward, given that I had no one to talk to like this. But it was nice. It made me want to find answers all the more for the sickness spreading at Haleshade.

"Do you think they'll listen to us in Sylvan Reach?" I asked after a while, my voice tinged with doubt. "What if they turn us away? After all, they're not the most… welcoming of people."

Griffin weighed my words, his expression thoughtful. He ran a hair through his hair, mussing the chestnut waves before tucking his hands in his pockets. "We won't know until we try," he replied, his tone deceptively casual. "I can only hope that there are good people who will listen to us there. And if not, we'll find another way to help Haleshade."

Hours later, the journey to Sylvan Reach had worn us down, the day's light dwindling as we ventured deeper into the thickening forest. Shadows stretched and flowed into the creeping darkness, reaching out as though to entangle us forever in the night.

"Griffin," I whispered, my voice barely audible over the rustling leaves and distant hoots of owls. "We need to stop here for the night. It's not safe to travel further in this darkness. Sylvanwood Forest has its own magic to it and the creatures that live here."

He nodded, his eyes scanning the dense undergrowth around us with a tinge of unease. I felt his intense aura flare as though daring any nefarious creatures to make themselves known. I could almost see it in the growing darkness, a tinge of gold around his body. "Yeah, you're right. Let's find a clearing where we can set up."

We located a small glade bathed in the moon's feeble light, a sliver of refuge in the encroaching night. Griffin gathered dry twigs and sticks for a fire while I unpacked our sparse supplies, my mind racing with the weight of what lay ahead.

As we worked in silence, the forest seemed to press in around us, alive with unseen movement. Each crack of a twig or whisper of wind through the leaves sent a shiver down my spine. I glanced at Griffin while I sorted the bedrolls.

His dark brows were furrowed in concentration, the budding firelight flickering across his face and igniting the sunlight of his eyes as he stoked the flames. The warm glow on his face was accentuating his strong features. I caught myself staring and glanced away, a blush creeping up my cheeks.

Get it together, Lyra. The first guy who shows even the slightest hint of kindness and you're over here blushing like a schoolgirl, I thought to myself angrily.

Despite my resolve, my gaze was drawn to him again just a few minutes later. As I observed him through my lashes, a soft flutter erupted in my stomach. He was such an irritating man, and yet I just couldn't keep myself from watching him. What was it about him I couldn't let go of?

"Lyra," Griffin said softly, breaking the uneasy quiet and pulling me from my thoughts. "We're getting closer to Sylvan Reach. How are we going to approach it? I know you said that you had a… complicated relationship with the people there."

A beat of silence. I didn't quite know what to say to this and had hoped to have a bit more time, but I supposed now was as good a time as ever. I sat down on my bedroll and Griffin did the same to his own.

Despite that, I hesitated, my fingers worrying a loose thread on my cloak. "There's something I haven't told you," I began, my voice faltering as I glanced nervously at the shadowy canopy above. "In Sylvan Reach, I won't be myself. I can use my magic to disguise my appearance, to blend in as someone else."

His brow furrowed deeper, concern etched into the lines of his face. " What do you mean? Is this what makes your magic forbidden? That you can become someone else?"

"Yes, it's exactly that," I said with a sigh. I was already so tired of this, and we hadn't even gotten close to our destination yet. I scrubbed a hand over my face in frustration. "But it's what I have to do. If they knew who I was when we arrived, they wouldn't hesitate to turn me away, or worse. For you too, since you're traveling with me. Lucky you."

Griffin's eyes were like molten honey, his hand reaching out to grasp mine. The simple touch sent a jolt through me, and I quickly pulled my hand away. He hesitated, then slowly let his hand drop to his side.

It was so warm where our skin had touched. The feeling of his hand on mine lingered, and I definitely didn't want him to do it again. *Get it together.* "Lyra, we'll figure it out. Don't worry. You have me on your side, at least." He sat back, watching the fire smoke curl up into the aether.

He seemed so confident, yet even so, a nagging sense of foreboding lingered. The forest seemed to hold its breath, every rustle and whisper carrying a chilling undertone. As the fire crackled and cast dancing shadows, I couldn't shake the feeling that unseen eyes watched our every move, waiting for the opportune moment to strike.

"We should keep watch tonight," Griffin suggested, his gaze following the same path as mine. His voice was low, rumbling through my ears. "Just to be safe."

I nodded silently, pulling my cloak tighter around me. A chill had settled deep within me, a vivid reminder of the trials awaiting us in Sylvan Reach. I could only hope we would remain safe from the things that lurked in the shadows. A shiver traced down my spine, my nerves jumbled.

Everyone knew you shouldn't be out and about in Sylvanwood Forest at night. The trees swayed even without a breeze, creaking ominously. The forest was hungry, the magic ancient and yearning. But we had no other choice.

As the night deepened, the forest seemed to grow restless. Strange sounds echoed through the trees, like whispers carried on the wind. My heart was racing, adrenaline coursing through me. It would be impossible for me to sleep like this.

If only I was a mage with transportation abilities, if such a thing existed. We could have already been there by now, I thought with a sigh. Griffin seemed just as on edge as I was, his back straight and his gaze alert, tracking every shadow. He seemed to instinctively place himself between me and the darkness, as though protecting me from any danger that may linger. My throat grew tight with emotion. Even such a simple gesture was out of the realm of what I was used to, and I didn't know how to feel about it.

"We should talk more about what awaits us in Sylvan Reach," Griffin suggested quietly and turned to face me, breaking the tense silence that had settled over our camp.

I swallowed hard, avoiding his gaze and looking up to see the stars winking through the trees. "I've been hiding my abilities for years," I confessed, my voice raw. Talking about this made me feel so… exposed.

"I don't think that the people within Sylvan Reach will be able to tell that it's me. So we'll head for the apothecary and hope for the best. That they will know what we can do to help the villagers back in Haleshade." Reluctantly, my gaze slid back to Griffin.

He nodded solemnly, understanding reflecting in his expression. "You've had to protect yourself," he murmured, his gaze flicking towards the shadows beyond our campfire's reach. "But we'll be stepping into the heart of the Arcane Order. Are you sure you're ready?"

A lump formed in my throat as I mulled over his question. Everything felt so uncertain. I had to face these people again, and I didn't know how to feel. How I would feel in the moment. What I would do if my parents were there? Could I even face them, in disguise or not? My fingers worried the edge of my shirt, anxiety eating through me. How could I pretend like nothing happened, like they were any other people? Although, I guess after so long, they *were* just like any other people to me. Tears pricked my eyes, but I blinked them away. Now wasn't the time to break down.

"I have to be," I replied finally, after a long pause, meeting his gaze with resolve. "For the sake of those in Haleshade and for my own peace of mind."

The wood in the fire split with a *snap*, sparks swirling into the night sky. Apprehension and resolve warred within me, but I quashed those feelings and pushed them deep down inside of myself. If I kept thinking about it, I would find a reason not to go. Any reason at all. But I had to push through.

Griffin's hand twitched as though he wanted to reach out to me again, but it stilled. "We'll face it together," he vowed, his voice surprisingly reassuring. I had to wonder why he was so adamant about this. About us. Like we were actually a team. Like he wasn't just stuck with me because I was the only person with an idea of how to fix this. I just felt confused about it. I mean, how else was I supposed to feel?

With a deep breath to settle my mind, I nodded, steeling myself for the trials ahead. The forest seemed to hold its breath, becoming still and silent. As we settled in for the night, I couldn't shake the feeling that we were being watched, that something beyond our understanding lurked just beyond the flickering firelight.

Sleep eluded me as the night wore on, that feeling of eyes on my back never leaving me. I opted to take first watch while Griffin slept on the other side of the campfire. Without the distraction of another person, the sounds of the night seemed amplified. Every snap of firewood, every rustle of leaves, seemed to echo in the quiet of our little circle of light. As I watched Griffin sleep, his features softened in the firelight, I felt a surge of protectiveness. The urge to brush a stray lock of hair from his forehead was almost overwhelming, and I had to clasp my hands tightly together to resist.

I'd never seen him asleep before, and listening to his quiet snores was almost endearing, as well as a little amusing. A faint smile touched my lips. He didn't seem the type to snore. I wondered if he knew he did. I couldn't help but think about how things might be different if I wasn't who I was. If I hadn't been cursed with this 'gift'. Would he and I be friends? More?

That thought surprised me. I'd never really thought about being with someone in a romantic way. I mean, of course, I'd fantasized about being in a relationship, but it always seemed so far and away. Exactly that, a fantasy. Not grounded in reality.

Hours passed before the sun started to slowly rise into the sky. The first light of dawn crept over the horizon, painting the sky in soft hues of pink and lavender. As the minutes passed, these pastel colors deepened into rich oranges and golds, the sun's rays piercing through the remaining darkness. The landscape gradually awakened under this warm, golden glow, shadows retreating and revealing the world in a fresh, new light.

I quietly plod over to where Griffin still lay sleeping and crouched down to gently shake him awake. His eyes shot open, and he sat straight up, causing our heads to knock together. Stars burst behind my eyes and I saw black for a second, falling back on my butt with a cry.

"What the hell, Griffin? I was just waking you up so I could take a nap before we head out." I snapped, rubbing the goose egg that was already forming on my forehead.

His cheeks ruddy with embarrassment, Griffin rubbed his own head, muttering, "I thought something was happening." He looked like a pouting child, crossing his arms.

Our eyes met and my anger dissolved like smoke in the wind, a laugh bubbling up my throat at the ridiculousness of this situation. Griffin chuckled as well, his cheeks still tinted pink and stood, coming to offer me a hand up. Our laughter subsided, but the warmth in Griffin's eyes remained.

He held out a hand to help me up, but I pushed it away and stood up on my own. "I've got it. I don't need your help." Despite my words, a hint of a smile twitched at my mouth.

"You okay?" he asked with a smile, his sunshine eyes still dancing with mirth.

Even though my head was throbbing, I couldn't stop myself from playfully pushing his shoulder. "I'm fine enough. You're a fool if you think that's enough to keep me down."

The silliness of the situation really broke the tension that had been lingering between us. Things were still awkward as ever, but Griffin seemed to have finally loosened up.

Meanwhile, I finally felt secure enough to take a quick nap before the sun rose high overhead. I lay down on my bedroll, which honestly wasn't much better than the ground, but it would have to do. Feeling a pain in my back, I reached under the bedroll to find a pebble had snuck its way underneath.

That ghost of a smile still traced my lips as I quickly fell asleep, finally feeling secure now that Griffin was awake. We would be okay. The forest wasn't so scary during the day.

If you could ignore the hint of magic that raised the hair on your arms, that is.

CHAPTER 6

As the sun rose high in the sky, I woke to the soft rustling of leaves and the gentle chirping of birds. My body was still heavy with sleep, and yet I felt more comfortable than I should have, having slept on the hard forest floor. The fire from the night before had long since died out, leaving only a few glowing embers. Griffin had his back facing to me, tending to his gear.

The sunlight caught the powerful lines of his shoulders, tracing the planes of muscle beneath his shirt and highlighting the precision in his movements. I swallowed hard, more aware than ever of the distance between us. This was definitely a new territory for me—I wondered if he felt the same, then banished the thought. It didn't matter if he did, it wasn't like I could do anything about it. I stretched and yawned, feeling the stiffness in my muscles from my nap on the forest floor.

"Morning," I greeted, my voice husky with sleep. I could only hope I wasn't snoring.

"Morning, Lyra," Griffin replied, still turned away as he packed his bag of supplies. I could hear a smile in his voice. "Sleep well?"

I nodded, though my dreams had been restless. Screams and the flash of blades and explosions of magical energy ran through my mind like a gust of wind, there and then gone just as quickly as I stretched any last grogginess from my muscles. Realizing he couldn't see me, I replied, "As well as I could have. Ready for the last stretch of our journey?"

Griffin glanced over his shoulder at the scowl on my face and chuckled, shoving his hands into his pocket and looking casual as always. It irritated me for no good reason and I felt a wrinkle form between my brows.

He didn't hesitate when he said, "Ready as ever. We've got one more day to Sylvan Reach. Hopefully, we'll make good time."

We packed up our camp quickly, the routine of it becoming almost second nature. As we set off, the forest seemed less foreboding in the daytime hours. As the sunlight enveloped the surrounding forest, it transformed everything into a picturesque scene with its warm hues. It was a stark contrast to the ominous atmosphere of the previous night. Thinking about what may lurk in the trees at night caused a lick of fear to travel up my spine.

Beside me, Griffin's usually stoic demeanor seemed to melt away as the afternoon sun cast a soft, golden light on his features. I found myself captivated by the way the sunlight played across his face, highlighting the powerful line of his jaw and the warmth in his amber eyes. A strange flutter stirred in my chest, and I glanced away, confused and all the more frustrated by my reaction.

He and I could never work, I assured myself. For one, I didn't even know if he was interested in me in that way, and for two, it wasn't worth the risk to his safety. I turned my attention to the path ahead.

My thoughts drifted to my home village in Sylvan Reach instead. I never thought that I would return to this place. Much less to bring anyone here to see it. Shame brought warmth to my cheeks. Twisting a sleeve of my cloak around my fingers, I was determined to look anywhere else but at Griffin.

I could only imagine what he thought about me. All I seem to have done since we met is burden him, and when he finally needed me to help with Haleshade, I had nothing to give. And now here we are, on our way to my childhood village. I choked back a laugh at the absurdity of it all.

We walked in tense silence, the only sound the shuffling of our feet as we walked along the path. Regardless of the memories that lingered, it really was beautiful here. The forest was a living tapestry, where sunlight streamed through the canopy, casting soft, dappled patterns on the forest floor.

The trees stood tall and proud, their leaves rustling softly in the warm breeze. There was a subtle hum in the air, an almost tangible presence of magic that made the very air feel alive. It spoke to my magic. The sensation was like the mana was stretching against my insides, urging me to use it, to unleash it. But I refused, not until I needed to. I couldn't justify it, no matter how good it felt.

The flowers that dotted the underbrush seemed to glow with an inner light that was just barely noticeable if you really looked closely at them. It was a place where the ordinary and the extraordinary coexisted in perfect harmony, and I felt a deep connection to the magic that pulsed through the very heart of the forest. I just wish it hadn't cursed me with this ability. Transformation. I scoffed and Griffin slid his gaze over to me.

Griffin finally spoke, interrupting my thoughts. His voice, low and rich, sent an unexpected shiver down my spine. I tried to focus on his words rather than the way his presence seemed to fill the space between us. "So, tell me more about Sylvan Reach. What's it like?" He hiked his pack a little higher on his shoulder, eyes intent on my face while we walked along.

I took a deep breath, memories flooding back and causing my breath to hitch a little. Most of the memories I had of that place were awful. "It's beautiful, in a way that's hard to describe. The village is nestled deep in the forest, surrounded by these huge, ancient trees. Everything there feels…alive with mana in a way I've experienced nowhere else. And you grow up that way, feeling in tune with that energy flowing through everything. Everyone."

Griffin listened attentively, his eyes turning to the path ahead. His voice was soft when he asked, "It sounds like a special place. Why did you leave?"

I hesitated, the question hitting a little too close to home. "I… didn't really have a choice, to be honest. When I was about 15 or 16, a boy saw me using my magic out here in the woods. I thought I was safe, and that I was being careful, but… not careful enough, I suppose. It's still home, in a way, but I have no pleasant memories of being there. I'm just hoping that it will be worth the trip there. That we find something useful to combat this sickness."

Griffin nodded, his brow furrowed. "I get it. There's a reason that I'm the only one of my kind at Haleshade. I had to escape something, too."

Silence lapsed between us again while we walked along, both lost in our own thoughts. I stole a glance at Griffin, my eyes tracing over his dark wavy hair, his honey eyes and the scruff on his face that appeared over the course of the last day of our travel. I felt a sense of ease around Griffin, a feeling that had grown a lot over the past few days.

There was something about the way he moved, the quiet strength in his gestures, that made me feel safe. I caught myself watching him more often than I'd like to admit, drawn to him in a way I couldn't explain. I didn't want to think too hard about it.

As the sun climbed higher, we reached a clearing and took a break. Griffin handed me a water flask, and I took a grateful sip. I murmured my thanks and handed it back to him before wandering over to a large, semi-flat rock to climb up on and take a rest. My legs and feet were just starting to really ache, so it felt like perfect timing.

"No problem," he replied, his eyes crinkling at the corners as he smiled, a chuckle escaping him as he watched me scramble up the rock.

I huffed a little as I settled onto the smooth, weathered surface, leaning back on my arms. "So, do you have any fun stories from your childhood? Something to pass the time?"

Griffin thought for a moment while rubbing his hand over the stubble dusted along his angular jaw, a slow grin spreading across his face. The sight of his smile, rare and genuine, made my heart skip a beat. I found myself wishing I could see it more often.

"Well, there was this one time when I was about ten, just a lad. I grew up in Duskforge where I had this friend, Nolan, who could Shift into a hawk. We played a prank on the town's blacksmith, who was notorious for his bad temper."

I sat forward, interested. "What did you do?"

Griffin's grin widened. "We snuck into his forge and hid his tools all over town. Nolan flew around, dropping them in the most ridiculous places—on rooftops, in the market stalls, a wellspring, even in the town fountain. The blacksmith was furious, shouting his way all across the town, but he never found out it was us. We thought we were so clever."

I snickered, imagining the chaos. "Did you ever get caught?"

"Not for that, no," Griffin said with a snort. "But we did get into plenty of other trouble. Like the time we tried to build a raft and sail down the river using random wood we found just outside of town. The wood was half rotten, and the raft fell apart almost immediately. We ended up soaked and covered in mud, clawing our way up the riverbank. Our parents weren't too happy about that one."

I shook my head, smiling despite myself. "I never took you for such a troublemaker, Griffin."

"There's a lot you don't know about me," he teased, his eyes twinkling as he gave me a wink. He was being so playful, I didn't know how to respond. I was used to Griffin keeping himself distant from me, but slowly he was chipping away at the armor I surrounded myself with.

I was scared. But I didn't want to keep holding myself back. My time with Griffin meant something, no matter how much I wish it didn't. But I wouldn't hope for the best. I would just let come what may.

We continued our journey after about a fifteen minute break, the conversation flowing easily between us. Griffin shared more stories from his past, tales of hunts and adventures that had me laughing and shaking my head. There was a warmth between us, a growing camaraderie that felt natural and comforting.

Eventually, after some hours of walking, we stumbled upon a lively brook, its gentle burbling inviting us to rest and enjoy our lunch. Griffin caught a few fish with a sharpened stick, his movements swift and precise, while I gathered some herbs and edible plants. We cooked the fish over a small fire, the smell making my stomach growl audibly. My cheeks heated when Griffin chuckled at the sound.

Once the food had finished cooking, I couldn't contain myself and sank my teeth into the perfectly cooked fish. "This is delicious," I said once I finished chewing. "You have a talent for cooking over a campfire. Call me impressed."

"Years of practice," Griffin replied, looking quite pleased with himself. "I'm glad you like it."

We ate in companionable silence, the sounds of the surrounding forest all around us. I couldn't help but notice how natural it felt, sharing this moment with Griffin. Our eyes met over the fire, and I glanced away, my cheeks warming from more than just the fire's heat. I felt a sense of peace, a rare moment of contentment. It was easy to forget the troubles ahead, to simply enjoy the moment.

I pushed all thoughts of Sylvan Reach out of my head and watched Griffin instead. His skin had a gentle sheen of sweat from fishing and cooking over the open flame and he kept pushing his dark locks of hair out of his eyes, bringing my attention to his face.

The past day of travel already showed, his skin looking sun-kissed. I glanced down at my own arms, still pale as ever. He was lucky it was so easy for him not to look like a specter in the night. I sighed.

After lunch, we doused the campfire and continued on our way, the path winding through the forest. The sun filtered through the trees, the pattern of shadows dancing on the ground. I found myself walking closer to Griffin, our arms occasionally brushing.

As the afternoon wore on, the conversation turned to lighter topics. Griffin told me about his favorite places to hunt, the best spots for fishing, and the time he had to chase a stubborn deer for hours. I laughed at his stories, feeling a warmth blossoming in my chest that had nothing to do with the sun.

"You know," I said, a teasing glint in my eye, "I think you might just be a bit of a rogue."

Griffin raised an eyebrow, a smile playing at his lips. "A rogue, huh? I don't think I've ever been called that before."

"Well, there's a first time for everything," I replied, grinning.

He laughed, a deep, rumbling sound that made my heart

flutter. "I'll take it as a compliment."

As the sun dipped toward the horizon, the light took on a scarlet hue, painting the forest in warm colors. The fading light cast a soft glow on Griffin's features, and I admired the way it highlighted the strong lines of his face. When he caught me looking, I quickly averted my gaze, feeling a warm blush creep up my neck. I felt like a child with their first crush, unable to keep my eyes from Griffin for long. The air was cool and crisp, the promise of evening lingering in the shadows.

"We should find a place to set up camp soon," Griffin said, looking around. "It's getting late."

I nodded, feeling a pang of disappointment that the day was ending. "Yeah, you're right. Let's keep an eye out for a safe spot."

We walked in comfortable silence, the lighthearted mood of the day lingering. Eventually, we found a small clearing surrounded by trees, the ground covered in soft moss. It was a perfect spot to set up for the night.

We worked together to set up our tents and gather firewood, the routine familiar and comforting. The sun dipped ever lower until nightfall crept in, casting the world into gloom.

Later, as we sat by the fire, the darkness of the forest seemed to close in around us, the trees casting long shadows. There was an eerie stillness in the air, a sense of something watching from the depths of the forest.

I shivered, pulling my cloak tighter around me as the brightness of our day together drifted away into shadows. "Do you ever get the feeling that we're not alone out here?"

Griffin's gaze met mine, reflecting the violet of my eyes

back at me, his expression serious. "Sometimes. The forest can be…unpredictable. But we're safe here. I'll keep watch tonight, just in case."

I nodded, grateful for the opportunity to get some restful sleep. "Thanks, Griffin. I appreciate it."

He smiled, the tension easing from his shoulders. "It's what I'm here for."

We sat in silence for a while, me reading a book from my pack that I brought from our home and Griffin carving a piece of wood with the carving knife he carried in his pocket, the fire crackling between us. The sense of camaraderie from earlier in the day lingered, a comforting feeling amid the encroaching darkness.

"Tomorrow, we'll reach Sylvan Reach," I said, my eyes finding his and breaking the silence. "It's strange to think about going back after all this time."

Griffin nodded, his expression serious. He sat the carving knife and wood down on the moss-covered ground next to his crossed legs. "It'll be okay, Lyra. We'll find the answers we need. And whatever happens, we'll face it together."

His words were reassuring, a promise of support and understanding. I felt a flicker of hope bloom in my chest. Maybe we would find exactly what we needed, and this trip would have been worth it.

As the fire crackled and the shadows danced, we prepared to settle in for the night. The surrounding forest was alive with the sounds of night, but the nearness of Griffin beside me was a steady, reassuring anchor, leaving me without fear.

The conversation turned to our plans for approaching

Sylvan Reach. "I'll need to disguise myself," I explained. "The villagers can't know it's me. It could be dangerous."

Griffin looked concerned, but nodded, crossing his powerful arms. "What do you have in mind?"

"I'll use my magic to transform," I said, feeling a pang of fear at the thought before I shook it off, refusing to be deterred when we're so close. "I'll make myself look different, someone they won't recognize."

Griffin's brow furrowed. "Isn't that risky? What if something goes wrong?"

I smiled, almost reassuringly enough to convince myself too. "I've practiced, I can do it. Besides, it's the best way to avoid trouble."

He sighed, running a hand through his hair. "Alright. Just promise me you'll be careful."

"I will," I said softly. "Thank you, Griffin."

As the night deepened, the towering trees around our camp seemed to close in, the shadows growing ever longer and darker. There was an ominous feeling in the air, a sense of something lurking just out of sight. We both felt it, the unspoken tension that kept us on edge.

"I'll keep watch," Griffin said, his voice steady, fearless. "Get some rest, Lyra."

I nodded, my lids already heavy. Awake one minute, and the next, sleep took hold of me in an iron grip.

I jolted awake to the sound of an unearthly screech and Griffin's shout, my heart pounding. Griffin was engaged in a violent battle with a large, sleek creature, its body shimmering with an otherworldly luminescence that seemed to shift and change with the forest's shadows, making it almost seem like a trick of the eye. Its antler-like horns and glowing green eyes looked like something out of legend—some type of beast. What was it doing here in Sylvanwood? I wracked my brain to see if I remembered any creatures like this I may have heard of before, but came up empty.

"Stay back!" Griffin growled as I scrambled to my feet on shaky legs, his voice a mix of human and werewolf. His form was caught between shifts as he fought.

The beast moved with impossible speed, dodging Griffin's attacks effortlessly. Its eyes locked onto mine for a moment, and I felt a wave of fear and nausea wash over me, the creature's will invading my mind, scratching and scraping against whatever meager mental barriers I'd enacted until Griffin caused it to look away with a clawed swipe to its jaw.

Griffin lunged at it again, but the beast dodged and instead darted towards me, knocking me to my back with a blow from its enormous paw. In a desperate move, I aimed for its eyes with my free hand, digging my fingers into its left eye socket. There was a *pop,* and the creature recoiled with a human-like scream, blood and viscera gushing from the damaged orb of its eye.

Griffin seized the opportunity, his powerful claws slashing through the air. The creature swung wildly towards him and sank its teeth into his forearm, ripping a bellow from Griffin as the flesh tore easily under its powerful jaw. My magic surged within me and before I knew it, I was bounding towards them on powerful paws. This was unlike any transformation I'd ever experienced. It was raw, primal, and my instincts took over. The surge of power was almost intoxicating, the world exploding into colors and scents I'd never experienced before. But before I could even think about how I felt, my fangs poised to sink into the beast's thick hide around its neck. As I clenched my immense jaws, the sudden pull startled the creature into letting go of Griffin.

Despite the animal's immense strength, I found its weight to be lighter than expected as I aggressively shook its entire body like a dog with a chew toy. I threw it to the ground and stomped on its torso, hearing a crunch as I did. It scrambled to its feet, teeth bared and with blood pouring down the left side of its face. The beast loosed another unearthly scream and tore off into the forest, its fur blending seamlessly as soon as it reached the shadows.

I looked to where Griffin stood cradling his damaged arm and my eyes met his. The world looked different in whatever form I had become. Everything was sharper, more vivid, with a clarity I had never experienced before. I had no idea what I was, but in this form, his eyes were still a warm golden hue, now even more radiant, like morning sunshine over a blanket of fresh snow. The immense detail I was seeing made everything feel surreal and almost dream-like.

Griffin loosed a shuddering breath, breaking eye contact. All the adrenaline quickly flowed out of my body, leaving me shaking as my mana drained away and, with a crash, I fell to the ground as a young woman once again, my ivory tresses fanned out around me.

CHAPTER 7

I lay there panting, dizzy as my eyes readjusted to the world, as I had always seen it, in much less detail than before. My vision as just a mage felt so muted, the world dulled as though obscured by a fog. And there were so few colors now. I sighed, disappointed that I couldn't see the world so vibrantly all the time. Whatever creature I had become, I don't think it was from Aethralis. But I would have to figure that out once we were out of the immediate danger of the monstrous beast coming back.

"What the hell?" I asked incredulously, my voice trembling. "What in the world was that?" I threw an arm out in the direction the mysterious animal had disappeared off into before flopping it back into the dirt, my muscles exhausted.

"Some kind of Fae beast if I had to guess," Griffin ground out, the sound guttural and raw, his body contorting and the sounds of snapping bone and muscle filling the air as he became fully human again, his eyes scanning the darkened trees. The scent of blood became stronger, churning my stomach. "That's probably what we've sensed stalking us for the last couple of days."

The weight of Griffin's words sank in. I had felt that something was off, but never did I imagine it was something as dangerous as a Fae beast. I had to wonder what it was even doing here, given that as the name suggests, they usually live near the Fey where they worked as guardians of the forests. Some even had pacts with the beasts that increased the power of their Fey mana and helped them to attune even further with nature.

The scent of its magic lingered in the air, the smell of rotting vegetation making me curl my lip. There was something else going on, I could feel it. I just had to figure out what it was. First the sickness, now a Fae beast wandering Sylvanwood? There was no way it was a coincidence.

As I lay there, still reeling from the attack, Griffin's voice cut through my daze.

"Lyra, what was that?" His voice held concern and no small amount of awe. "I've never seen anything like… that."

I blinked slowly, trying to process his question. My entire brain was in a fog right now, and my thoughts were incredibly sluggish. "I have no idea. Nothing like that has ever happened to me before."

Griffin's brows shot up. "Never? I thought you had the ability for transformation?"

A beat of silence lapsed as I tried to look for the right words.

"I can, yes, but this was different. Usually I have to picture what I'm trying to become. I have to imagine it in my mind's eye and then allow my magic to come forth. This was more…

instinctual. It just… happened." I picked my hand up from the ground and turned it this way and that, just to make sure I was really myself again.

Slowly, Griffin nodded. He hissed out a breath as he shifted his wounded arm. "Whatever it was, it was damned impressive. I mean, that you basically took on that entire Fae beast on your own…" he trailed off, but I could hear the implied words. If I could do this, what else could I do?

I shook my head to clear my thoughts and dragged slowly myself to my feet, making my way over to Griffin. He clasped his arm to his chest, but I slowly pried his fingers away. It was worse than I had initially thought.

The beast's teeth nearly reaching bone. It was a grisly sight, and I had to swallow several times as my mouth filled with moisture, my stomach contents threatening to empty. I cleared my throat and jogged over to my forgotten pack, pulling out a small medical kit containing a small tincture from Louise, some cloth bandages and some needle and thread.

"I'm going to warn you in advance, I am not good at this," I said, directing Griffin over to a nearby stump where I knelt down in front of him. He slowly sat, sweat beading on his forehead. I could only imagine the pain he must be in.

I thrust the tincture towards his mouth. "Here, drink this. Louise gave it to me a while ago, just in case we needed it. It should help with any pain and help with the healing process."

Our eyes met as I tipped the small vial against his lips, and he drank the iridescent liquid. His throat worked as he swallowed it down, his tongue darting out to catch any remnants on his lower lip, drawing my attention to his mouth. The moment was so incredibly intimate and I became flustered, my fingers trembling just a little.

My face warmed, and I looked away, heat spearing low in my belly. Why was I feeling this way? Especially now of all times! What was wrong with me?

I took a deep breath and let it out, threading the needle and shaking off those thoughts. "I'm sorry in advance. This is definitely going to scar, but I'll at least help to close the wound as well as I can."

"I trust you." Griffin's voice was low and husky, his eyes sliding closed from the pain. The medicine would take time to take effect.

Without the sun, it was much more difficult to prepare, however I was determined. I'd never tried something like this, but… A whisper of magic improved my night vision by changing my eyes closer to a cat's, which helped immensely. My eyes strained almost immediately with this limited transformation, but it would have to do.

With Griffin's permission, I first cleaned the wound with the water remaining in our waterskin, then I set to work on closing the wound as best as I could. I wasn't able to do it perfectly, but my work was still better than nothing. The jagged lines were stitched back together roughly because of missing flesh, despite how careful I was during the process.

His face was pale and drawn, the lines of red on his arm

standing out staunchly against his skin and the gaps in the stitching causing rivulets of blood to run down his fingertips.

I took the bandages from the pack and bound his arm as tightly as I could to try and prevent any further blood loss and sat back on my haunches, wiping my hands on my cloak and releasing the magic I had been maintaining to help my vision. Everything immediately became much darker and I was temporarily blinded, blinking my watery eyes.

"I'm sorry I couldn't do more. There weren't many clean cuts from the bite." I said with a frown, guilt tugging at my heart. I wished now more than ever that I had a healing ability instead of this stupid transformation 'gift' I was given.

"We need to keep moving," Griffin said slowly, his voice low and gravelly. "It might come back, and next time we might not be so lucky."

I looked up at his face, his eyes still closed and his face just so pale and wan. We couldn't travel like this. I at least had to give time for the medicine Louise gave us to kick in and give Griffin some relief.

I slowly shook my head until I remembered he couldn't see. "No, we can't right now. Not with you like this."

Griffin tilted his head down to look at me, bleary-eyed. "I don't want to risk being out in the open right now. Moving along will put us into a safer position in case the fae beast comes back. I don't want to put you at risk."

I scoffed lightly. "Put me at risk? You're the one who was hurt! At least wait until Louise's tincture helps with your pain.

It shouldn't be long." I crossed my arms in defiance, standing up and leaning over Griffin. "Just rest. I'll keep watch."

Griffin's gaze narrowed as he leered up at me before his eyes seemed to slide shut of their own accord. He lay his upper body back on the large stump and left his feet planted on the ground. I sat next to his legs and leaned back, my cloak giving me a bit of cushion against the rough bark that would otherwise scratch my skin. I turned my eyes towards the dark, starless sky, desperately hoping for the night to end.

Time crept slowly by as I kept watch over Griffin. His ragged breathing slowly steadied and became deeper, more relaxed. Subconsciously, I matched my breathing to his, as though I could share his pain, though I knew it wasn't possible. I could only imagine the agony he was in with a wound like that. I hadn't expected that the medicine would take so long to work. The delay must be because of the additional healing properties imbued within it, if I had to guess. We had to rush to Sylvan Reach. Not only would he be safe there, but we could get him looked at by a healer.

I reached out and grasped Griffin's knee. With no response from him, my heart pounded nervously in my chest. I shook his knee more intensely, and he stiffened, sitting up quickly before hissing in pain. Cradling his arm against his chest, his gaze darted around before falling on me sitting next to him on the ground.

"Everything okay?" he asked, glancing around at the darkness of the surrounding woods.

"It's fine. I just figured enough time had passed that we should be good to get going. The last thing I want is for you to get some kind of infection from that bite." I quickly stood, gathering the rest of our things into our packs and shouldering my bag, choosing to carry his instead.

Griffin quietly huffed, but chose not to say anything. Smart man.

We moved quickly, the surrounding forest a maze of ancient trees and dense undergrowth. My senses were on high alert, every rustle of leaves and snap of twigs setting my nerves on edge. Griffin stayed close, his woodsy, leathery scent comforting. I ignored the light hint of blood that wafted from him as well.

"Have you encountered one of those Fey beasts before?" I asked, trying to clear my jangled nerves.

"Once," Griffin replied, his voice tight with pain while we strode through the brush, trying to find a fresh path to Sylvan Reach. "Years ago, a little ways outside of Duskforge. It was weaker, younger. Still, it took a group of us to drive it off."

His words did nothing to reassure me. The Fey beast we had just faced was neither weak nor young, but it had only taken us two to fend it off. I had to wonder if the creature he fought was maybe a different type of Fey beast. I couldn't help but wonder if the one that attacked us so abruptly was still out there, watching and waiting for another chance to strike.

The time passed in a blur of cautious steps and hushed whispers. The forest was a living entity, its magic thrumming just beneath the surface, but right now it felt more like a predator, lying in wait. Despite my exhaustion, I forced myself to stay alert, my magic simmering just below the surface, ready to be called upon if needed.

Griffin's voice startled me, adrenaline immediately spiking through my body. "Hey Lyra, about your transformation earlier." He paused.

My brows furrowed, and I became impatient when he didn't continue, so I prompted, "What about it?"

"What was it like? Becoming something like that?" His voice held a cautious curiosity, as though he was worried about offending me somehow.

I had to think about it. The entire fight with the Fey beast was a bit of a blur. "I don't think transforming for me is like Shifting for you. It's not painful, but usually there's a lot more effort that goes into it than this time."

He mulled over the words and then nodded thoughtfully. "I suppose it wouldn't be the same for you. It's a different type of magic that allows you to change after all, rather than an innate ability you're born with."

"Exactly. But this was kind of almost like a dream. I didn't think about it. It just happened. Suddenly, I was some kind of… monster." I shuddered, remembering the thought. The primal energy within me had been exhilarating in a way that I couldn't admit aloud. It was terrifying in its intensity, but it was *my* power that saved us. That saved Griffin. Part of me wanted to chase that feeling, but the more logical side of me knew I could never. That desire scared me almost as much as the transformation itself. I knew I could lose myself in that wild magic, and that horrified me.

There was much more to my ability than I knew, and this proved it. I didn't even know what kind of monster I had become and yet my magic just knew how to transform me into exactly what we needed.

I filed away those thoughts for later. Right now, we needed to focus on getting to Sylvan Reach as quickly as possible.

As dawn broke, the oppressive darkness gave way to a soft, golden light that worked to grant a false sense of security.

The change was almost magical, the forest shifting from a place of hidden threats to one of ethereal beauty. Birds began their morning songs, the melodies a welcome contrast to the tension of the night.

We paused to catch our breath, the anxiety easing slightly with the arrival of daylight. Griffin glanced at me, his eyes filled with concern.

"How are you holding up?" he asked, his voice softer now.

"Me? I'm fine. More importantly, how's your arm?" I put my hands on my hips, eyeing the bandages.

He shrugged. "I'm managing. The bleeding has slowed, so that's good. Still hurts like a bastard, though."

"We're close to Sylvan Reach finally. I just need to disguise myself and we can head there." I pointed over the ridge a short way away, where you could just barely see the tops of buildings peeking over, anxiety twisting my insides into knots.

But I had to be strong, especially for Griffin. The longer we took to get him to a healer, the more likely it was for him to get an awful infection from that bite.

"So, how does it work?" he asked finally, his gaze intent on my face.

I chewed my bottom lip and wrung my hands together before bracing myself. "I can't just change myself willy-nilly. When I am becoming an entirely different person, it has to at least be someone I've seen before. So I was thinking about becoming Louise. She would have a reason to come here, and because she's a mage, it wouldn't be surprising for her to show up."

Griffin was silent, assessing. Finally, he nodded. "It makes sense. It's dangerous though. What if Louise knew someone here?"

"I can bluff my way through it. Just tell me as much as you know about her."

Griffin didn't waste any time giving me all the details he knew about Louise. That she'd been in Haleshade at least five years, given that she'd been there when he had first moved there. She had never left except once two years ago, where she was gone for about three days and returned with nothing to say about it. He continued on and I took in as much detail as I could before taking a deep, centering breath.

It had been a long time since I used this ability in particular. Becoming another person always stressed me out, as it should. But I refused to be deterred. The people in Haleshade needed me. And even more importantly, Griffin needed me. I couldn't let him down.

Inhale.

Exhale.

Inhale. I pulled my mana to the surface.

Exhale. My magic cascaded over my body, leaving Louise in my place.

I turned my moss-colored eyes to Griffin, and his mouth was agape with surprise. He quickly schooled his face into more neutral features, but I couldn't help a small smile, proud that I'd surprised him. I could only hope that I could do this. That we could do this. I straightened my spine and prepared to walk into Sylvan Reach.

CHAPTER 8

I stood at the edge of Sylvan Reach, the familiar trees casting long shadows in the late afternoon light. It felt like being surrounded by old friends. I was always more at home in the trees than I was in the village.

The air was thick with the scent of pine and earth, but today it felt different. *I* was different. My body felt older, creakier. Whenever I took on the form of someone else, it was almost like I became them. Their ailments, their aches and pains all became mine until I released the form. I absently wondered if I would have been a talented healer if this ability wasn't so hated. Griffin stood beside me, his eyes scanning the village ahead.

"We're almost there," I said, though the voice that escaped me was that of Louise. My heart raced, climbing into my throat, choking. "Remember, we need to find out more about this sickness. And I need to keep up this… appearance."

Griffin nodded, his gaze shifting to me with a mixture of

concern and determination. He reached over and touched my shoulder, his hand warm and leeching away the chill that had settled over me. "We'll be careful. Just stick to the plan."

As we stepped into the village, the first thing I noticed was the subdued atmosphere. A somber quiet had settled over Sylvan Reach, snuffing out the usual bustling energy. There were no children yelling in the streets, parading about their newly discovered gifts. No murmured conversations or hawking of wares in the village center. Villagers shuffled about with wary glances, their faces drawn with worry and their children clutched to their bodies. It was disconcerting, to say the least.

We walked along the main street, the sound of our footsteps echoing off the stone buildings. I kept my head high, trying to exude the confidence Louise always had in Haleshade. It wasn't long before we attracted attention and my heart immediately stuttered into an unsteady rhythm. Whispers followed us, and I could feel eyes boring into me.

"Lou?" a woman's voice called from a nearby stall. "Louise, is that you?"

I paused in my stride, swallowing hard. Slowly, I turned to face the voice. It was Marla, the baker's wife. It looked as though she was just about to enter the bakery.

Marla had grown old in the time since I had last seen her. Her blonde hair was peppered with gray, her fair skin thin and creased with age. She approached us, her dark eyes huge and owl-like behind thick spectacles. She brought with her the scent of warm bread and tea spices. "I didn't know you were back in the village."

I forced a smile, hoping it looked natural. "Yes, Marla. I thought it would be for the best if I returned for a visit."

Marla nodded, but despite her age, her gaze was sharp. My palms became slick with sweat and fought the urge to wipe my hands on my skirt. "You've been away for a long time. It's good to see you. Keeping healthy? There's a sickness going around, you know."

I nodded slowly. "That's actually why I'm here."

Her shoulders sagged, and her gaze became melancholic. "It's been terrible. So many have fallen ill, and we don't know why. Some say it's a curse."

Griffin stepped forward, his presence a silent support. "We're looking for information. Anything that might help us understand what's happening."

Straightening, Marla glanced at him as though only just noticing his existence, then back at me. "Well, you'd best speak with Elder Brynn. She's been trying to find answers. She's over by the old university building, tending to the afflicted. There have been so many ill, we had to convert it into a temporary hospital."

"Thank you, Marla. We'd better hurry there," I said, relief washing over me now that I had an excuse to leave. We quickly made our escape, murmuring our goodbyes to Marla as we went.

As we continued towards the university, I could feel the villagers' eyes boring into us no matter where we were in Sylvan Reach. Some people recognized Louise and greeted me warmly, while others watched with suspicion and avoided us entirely. I did my best to avoid prolonged conversations, just to reduce any risk of discovery.

When we reached the makeshift hospital, the scene inside was heartbreaking. Rows of beds lined the walls, each occupied by a suffering villager. The air was thick with the scent of herbs and the acidic tang of potions. The room was filled with a constant hum, the nearly inaudible murmurs of the sick and their families.

I may not have met Elder Brynn before, but I recognized the authority she carried herself with. She was directing a small group of mages on how to alter their care to suit the changing needs of the sick.

At first glance, she was short and plump, wispy hairs escaping her bun to curl into her cheeks, softening the harsh edge of her expression. Despite the severe look she had, her voice was kind and soothing.

She also wore a set of sapphire robes. As we got closer, I saw that Elder Brynn wore an intricate diamond-encrusted brooch in the shape of a, eight-pointed star, encircled by a ring of runes.

At the center of the star was an open book, its pages filled with arcane symbols, symbolizing her high rank within the Arcane Order. My mouth went dry as we approached, and I quickly cleared my throat.

Her eyes widened slightly when she saw me. "Louise? It's been ages. I hadn't heard that you were coming." Elder Brynn's gaze flickered over me, lingering just a second too long, as though she was searching for something out of place.

"Usually you send word in case we need you to bring any supplies from outside the forest. What brings you here?"

Taking a deep breath to quell the anxiety currently twisting my insides, I inclined my head respectfully. "Elder Brynn, I've heard about the sickness. I didn't send any foreword that I would arrive because I wanted to see what we had learned about it so far and whether I could be of any assistance."

She studied me intensely for a moment before nodding. My skin prickled under her gaze, and I fought the urge to squirm. She finally broke her gaze, and I breathed a quick sigh of relief. "We need all the help we can get. Follow me."

Before turning around, the elder's eyes skated over Griffin, slightly behind me. Her eyes rounded with a hint of surprise. "You're injured?"

Griffin reached a hand up to the back of his neck and rubbed it. "Ah, yeah, about that…" His gaze slid towards me before returning to the elder. "We were actually attacked by a Fey beast on the way here. We just barely managed to fight it off."

A gasp escaped Elder Brynn and her hand flew to cover her mouth. "A Fey beast? Here in Sylvan Reach? That's concerning. What the hell could something like that be doing here? They usually stay in the Starfall Veil."

My confusion must have been apparent on my face because she clarified, "Starfall Veil is the realm of the Fae. It's kind of similar to Sylvan Reach in that it's primarily a large magical forest, but it's separate from us. And most Fey beasts are tied to a master, so if a Fey beast is running around here…where is its master?" She loosed a shuddering breath, as though the very thought was awful in itself.

Then Elder Brynn led Griffin towards an empty cot nearby. He went obediently and settled on the cot. His face was already paling, so I'd guess that Louise's potion was wearing off.

"Let me get a look at this wound of yours. Was it teeth or claws?" she bustled around, efficiently gathering supplies.

"Teeth," I said, before Griffin could even open his mouth. Elder Brynn sent a knowing look my way. Her lips lightly quirked in a smile.

With great efficiency, she removed the bandages and sucked some air through her teeth at the sight that greeted her. "This looks positively awful."

Despite the pain he must be in, Griffin chuckled. "I'm hoping it looks worse than it is. I can still move my fingers after all." He wiggled his fingers to demonstrate his point.

Brynn clucked her tongue and strut over to a cabinet full of potions, herbs and vials. "I've not seen anything like this in a long time," she said over her shoulder. "You're going to be incredibly lucky if there isn't already an infection starting."

She soon returned with two bottles. One held a thick, sludgy green-black liquid, and the other looked like ordinary water. Forgetting myself, I cocked my head in confusion as to what these glass bottles could contain.

Luckily, the elder didn't notice the look on my face and instead explained to Griffin, "This will go on the wound," she said, gently shaking the container that looked to have water in it. With a *thoomp* sound, she popped the cork and poured it over his wound.

A scream ripped its way from Griffin's throat, and immediately my heart pounded in my ears. I rushed over to his side and looked at his arm. There was a black smoke pouring from the wound and the liquid hissed and spit as though it were acid eating through his skin, although there was no evidence of that.

"Just as I thought," she murmured. "An infection was already spreading from this wound." She caressed his forehead and his screams quieted to pained whimpers. It hurt my heart to hear Griffin like this. I didn't realize he was in this much pain, how much he was holding back just so we could make it here. A wave of guilt swept over me and I looked around the room instead, though I reached my hand out to touch Griffin's arm and give at least a small measure of comfort.

The other mages in the room turned towards us, blatant curiosity written across their faces, but the elder shooed them away and continued to work. She uncorked the sludgy looking liquid next, holding it to Griffin's mouth. "This will help with the pain and healing. It has a sedative effect."

Griffin didn't even hesitate and choked down the thick, viscous liquid. He gagged on the taste, but within moments, his face relaxed. "This is some powerful stuff."

"Yes, and you'll be sleeping well in no time," she said, pushing his shoulders back so that he laid down on the cot.

"This will be good for you to settle in before dragging you two into the thick of it," Elder Brynn said, dragging a stool over so that I could sit near Griffin. "I'll be back to check on you two soon. I hadn't realized the journey was so treacherous. This will also give me some time to check around regarding that Fey beast."

Without even giving me time to respond, she bustled away. The other mages gave us a wide berth, and I glanced over at Griffin. He was already asleep, snoring away. A hint of a smile lifted my lips.

It was a couple of hours when Elder Brynn returned. Griffin was awake and seemed to be doing much better, his color back in his cheeks. I had re-bandaged his wound with some nearby gauze and it did not resume bleeding.

Surprisingly, it was no longer angry and red. I knew Werefolk healed quickly, but I had no doubt that it was doing so much better because of the potions that Elder Brynn had provided.

She led us to a quieter corner of the room, away from prying ears. "Despite my best efforts in determining where and how the Fey beast arrived here, no one has seen or heard about it before you. The Arcane Order will keep watch to ensure that the village stays safe." Elder Brynn assured us.

"Now, back to the reason you are here. The sickness started a few weeks ago," she began, her voice low. "At first, it was just a few cases. But it's been spreading, and we can't find a cure. The symptoms are strange, almost… *otherworldly.*"

Griffin frowned. "Otherworldly? What do you mean?"

Elder Brynn hesitated, glancing around before continuing. "There are rumors… whispers of dark magic. Some believe it's the work of a powerful mage."

My heart sank to my stomach. "Has anyone tried to find the source? Any clues?"

She shook her head slowly. "We've tried, but it's like chasing shadows. Every lead seems to turn into a dead end."

I exchanged a glance with Griffin, his dark brows lowered with concern. This was more serious than we'd thought. "Is there anyone who might know more? Someone who's been looking into this?"

Elder Brynn nodded slowly. "There's one. A healer named Thorne. He's been treating the sick and studying the illness. He lives on the outskirts of the village, near the old oak."

"Thank you, Elder Brynn," I said, my mind already racing with possibilities.

As we left the makeshift hospital, Griffin turned to me. "We should visit Thorne as soon as possible. If anyone has answers, it might be him."

I nodded in agreement. But as we made our way to Thorne's home, I couldn't shake the feeling that we were being watched. The villagers' wary glances and whispered conversations followed us like shadows.

As we approached Thorne's house, a sense of unease washed over me. The small, weathered cottage stood amidst a colorful array of medicinal herbs and plants, their fragrant aromas mingling in the air. I hesitated, my heart pounding in my chest.

What if he saw through my disguise? What if he recognized me? The creaking of the old wooden porch beneath our feet echoed in the quiet surroundings, amplifying my anxiety. I couldn't help but wonder if Thorne knew Louise too well, if he held any clue to our connection.

The weight of uncertainty pressed upon me, making me question how we would ever escape from this potentially dangerous encounter.

Griffin rolled his shoulders, trying to ease some of his own tension. "We'll get through this. Just remember why we're here."

I took a deep breath and knocked on the door. Moments later, it creaked open, revealing a tall, thin man with sharp features and dark, intense eyes. His blonde hair was pulled back away from his face with a leather thong and shorn on the sides, and he wore simple brown breeches and a stained white linen shirt. He looked vaguely familiar, though I couldn't place where I'd seen him before.

"Louise?" His voice, soft yet commanding, was cautious, as if unsure whether to believe his own eyes.

"Yes," I replied, forcing a cheery smile. I didn't know how well Louise knew this man. He was a healer though, so I could assume they were at least colleagues at one point. "I heard from Elder Brynn that you've been treating and researching the sickness. We need your help."

Thorne's gaze shifted between Griffin and me, his expression unreadable. "And who is this?" he asked, looking over my shoulder to where Griffin stood.

"This is my traveling companion, Griffin. He is one of the Werefolk. His protection was needed to traverse the forest on my way here."

After a pause and a searching glance, he stepped aside and gestured towards the inside of his cottage. "Come in. There's much to discuss."

As we entered the dimly lit room, filled with shelves containing jars of herbs, tinctures, and medical instruments, I couldn't shake the feeling that we were on the brink of uncovering something significant. The air was thick with the scent of medicinal plants and a faint odor. The smell of sickness, cloying and unpleasant. I wrinkled my nose.

Thorne led us to a workspace in the center of the room that had a large table and a couple of simple wooden chairs. The tabletop was rife with various remedies and notes scattered about. The papers had drawings of creatures afflicted with various maladies, some with tumors, others with mottled skin, others that appeared normal but seemed to have more extensive documentation.

I pried my eyes away from the pages and turned to Thorne. He gestured for us to sit, and I slowly settled into one of the chairs, my body aching. Louise must be very resilient to work as much as she does with a body that becomes sore so quickly. Griffin chose not to sit, instead standing next to one of the many rows of bottles, potions, and tinctures. Thorne wandered over to the shelf and picked up a large, round potion bottle, swirling the incandescent fluid within. His eyes held an intense look as he held the glass up to the light.

"What have you found?" Griffin asked, wasting no time.

Thorne sighed, putting the bottle down with a *clink* and sinking into the remaining chair, rubbing his temples. He leaned forward and put his elbows on the table, crumpling the paper with an exasperated sound. "It's not good. This sickness, it's unlike anything I've seen before. I've been treating patients and studying the symptoms, but nothing seems to work."

I leaned forward and braced my arms on my knees, my heart pounding. "Do you think it's something beyond natural causes?"

Thorne nodded slowly, leaning back in the chair and rubbing his neck. His eyes looked haunted, empty. "It's possible. The way it spreads, how it resists treatment...it all points to something unnatural. I've even consulted some old medical texts, looking for similar cases in the past, but nothing quite matches." He gestured to the many pages littering the table, the sheets covered with notes in black ink and strange illustrations.

"So what do we do if nothing seems to match? Is there anything we can do to stop the spread?" Griffin asked.

Thorne hesitated, his dark eyes flicking to me, the inky blackness unnerving. "There might be. I've been working on a potential cure, but it's experimental and risky. It requires incredibly rare ingredients and... a unique approach."

I swallowed hard. "What kind of approach?"

He shook his head. "I'm still working out the details. But it's clear that it won't be easy. It might even be dangerous."

Griffin's jaw tightened. "We'll do whatever it takes. Just tell us what we need to do."

Thorne studied us for a moment, then nodded. "Very well. I'll prepare what I can. Meet me here tomorrow at dawn. We'll need all the time we can get."

As we left Thorne's cottage, the weight of his words hung heavy in the air. The sun was setting, casting long shadows over the village. I glanced at Griffin, his expression mirroring my determination and fear.

"We're in this together," he said in a hushed tone, ever aware of the ears that may be listening in Sylvan Reach. "No matter what."

I nodded, my resolve hardening. "We'll save them. I won't let this sickness destroy my home."

As we made our way back to the village center, I couldn't shake the feeling of being watched. The villagers' wary glances followed us, and I knew that maintaining Louise's facade would only get harder. But I had to try. For the sake of Haleshade and all others afflicted by this terrible sickness.

That night, as I lay in a cramped, rented room, sleep eluded me. My mind raced with thoughts of the ritual, the sickness, and the sacrifices we might have to make. But one thing was evident: we couldn't afford to fail. No matter what may come my way, I was determined to see it through and save Haleshade.

CHAPTER 9

The first rays of dawn crept through the dusty window, painting the room in hues of gold and amber. I hadn't slept, my mind a whirlwind on repeat of everything that could possibly go wrong during our time here. As I rose, my sore muscles protested, a reminder of the long journey that had brought us here, along with the form I still wore.

Since I have never worn another's appearance for so long, I didn't know if I would wake up looking like myself or not, and I couldn't risk being found out. Padding over to the small bathroom attached to my room, I splashed cold water on my face, the shock helping to clear the fog of sleeplessness.

Louise's mossy green eyes stared back at me from the mirror hanging in front of the sink, dark circles marking my face from the lack of sleep. My mana was being drained like never before, holding this form for so long, and it caused a bone-deep ache. I had to wonder how long this could go on before I just couldn't do it anymore. Not like I had a choice right now, though. If anyone found me as, well, me in this village, I'd be jailed, or worse.

I quickly dressed in a warm sky blue dress and shrugged into my cloak, mentally preparing for this trip back to Thorne's cottage. I quickly brushed through my hair and pinned it back into a simple twist. Taking a deep breath, I made my way from my room to the exit of the inn.

Outside, the air was crisp and held a light fog, carrying the scent of dew and pine. Griffin waited, his broad shoulders tense, eyes scanning the quiet street. Without a word, we set off toward Thorne's cottage, our footsteps echoing in the early morning stillness.

As we turned onto the main street, a gasp caught in my throat. Griffin stopped me with a hand on my elbow, his brows raised. "What is it?"

I couldn't force the words, but I couldn't turn away from them. My parents were just a few paces ahead. They looked different from what I remembered. The faces that lived in my memories didn't exist anymore. There were deep wrinkles carving grooves around their eyes, their mouths. My mother's once-rich chestnut-colored hair was now streaked liberally with gray, and my father's shoulders, once proud and strong, now sagged under an invisible weight. I absently wondered if they missed me. I rubbed a hand against my chest as though to assuage the ache that bloomed there.

I was just standing there in the middle of the road and before I could get it together, my mother's honey-colored gaze landed on me and her eyes lit up. "Louise!" she called, completely unaware of the pain her voice caused me. My father turned too and a familiar smile spread across his face, something I'd rarely seen since that awful night when I was 'gifted' this power. I never thought I'd see them again and here they were, right in front of me.

And yet… I couldn't even show my true face. I couldn't trust that they wouldn't out me to the rest of the village. I quickly turned away as though I hadn't heard her. My heart was shattering and my breath hitched in my throat. Concern etched across Griffin's face. Tears filled my eyes and fell before I could catch myself. Luckily, Griffin acted quickly, ushering me down a nearby alleyway. We just kept walking until we reached the outskirts of town where it was quiet.

Fat tears rolled down my cheeks the entire way despite how furiously I tried to stop them. As soon as we were alone, Griffin gripped my shoulders tightly and turned me to face him. "Are you okay? What happened, Lyra?" he asked softly, the worry plain on his face.

I swallowed thickly, unable to force the words out before a sob escaped me. Before I knew what was happening, I was surrounded by the scent of wood and leather and it was *warm*. Griffin's arms were wrapped around me and I just cried and cried until I couldn't anymore.

After I got myself back together, I awkwardly pulled myself from Griffin's arms. I refused to admit to myself how much I wanted to stay wrapped in his embrace and just forget everything. But my life could never be that easy, and I could never have him for myself. I had to keep reminding myself of that. Just the fact that I had to be here disguised as Louise was enough to cement that fact.

"Those people who called out to me were my parents," I said before I could talk myself out of it.

"Your parents?" he repeated.

"Yeah… and I just didn't expect to see them here. I don't know why, given that I knew when I was here last, they still lived here. It was just harder than I expected seeing them." I admitted, my voice cracking.

Griffin's eyes held sympathy, and it angered me for a reason I couldn't explain.

"Don't you dare pity me, Griffin. I don't need them or anyone else. It's been just me for years and I've suffered through life this long with no one," I said bitterly, full of vitriol.

He shook his head, "I don't pity you, Lyra. I admire you. It must have been hard, leaving as basically a child."

I refused to admit that yes, it had been hard, and I held so much fury in my heart about the unfairness of it all. "It's just unfair. It's all unfair. Why couldn't I have gotten a normal gift? Why did I have to get this damn *curse*?" I spat, venom flowing from my words.

Griffin's words were soft as he said, "Lyra, it's who you are. You can't change it, no matter how much you want to. And if not for that, you and I likely wouldn't have met. And I think that would have been a damn shame."

My heart stuttered at his words, and my gaze snapped

up to his. His eyes were like sunshine chasing away the clouds surrounding my heart, and I couldn't help but curse him for it. I couldn't afford this weakness. I didn't want to be hurt again. To lose yet another person who I cared about.

"Forget it. Let's just get to Thorne's house before he changes his mind," I murmured, all the fire gone from my words. My shoulders sagged as the weight of my feelings dragged me down. Griffin reached out as though he were going to touch my arm, but then his hand dropped and he nodded. We started back towards Thorne's house, careful to avoid the street we'd seen my parents earlier.

Thorne's door creaked open before we could knock, as if he'd been waiting. The healer looked even more haggard than the day before, dark circles under his eyes a testament to a sleepless night.

"Come in," he said, his voice hoarse. He cleared his throat. "There's much to discuss."

The cottage interior was a chaos of papers, books, and vials. Thorne led us to a cleared space at the center, where a large map of Aethralis lay spread across the table. He pointed to a region in the north, his long finger tracing the outline of a territory I'd only heard whispered about, as no one dared to go there.

"Vespara," Thorne crooned, his voice barely above a whisper as he touched the letters scrawled on the parchment. "The kingdom of vampires."

Griffin tensed beside me and crossed his arms, brow furrowing. "What does Vespara have to do with the plague?"

Thorne's dark eyes gleamed with a mixture of excitement

and trepidation. "Everything, potentially. I've been analyzing reports from across Aethralis, and there's a pattern. The sickness... it doesn't touch Vespara."

The implications of his words hung heavy in the air. Placing my hands on the table, I leaned closer to the map, studying the territory of Vespara. There wasn't much there aside from the name. Seems whomever created the map had not actually attempted to go there, not that I could blame them. Vampires have always had a certain reputation, after all. "You think the vampires are immune?"

"It's more than that," Thorne replied, shuffling through a stack of papers. He pulled out a worn parchment, covered in spidery writing. "This is an account from the last great plague from centuries ago. It mentions a cure derived from the blood of the undying."

Griffin frowned and ran a hand through his hair, exasperated. "Vampire blood? That's your cure?"

Thorne nodded, his eyes bright with excitement and a wide grin stretching his lips. "Not just any vampire blood. We need the blood of a living vampire - one of the royal family of Vespara."

The room seemed to spin around me as his words sank in. "You want us to go to Vespara and... what? Ask a royal vampire for a vial of blood?"

"Precisely," Thorne said, his eyes locking with mine and trapping my gaze. The darkness held there felt deep, unfathomable. A shiver raced up my spine. "And not just any vampire. You need to find the young prince. He's rumored to be more... approachable than the rest of his family."

Griffin's hands clenched into fists and he took a step towards Thorne, his voice lowering to a growl. "This is madness. We can't just walk into a vampire kingdom and expect to leave alive, let alone with royal blood."

Thorne's gaze didn't waver. "It's the only way," he said, his grin falling away, voice low and urgent. "The plague is spreading faster than we can contain it. Without this cure..." He paused and sighed, finally breaking eye contact to look at the sprawl of papers in front of us. "Without this cure, Sylvan Reach - all of Aethralis - will fall."

The words hung in the air, heavy and ominous. I felt as if the ground had suddenly shifted beneath my feet, the world tilting on its axis. Beside me, Griffin went rigid, his face a mask of shock and disbelief.

"What do you mean, all of Aethralis?" "Griffin demanded, his voice filled with disbelief." "Last we heard, it was just a few isolated cases in the outlying villages."

Thorne shook his head grimly, reaching for a stack of papers on his cluttered desk. He spread them out before us, and I felt my heart sink as I took in the contents. Maps, charts, hastily scribbled notes - all painted a picture far more dire than I had imagined.

"These are reports from the past week alone," Thorne explained, his finger tracing a line that snaked across the map of Aethralis. "The plague started here in Sylvan Reach. Then it slowly crept to the nearby villages, however by now it has touched every village, city and kingdom in Aethralis. This will only continue to get worse."

The more that Thorne spoke, the more I got the feeling that his dark eyes were tracking my movements. How I may hesitate a fraction of a second too long before responding to her name. But it was so fleeting of a feeling, I ignored it. I needed to pay attention to the issue at hand.

I leaned closer, my eyes scanning the documents. Names of towns and villages I knew and traveled through myself, now marked with ominous black Xs. Population numbers, dwindling at an alarming rate. Descriptions of symptoms that made my stomach churn.

"But... how?" I whispered, my voice barely audible. "How did it spread so quickly?"

Thorne's expression was grim. "We don't know. It's as if the disease has a mind of its own, seeking new victims. No quarantine has contained it. No treatment has shown any effect."

Griffin slammed his fist on the table, causing us both to jump and turn towards him. His golden eyes radiated with a rage I'd never seen in him before. "Why weren't we told? Why keep this hidden?"

"To prevent panic," Thorne replied, his voice tired. "The Order thought they could contain it, find a cure before word spread. Especially since it seems to have a magical source. But now..." He gestured helplessly at the papers before us.

The weight of the situation pressed down on me, making it hard to breathe. All of Aethralis... millions of lives hanging in the balance. And somehow, impossibly, the key to saving them lay in the hands of the vampires of Vespara.

I closed my eyes, feeling the enormity of the responsibility settle on my shoulders. When I opened them again, I saw both men watching me intently, waiting for my response. The fate of our world seemed to hinge on my next words.

Taking a deep breath, I forced myself to focus, to push past the fear and shock. "How do we even get into Vespara?" I asked, my voice steadier than I felt.

The question hung in the air, heady and dark. As Thorne opened his mouth, a weight settled in my gut. This was impossible. There was no way.

A smile flickered across Thorne's face, enigmatic and unsettling, as he pushed away from the table. "That's where things get... interesting." His ebony eyes bore into mine, a knowing glint that made my skin prickle with unease. "Tell me, Louise, have you ever considered how fascinating the concept of identity is?"

The abrupt change of topic caught me off guard. "I... what do you mean?"

Thorne paced, his movements slow and deliberate. "Identity. The essence of who we are. It's not just in our blood or our bones, is it? It's in the way we move, the cadence of our speech, the flicker in our eyes when we're caught off guard." He paused, turning to face me. "Wouldn't you agree?"

My mouth immediately went dry and my eyes briefly touched on Griffin before returning to Thorne. "I suppose so."

"You see," Thorne continued, his voice taking on a scholarly tone that did nothing to ease the growing tension in the room, "I've always been fascinated by the minutiae of behavior. Otherkind, animals, human, it doesn't matter. As a healer, it's essential to notice the small things. A slight tremor in the hand, a hitch in the breath - they can tell you so much about a person's condition."

Griffin shifted beside me, his discomfort palpable as he moved to stand at my shoulder. Tension rolled off him in waves. "What does this have to do with getting into Vespara?"

Thorne's eyes never left mine. "Patience, Griffin. I'm getting there." He took a step closer to me. "Louise, do you remember when you were ten, and you fell from that old oak tree by the river? Do you recall the scar it left on your left palm?"

My heart thundered in my chest. I fought to keep my expression neutral, but I could feel a bead of sweat forming on my brow. My left hand clenched into a fist, seemingly of its own volition. Thorne paid it no mind.

"Or perhaps," Thorne pressed on, his voice softening, "you remember the winter when you were fourteen, and that terrible cough kept you bedridden for weeks? The way your voice was hoarse for months afterward?"

Griffin's confusion was evident in his voice. "Thorne, what are you-"

"Quiet," Thorne cut him off, still focused entirely on me. "I'm curious to hear Louise's recollection of these events. After all, they were quite significant moments in her life. Weren't they, Louise?"

The room felt too small, the air too thick. I struggled to find words, my mind racing and my breath quickening. "I... I don't..."

"No?" Thorne's eyebrow arched. "That's strange. Because I remember them quite vividly. You see, I've known Louise since she was a child. I've treated every scrape, every fever, every ailment. I know the map of her life written on her body."

He leaned in closer, his voice dropping to barely above a whisper. "So tell me, why is it that when I look at you, I see a stranger wearing a familiar face?"

The silence that followed was deafening. I could hear my heartbeat loudly in my ears, my right hand drawing into a fist to stop the trembling. Griffin stood frozen beside me, the implications of Thorne's words slowly dawning on him.

"Who are you?" Thorne asked, his voice low but unyielding. "What power do you possess that makes you believe you can walk into the realm of vampires and emerge unscathed? What... unique talent allows you to wear a face that isn't your own?"

I felt the walls of my carefully constructed world crumbling around me. Thorne's gaze held me captive, filled with a mixture of curiosity, hope, and something else I couldn't name.

"How long?" I managed to whisper, my voice barely audible.

A sad smile touched Thorne's lips. "Since the moment you walked through my door. You may wear Louise's face, but you can't capture her essence. Not to someone who knows her as well as I do."

Griffin's voice cut through my shock, however he held firm to our ruse. "What's going on? Louise, what is he talking about?" His fiery gaze never moved from Thorne's face, gauging his next move.

Thorne finally broke his gaze from mine, turning to Griffin. "She's not Louise, my friend. She never was." He looked back at me, his gaze sharp. "It's time to drop the illusion. Show us who you really are... Lyra."

Griffin stepped forward, positioning himself in front of me as a trickle of his intense aura flared around us, the scent of leather and citrus blooming in the air. "If you know who she is, then you know what she can do. How dangerous it would be for her in Sylvan Reach, much less in Vespara."

"It's precisely because of what she can do that this plan has a chance of succeeding," Thorne countered. He turned to me, his expression softening. "Lyra, your ability to transform... it's the key to infiltrating Vespara. You can become someone the vampires would welcome, someone who could get close to the royal family."

The room fell silent as I processed his words. The risk was enormous, but so was the potential reward. If we could find a cure...

"I'll do it," I said, my voice steadier than I felt.

Griffin's face darkened and his words left him in a growl. "Lyra, no. It's too dangerous."

I placed a hand on his arm, feeling the tension in his muscles. "We don't have a choice, Griffin. If there's even a chance this could stop the plague, we have to try."

Thorne nodded, wandering over to the other side of the table and taking a seat in the chair waiting there. "Thank you, Lyra. I know I'm asking a lot, but this could save countless lives."

He leaned over, pointing to a location just outside Vespara's borders. "There's a small trading post here, frequented by vampires and various Otherkind. It's your best chance of making contact and finding a way into the kingdom."

Griffin's jaw clenched. "I'm coming with you."

I shook my head. "No, it's too risky. If something goes wrong, one of us needs to be free to continue the search for a cure.”

His eyes met mine, a storm of emotions swirling in their warm honey depths. After a long moment, he nodded. “Promise me you’ll be careful.”

“I promise,” I said, trying to inject more confidence into my voice than I felt. It felt odd, making a promise like this to him. I knew that no matter what, I would try and return just so I wouldn’t let him down.

Thorne cleared his throat, and I begrudgingly looked away from Griffin’s all-encompassing gaze. “There’s one more thing. The blood needs to be fresh, and it needs to be willingly given. Force or trickery will negate its healing properties.”

I furrowed my brow. “That doesn’t make sense. Why would the properties of the blood change just because it is not willingly given?”

Thorne loosed a sigh. “I couldn’t tell you. Vampires have a particular magic of their own relating to their blood. Maybe that is why their blood has never been harnessed in this way before.”

I let out a humorless laugh. “So not only do I need to get close to a vampire prince, but I need to convince him to willingly give me his blood? Anything else?”

Thorne’s expression was grim. “Just this: be wary of the young prince. He may be more approachable than his kin, but he’s still a vampire. Don’t let your guard down, not for a moment.”

As the sun climbed higher in the sky, we finalized our plans. Thorne provided maps, what little information there was to be found on Vesparan customs, and a small vial for the blood. Griffin reluctantly agreed to stay behind, coordinating with Thorne and continuing to search for alternative cures.

As I prepared to leave, gathering supplies and steeling myself for the journey ahead, I caught sight of my reflection in a small mirror hanging on the wall between the many shelves lining the room.

The face of Louise looked back at me, a stranger wearing my determination. I took a deep breath, letting the transformation fade for a few seconds. For a moment, I saw myself - Lyra, the girl who had been forced from her home, now preparing to walk into the den of monsters to save it.

"Ready?" Griffin asked from the doorway, his voice tight with concern. He had an unidentifiable emotion lurking behind his eyes and I didn't know what to say or do. Would he be okay while I was gone? Was this a mistake? Should we just run?

I said none of these things. Instead, I just nodded, shouldering my pack and disguise again firmly in place. "As I'll ever be."

We stepped out into the sunlight, the village of Sylvan Reach spread before us. In the distance, I could see the effects of the plague - shuttered windows, empty streets. The weight of my mission pressed down on me, a constant reminder of what was at stake.

As we reached the edge of the village, Griffin pulled me into a fierce embrace. "Come back," he whispered, his voice rough with an unnamed emotion. Startled, I returned his embrace. "Whatever happens, just come back."

Our hug lingered, incredibly warm and comforting. As we pulled back, chill air slipped between us and I shivered. "I will. I promise."

Before I could turn to leave, Griffin's hands shot out, grabbing my jaw in a caress. A small gasp escaped me from the surprise and he drew me in close. His eyes were like sunshine, luminous and beautiful. And like sunshine, my skin warmed in their presence as his gaze traced over my skin.

Panic didn't have time to set in before his lips were on mine. The sensation was shocking. Gentle, warm, a little scratchy from his stubble. His mouth was gentle but insistent, leaving little room for me to resist. Not that I wanted to in that moment. My eyes slipped closed, and I melted against him. It lasted only a moment and then we reluctantly had to separate.

My mouth still tingled when reality crashed back into me. This single moment might be all we ever get. I was willingly wading into dangerous waters and I may never return. Part of me wanted to cling to him, to take this little slice of normalcy, of intimacy, and never leave. But I couldn't. Being cowardly wouldn't just hurt me, it could hurt countless others. I needed to be strong, and there was no room for this weakness. His hand reached for me as I stepped away.

"I'll… I'll be back. Be here when I arrive." I murmured, then with one last look, I pulled my cloak around me like a shield and turned on my heel to leave. Griffin didn't respond, just looked like there were so many words left unsaid. I could only hope that I would hear them when I returned, whatever it may be. But for now, I had no choice but to leave.

With a last look at Sylvan Reach and at Griffin's worried face, I turned north. Somewhere beyond the horizon lay Vespara, and within it, a vampire prince who held the key to saving Aethralis. Every step took me further from everything I knew, towards a kingdom of shadows and blood.

But I was Lyra, one of, if not the last, transformation mage. I had faced fear and prejudice, had fled my home and found a new purpose. Now, I would face the vampires of Vespara, would look into the eyes of the young vampire prince himself. And somehow, someway, I would return with what we all hoped was the cure.

The road stretched before me, long and uncertain. But I took that first step, and then another, my resolve growing with each passing moment. The fate of Aethralis hung in the balance, and I would not let it fall.

CHAPTER 10

The setting sun painted the sky in bruised hues of crimson and purple as I stumbled over the crest of the last hill. It had taken me weeks of travel to get here, carefully following the map drawn out for me by Thorne. My muscles screamed with each step, a constant reminder of the countless miles between me and Sylvan Reach.

The pack on my back felt like it was filled with stones, its straps cutting into my shoulders. I adjusted it for the hundredth time, wincing as the rough fabric pulled against my raw skin even through my cloak and dress.

Wind whipped across the stark landscape, throwing loose waves of hair that escaped my hood into my eyes and carrying the bite of approaching winter. The air was filled with the faint scent of decay. My lips were dry and cracked, my mouth felt as though it were filled with sand.

Gone were the lush forests I was used to, with their comforting canopy and familiar sounds. Instead, scraggly barren shrubs clung desperately to rocky soil, their branches rattling like old bones in the relentless gale. As darkness crept in, shadows seemed to writhe in the corners of my vision, putting me on edge.

I glanced over my shoulder more often than I cared to admit, my hand instinctively reaching for the dagger now at my hip. I picked it up along the way after receiving one too many suspicious looks during my trek up north. Figured it would be better to have it and not need it than to need it and not have it.

I inhaled sharply, the frigid air stinging my lungs and leaving a metallic taste in my mouth. The loneliness of this mission weighed heavily upon me, and I hugged myself tightly, trying to gather my resolve. I was really missing Griffin right about now. He seems like the kind of guy who would just exude heat. Unbidden, the image of us curled together under a fur danced across my mind and my breath caught in my throat. A blush crept up my neck, and I vigorously shook the thought out of my head.

Griffin's face flashed in my mind - his furrowed brow, the worry in his eyes as we said our goodbyes. "Come back," he'd said, his voice tight with concern. The memory of our parting was both a comfort and a source of anxiety. I could almost hear his rumbling voice as he cautioned me about the dangers ahead. His absence made the risks feel almost insurmountable.

With that ever-so-happy thought, I sighed. My feet moved mechanically, one in front of the other, driven by a rhythm born of weeks on the road. The monotony of travel had become both a blessing and a curse. It dulled the sharp edges of fear but left my mind free to conjure increasingly awful scenarios of what may lie ahead. By this point, I feel like I could write an entire horror novel with all the haunting ideas I'd had running on a constant stream through my mind.

Each step sent shockwaves of pain through my blistered and bruised feet, the discomfort a constant companion on this lonely journey. It honestly felt like I'd been traveling for years as opposed to a few weeks. Everything seemed to blend together despite the changing scenery. Every day felt the same, with varying degrees of anxiety depending on what I may come across. It reminded me too much of the time before Haleshade, when I was always alone.

I traveled for six years by myself, always too scared to get close to anyone. And once I finally did, here I was, back on my own because of some stupid sickness. It felt so unfair. A sting hit my eyes, but I bit my lip, determined not to cry. I was almost there, and then I can focus on moving forward, so I can get back to my home…and to Griffin.

As I drew closer to Vespara's borders, the very air seemed to change. It grew thick and heavy, each breath sinking into my lungs and making me fight to keep my breathing even, suffocating me. Black spots swam in my vision while I struggled to adjust. I braced my hands on my knees and took deep, open breaths, and after an intense few minutes, I breathed just a little easier. My magic coiled beneath my skin, poised to strike as though sensing the inherent danger.

Wisps of fog curled around my ankles, cold tendrils that seemed to reach for me with malevolent intent. An unnatural chill settled deep in my bones, making me shiver despite the many layers of clothing I'd thrown on as the temperature had dropped.

Stories of vampires echoed in my head, each tale more terrifying than the last. I wondered if the mist itself might be alive, drawn to what might be a hapless victim with nowhere to go except onward into Vespara. The thought sent a lick of fear up my spine, and I fought to keep my legs from shaking.

Through the gathering gloom, I spotted the outpost Thorne had sent me to find. *Finally.* It felt like I'd never make it here. My eyes traveled along the valley below, where there was a jumble of weathered buildings that looked like they might topple in a strong breeze. None of the styles of the buildings quite matched, making it appear that the outpost had grown slowly over a period of years.

Flickering lanterns cast long, dancing shadows across crumbling walls stained with age and neglect. I supposed the buildings may not have been built to last, given how many of them seemed to collapse under their own weight. Figures darted between buildings, some with unnatural speed, their movements too quick and fluid to be entirely human. The sight sent a shiver down my spine, a stark reminder of the Otherkind known to dwell here.

So this was Sindonil, the last neutral ground before Vespara. The one spot where Otherkind of all types could come and trade with the vampires of Vespara. I had to wonder if these people were just incredibly desperate or stupid. Desperation drove me, after all. I couldn't help but feel sorry for those who may wander to this outpost without being aware of what it contained.

The air seemed charged here in a way I couldn't explain.

The hair on the back of my neck stood on end like I was being watched, but I refused to stop. Not when everyone relied on me.

I looked to the left and right. There was a wall going as far as the eye could see in either direction. I had to wonder how well they could maintain it, but I supposed it didn't matter. Looking at the massive sheet of rock, I had to wonder. Was it to keep vampires in… or their prey from being able to escape? The thought made me shudder, my stomach flip-flopping.

I paused at the top of the hill, my hand unconsciously reaching for the silver locket around my neck. A 'gift' from Thorne. The metal was cool against my fingertips as I traced the intricate engravings, feeling every curve and line. Inside lay a tiny, empty vial - my one hope of salvation for Aethralis. I closed my eyes, drawing strength from the weight of it against my chest, trying to channel the determination that had carried me this far.

"You can do this," I murmured, my voice sounding small and lost in the vastness around me. The words hung in the air, quickly snatched away by the hungry wind. I took a deep breath, feeling my form shimmer slightly at the edges - a reminder of the power thrumming just beneath my skin.

My vision blurred momentarily, the world around me taking on a silvery sheen as my transformation magic fought for release. I clenched my fists, nails digging into my palms, willing the magic to subside. Now was not the time to lose control, not when I was so close to the heart of enemy territory. Taking a deep breath, I steeled myself and started down the hill. The angle of the hill was steep and my legs were screaming in pain, nearly causing me to tumble down. I caught myself, straightened, and continued more carefully to the road below.

As I approached the outpost's gate, the scents hit me like a wall: wood smoke from dying fires, the acrid tang of unwashed bodies, and something sickeningly sweet that made my stomach churn. Underneath it all was a metallic odor that I desperately tried not to identify as blood. I used my mana to enhance my senses, immediately regretting it as they painted a vivid picture of the horrors that might await me.

A gravelly male voice cut through the darkness, startling me despite my heightened awareness: "State your business, traveler."

My heart hammered in my chest, its frantic rhythm surely audible to whoever—or whatever—lurked in the shadows beyond the gate. Eyes wide in an effort to glimpse the person speaking, I swallowed hard, tasting fear and exhaustion, before forcing my voice to remain steady. "I seek passage to Vespara for trade," I said, the practiced words falling from my lips with a confidence I didn't feel. My lips were so tightly pursed that they felt numb. "I have business with the royal court."

Silence stretched for what felt like an eternity and tension coiled tightly in my belly. The wind died down, as if the very elements were holding their breath in anticipation.

The lack of response was eerie and put me on edge. I stood perfectly still, fighting the urge to fidget or worse, to turn and run back the way I had come. I felt the guard's eyes heavy on my face. Then, with a groan of protesting metal that set my teeth on edge, the gate slowly swung open.

As I crossed the threshold, a wave of magical energy washed over me, foreign and invasive. It probed at my defenses, seeking weaknesses, and I gritted my teeth against the assault. My mana rose to meet it, a warm counterpoint to the barrier's icy touch.

The sensation was awful, the energy causing my skin to itch and burn while my power fought to escape. It felt like I was being skinned alive, tears springing to my eyes and a scream catching in my throat, but luckily, it did not last for long. As my magic rebelled against this foreign invader, I feared my eyes might betray me, shifting to their telltale violet, and I closed my eyes tightly.

But the moment passed, and I breathed a silent sigh of relief, rolling my shoulders to release the tension. Slowly, I opened my eyes again and glanced around at the dirty streets and dilapidated buildings beyond the interior of the gates.

There was no going back now. Whatever fate awaited me in the kingdom of Vespara, I would face it head-on - for Aethralis, for the future I desperately hoped we could still save, and for the trust Griffin and the others had placed in me. With each step into Vespara's domain, I left behind the little girl ostracized from Sylvan Reach, afraid of everyone and everything, and became someone else entirely—a woman walking willingly into the lair of monsters, armed with nothing but her wits, her magic, and a desperate plan that simply had to succeed.

The gate clanged shut behind me with a finality that sent a shiver down my spine. I took a deep breath, remembering Thorne's insistence that I use my transformation abilities to blend in. "You'll need every advantage," he had said, his eyes glinting with an intensity I couldn't quite place. "Become someone they won't suspect. Someone with a reason to be there."

With a subtle flex of my will, I felt my body shift and change. My hair darkened to a deep auburn, my eyes shifting to a piercing green. My features rearranged themselves into those of a minor noble I had once glimpsed at a market fair. It was an unsettling sensation, wearing another's skin, but Thorne had been adamant. At least this woman was young. No aches and pains this time like I had dealt with as Louise.

As my eyes adjusted to the gloom, the true nature of this place revealed itself. What I had mistaken for haphazard construction was, in fact, a deliberate hierarchy etched in stone and wood.

"First time in Sindonil I take it?" a smoothly accented, masculine voice asked from my left.

I turned to see a vampire materialize from the shadows of a nearby building, his gait confident and casual as he strode over to where I stood. His clothes were of fine make, though worn, and he carried himself like someone who knew he belonged here. His hair was so blonde it was almost white and tied back at the nape of his neck.

But it was his eyes that gave me pause. They didn't hold the predatory gleam that I expected after looking at the nearby, more gaunt, vampires. Instead, they held a simple curiosity in their warm brown depths. Everything about him seemed meticulously crafted to put someone at ease, which left me more wary than ever. *This* was a true vampire. I could only imagine the droves of innocent people who had been taken to their death by this man. A chill worked its way up my spine at the thought.

"Is it that obvious?" I asked, trying to keep my voice steady even as my hands wrung the fabric of my trousers beneath my cloak. Silently thanking Thorne for his foresight, I realized how much more conspicuous I would have been in my true form. I would have stuck out like a sore thumb, given that many of the Otherkind here seem to have dark hair and dark eyes. They all seemed to be cut from the same cloth in a way that disturbed me.

He chuckled, pushing himself off the wall and approaching me. "To those who know what to look for, yes. I'm Varen. Think of me as a…greeter of sorts here in Sindonil. Guiding the poor souls who make their way here. And you are?"

"Olivia," I replied, the lie slipping out smoothly. "Of Alton Village."

This village was just a small, nondescript place I'd briefly visited during my travels before reaching Haleshade. I highly doubted that Varen or anyone here, actually, would have even heard of it, much less been there.

Varen's pale brows rose slightly, though he didn't question it. "I see. Interesting. Well, Liv, allow me to give you a quick lesson in Vesparan society. You'll need it if you want to survive here." The casual way that this man addressed me really rankled me and put me on edge.

He gestured to the surrounding hovels with a flourish. "What you see here are the dregs of the kingdom, the lowest caste. Vampires so far removed from the royal bloodline that they're hardly more than animals. Barely worthy of the name 'Vampire', to be honest. They serve with manual labor and... other things. That's why they aren't even within the walls of the kingdom anymore." He leaned in towards me and said the last in a stage whisper, earning more spiteful looks from the wanderers nearby. He looked at the faces near us with pity. I couldn't tell if he was being genuine or not.

I couldn't help but notice the hunger in the eyes of these 'lower caste' as they darted furtive glances our way. I had a strange amount of guilt seeing these turned humans. They didn't ask to become immortal blood-drinkers, and yet here they are, being treated as garbage by those who made them this way. It struck a chord within me and I pushed down my rising anger at those who made them.

Varen continued, unaware of my inner turmoil, gently pressing a hand to my lower back as he guided me deeper into Vespara. We approached a towering inner wall, its surface smooth and imposing. Guards flanked a massive iron gate, their eyes scanning us with predatory intensity.

Their gaze fell upon Varen, quickly skittering away while they opened the gate without even a question. It made me wonder just who Varen is to move through the gates of Vespara with such ease. I got the feeling it was not the same for the other vampires here.

"The first barrier," Varen explained as we passed through. "It separates the lesser-than from the middle castes. We will actually enter the kingdom once we pass over this threshold." He bowed with a flourish that seemed just a bit too fluid, and I hesitantly walked past the guards.

Beyond the wall, the transformation was stark, and I came to a stop, glancing around. Varen stopped next to me, a wry smile on his face. Gone were the ramshackle hovels, replaced by sturdy buildings of stone and wood. The vampires here moved with purpose, their clothes finer and their bearing more composed. We were given hardly a glance from the passers-by, which was refreshing compared to the desperate, agonized and hungry looks from those beyond that first gate.

"This is where the middle castes reside," Varen said, gesturing to the bustling streets. "Merchants, artisans, those with some claim to noble blood, however distant. They're the engine that keeps Vespara running. As long as they have value, they can stay. Otherwise, it's out there with the rest of them," he said with a shake of his head.

As we traversed this section, I noticed another wall looming ahead, even grander than the first. Its surface gleamed with a pearlescent sheen, and atop it stood guards in armor so highly polished that it seemed to shimmer with an inner light.

"The second barrier," Varen murmured, his voice tinged with distaste. "Beyond lies the domain of the upper castes, those closest to the royal bloodline. They hold the actual power in Vespara."

Through the gate, I glimpsed opulent manors and manicured gardens. And there, rising above it all, stood a castle of midnight-black stone, its spires piercing the sky.

"The royal family resides there," Varen said, noticing my gaze. "Few ever see the inside of those walls."

"It's... not what I expected," I stated, taking care to keep any judgement out of my voice.

Varen laughed, but there was no humor in it. "That's putting it mildly. Our entire society is built on the purity of blood. The closer you are to the royal family, the more power and privilege you have. It's a system that's held for centuries, though not without certain... tensions."

Just as Varen spoke, a commotion erupted near the first wall. A young vampire, his clothes tattered and his eyes wild with desperation, had somehow slipped through. He sprinted towards the second inner gate, his voice cracking as he cried out.

"Lord Caelius! Please, I beg an audience!" He fell to his bony knees, trembling. The sound of his knees hitting the stones made me cringe. His matted black hair fell over his face like a sheet. "The blood rations... they're killing us! We haven't had fresh blood in weeks. It's all spoiled, rotten. We can't keep living like this! Please, we need something fresher. I'll work double shifts at the factory!"

An immortal I assumed was Lord Caelius materialized before us, his pale skin almost luminous in the lamplight. His lip curled in disgust as he regarded the young vampire. "You would dare to suggest that the blood provided to your caste is inadequate?" he snarled, his voice dripping with contempt. "Perhaps if you and your ilk worked harder, you'd earn better quality. Your weakness is not our concern."

The young vampire's face contorted with a mixture of anger and despair. His fingers curled like claws as he reached towards Caelius, but whether to beg or to attack, I couldn't tell. His voice cracked, the sound thick with exhaustion. His bright blue eyes shone with unshed tears as he raised his face to the elder vampire. "But my lord, the factories... the conditions are worsening. We're worked to the bone, and for what? How can we serve Vespara if we're too weak to stand?"

In a flash, Caelius had the young vampire by the throat, lifting him off the ground. The younger vampire clawed desperately at Caelius's arm, choking, his face reddening quickly. "You forget your place," Caelius hissed, fangs flashing. "You exist only to serve us. Be grateful for what you're given, or perhaps we'll find more... cooperative replacements for your entire sector."

With terrifying force, he flung the young vampire back towards the gate. He hit the ground hard and slid into the wall, the crack of a bone slicing through the air. Pained screams poured out from the younger vampire's mouth, but before I could even try to help, the guards quickly closed ranks, dragging the unfortunate soul away, his cries of protest and anguish fading into the distance.

I kept my face carefully neutral and turned away from the awful sight. I was meant to be a noble and couldn't be phased by such brutality.

With screams still ringing in my ears, Caelius turned back to us, straightening his immaculate jacket and pushing back his dark hair away from his face as if nothing had happened. The lord had a severe look, the planes and angles of his face razor-sharp. He had an aristocratic nose and wore high fashion clothing…for the 1800s.

He wore pale trousers with a white long-sleeved shirt and a tailored waistcoat the color of blood, along with boots that had narrow, pointed toes. My gaze snapped back up to his face. His pleasant mask slipped back into place with practiced ease, but I could see the cold fury still simmering beneath the surface.

"Lord Caelius," Varen murmured, bowing his head slightly. "Lord of this district."

Caelius turned to us, his eyes like flecks of obsidian. "Varen," he acknowledged with a nod, then fixed his gaze on me. I felt very much like prey under the intensity of his stare, fighting not to show weakness. "And who might this be?"

"Olivia of Alton village," I replied, forcing myself to meet his gaze. "I seek an audience with the royal court."

Caelius raised an eyebrow, a smirk playing at the corners of his mouth. He gestured for Varen and I to follow him through the final barrier into the highest of Vesparan society. As we walked, he glanced towards me. "How fascinating. And what business could a creature such as yourself possibly have with our esteemed rulers?"

I worked to keep up with the pace at which Caelius walked. I wasn't certain where he was leading us, however, I had no choice but to follow. My mind raced. The brutality I'd just witnessed confirmed my worst fears about Vesparan society. But it also revealed the deep fractures within—fractures I may be able to exploit.

"Perhaps," I said carefully, "we could discuss my business over a drink? I'm sure a lord of your standing must have exquisite taste."

Caelius' eyes glittered with interest and no small amount of suspicion. "Indeed," he purred. We stopped before a large, extravagant manor. It had a weathered stone facade, adorned with intricate carvings, stretching high towards the sky like a mini castle.

There was a wraparound veranda, supported by ornate columns twined with night-blooming jasmine. The home was beautiful and terrifying. It had enough space to fit all the villagers back in Haleshade and then some.

Lord Caelius gestured to the door with a flourish. "Do come inside. I find myself most curious about what brings a being like you to our fair kingdom."

As I followed him into the manor, Varen caught my eye. His expression was a clear warning: tread carefully. I had entered a realm balanced on a knife's edge, where one wrong move could send me plummeting into darkness.

But within that precarious balance lay opportunity. If I could navigate the treacherous waters of Vesparan politics, playing the castes against each other... perhaps there was hope for my mission after all.

The manor's heavy door closed behind us with the finality of a tomb, sealing me in with predators who saw me as nothing more than prey. I took a deep breath, steeling myself for the performance of a lifetime. The real game was about to begin.

CHAPTER 11

The heavy doors of Caelius' manor swung shut behind us with a resounding thud, sealing us in a world of affluence that stood in stark contrast to the grim reality just beyond these walls.

My eyes darted around, taking in the tapestries that adorned walls of polished marble, their intricate designs seeming to tell tales of Vesparan history. Crystal chandeliers hung from the ceiling, their light dancing off the polished surfaces in deceptively cheerful rainbows.

A sickly sweet scent of incense permeated the air, but underneath, I caught the faint metallic tang of blood. My stomach churned, and I swallowed hard. I took a silent breath and lifted my chin, refusing to be cowed now.

Caelius glided across the floor, his movements graceful and predatory. He gestured towards a set of ornate double doors. "Come, let's chat somewhere more... intimate."

I followed, the plush gray carpet muffling my footsteps.

Behind me, I could hear Varen's steady breathing, a reminder of his unwelcome presence. I can't be certain why, but something about how he's been trailing along irked me. I pushed the feeling aside. Annoying or not, I needed all the allies I could get in this den of vampires.

I just couldn't help but feel that him following me here was odd. I slid a glance his way. His warm brown eyes were looking straight ahead, his face carefully passive. He said that he was just a greeter and yet, he can traverse all the different castes within Vespara? Something about that felt wrong to me if he was just a simple vampire from a lower caste, but I didn't have time to think about that too much before we entered through a large, heavy door.

The study we entered was a book lover's dream—or nightmare. I glanced around the vast room. The scent of inked parchment filled the air. Floor-to-ceiling shelves bowed under the weight of works ranging from ancient, crumbling tomes to sleek, modern volumes. The floor was dark oak, so heavily polished that it gleamed in the lamplight.

It had far too much space just for a study. It held an entire library's worth of books. I absently wondered if Caelius actually read any of these books or if they were all just for show. Finally, my eyes landed on Lord Caelius, where he strode further into the room.

At the center stood an oversized desk, also made of the same dark, polished wood that seemed to grow out of the floor itself. It was definitely lavish, but I couldn't deny that this room had made an impact. It made you feel small, lesser-than, which I have no doubt was Caelius's intent.

As I took in the surrounding room, a chill ran down my spine. I had to wonder how many people had died to get Caelius here? Some tomes on the shelves were ancient, their spines cracking and crumbling with age. Were they his to begin with? Were they stolen? How did Caelius get into this position of power? It made the sweet, metallic scent of blood lingering in the air all the more horrifying.

Caelius slid into the high-backed chair behind the desk, his movements fluid. He gestured to the chairs opposite. "Please, make yourselves comfortable."

As I sank into the plush leather, Caelius braced his arms in front of him and leaned forward, his obsidian eyes glittering in the warm lamplight. "So, Olivia of Alton village. What brings a human to the heart of Vespara? We rarely entertain your kind here." His thin lips curled into a smirk. "At least... not for conversation."

I suppressed a shudder and lifted my chin, channeling every ounce of noble bearing I could muster. "I come seeking help, Lord Caelius. My village faces a threat unlike any we've seen before."

Caelius raised an eyebrow, his interest clearly piqued. "Oh? And what sort of threat would drive a human to seek aid from vampires?"

"A plague," I said, my voice steady despite the nerves churning in my stomach. "One that defies all our healers' efforts to cure."

"Interesting," Caelius murmured, his eyes narrowing. "And why should Vespara concern itself with a human plague?"

I leaned forward slightly, meeting his gaze. "Because it's not just humans who are falling ill. This disease... it doesn't discriminate. Nearly all the Otherkind races have succumbed as well, and it just continues to spread. If left unchecked, it could threaten every race in Aethralis."

A heavy silence fell over the room. I could feel Varen tensing beside me, but I kept my eyes locked on Caelius. His face was an unreadable mask, but I could almost see the gears turning behind those dark eyes.

"By the blood," Varen breathed, his voice a mix of awe and fear. "I've never heard of such a thing. Olivia, what exactly does this plague do? How does it spread?"

I turned to Varen, noting the genuine concern in his eyes. Caelius, too, leaned forward, his interest clearly ramping up.

"Perhaps," Caelius interjected, his tone measured, "you could elaborate on this disease. Its symptoms, its progression. We need to understand the full scope of this... threat."

I nodded carefully, steeling my nerves. As I prepared to weave the tale that Thorne and I had carefully constructed, I silently prayed to whatever gods may be listening that my hastily concocted story would hold up under their combined scrutiny. The fate of Haleshade—and possibly all of Aethralis—depended on my performance in this room.

I took a deep breath, centering myself before speaking. "The plague begins subtly," I explained, recalling the symptoms I'd witnessed in Haleshade. "Fatigue sets in first, followed by a strange disorientation. Victims report feeling disconnected from time itself, experiencing moments as if they're stretched or compressed."

Caelius's dark eyes traced my face as I spoke. "Go on," he urged, his voice low and intense. His gaze was sharp as a dagger against the pulse in my neck. I swallowed hard.

"As the disease progresses, more unusual symptoms manifest," I continued. "Their senses become erratic—one moment, a victim might hear a whisper from miles away, the next, they're blind to what's right in front of them."

Varen shifted in his seat, his pale brows furrowed. "I've never heard of anything like this," he murmured.

I nodded grimly. "Neither had our healers. But the most disturbing symptom is the last. The victims fall into a catatonic state, unresponsive to the world around them. It's as if... as if their very life force is being drained away."

Caelius' eyes narrowed. "And you say this affects more than just humans?"

"Yes," I replied, silently thanking Thorne for practicing a conversation just like this one with me over and over to ensure I was as prepared as possible. "We've seen it in mages, in Werefolk, even in a Fae Beast we saw in passing during our travels. No race or creature seems immune."

A heavy silence fell over the room. Caelius stood, moving to a window that overlooked the city below. For a long moment, he said nothing, his back to us as he gazed out at Vespara.

"If what you say is true," he finally said, his voice carrying over to us despite his nearly whispered words, "this could indeed pose a threat to our kingdom." He turned back to face us, his expression grave. "But I can't imagine how we could possibly be of assistance to you if you say that this plague could affect vampires as well."

My heart fluttered in my chest and I knew Caelius was aware when he dropped his gaze to my throat and back. I swallowed thickly and pressed on. "I have made contact with one of the most skilled healers in Aethralis. He believes he can create a cure with help from the royal family."

Caelius returned to his seat, his movements graceful yet predatory. "I will send a team to your village to verify your claims. If they confirm the existence of this plague, then we can discuss the possibility of an audience with the royal family."

My heart skipped a beat. This wasn't part of the plan. I couldn't be sure that there was a plague-ridden village for them to investigate. I hadn't been to Alton in over a year.

"My lord," I said, thinking quickly, "while I appreciate your thoroughness, time is of the essence. More fall ill every day. Perhaps there's a way to expedite the process?"

Lord Caelius's gaze was hard as he assessed me. My magic surged beneath my skin and I felt a bead of sweat slip down my spine. I concentrated hard to calm my stuttering heart and to shove my magic back down deep before I lost control and my facade fell away. The pressure was immense.

As if sensing the tension between us, Varen cleared his throat. "If I may, Lord Caelius," he interjected, "I've heard rumors of a royal prince who takes a particular interest in matters outside Vespara. Perhaps he could be persuaded to grant an initial audience?"

Caelius shot Varen a sharp look, but seemed to consider the suggestion. "You speak of Prince Aldric," he drawled. "He is... unconventional in his interests. It's possible he might be intrigued by this situation." He waved his hand as though dismissing the thought.

But I couldn't let this chance pass me by and I latched onto this new possibility. "If there's any way to arrange a meeting with Prince Aldric, I would be most grateful," I said, trying to keep the desperation out of my voice.

Caelius studied me intently, his dark eyes peering into my very soul. I fought the urge to squirm under his gaze, instead meeting it with what I hoped was an appropriate mix of determination and deference.

"Very well," he said at last. "I will send word to the palace. If Prince Aldric is interested, he may grant you an audience. But be warned, Miss Olivia—the prince is not to be trifled with. If he suspects any deception..." The threat was clear. I knew I needed to tread carefully.

"I understand," I blurted before catching myself. I said the next more slowly, "I assure you, my intentions are genuine."

Caelius nodded, then rose from his seat. "You will stay here as my guest while we await a response from the palace. Varen will show you to your quarters."

As we stood to leave, Caelius fixed me with one last penetrating stare. "You're either very brave or very foolish to have come here, Lady Olivia of Alton. I do hope, for your sake, that your visit proves... fruitful," he said, his voice a purr that set my teeth on edge. He was a predator in every sense of the word, and he wanted me to know it.

The subtle threat in his words wasn't lost on me. As Varen

led me from the study, I couldn't shake the feeling that I had just stepped onto a chessboard where every other piece was poised to strike. One false move, and it would all be over.

But as we walked through the opulent halls of the manor, I steeled my resolve. I had come too far to falter now. Somewhere in this den of predators lay the key to saving Haleshade—and I would find it, no matter the cost.

Varen led me through a maze of corridors, each more lavish than the last. The walls were adorned with intricate paintings that were masterfully made. I could only imagine the money that went into this place. My lip curled in distaste while thinking about how the money from a single painting could have helped entire families in the lower districts.

"How do you know Lord Caelius?" I asked before I could stop myself.

Varen's amber eyes slid over to me. "I know everyone there is to know, more or less. My job requires it."

I thought on that for a moment before blurting, "Why is Lord Caelius asking you to bring me to my room? That doesn't sound like the job of a guide."

Varen sighed, the sound melancholic. "They use me as they please. I am a greeter, guide, factory worker, butler, *slave*. It's whatever they request of me. I know all the nobles' homes because of this. They've all had use for me at one time or another."

My stomach sank, and guilt pricked at me. "I'm sorry, Varen. That sounds like a hard life."

Varen's eyes flickered with an emotion that I couldn't quite place as he said, "In this place, Liv, things are rarely as simple as they appear. Hold on to that and don't let your guard down. Not for anyone or anything."

With those last cryptic words, my gaze fell to the ground as we continued our walk through the winding corridors, no sound but our steps lightly echoing off the stone walls.

The farther we ventured into Lord Caelius's abode, the colder and colder the air seemed to get until I could almost see my breath. A shiver traveled up my spine as nervous sweat cooled on my skin.

"Here we are, Liv," Varen said finally, breaking the silence and stopping before a heavy wooden door. "These will be your quarters for the duration of your stay."

The door swung open with a soft creak, and I stepped into the room, my footsteps muffled by a plush cream-colored carpet. Moonlight filtered through the crack between heavy, black velvet curtains, casting long shadows across the space. My eyes were drawn to a massive four-poster bed, its dark wood gleaming in the dim light. Crimson sheets spilled over the sides, pooling on the floor like a river of blood.

I ran my fingers along the ornate wallpaper, tracing patterns that seemed to shift and move in the flickering candlelight. Crystal decanters on a nearby table caught the light, their amber contents promising both comfort and danger.

As I moved to the window, I pushed aside the heavy curtains

and my gaze fell on the gardens below, beautiful even now. Night-blooming flowers filled the space, all turned towards the moon. I felt around for a latch and found none.

Looks like the windows in this room are sealed.

A pit opened up in my stomach and I turned back towards Varen, fighting panic.

"I trust you'll find everything to your liking," Varen said. His tone was casual, but his eyes were intense. "If you need anything, simply ring the bell by the bed. Someone will attend to you... eventually."

I nodded, trying to mask my unease. "Thank you, Varen. You've been most helpful."

He smiled, but it didn't reach his eyes. "Of course. That's what I'm here for. Oh, and Liv?" He paused at the doorway, his expression turning serious. "A word of advice—don't wander. The manor can be... dangerous for those who don't know their way around. Especially during a time like this."

"A time like this?" I asked, fear spiking through me.

Varen's expression grew dark. "Let's just say that the court is… unsettled. Not everyone is happy with the way the kingdom is ruled now and the lower castes are rebelling, as you saw earlier. It would be wise to tread carefully and not cause any trouble," he murmured.

Before I could ask anything else, he closed the door. I heard the distinct click of a lock, confirming my suspicions. I was a guest, yes, but also very much a prisoner.

Taking a deep breath, I struggled to calm my racing heart.

I was in the heart of Vespara now, surrounded by creatures who would drain me dry without a second thought. Not to mention that ominous warning from Varen. Just what was happening here? What had I fallen into?

But I couldn't afford to falter. Not now, not when I was so close. I took off my cloak and draped it over a chair, resisting the urge to panic. Instead, I began methodically exploring my new surroundings, searching for anything that might be useful. The room was well-appointed, with a writing desk, a small bookshelf, and an ornate wardrobe. But it was also clearly designed to keep its occupant contained.

The silence in this place was deafening. There were no murmurs from nearby vendors, no footsteps echoing out from the cobbled streets, no children's laughter ringing out in the air. It was incredibly eerie and made me feel like I was the only living person in this place.

As I ran my fingers along the spines of the books, a soft knock at the door made me jump. "Come in," I called, trying to keep my voice steady.

With a click of the lock, the door opened to reveal a young girl, her eyes downcast and her posture submissive. She looked young, maybe 15 years old, with auburn hair in a twist on top of her head. We briefly locked eyes and my breath caught in my throat. She moved with the telltale unearthly grace of vampires. She wasn't quite as elegant as Varen or Caelius, making me wonder just how old she truly was.

I couldn't help but speculate if she was one of the lower caste being used just like those outside of the walls. What would drive someone to turn a child into an immortal creature? I thought with disgust.

She carried a tray with what appeared to be food and drink. "Your evening meal, my lady," she murmured, setting the tray on a small table. The telltale fangs of vampires—hers were short, blunt. Had they been filed down? Disgust filled me on her behalf. How could they treat their own like this?

I watched her carefully, noting the way she moved—efficient but fearful, as if expecting punishment at any moment. "Thank you," I said softly. "What's your name?"

She looked up, startled, her bright blue eyes wide with surprise. "E-Elena, my lady," she stammered.

"Elena," I repeated, offering a small smile. "Thank you for bringing this, Elena. I appreciate it."

She stared at me for a moment, clearly unused to such treatment from guests. Then, with a quick bow, she hurried towards the door. Panic set in at the thought of being alone here.

"Elena," I blurted before she could leave.

After a moment's hesitation, she slowly turned to face me, though her eyes remained downcast. I noticed a gentle tremor in her hands, as though she were expecting a reprimand. *Or worse,* my mind whispered, unbidden. My tone softened.

"How long have you been here? Do you have any family?"

Elena's eyes grew round. "I—I shouldn't speak of such things, my lady. Please, have a good meal. I must be going." Without another word, she almost ran from the room. My heart ached on her behalf. There was such palpable fear in her voice.

Left alone again, I approached the tray cautiously as though it may reach out and bite me. The food looked and smelled delicious, but I couldn't shake the paranoia that it might have been tampered with somehow.

Still, I knew I needed to keep up my strength. I picked at the meal, then waited to see if I felt off. When nothing happened, I took the risk and ate with relish. I hadn't had a decent meal in such a long time. My time at Haleshade felt like a lifetime ago at this moment.

As the hours grew later still, the room grew darker, the heavy curtains blocking out even the faintest starlight. I lay on the bed, fully clothed and alert, my mind racing with plans and contingencies. Sleep seemed impossible, but I knew I needed rest if I was to face whatever challenges tomorrow would bring.

Just as I was about to drift off, a faint sound caught my attention. It was barely audible—a soft scraping, as if something was moving within the walls. I froze, straining my ears. There it was again, closer this time.

My heart pounded as I slowly sat up, eyes scanning the dimly lit room. I held my breath and strained my ears. The noise stopped, leaving only the oppressive silence of the manor. But I couldn't shake the feeling that I wasn't alone, that something was watching, waiting.

At that moment, the true peril of my situation hit me full force. I was deep in enemy territory, surrounded by creatures that

I barely understood, playing a game with rules I didn't know. And somewhere out there, beyond these suffocating walls, was Prince Aldric—my best hope and potentially my greatest threat.

As I lay back down and loosed my held breath, every sense on high alert, I longed for the simple safety of Griffin's cabin and his powerful presence beside me. But I pushed those thoughts aside. I had a mission to complete, a village to save. And come morning, I would face whatever Vespara threw at me with all the courage and cunning I could muster.

The game was far from over. In fact, it had only just begun.

CHAPTER 12

It had to be just after midnight when a hard knock came at the door, startling me out of my fitful sleep. I quickly raced to the bathroom and made sure that nothing had changed about my appearance before slowly approaching the door.

"Yes?" I called.

"Hello, my lady. Lord Caelius has requested your presence for dinner," a soft voice responded. I recognized it as Elena. A soft lock clicked as she opened the door.

"Dinner?" I asked. "I've already had my evening meal."

"Ah yes… but Lord Caelius and the others have not," she said, her sapphire gaze sympathetic. Her posture was hunched, as though trying to shrink away into nothing. "He wishes to have your company and further discuss things."

"I see. What would he have me wear?" I asked. I hadn't prepared for something like this.

"He sent me with a gown, my lady. It is just here," Elena

said, gesturing to a cart just outside of view. A black garment bag large enough for a dress hung from it. "I am here to get you ready and to bring you to him."

She picked up the bag and opened it, presenting a gown so beautiful that it made my breath catch in my throat.

The dress was a deep, midnight blue made of layers of silk chiffon that seemed to absorb the light around it. As I hesitantly reached out to touch the fabric, it shifted beneath my fingers, causing tiny crystals embedded throughout to catch what little light there was in the room and twinkle like distant stars.

The bodice was adorned with delicate silver thread which would accentuate the delicate column of my throat. It had sheer, flowing sleeves. In any other situation, it would be a dream to wear a gown like this. However, in these circumstances, I wanted no more attention drawn to me than there was already.

Elena shut the door behind her and herded me towards the dressing table with surprising swiftness. "We have no time to waste, my lady. We cannot keep our Lord waiting," she murmured.

Elena undressed me with rapid efficiency despite my protests. With no other choice, I reluctantly slipped into the gown. It felt cool against my skin and incredibly soft. Looking back at myself in the mirror, I saw that there was an incredibly low dip in the dress with almost my whole back exposed. I swallowed thickly, uncomfortable. As I turned this way and that, the dress hugged every curve tastefully.

There was a high slit I hadn't noticed before, showing what would be an enticing amount of thigh. I barely recognized myself in this outfit. How had Caelius even known my size? My skin was crawling, and I felt incredibly exposed.

"You look lovely, my lady. Let me just fix your hair," Elena said, quickly pushing me into the plush seat in front of the dressing table. With almost preternatural speed, she pinned my hair into an elegant mass of curls atop my head, dotted with more of the same crystals embroidered into the gown. I looked like I had just been plucked from the night sky and given form. It was a magical feeling, despite the circumstances. As a final touch, Elena put light makeup on me that would accentuate my eyes and ruby red lip stain.

I felt incredibly conflicted. This was a gorgeous outfit, but could I really allow myself to be put out there like a raw steak in front of hungry wolves?

I didn't have a choice, I reminded myself sternly. I had to ensure that I got what I needed so that I could return to Sylvan Reach without being empty-handed. And that meant I had to play their game. I knew what Caelius was doing. He was trying to rattle me so that I would either admit to whatever lies he thought I was telling, or I would be too afraid to stay. But I wasn't about to be so easily shaken. I *would* get what I came here for. No matter what.

Elena offered her arm, and I took it. She was trembling— and so was I.

Elena led me down a series of halls until we reached a ballroom. This home was ridiculously large, even bigger than what it looked like from the outside. At one point, we saw a puddle of darkness, with a servant scrubbing the marble floor furiously.

"If any of the high-born see this, they'll have my head…" they muttered, and I caught the flash of fang. Filed down, just like Elena. I felt sick.

Once we reached our destination and breached the threshold, Elena quickly bowed and retreated, as though in fear of her life. And honestly, maybe she was. How she acted wasn't normal. It broke my heart. She seemed so kind, too young to be taken as one of the undead.

As she closed the heavy doors behind me, my gaze flit across the room and my heart jumped into my throat. Everywhere I looked were vampires in various states of undress, with humans draped across their laps, or sprawled on settees, or engaged in carnal acts. My cheeks heated, burning hot. There was an erotic thrum of live music in the background, full of bass. The band looked to be human, but I couldn't tell from this far away.

I felt a few sets of eyes land on me, and I fought the urge to run. Instead, I raised my chin and strode towards one of the tables set with various fruits and meats. The meats were almost raw and bloody. My stomach churned, and I instead picked from a bunch of green grapes, popping them in my mouth and avoiding making eye contact with anyone. They burst apart in a wash of sweet juice, surprising me. I didn't figure vampires would care about the quality of their produce, but I guess I was wrong.

Once I collected myself and prepared for the sight in front of me, I looked around the room, trying to see Lord Caelius. I found him seated at the head of the middle table with a human woman straddling his hips with her head lolled to the side, an expression of ecstasy on her face. She had her satin, cream-colored dress hiked up around her thighs and was moving against him with wanton abandon. My mouth dropped open and I couldn't look away. It was like watching a horrible accident in live action. Caelius's eyes were closed, his mouth moving against her throat.

My mouth went dry, and I fisted my hands, the pain of my nails biting into my palms enough to snap me out of it. I couldn't just stand here gawping like a fish at these people. Instead, I kept my gaze moving across the crowd. I was surprised that there would be so many vampires here, although I suppose with an eternity ahead of you, why not engage in a bit of debauchery? It's not like there's much else you can do.

There was a burning at the back of my neck, like someone's eyes were boring into me, and I turned around, trying to find the culprit. I scanned the sea of faces and glimpsed silver for just a moment before they were lost in the crowd. There was a strange pang deep inside of me, almost like I was missing something. But what?

Before I could think on that any further, a cool touch on my arm jolted me and I spun around. Caelius. He had a smear of bright red blood down his chin and his obsidian eyes were bright, his cheeks flushed. He smiled widely, flashing fangs, as he gestured around the room. "Hello, Miss Olivia. Enjoying yourself?" he asked.

I was flustered, caught by surprise. I hated that feeling. "Of course. What's not to like?" I asked in return, keeping my tone casual.

"Would you like to… partake?" Lord Caelius asked with a sly smile.

My skin crawled, and I shook my head a little too aggressively before I caught myself. "No, thank you. I'm not here for fun. Just business. I was told that you wanted to talk?" I asked flatly.

A flash of displeasure crossed Caelius's face, and he opened his mouth to speak, but a servant appeared next to him and whispered something in his ear. Caelius's mouth closed with a snap and he frowned, his brows furrowed.

"Excuse me. I've been summoned by the prince. Please, enjoy the party," he said with a slight bow.

The prince was here?

I turned in a slow circle, looking again at the different vampires. Was he the auburn-haired vampire with long, wavy locks, currently being… serviced by several humans, both men and women? Was he the blonde against the far wall with ice-blue eyes scanning the crowd, same as me? The blonde's gaze stopped on me and he smiled with some fang as he looked my body up and down. I felt incredibly exposed under his gaze. This dress did not hide enough. My pulse raced, and I quickly looked away. I hated being around this many predators. I couldn't protect myself without giving away my abilities, so I had to play it safe.

Turning back towards the food table, I picked at some more grapes, the sweetness bursting in my mouth. I closed my eyes against the taste. It had been a while since I had some good, fresh fruits. Most of my meals on the way here had been dried meats and breads, when I could eat, that is. It was a rough trip to get here. I shuddered at the reminder of the chilly nights, the times I had to go to sleep hungry. Picking up the bunch, I kept popping them in my mouth like candy. Someone cleared their throat next to me and I jumped, my eyes snapping open to find the source of the sound.

It was the blonde vampire. He was incredibly tall and lean. He smelled of spiced wine and apples. It was incredibly pleasant, I thought with irritation. This must be how they lured humans in. Had to be pheromones or something.

"Hello there," the mysterious vampire said, his voice rumbling through me and sending tingles along my skin. What the hell? Who was this guy? This was *definitely* how they lured humans in. Gods damn it.

I gave my head a slight shake and straightened my shoulders. I was not about to melt into a puddle in front of this guy. "Hello. I am not looking for company. Please look elsewhere," I said with a sniff.

His pale brows rose, and he smirked. Were all vampires so haughty? They seem to find themselves irresistible. What a pain. His eyes rose to something beyond my shoulder, and he stiffened, wordlessly slipping back into the crowd like a shadow. I frowned and turned to see what had startled him, but a heavy pair of hands fell on my shoulders, forcing me to stay facing forward.

"Why, whatever are you doing here?" a smooth male voice murmured against the shell of my ear. The warmth of his breath brushed the side of my face. The scent of storms and moonlight filled my senses. A shiver raced down my spine, and a flood of warmth filled me at the sound. Just what were these vampires *made* of? It's like they were incubi, just out there to ruin all men and women they set their sights on. Life was so unfair.

My eyes fluttered closed before I cleared my throat, shoving these feelings away. It's just a physical reaction, I assured myself. The reminder of Griffin's kiss still burned my lips, a reminder of the promise that I'd made to return to him. I couldn't sit here, feeling drawn to another man like Griffin didn't even matter. "Minding my own business. What about you?" I asked snarkily. I craned my head, but the man dodged my view with a dark, rough laugh, the sound curling in my stomach like a nest of butterflies.

My breath caught as he pressed himself against the exposed skin of my back. He was warm, incredibly so. Was this man a vampire? Or a human? I couldn't tell from this angle. Part of me wanted to melt against him and enjoy this touch, and that terrified me more than anything. I knew what this man could be—if he was a vampire, he could kill me as easily as swatting a fly. I tried hard to conjure Griffin's sunshine eyes, warm and bright, his scent of leather and wood, but it felt distant, murky, whereas this man's touch burned against me like a brand. He nuzzled my hair with his nose and inhaled.

"You smell lovely, my dear. So warm and comforting. It suits you, I must say," he said, his voice soft and seductive. My heart beat wildly against my ribs from the sound.

"I'm just looking around at the newcomers," he said, his voice intoxicatingly deep and melodic.

"I'm here to meet with a prince. And much like I told the other guy, I'm not looking for company," I said, but my voice was breathy. How could I be so easily won over? Did I truly have no shame? I tried to step away, but his grip didn't loosen, leaving me trapped.

The man chuckled, his hands leaving my shoulders to wrap around my waist instead. I could feel the heat of his hands through the layers of fabric draped on my body, and he swayed with me gently in time to the music. He was surprisingly gentle, the touch the softest of caresses sending goosebumps across my skin. My breath hitched at the light contact. Was it like this for all vampires? The thought horrified me. No wonder these humans were here. It would be easy to become addicted to this. Far too easy.

"A prince, hmm? I see. That's okay. I'm not looking for company either. Or at least, not the kind you're thinking of," he said, a smile in his voice. His head was still atop mine and I couldn't turn to look at him, but I caught a hint of raven black hair that tickled my cheeks.

"Who are you?" I asked, curiosity burning within me. I shouldn't care, but some part of me was dying to know.

"You'll find out soon enough. For now, I should leave you. Otherwise, I'll have to take you," he murmured with another husky laugh.

I opened my mouth to respond, but before the words had left my mouth, he was gone. Bereft in a way I couldn't explain, I went on the hunt for some wine.

Caelius seemed inclined to ignore me, thank the gods. I'd spotted him a few times, but he didn't approach me again. I had my fill of fruits and pastries, and maybe more than a couple of glasses of wine. Just enough to take the edge off. My mystery suitor never came back, nor did the blonde vampire. My mind kept replaying his touch and how it made me feel, despite my attempts to quash the memory. I thought of Griffin instead, though in this moment, his face was hazy.

I scowled. This entire trip was for not only Aethralis, but for him. I shouldn't be thinking about another man and how he made me feel. Did I have no shame? Rolling my shoulders, I had to reason that it was the vampire's influence. They had to get other species to agree to feedings somehow. Otherwise, they'd be forced to capture or kill their prey, and that's not exactly a good look for them. Nor is it sustainable.

Maybe they just had an ability for hyper-arousal or something, I thought while crossing my legs under the table. This was ridiculous. I felt like a cat in heat watching all the couples together. There was a large grandfather clock near the entrance of the room that showed the time as 3AM. I'd been here long enough, I decided. I got to my feet only a little unsteadily and made my way towards Caelius. He wanted me here. I'd at least tell him I was going to ask for an escort back to my room. Felt like the gracious thing to do.

Caelius had his face buried in yet another neck, this time a man's. He was slender, graceful. Beautiful, really, with alabaster skin and white-blonde hair. He lovingly stroked Caelius's shoulders as he drank, a moan slipping from his lips. This could not be more awkward, but I cleared my throat, anyway. Caelius's eyes found mine, looking like chips of obsidian. He released the man and gave him a shove to the side, like trash on the side of the road. I felt bad for the man as he stumbled and fell, though he laid there and cried out softly, his entire body trembling in whatever ecstasy the bite gave him.

I ripped my gaze from the man's form and turned back to Caelius. I gave a brief curtsy. His gaze roved over my body, stopping at each curve and valley.

"Have you changed your mind?" he asked, licking a droplet of blood from the side of his mouth.

"I have not. But I would like to retire to my room," I said, my hands clasped in front of me.

Caelius' booming laugh surprised me and evidently some of the other vampires, too, given how they turned to look at us. "You wish to retire? Well, who am I to refuse someone who asked so nicely?" he said with a smirk. "You have someone watching out for you, it seems. I had hoped for a bit more… entertainment." Caelius said with a smarmy smile. Revulsion filled me, nausea churning in my stomach, though I kept my face carefully impassive.

He snapped his fingers, and Varen appeared, seemingly from nowhere. He carefully took my arm and led me through the throngs of vampires still feeding. Some laid next to unnervingly still bodies, and others appeared to be sleeping off their meals on the various plush furniture around the room. The fruit no longer seemed to settle well, and I swallowed hard. Seeing these people with their bellies swollen like ticks while the surrounding humans treated them like their drug of choice was incredibly unnerving.

My mind went back to the man who had come up behind me. He didn't seem to be like the rest of them. He could have tried to coerce me into giving him my blood, or worse. And yet, he didn't. Why? The thought unnerved me. Griffin had shown me nothing but kindness, giving me a home and a chance when I had no one and nothing. And how did I repay that? By having my head turned by the first man who showed me attention.

I told myself that it was just some vampire charm or preternatural allure, but it felt like an excuse. The worst part about it, I couldn't stop wondering. Would I see him again? Would I know it if I did?

CHAPTER 13

Sunlight streamed through the gap in the heavy curtains, casting a golden line across the opulent room. I hadn't slept, my mind a whirlwind after last night, even after the wine. Varen had led me back to my room and left as quickly as possible. I didn't know whether it was to return to the ballroom, or what his intentions were. He didn't speak to me the entire time.

My limbs were heavy with exhaustion and the constant strain of maintaining this form left me drained in a way I'd never experienced before. I didn't know how long I could keep this up, but I feared releasing this form until I knew I was truly alone.

The soft scraping sounds from the night before had ceased with the dawn and I think I found the culprit with the sun. Mouse droppings. I almost laughed with relief, but I was still too wound with tension.

I sat up, running a hand through my tangled hair. In the harsh light of day, my mission seemed more daunting than ever.

I was trapped in a gilded cage, surrounded by creatures who, though dormant now, would drain me dry if they knew my true nature. For a moment, doubt crept in. What was I really doing here? Was I foolish to think I could outsmart an entire kingdom of vampires? Slowly, I got to my feet and disrobed, taking off the dress from the night before and carefully unpinning my hair until it fell into a mass around my shoulders. I put on my own clothes, feeling much more comfortable. While the outfit had been beautiful, it wasn't really me.

I closed my eyes, picturing the faces of those I'd left behind in Haleshade. Griffin, waiting for me. The villagers, their bodies wasting away from the mysterious plague. Thorne, working day and night to solve this plague. My parents. They were all counting on me.

Taking a deep breath, I steeled my resolve. I hadn't come this far to falter now. Whatever challenges lay ahead, I would face them. For Haleshade. For all of Aethralis. And, I realized with a start, for myself.

I wanted to do something good, to prove everyone wrong who ever thought that just because I was gifted with this transformation ability that I would be doomed to cause untold destruction, just like the mage who held this power before me.

The hours crawled by, each minute feeling like an eternity. I paced the room, leafed through books, and peered out the window at the sun-drenched gardens below. The manor was eerily quiet during the day, with only the occasional sound of a human servant passing by my door. Every once in a while, my mind returned to the mystery man from last night. My heartbeat quickened in my chest. Why couldn't I stop thinking about him? Just who was he?

As evening approached, anxiety built in my chest. Soon, the vampires would awaken, and I would once again be at the center of their dangerous game. Absently, I wondered how many vampires were here, in this building with me right now. If they turned on me, I wouldn't have a chance in hell and the thought was terrifying, but enough to keep me from falling asleep at least.

Just as the last rays of sunlight faded from the sky, a soft knock at the door broke through my thoughts. "Come in," I called, straightening my posture and schooling my features into a mask of calm.

The lock clicked, and Varen slipped into the room, a tray of food balanced in one hand. His amber eyes scanned my face, a mix of curiosity and wariness in their depths.

"Good evening, Liv," he said, setting the tray on a nearby table and picking up the old food tray. "I trust your day was... restful?"

I forced a smile. "It's Olivia. As far as your question goes, it was as restful as can be expected after last night's... events."

Varen nodded, his gaze never leaving my face. "I imagine it must be quite a change. Tell me, what made you decide to come to Vespara? It's not a journey many humans would willingly undertake."

His tone was casual, but I could sense the underlying tension. He was fishing for information, probing for any inconsistencies in my story. I would have to tread carefully.

"Desperation can drive people to unexpected places," I replied, moving to inspect the food he'd brought. "When your home is threatened, you'll seek help wherever you can find it."

Varen hummed thoughtfully, leaning against the wall. "And you believe Vespara holds the key to saving your village? What makes you so sure?"

I turned to face him, meeting his gaze steadily. "I've heard rumors of Vesparan blood's healing properties. Given the magical nature of the plague we face, it seemed worth the risk to investigate. I don't want to leave any stone unturned, no matter how unlikely it is to bear fruit."

A flicker of surprise crossed Varen's face, quickly masked. His eyes narrowed slightly, but his tone was casual. Too casual. "Interesting. And how exactly did you come by such information?"

I felt the conversation balancing on a knife's edge. One wrong word could unravel everything. But as I opened my mouth to respond, a commotion in the hallway outside caught our attention.

The sound of hurried footsteps and muffled voices grew louder, drawing both our attention to the door. Varen's posture stiffened, his eyes narrowing as he listened intently.

"Stay here," he murmured, moving swiftly to the door. He cracked it open, peering into the hallway.

I held my breath, straining to hear what was happening. My heart raced, mind spinning with possibilities. Was this what Varen had warned me of last night? A rebellion from vampires from the lower caste? Had they somehow found me out?

Varen exchanged hushed words with someone outside, his expression grave. After a moment, he closed the door and turned back to me, his face unreadable.

"It seems there's been a development," he said, his tone carefully neutral. "Lord Caelius requests your presence immediately."

A chill ran down my spine. "What's happened?"

Varen shook his head. "I'm not privy to the details. But I suggest you prepare yourself quickly. Lord Caelius is not known for his patience."

As I hurried to make myself presentable, smoothing my hair and straightening my clothes, Varen watched me with a calculating gaze.

"You never did answer my question, Liv," he said, his voice deceptively soft. "About how you came by your information on Vesparan blood."

I paused, meeting his eyes in the mirror. "Some secrets are best kept, Varen. Especially in a place like this."

A faint smile tugged at his lips. "Indeed. You're learning quickly." He moved to the door, gesturing for me to follow. "Let's not keep Lord Caelius waiting."

As we made our way through the winding corridors, the oppressive silence of the manor pressed in around us. Unlike yesterday, where the halls were mostly abandoned, today servants scurried past, their eyes downcast, while guards stood at attention, their gazes following our every move.

We reached Lord Caelius' study, the ornate doors looming

before us like the maw of some awful beast. Varen knocked twice, then pushed the heavy doors open without waiting for a response.

Lord Caelius stood by the window, his back to us as he gazed out over the city. The air in the room was thick and oppressive, the scent of ink and parchment not enough to cover the cloying scent of copper lingering in the room on the clothes of several vampires I'd never seen before.

Their eyes were intense as they roved over me with a mixture of polite curiosity and barely concealed hunger. There was a mix of male and female vampires, all in various noble attire straight from the Victorian era. I had to wonder if they all had some kind of dress code or something.

The thought almost caused a hysterical bubble of laughter to burst from me, but I tamped it down and cleared my throat instead. I schooled my features into an expression of impassiveness as I looked slightly past each of them.

"Ah, Miss Olivia," Caelius said, turning to face us. His eyes gleamed with an unsettling intensity, trailing up and down my body with some disappointment at my change in clothing. All the better not to appeal to someone like him. "How fortunate that you're here. We've just received some... interesting news from the outlying territories."

My heart pounded in my chest, but I forced my voice to remain steady. "Oh? What kind of news, my lord?"

Caelius' lips curled into a wintry smile. "News of a plague, my dear. One that sounds remarkably similar to the one you described." He took a step closer, his gaze boring into mine.

"Perhaps you'd care to explain how you arrived just in time for this plague to be in danger of afflicting our own citizens? Seems like quite the coincidence, now doesn't it?"

I felt the weight of every eye in the room upon me. This was the moment of truth. Everything hinged on what I said next. Taking a deep breath, I prepared to give the performance of my life, praying that my hastily constructed story would hold up under their scrutiny.

"My lord," I began, infusing my voice with a mix of relief and urgency, "this is precisely why I came to Vespara. The plague has spread faster than we anticipated. I had hoped to reach you before it became a widespread threat, but it seems I was too late."

Caelius' eyes narrowed, searching my face for any sign of deception. "And you believe Vespara holds the key to stopping this plague? What makes you think that?"

I nodded emphatically. "I do, my lord. As I said before, I am working with one of the best healers in all of Aethralis, and he is the one who told me to seek out the royal family. If there's any hope of a cure, he believes it lies within your kingdom."

A tense silence fell over the room as Caelius considered my words. I held my breath, acutely aware that my fate—and the fate of so many others—hung in the balance.

Finally, Caelius spoke. "It seems, Miss Olivia, that your warning was more timely than we initially believed." He turned to the other vampires in the room. "We will have to bring this to Prince Aldric's attention. It seems that we will have to have a discussion, after all."

As the others hurried to carry out his orders, Caelius fixed me with a penetrating stare. "I hope, for your sake, that your faith in Vesparan blood is not misplaced. The coming days will prove... interesting."

As silence lapsed, my thoughts turned to Prince Aldric. I had to wonder what kind of person—no, vampire—he was. He had enough of a reputation for Thorne to have heard of him, which was no small feat. But was it true? Would he be willing to listen, to hear out a stranger from another kingdom? My stomach sank as I considered the possibility of failure. I'd come so far.

Despite the drain on my mana, the spike in adrenaline caused my magic to tingle beneath my skin as though ready to burst forth. I fisted my hands, my nails digging hard into my palms, just shy of drawing blood. This would not be the place to lose control, no matter how hard it was to maintain this form.

Feeling Caelius's eyes on me, I suppressed a shudder. "I look forward to meeting with his Highness."

Caelius huffed out a dry laugh and dismissed me with a wave. I gave a slight bow and turned away, Varen silently following beside me. I felt as though I had just been given a gift in that this conversation was over and I had a chance to recuperate from all the adrenaline.

As Varen led me back to my room, I couldn't shake the feeling that I had just stepped onto a much larger and more dangerous stage. The game had changed, and the stakes were higher than ever.

But as fear threatened to overwhelm me, I thought of Haleshade, of Griffin, of all those counting on me. I had come too far to turn back now. Whatever challenges lay ahead, I would face them. For the sake of those I'd left behind, and for the future of Aethralis itself.

CHAPTER 14

After Varen returned me to my room and locked the door behind me with not even a word exchanged between us, I finally acknowledged that I needed to sleep. I crawled into the bathtub of the attached bathroom with a pillow and covered myself as much as possible with my cloak so that even if I were being spied upon, they wouldn't be able to see my face or body changing.

With an immense amount of relief, I released the form my body was in for the last day and a half. My entire body ached like an overworked muscle, and I was so incredibly drained. I don't think I'd had to work so hard to maintain a form ever in my life. Between the intense amount of adrenaline, the feeling of constantly being on edge and surrounded by death, it was no small feat that I could keep composure and avoid exposing myself in such a way. It didn't even take five minutes before I had fallen into a deep and dreamless sleep.

I was abruptly awoken by my cloak being ripped from my body. A scream ripped its way from my throat before I could contain it and I came face to face with Varen. His expression was a carefully constructed mask, and I didn't have time to disguise myself. Horror and fear choked me as his gaze roved over my body.

"Just who are you, *Liv*?" he asked, menace radiating from the words.

My mouth opened and closed soundlessly. What could I say? What did I do? Despite my magical reserves being dangerously low, I felt a weak surge of power and pushed Varen away with as much force as I could muster. He didn't expect the show of force and stumbled away from the tub, giving me an opportunity to jump from the tub and race for the door. While Varen caught himself, I managed to slam the door and quickly drag the cloak over my form, lowering the hood as much as possible while I dashed for the exit.

Varen was hot on my heels, however, and I had to push myself faster and faster. I tried to call upon my magic to change forms, to help me, and my reserves were just so drained that all it did was make my skin tingle uncomfortably without change. I cursed this ability more than ever before. When I truly needed it, I couldn't do anything about it. The sound of pounding footsteps behind me made my heart race faster and faster until I felt like it would explode.

I rounded a corner and took a chance, ducking into one of the open doorways and silently slipping the door closed before Varen could capture me. I held my hands over my mouth to capture my ragged breaths and fought to slow my racing heart.

Certainly he must be able to hear it as it's so loud in my ears. Crouching low to the floor, I sought a place to hide. My eyes wide, I glanced around the room to find yet another bedroom. The room smelled incredibly masculine, and the colors contained within were all golds, scarlets and deep oranges.

I noted with rising horror that the sheets were rumpled as though someone had recently slept within them, but I didn't have a choice. I saw an open door and dove through it, finding a closet. Quickly making my way inside, I tucked myself in the back of the closet and piled clothes on top of myself. I kept the door just barely cracked so that I could see if anyone was to enter the room.

I don't know how long I remained there before someone entered the room. Taking deep, silent breaths, I fought to remain calm. I couldn't afford to panic or I was as good as dead. It was someone I didn't recognize. A tall, dark-haired vampire.

He wore a simple outfit of fitted black pants, cap toe boots and a dark gray shirt that clung to the musculature of his chest, exposing a dusting of fine black hair. His skin was lightly tanned, and he silently stalked around the room before coming to stand at the very closet where I was hiding.

He inhaled deeply, scenting the air, and to my dismay, his eyes fell on me almost immediately.

His voice was deep and rumbled across my skin like a caress as he said, "And who might you be, then?"

Against my will, my body reacted and a warmth spread low in my belly. A gasp caught in my throat and I didn't know what to say. My eyes tracked up this vampire's lean, muscled body to his face and any words I may have tried to string together withered away. Death had silver eyes, luminescent like moonlight. I found myself unable to look away, trapped in the swirling depths.

He seemed just as entranced before a thump in the hallway pulled our attention, both of us turning towards the open door. I heard Varen's voice pour in from the doorway and saw his shadow stretch across the floor. "We are continuing to search for the fugitive. Please remain in your room until she is captured for your own safety."

The man's full lips quirked, but surprisingly he winked at me, then closed the closet door, throwing me into pitch black. His melodic voice rang out, "Yes, yes, Varen. I'll hide away like a good boy." The tone was teasing, and I heard Varen huff out a laugh in response, then the click of the door closing. Suddenly, it was just me and him.

The closet opened a moment later, and there was a teasing smile on the man's lips. I didn't know what to say or do, so I did nothing and just sat there in shock.

"Are you going to kill me?" I blurted, before I could think better of it.

He laughed, surprising me. The sound was rich and genuine. "Now why would I do that when things only just became interesting?"

I wasn't sure what to say to that, but didn't get much of a chance to say anything regardless before the man's callused fingers wrapped around my wrist and dragged me from the pile of clothes I'd attempted to hide in, pulling me flush against his hard, angular body.

All of my breath left me in a *whoosh* and I looked up to see him smiling down at me, fangs on display. My heart thumped painfully in my chest at our proximity. It was such a sharp contrast to Griffin, who felt warm and *safe* and comfortable.

The thought of Griffin was like a cup of cold water poured over my head and immediately I felt guilty for my body's betrayal. We had only just started to become close and here I was, practically panting over a man who was likely my enemy.

I tried to pull my magic to the surface, but it sputtered and died before becoming anything tangible. I was still too low on mana to use my magic to defend myself. The thought caused my stomach to sink as though it were full of rocks. If he were to decide to hurt me, I'd be at his mercy.

The man's fingers were like a manacle around my wrist, unyielding, and his other hand settled on my waist. He was… surprisingly warm for a vampire. Up close, his skin looked even more sun-kissed, and a chuckle escaped his lips as he saw me staring.

"Who are you?" The words escaped me, unbidden, as I looked up into his eyes yet again. "Your voice sounds familiar."

"Who am I? That should hardly matter. The real question is, who are you, love?" His lips were still quirked up in a smile as he asked. He seemed to deliberately ignore my second point.

His gaze was warm despite the underlying steel of his grip. He was definitely unlike any vampire I'd met thus far. All the others seemed very full of themselves, lording themselves over all others, whether vampire or not. But this man seemed much more... *human*, I thought hesitantly.

He was gazing at me expectantly, and I found myself telling him the truth, almost as though I were compelled to do so. It felt somehow... wrong to lie to him. "My name is Lyra. I'm a mage, and I've come from far away to ask the royal family for help."

His dark brows rose in surprise and his smile grew devilish. "The royal family, hmm? What could you possibly want from one of them?" His voice held a trace of disgust, which surprised me. His gaze on me grew intense and my mind became a little fuzzy.

"I was told that there was a prince who would listen to me. Aldric. There's a plague spreading across Aethralis and the healer that I have been working with has told me that he believes royal vampiric blood is the key to finding a cure for this sickness." I was rambling, all the words escaping me as though I had no control.

Was this the magic of vampires? I felt as though my soul itself was being bared before this man, and the feeling sent chills down my spine. It was so much different from the blatant eroticism of last night. This was much more personal, intimate.

As though sensing this, the man's hand slid from my waist to the small of my back, raising goosebumps along the way. The touch was casual and languid in a way that I did not expect, and warmth crept up my cheeks. "Stop." This touch reminded me of another. The vampire from the party? He had dark hair, just like the man who grabbed me from behind.

"Stop? Are you sure about that? You seem to enjoy it," he said teasingly.

"I don't even know who you are!" I snapped, trying to extricate myself from his grip. Surprising me yet again, he simply let me go. I stumbled back and put some distance between us. Now was not the time to lose my head just because this may be the most frustratingly attractive man I'd ever met.

That thought sent a stab of guilt through me, Griffin's face crossing my mind. I looked away, but the man reached out to capture my jaw, the calluses of his palm rough on my skin as he turned me back to face him. I jerked my chin from his hand. The man seemed entirely unbothered, which made me all the angrier.

"You're looking for Aldric, right?" he said with another lazy smile. "Well, you've found him." He gestured grandly towards himself.

"You?" I asked, my mouth falling open before I caught myself and snapped my jaw closed with a *click*. "Then can you help me?" I asked urgently. "I need you to give me some of your blood."

He shrugged casually, sounding almost bored as he said, "Now, why would I do that?"

Fury instantly suffused me, and I bristled. "I need you to help me with this gods-damned plague that's spreading across Aethralis! People are dying and you're our only choice."

My anger only seemed to amuse him, and I grit my teeth when he laughed. "And if I give you my blood, what will you give me? Royal blood isn't exactly easy to come by, you know."

"Give you?" I asked, incredulous. "What would you even want?"

"You said you're a mage, right? I'll trade you. My blood for yours," he said with a teasing wink.

The words rocked me for a minute, and I had to consider if he was serious. If he was, is that something I could do? *Why would he want* my *blood? Was it just to have power over me?* I thought. I couldn't just sit on that question without an answer.

"Why would you want my blood?" I asked. "I can't imagine it would be desirable for a royal vampire who could have whatever type of blood he wanted."

"Don't think too much about the royalty aspect of it all. I'm just a man. A man who knows what he wants. And right now, it's your blood. After all, it's not often that we come across mages in Vespara. Most know to keep their distance after the last of your kind to make their way here. So consider it a treat for me," he said, his smile lazy and seductive.

The last mage to come here, huh, I thought. I had to wonder how long ago that was. I knew vaguely that at some point the last transformation mage had made their way here.

He again drew close to me, and my breath caught, my thoughts escaping me like smoke through my fingers. I hated that my body was reacting to Aldric's presence. It felt like I was betraying Griffin somehow, even though we weren't *really* together. That kiss meant something to me. I stepped back, putting some distance between us.

The first sign of displeasure crossed Aldric's face, and he released a heavy sigh. His eyes were molten with a hunger that took my breath away. He inhaled deeply, clearly scenting the air, and his tongue darted out to wet his lips. A small, dark part of me was excited by that look, and I felt disgusted with myself.

"Lyra," he murmured, his voice low and husky. My name sounded like a prayer on his lips, and a tingle spread through my core in response. "Your blood smells intoxicating in a way you wouldn't believe. You're hurting my feelings, running away from me like this."

My mouth went dry, and I gripped the edge of my cloak, twisting it between my fingers as I took another step back, finding my back against the wall. "W-what do you mean?"

"There's just something about it. Mage blood is rare enough in this place, but yours… It smells different. Powerful." His gaze was heavy, hot. I'd experienced nothing like this before. Such palpable desire from a man. Goosebumps raised along my skin and I felt bare under his stare. Naked.

He took a step closer, and a small gasp left me, my pulse jumping. His gaze dropped, watching my fluttering heartbeat in my throat before returning to my eyes. Before I knew what was happening, he had caged me in. Griffin's face flashed in my mind and I closed my eyes tight, turning away from Aldric's intensity. "Stop." I said, but the word was breathy.

Despite my wavering voice, he did. His scent enveloped me like a stormy night—wild, untamed. Electric. The warmth of his breath fanned across my cheek, carrying the promise of untold power barely contained within. We stayed like that for what could have been minutes or hours, but soon Aldric's husky voice rumbled against my ear like faraway thunder, causing me to shudder.

"So, what do you say, love? My blood for yours," he murmured.

I couldn't—wouldn't betray Griffin, no matter what. I kept repeating that in my mind like a mantra. My body's reaction is biology. It meant nothing. I could control my own responses. I took a slow, deep breath. It worked against me, bringing with it more of his musky, earthy scent.

"And if I agree, what would you do with it? What would happen?" I said, proud of myself for how the words didn't waver. "I've seen what happens when people are bitten by vampires. They—it's—,"

I couldn't formulate the words.

"I won't do anything nefarious. I just want to… taste you," he said. Opening my eyes, they went round with shock. His lips curled into a smirk, but his gaze was hypnotic, drawing me in.

I would be doing this for Griffin if I said yes. For Aethralis. To cure this plague and save so many lives. But I also couldn't deny my curiosity, and I hated myself for it. Reaching between us, I put my hand on his chest to get some distance between us. I could feel the hard plane of muscle beneath my hand as I tried to push him back. He didn't budge an inch, although his lips quirked up. I snatched my hand back.

"We're running out of time, dearest." As though to punctuate his words, I heard Varen's voice faintly from beyond the door, barking orders to search all the rooms again.

"Don't call me that," I said, venom lacing the words. No matter how I felt, I wouldn't lose myself now. "Do you swear you will help me with this plague by willingly offering your blood?"

Being angry was easier than facing this awful magnetic force between us. Aldric was right, we were running out of time, so I needed to decide fast.

"Of course. I swear it. My blood for yours. A fair trade, no?" he purred. He leaned in, his face mere inches from mine, and his gaze dropped to my lips. For a moment, I thought he might kiss me. The realization that I wanted him to shocked me to my core. What the hell was wrong with me?

"I'll do it." I said, my voice stronger than I felt. My insides were trembling with anxiety, yes, but also with insatiable curiosity. "But just blood. Nothing else. And only this once." I didn't know how this would affect my magic, much less anything else. I didn't want to take any unnecessary risks, or promise anything more than I could deliver.

Aldric looked like a cat with a bowl of cream. His smile was alight with anticipation as he reached a hand up to cup my cheek, his other arm caging me against the wall. "You have my word, Lyra. Now, shall we seal our bargain?"

I wished Griffin were here. Would he understand why I had to make this choice? Would he want nothing to do with me once he found out? The very thought sent shards of ice through me.

Aldric's face dipped towards mine, and adrenaline roared through me. I couldn't help but wonder if I was making the biggest mistake of my life, but I had no choice.

I braced myself.

CHAPTER 15

Aldric's touch was surprisingly gentle. His lips traced my jaw and my breath hitched.

"Only blood and nothing else, remember?" I rasped. My mind went to the ballroom, watching the couples in an erotic embrace. I had to maintain control.

Just when I thought he would kiss me, he lightly tilted my head to the side. Anticipation flooded me and, despite my best intentions, my core became liquid. Aldric lifted his head and gave me a knowing smile, as if he could sense it. And maybe he could. Who knows? My cheeks flushed with embarrassment at the thought.

His head dipped again, and I felt his hot breath on my bare throat. A shudder traveled up my spine, and I resisted the urge to stiffen against Aldric. I feared it would hurt more then. I mean, it had to hurt, right? Being bitten? My mind was racing, and I began to tremble.

"It won't hurt at all, love," Aldric murmured against my skin as though he could read my thoughts. "You might find you like it." I felt wetness against my pulse and jolted when I realized it was a languid brush of his tongue on the flesh there.

I am doing this for Griffin. I am doing this for Aethralis. This isn't for me. I kept repeating this in my mind to stay sane and not lose myself in this moment. It was so difficult to keep my wits about me when my body was being wound tighter than a spring. A nearly painless prick at my throat caused me to gasp aloud, and Aldric reached up to cover my mouth and smother the noise.

I felt his tongue working against my throat and warmth suffused my body. A wave of uncontrolled pleasure radiated from my core and a muffled moan escaped my lips. An answering groan rumbled from Aldric and he pressed even closer, our bodies flush against each other.

I writhed against him. I wasn't sure what I wanted, what I needed, but I couldn't contain myself. As if in answer to my movement, Aldric pushed his leg in between mine and I ground myself against him instinctually, trying to relieve this ache inside of me.

My hands reached up and tangled themselves in his hair, getting lost in the inky strands as I clutched his head to me. I felt a hard length against my hip and the sensation was almost too much for me to handle. Every noise coming from my lips was muffled against his hand and seemed to drive Aldric further into a fever pitch. He drank heavily and my head went fuzzy, almost like I was wine drunk.

My limbs felt heavy, and I strained against Aldric's touch.

As though realizing he was taking too much, Aldric abruptly released me, disentangling me from him and putting several feet of distance between us. His eyes were wild, and he was panting. A rivulet of blood trailed from the corner of his mouth, and I had the insane urge to lap it up.

The sudden chill against my skin had me shivering. Knees weak, my body was on fire and I had no way to put it out. A frustrated whimper left me and shame flared within me. Through the haze, the thought drifted through my mind that Griffin would never forgive me for this. I was doing it for all the right reasons, but I couldn't deny how it made me feel.

Aldric pushed a hand through his hair, his breathing ragged. His eyes were alight with desire, swirling like liquid mercury, and I felt the same pull. My gaze dropped, seeing evidence of his arousal straining against his pants. I quickly looked back up at his face and he smiled devilishly in response.

His head cocked suddenly as though he were listening to something outside of the room and he was suddenly in front of me with preternatural speed, blocking me with his body as he turned to face the entrance to the room, wiping his mouth and leaving a smear of blood on his hand.

My gaze snapped to his, and I struggled to regain my composure, all the more difficult with his sudden proximity. He winked as he dragged his tongue over the last hint of blood on his hand. My thighs clenched in response to the sight.

The air between us virtually crackled with unspoken tension. I opened my mouth, though I had no idea what I would say. That didn't matter though, because before I could even fumble over my words, a quick knock rang out. The door abruptly opened without pause, Varen striding in without waiting for an answer.

"Highness, despite our best efforts, the woman has esc—," he paused, catching sight of me lingering behind Aldric. "What the hell is this?" His expression darkened and fear extinguished any lingering effects of the bite that Aldric and I shared.

With a casual tone to his voice, Aldric said, "Oh her? She's my new friend. I assume you two have met." He chuckled softly, much to Varen's chagrin.

"Highness, this woman could be extremely dangerous. She's a transformation mage," he said through a clenched jaw. I was startled to realize that he knew exactly what my ability was. But then he said, "You recall the last mage who had this ability and came here. Don't be foolish."

I had no words, and I glanced from Aldric to Varen. Aldric was unnaturally still, but he maintained his position in front of me, seemingly protecting me from Varen. I had no idea why he was choosing this stance. He didn't know me at all. For all he knew, I could very well be after something nefarious.

I tamped down the side of me that purred in satisfaction at his protectiveness and instead questioned just what was up with this guy. There was just… something about him that felt so different. I didn't know what to think, what to do. But some part of me trusted him and I had to follow my gut.

I spoke out before I could stop myself, my voice soft, "Varen, I know I had to deceive you, but I had to see Aldric, and I was too afraid to come here as a lone mage. My intention isn't to harm anyone. I just want to help the people of Aethralis survive. You know the plague is real, and Aldric is our best chance."

Varen's gaze settled on me and I thought his gaze softened ever-so-slightly before he said, "Deceit is deceit. I can't trust you with the safety of our crown prince. It is my duty to keep him safe and in line. I may be old, but I am not a fool."

A laugh, loud and hearty, erupted from Aldric, startling both Varen and I. Varen's amber eyes narrowed into slits as he regarded Aldric. "Just what is that about?"

Aldric wiped a tear from his eye, still smiling, before he said, "There's nothing you can do, Varen. We've struck a boon. I'm indebted to her and I must repay."

Varen looked so shocked that it would have been funny in any other situation, but he quickly recovered with a scowl. "What do you mean, you've struck a boon?"

"It's exactly as I said, Varen. I must travel with her back to this healer so that I may assist in developing a cure." He glanced over his shoulder at me with a wink. I was stunned silent, mouth gaping like a fish before I snapped my jaw closed. I instead found myself nodding along.

"It's true. We struck a boon, and he promised to help me in exchange." When Aldric moved aside, I glanced up at his eyes to see them alight with mirth. He seemed way too happy about this situation. My curiosity was piqued, but I filed this aside for later.

Varen's gaze fell to my throat and his fists balled at his side when he saw the mark that must be left there. I could still feel the warmth of Aldric's mouth there, cooling in the chill air. A blush crept up my cheeks and when Varen stepped forward menacingly, I instinctually tried to summon my magic. Aldric shot Varen a threatening look, and he stopped in his tracks, though fury was plain on his face.

Not even wisps of my magic of it remained, and horror filled me. My face fell. What could this mean? Did I lose my powers? Is this what it means to share your blood with a vampire? Is this why no mages ever traveled to Vespara? I felt… empty inside. As though something that was intrinsic to my being was just gone. What if it didn't come back?

Some vulnerable part of me was exposed, and I hated it. My magic was like an armor that I always wore and yet I had been stripped bare without realizing it. And I felt like a fool. A void had been opened deep within me. Had I made a terrible mistake?

My adrenaline spiked, and panic filled me. Aldric moved quickly, enfolding me in his arms. I didn't know what to do and so just stood stiffly in his embrace. The scent of storms and nature enfolded me and it calmed some feral part of me that was crying out.

The effect that Aldric had on me was heady. I didn't understand what was going on. However, he murmured something in my ear that had me going stock-still. My gaze shot up to his and his eyes had darkened to the color of smoke. He cast me a reassuring smile.

"Well, Varen. You are dismissed. I will depart from Vespara within the next day," Aldric said with a purr, without breaking eye contact with me.

Varen sputtered a refusal and suddenly, the room went ice-cold. I could see my breath fanning out in front of me, and the sudden change was jarring. A darkness flit across Aldric's eyes and he slowly turned to look at Varen.

"I tolerated you because I found you less irritating than the rest. I told you, you are *dismissed*," Aldric said, his voice dominating and powerful. It brokered no room for argument. "And tell the rest of them about my departure."

Varen hissed out a curse and pivoted on his heel, striding angrily from the room. I heard the footsteps of several people following Varen wherever he was going, so Aldric and I were truly alone for the first time. No pressure. I looked up at him from under my lashes and found his gaze already raking over my body. Gods, what was with this guy? It was like he was starving and I was an all-you-can-eat buffet.

His earlier words came back to me and I strode over, closing and locking the door at the entrance to the room.

"You said that my power will leave me for a period after sharing blood with a vampire?" I crossed my arms, shaking with fury at myself and also at him for not telling me.

"Yes, love. It will return, however. It's part of what makes mage blood so alluring. You get to taste their power in a way that normal blood just can't compare to. It's like ambrosia," he said the last on a groan, a shudder of pleasure making its way through his body at the words and his eyes slipping closed. "Why do you think I would trade my own blood for it? You could turn me into an addict, you know," he said, cracking his eyes open to give me a playful wink.

I grit my teeth, my hands balling into fists. "Why didn't you tell me this before?"

Aldric feigned a hurt expression, a huff escaping his mouth, "Because, love, if I'd told you that from the jump, there's no way you would have let me taste you. And what a taste it was," he said with a sultry smile.

The memory of his lips on my throat caused an instant throbbing at my core, and I fought to keep from fidgeting from the sensation. Instead, I scowled. "You're a real snake, you know that? And what's this about traveling with me? That wasn't part of the deal."

Aldric slowly straightened, losing his playful edge. I saw something dark shifting behind his eyes as he said, "I need to get out of this place, Lyra. Our bargain was exactly what I needed to get a ticket out of here. After all, I never did say *when* or *where* I would give you my blood, now did I?" He shoved his hands in his pockets, back to his usual casual attitude.

A scream of frustration bubbled up, and I shoved the sensation down. This may very well be for the better. If Thorne needs more blood, I wouldn't have to come back to this place. But at the same time, what was I going to do? How could I bring this man to what was essentially Griffin and I's doorstep? And worse, what if Aldric elicits some kind of reaction when Griffin and I are together? A groan of dismay slipped from my lips and I scrubbed a hand down my face.

"Now, what's that about, love?" Aldric asked. He sounded genuinely concerned, surprising me. "Will it be so bad having me as a companion? I am going to help you, after all."

Some part of me wanted to reassure him. I had no idea why. And honestly, with the way he tricked me, he didn't deserve my reassurance. "You're still a snake," I repeated. Determined to get some distance from him, I said, "I need to go back to my room and gather my things if we are leaving soon."

A dry smile twisted Aldric's lips as he said, "Okay. I'll accompany you."

With my hands held up as though to ward him off, I walked backwards towards the door. "I don't need you to come with me."

"Oh, but you do, love. If you recall, Varen isn't exactly happy that I am going to be leaving Vespara. And how best would he keep me here than to eliminate the exact person I've struck a bargain with?"

Gods above and below, this man was so incredibly frustrating. I didn't know how I would make it the whole way back to Sylvan Reach without killing him. "You can't just follow me around everywhere, can you? I mean, you're a prince. Aren't you supposed to have a guard, not *be* a guard?"

With a mocking smile, he said, "Listen, Lyra. You may not know this, but I'm one of the very few living vampires left. Not many are more powerful than I. Varen was there mostly for show and to spy for me as needed to keep ahead of my family."

At my obvious confusion, he clarified, "I'm next in line, darling. There are plenty of naysayers within my family who would rather I die than take the crown. All the more reason to leave this place," he said bitterly.

"What does that mean, a living vampire?" I asked, curiosity taking hold of me before I could think better of it.

"It's how I maintain this delightful tan," he said with a smirk. Despite myself, my lips curved gently in a hint of an answering smile.

He continued, "Living vampires are the oldest race. The true vampires, if you will. We aren't weak to the sun or anything like that. It's what makes us harder to kill and why we've been the ruling family for so long." He shrugged. "But royalty has never been the life for me. The way Vespara is run is disgusting," he said. Anger made his voice go even deeper, more husky and infinitely more dangerous. I suppressed a shudder.

"You seem to hold a lot of resentment for your family," I noted.

Aldric cursed softly, running a hand through his inky hair. "Now's not the time, love. Not now. We can talk later."

"You seem to have a lot of trust in someone you just met. I mean, you're telling me an awful lot," I said cautiously.

"What can I say, love? There's just something about you. And I'm determined to find out what it is," he said.

Deep within me, an answering voice rang out that I felt the same way, no matter how hard I tried to deny it.

CHAPTER 16

Since I couldn't safely go gather my things from the other room, nor did I recall where my room was, frankly, Aldric led the way. I didn't know how he knew what room I had been in, given that he had just arrived after I did, but the room we arrived at was definitely mine.

I cast a sidelong glance at him. His long, raven-black hair was brushing over his shoulder. I fought the irrational urge to tuck it behind his ear and reveal his face. What was wrong with me? I had to get away from him somehow before I ruined everything between Griffin and I before it could even happen. A mournful sigh escaped me. I missed him. The scent of musk and leather, of nature, that surrounded him.

Aldric frowned. "Just what was that for?" he asked.

"Nothing. Just missing a friend." I said flatly, unwilling to disclose anything else. He didn't need to know anything more about me than he already did. I just wanted to get back to Sylvan

Reach, find the cure for this wasting plague, and move on with my life back in Haleshade. It felt like years since I'd been back and despite the short time I stayed, I truly felt as though I could make it my home.

Curiosity was plain on Aldric's face, but he wisely chose not to press. He stood outside the door as I went through the room, gathering my meager belongings into a pack and hefting it on my shoulder. Unbidden, my hand reached up to trace the column of my throat where Aldric's mouth had been. There were two small, raised bumps there. Just that simple touch sent a shot of pleasure through me and my breath escaped me in a hiss.

"You okay in there, love?" Aldric called out.

"Yes. And can you quit calling me that?" I grumbled. "I am not your love."

He peeked his head around the corner and shot me a dramatic, pained look. "You would deny me before even giving me a chance? I'm wounded."

I scoffed, "You're such a drama queen."

He chuckled and retreated around the corner, returning me to privacy. As much as he could, I supposed. Despite it all, it was nice of him to pretend to give me space. I wondered if he could feel how overwhelming this entire process had been. My entire body felt like I'd been through a meat grinder. My muscles were all sore, my magic was drained, I'd not slept well in days, and I'd given up who knows how much blood to some strange vampire prince.

What the hell was my life right now? I thought with a sigh. All I wanted was peace. That's it. Instead, here I am, about to make a trek halfway across the country with some vampire guy who's got the hots for me while trying to cure a plague that I have nothing to do with. All this, just so I can go back and live in some random far-off village in an attempt to get some quiet in my life and settle down.

I felt bitterness like never before right now. I felt trapped in this endless cycle. Finding a place for me to call home, just to get ousted for reasons beyond my control. I know that's not quite what happened with Haleshade and that I left more because of a sense of duty, but still. Why couldn't I just settle without all of this other external stuff going on? I cursed under my breath in frustration.

My entire life felt cursed. Maybe the elders who used to gossip amongst themselves about me were right. Maybe I was just doomed to a life of discourse. Tears pricked my eyes and threatened to spill over and I stormed over to the attached bathroom, throwing the water on in the faucet. I angrily splashed my face, scrubbing against my skin. The shock of the cold water helped me to gain a bit of clarity. Having a pity party wouldn't help with anything. It wouldn't help me feel better or to solve anything.

Sometimes it was just hard. *Life* was just hard. I refused to crumple beneath the weight of it all, despite that. I straightened, looking in the simple square mirror above the sink. My eyes were dark amethyst, dark circles beneath. My hair was a tangled mess and my skin was sticky with old sweat. I needed a shower. I figured now was as good a time as any. That was one thing I was grateful for. Given how opulent Lord Caelius's home was, he had all the modern amenities.

I turned the water on and as it warmed, I padded out to where Aldric still stood watch outside of my door.

He smiled when he saw me and my heart stuttered in response. I looked quickly away to the empty hallway and said, "I'm going to take a quick shower before we leave."

I heard the smile in his voice as he replied, "Room for one more?" His voice was low and husky. I sputtered for a moment, my gaze snapping back to him. His eyes held barely contained laughter, and I scowled. "Absolutely not. Contain yourself. Are you a prince or a bawd?"

With that, he could no longer contain himself and laughter rang out in the hall as I turned back towards the bathroom. The sound followed me in until I slammed the door, locking it. I peeled off my clothes in the now-steamy room. A delighted sigh slipped from my lips as I slid under the hot spray of the shower.

My muscles immediately started to relax under the beat of the water. Luckily, there were oils and soaps for me to use already in the bathroom. It smelled fresh and clean and that's all that mattered to me right now. As I washed, my mind wandered. I felt deep within myself, trying to spark my magic back to life. The barest flutter of power flowed from my soul and relief made me weak. I wrapped my arms around myself and just let myself exist in this moment. My mana was returning.

Thank the gods. I don't know what I would have done. It felt as though an integral part of myself was ripped away without my power. I was shocked to realize this, as I'd never seen my ability as anything but a burden. And yet, here I was, glad to feel its existence. I shouldn't have been so afraid of the loss, given that my power had never brought me anything but grief. And yet… it made me who I was. I wouldn't have met Griffin without it. I would absolutely never have traveled to Vespara, or to Haleshade. The losses that I've experienced and the hardship all led me to this place at this point in time.

Despite it all, I was grateful. I smiled as I thought about Griffin. His chocolate-colored hair, his sunshine eyes and the stubble dusting his jaw. My lips tingled as I thought back to our last meeting. The brush of his lips against mine. I couldn't wait to see him again. My fingers traced the line of my lips and I imagined him here with me in this shower. A soft sigh escaped me and heat curled low in my belly at the thought.

Why do I keep feeling this way? I'd dealt with passing crushes. I had a pulse, after all. But I'd never craved a man like I did now. I felt like a teenager all over again, every passing glance causing a flutter in my chest. But I couldn't deny the attraction I had for Griffin. I could only hope that he felt the same. A smile curved my lips. All I had to do was bring Aldric back to Thorne, and we could go back to Haleshade together. And maybe… maybe we could be together. I felt a blush creep up my cheeks and I quickly finished up in the shower.

Just for good measure, I turned the water ice cold, determined to get myself together. The chill took my breath away and my teeth were chattering before I stepped out and reached for a nearby towel hanging up, fluffy and white. Wrapping the towel around myself, I padded across the bathroom and looked down at my dirty clothing with disdain. I wondered absently if there was extra clothing anywhere in this suite.

I unlocked the door and came up short as my gaze drifted over to the bed, where Aldric was currently sprawled, his arms crossed behind his head.

"What the hell are you doing?" I snapped.

"Whatever do you mean? I'm just doing my due diligence as your guard, my dear," he said with a wink. "I'm here to defend you in case any salacious men come threatening to ravish you."

I rolled my eyes so hard I could practically see my brain. "The only salacious man here is you."

His hand grasped his chest as he gasped out, "Oh no, you've wounded me. Quick, come give me mouth to mouth. Lest I die here and now."

I shook my head, determined not to laugh. I refused to encourage this behavior. "Get out of here. I need to see if there is anything clean for me to wear."

He meandered off of the bed and slowly slipped from the room, his gaze lingering on me. "Don't take too long. Shame, really. I could have stayed, you know," he said with a wink. Luckily, he closed the door behind him and I sagged with relief.

He was so intense to be around all the time. And such a flirt! He had no shame at all. Although, I guess he wouldn't need any being royalty. He has probably been with half of the kingdom, the way he acts. And I wasn't upset at that thought at all. I shook my head, refusing to think about it any longer, and began to root through the drawers and closets in the room, finally finding an overlarge shirt and breeches that I could tie to fit. It was loose, but it would have to do. At least it wouldn't fall off of my body.

Once I was decent, I peeked my head out of the doorway to find Aldric casually leaned against the wall. He seemed entirely unbothered by his decision to leave. I had to wonder what his motivations were. He seemed to resent being here.

He seemed to be deep in thought. Without the sardonic smile that seemed a permanent fixture on his face any other time, he looked so… melancholy. It bothered me for a reason I couldn't explain.

"Are you okay?" I asked, hesitantly. I don't know why I was bothering to ask, but I just couldn't help myself.

"Of course. Why wouldn't I be?" he said nonchalantly, schooling his features into his usual playful expression.

I paused, unsure. But then I asked, "Why do you *really* want to leave Vespara, Aldric?"

He hesitated, caught off guard. "Let's just say not everyone wants to be a part of royalty. A part of—," he waved his hand vaguely to our surroundings, "—all of this. The politics, the treatment of the lesser vampires…"

I waited for him to complete his thought, but he didn't say anything else. Just shook his head. I didn't want to push him when the subject clearly made him uncomfortable, so I decided to change the subject instead.

"So, do you want to meet here in the morning?" I asked.

Aldric's gaze slid over me, taking in the ill-fitting outfit I'd been left with. His lips curved up, but it didn't reach his eyes. "Whatever do you mean? I can't leave you alone, Lyra. You're stuck with me."

Panic seized me at the thought. "What do you mean, I'm stuck with you? I stayed here last night without a problem."

"It's simple, love. It's the same reason I'm here outside your door right now. You need to be protected, and the only one I can trust to do that is me," he said with a wink. His smile seemed a bit more genuine and warm now, which was a relief.

I sighed, scrubbing a hand over my face. Exhaustion was truly setting in. Aldric seemed to notice, because he reached out to cup my cheek in his warm, rough palm, startling me into taking a step back. A flicker of something showed in his eyes, but it was so fast I may have imagined it. Aldric returned the sigh.

"You look like you're about to keel over and die," he said, completely straight-faced.

I scoffed in indignation. "You should talk. Your kind literally *are* dead."

Aldric held up a hand. "Ah, ah, ah. *Other* vampires are dead. Don't forget, I am a living vampire. See?" With that, he grabbed my wrist, pulling me flush against his body, holding me tightly to the hard planes of his torso. My cheeks immediately burned with embarrassment and I tried to pull away, but his hands cradled my head against his chest, gently but unyielding.

I was surprised to hear a heart beating. A bit quicker than it probably should have, but beating none-the-less. My eyes rounded with surprise and I twisted to look up at him. He released me, chuckling at my expression. "See? Very much alive."

"I—I see," I murmured, unsure of what else to say. That moment had felt so… intimate. I felt incredibly awkward and shifted on my feet. "Well, you're right. You seem to be alive."

Sensing the awkwardness, Aldric stretched and hiked a thumb over his shoulder. "So. Your place or mine?"

CHAPTER 17

After a heated argument, I took my small pack of supplies to Aldric's room in Caelius's estate. His room was larger and there was more furniture, so I figured I'd have more places to sleep. However, I couldn't be more wrong about that I found as I walked in, Aldric on my heels.

"So, where am I going to sleep?" I asked, eyes scanning the room for suitable chairs or sofas. There were several that I could probably use fairly comfortably, all in shades of orange, scarlet, or gold. I couldn't believe that I hadn't realized he was the prince before. This room practically screamed 'royalty'.

"What do you mean? In the bed, of course," he said, sounding offended.

"Where will you sleep, then?" I asked, glancing sidelong at him.

There was a pause, then a wicked smile as he said, "Why, in the bed. Where else?"

I immediately began shaking my head, holding my hands

up as though to ward off the words. "Nope, no. Absolutely not. We are not sharing a bed together."

As I thought he would, he held a dramatic hand over his chest as though I staked him right then and there. "You're always so hurtful to me, you know. In case you were wondering, yes, it does make you incredibly attractive." His teasing grin was back, although he still made an effort to look wounded.

"You are ridiculous," I said flatly, scowling. "We are not sharing a bed. I will take this sofa." I walked over to the sofa in question, a sunset-orange, plush sofa with silky-looking pillows, dropping my pack next to it with a huff.

Aldric followed along behind me with a frown. "You must think I'm no gentleman at all. I'll take the sofa if you insist. I can't have a lady uncomfortable in my bedroom," he said, surprisingly serious.

"You need to make up your mind, Aldric. I won't be sleeping in the bed if there's a chance of you crawling under the covers with me."

"What if I lay *on top* of the covers?" he offered teasingly. At the flat look on my face, he sighed. "Okay, okay. No more joking. I will be a good boy and stay over here, no matter how much I want to be pressed up against you."

My jaw fell open at his words, and a blush immediately bloomed on my cheeks. "Stop saying things like that. You know our deal was blood, just once, and nothing more."

He loosed a wistful sigh as he said, "I know, but it doesn't stop a man from wanting, now does it?" With that, he practically threw himself onto the sofa and settled himself in with one of the pillows, dropping the other few on the floor in front of him.

I cautiously grabbed my pack and brought it over to the bed, still rumpled from the night before. I traced my fingers over the sheets, unsurprised to find them incredibly soft and luxurious. Only something this fine would be fitting for royalty, I supposed. A thought crossed my mind unbidden of Aldric wrapped naked in these sheets as he slept, his raven-black hair spread across the pillows like ink.

I cursed under my breath and shook my head to clear the thought away. Aldric chuckled from his spot over on the love seat and I shot him a dark look just to find him laying with his eyes closed, curled up in the fetal position to make enough room for his long limbs. Seeing him contorted like that made me feel a pang of guilt.

I strode back over to the sofa and waited until he cracked open his eyes and looked up at me to say, "You take the bed. Please."

He immediately frowned and shook his head, closing his eyes again stubbornly, "Absolutely not. Either you alone get the bed, or you and I together share it."

"Aldric, you're going to be so uncomfortable curled up on that sofa. Take the bed," I insisted. The thought of him making himself uncomfortable for my benefit put me on edge. I didn't look too hard at why.

Wordlessly, he rolled over to face away from me. I could not believe how childish this man was being right now. "Aldric, you're being ridiculous. You are the crown prince of this entire kingdom. This is your room. Take the bed."

When he chose not to respond, I stomped back over to the bed and plopped my butt down on its downy softness. I wasn't going to keep arguing with him. I barely knew the guy. Who knew how he would react? Then again, I bet I knew. He'd probably just say something lewd to make me feel uncomfortable and then have that stupid grin on his face yet again before refusing to listen to me yet again.

Traveling with Aldric was going to be miserable if he kept this type of attitude and behavior up the entire time. While he lay silently over on the love seat, I reached inward to pull my magic. To my immense relief, I felt a response, my mana stretching and yawning like a cat under my skin.

It was both uncomfortable and an incredibly welcome sensation after so long without it. Not that I needed to use it at the moment, but it was good to know it was there in case I did. It was still weak yet, but I'm sure after a night's rest I would be back to normal. I didn't want to admit how much that comforted me.

I wished I were alone so I could take off these uncomfortable, strange clothes, but I didn't dare with Aldric here. Much less anyone else who could make their way into this room.

"Aldric," I called softly.

"Yes, my love?" he responded without hesitation. That response irked me, but I was starting to wonder if he referred to everyone like that. It seemed to be a habit for him that was hard to break.

"Don't call me that," I snapped, then asked, "Do we have to be concerned about anyone bursting into this room?"

"I can't help it, my dear," he said ruefully, slowly rolling back over in my direction. "It just comes out when I talk to you." I scoffed, but before I could bite out a response, he continued. "But in answer to your question, no. No one would dare to cross me now that I am leaving. Why would they bother?"

"To keep you here, to end your legacy, who knows?" I asked, ticking the different options off on my fingers.

"I think they'd be more than happy to see me go with no bloodshed. Although if they changed their mind, I'd be more than willing to show why I am next in line for the crown," he said, his voice low and dangerous. A chill traced its icy fingers up my spine, and I rubbed my arms to clear the sensation.

There was a beat of silence, then Aldric said, "Well, I'm going to get some sleep before we depart for… wherever we're going."

"I don't know if I'll be able to sleep. I'm worried about someone sneaking in here," I admitted.

He sighed and begrudgingly sat up. Then he got up, meandered over to the door and locked it, then glanced at me over his shoulder. At my uncertain look, he easily slid the wardrobe over the door and then gestured at it as if to say *Satisfied?*

My eyes went round with shock. Just how strong was Aldric? He moved that heavy piece of furniture like it was nothing. If he's offering to protect me, I realized I probably did not need to be as worried as I was and gave him a small nod.

Wordlessly, he slipped out of his boots and padded back over to the loveseat, practically folding himself in half to fit. I kicked off my own boots and drew back the covers, enfolding myself in its silky coolness. A small sigh of contentment escaped me. It had been so long since I'd been in such a comfortable bed. I snuggled deep and closed my eyes.

But sleep wouldn't come. I was bone-tired and my body was beyond its limits. And yet, something was niggling at me and keeping me from slipping into sleep. The thought of Aldric being so comically oversized over on the sofa was making me feel guilty, I realized. Rolling over, I tried to put it out of my mind. There was nothing I could do about it. He wouldn't let me take the sofa and I didn't want him in the bed with me.

Don't lie to yourself, a traitorous part of my mind whispered. I firmly shoved that thought away and rolled over again, my frustration rising. This would be much easier if he'd just swap places with me. After about fifteen minutes of rising anger, I sat up, flinging the blankets off. I strode over to where Aldric lay, to find him still awake as well. He turned his eyes on me and the intensity took my breath away. After a few seconds, I remembered to breathe and sighed.

"Get in the bed," I grumbled.

"Oh? Changed your mind, did you?" he asked, his voice husky.

I crossed my arms. "Don't make me change my mind again. The bed is big enough for both of us to have our own side and not even have to touch," I said, gesturing to the bed in question. It was indeed enormous. You could easily fit 4 grown adults in it. It seemed ridiculous to have a bed so large, but who knows what vampires got up to in the night, I thought with a shudder.

I stomped back over to the side of the bed I'd been laying in and was careful to ensure I was as far away from the other side of the bed as possible. I had to rest. Being exhausted and having to travel such a long way with a vampire who admits that my blood tastes good and is prized, not a good idea at all. And yet, all of my senses were on high alert when I heard the whisper of clothes hitting the floor and felt the bed shift ever-so-slightly as Aldric climbed in on the other side.

Closing my eyes, I snuggled into the blankets as much as I could and tried to ignore him. He loosed a sigh behind me and I felt him stretch out. *It had to feel better than that love seat,* I thought.

I started counting my breaths, breathing long and slow until drowsiness overrode my active mind. I heard gentle breathing start up from the other side of the bed and realized that Aldric was already asleep. All the more reason for me to sleep too, I thought. After a few more minutes, sleep finally overtook me and the world went dark.

I awoke with a bit of a start to a foreign sensation. A powerful arm was draped over my waist and I was tucked against a very male body. All of my nerve endings were entirely too aware of the hard planes of muscle against me. My eyes went wide, and I looked out into the room. It was dark, a hint of moonlight peeking through a gap in the heavy golden curtains. I wasn't sure how long I'd actually been asleep. I was still exhausted, and the feeling of this person behind me was very cozy and warm.

Giving into the impulse and snuggling back more into the warmth, I received a contented sigh in return. My lips curved up slightly and I fell back into a deep sleep.

Griffin stood over me, disgust plain on his face. I scrambled out of bed, only to find myself naked and sore. I looked around in horror to find Aldric laid out behind me with a Cheshire grin on his face.

"It's not what it looks like, Griffin! I'm just trying to get back to you," I cried.

"I trusted you. You were there to find a cure and instead you're whoring yourself out to some vampire? I can't believe that I wanted anything to do with you," Griffin spat.

My heart cracked in two and I looked around to find something to wear, something to prove that I was innocent, and there was nothing. A warmth trickled down to my breast, and I reached up and traced a fingertip to it, looking to see that I was bleeding. I looked for the source and there was another bite.

I looked back at Aldric in confusion, and his eyes had gone red with hunger. He attacked me, pinning me down with his weight on the floor as Griffin watched over his shoulder, loathing plain on his face. He turned and walked away as I cried out to him. Aldric bit into my neck viciously and I tried to use my magic, only to find it had abandoned me, too.

I awoke with a cry, jolting upright in bed. I was sweating like a pig, and raggedly ran a hand through my matted hair. What the hell was that about? Aldric groaned next to me and blearily sat up. We had been spooning, I realized. And I saw, with horror, that he was shirtless.

Oh gods. My eyes roved over his bare chest before I caught myself, shaking my head with disgust given the dream I'd just had.

"What are you doing over here? Go away," I said viciously, shaken up by my dream. My voice was wavering, and Aldric frowned.

"Are you okay, love?" he reached out a hand and laid it on my shoulder. I tensed.

"No. And I said get the hell away from me!" I hissed, kicking my way out of the blankets and standing, pacing away from Aldric.

Aldric held his hands up, placating. "Okay, okay. I'm here if you want to talk," he said. What was with this guy? He's supposed to be some evil vampire prince or whatever, but he's over here wanting me to talk about what's upsetting me? I didn't know what to do with him. It frustrated me. I didn't even want to travel back to Sylvan Reach with him, but I had to be sure he would make it to Thorne safely.

A bitter laugh escaped me. This was just horrible. This whole thing was awful. I clutched a hand to my chest as though that would help to ease the ache there. Just what was that dream for? Was Griffin going to hate me when I tell him what I had to do? Will he reject me and walk away?

I raced towards the door I suspected would lead to the bathroom and found that I was right, heading through the heavy door and closing it aggressively. I stomped over to the sink and glared at myself through my lashes. Tears filled my eyes, and I turned on the cold tap, splashing my face to hide my shame.

I scrubbed my face until the pressure behind my eyes stopped, and I was breathing heavily, hiccuping. Why? Why was I so scared about leaving this place and going back to Sylvan Reach? But I knew the answer. Griffin. I feel like I'd betrayed him. I didn't mean to. Didn't have much of a choice, but I felt the same. All I could do was hope that he would understand.

There was a comb nearby the sink, and I picked it up, noticing inky black strands caught in the teeth. I huffed and removed it, then tried dragging it through the tangled mop of my hair. As soon as the first tooth broke off in the matted strands, I felt like I was going to scream. I rummaged through the drawers of the sink cabinet and found a brush instead. I didn't care that it didn't belong to me, not right now.

The brush was a lot more successful in helping to eliminate all the tangles in my hair. Once it was back to its normal wavy softness without all the mats, I breathed a sigh of relief. I felt a little more like myself. I put my hair up in a simple twist and checked my reflection in the mirror. Redness lined my eyes, and I looked like a corpse. *Fitting*, I thought.

I didn't know how long I was in the bathroom before Aldric cautiously knocked. "You okay in there?" he called.

I pinched the bridge of my nose and took a deep breath before opening the door. "I'm fine. Had a bad dream. I'm sorry for snapping at you," I said begrudgingly.

"No problem, love. I'm glad you're okay," he said, though he still looked concerned. He'd donned a simple linen shirt and wore a fitted black pair of pants and his boots.

"We need to get ready to go," I said. "It's a long road to Sylvan Reach. Are we walking?"

Aldric shook his head. "I was thinking we could take horses. We'll still have to stop to give the horses a rest, but it shouldn't take as long as going on foot," he said.

I loosed a heavy sigh of relief. Walking the entire way up here had *sucked*. Felt like I'd walked forever and still had forever to go before I got here. "Okay, good. That works. Are you ready?" I asked.

"Yes, love. I don't plan to bring too much with me," he said.

"Can you *please* stop calling me pet names?" I said, forcing myself not to sound as angry as I felt.

"I'll try, Lyra," he said seriously. "It's just hard with you."

"Well, regardless of how difficult you find it, I don't want to hear you calling me anything other than Lyra again," I said, frustration leaking through.

Things were awkward yet again, and I cursed myself under my breath. I couldn't wait to have this trip done and over with.

"Let's go," I said. Aldric swept an arm towards the door in a grand gesture and I grabbed my pack of supplies. Aldric slung a small backpack over his shoulders and out we went into the night.

CHAPTER 18

Aldric had to be playing up the cliche of a vampire prince, I thought to myself as I looked at him, sat astride a huge, black-as-night Vesparan horse. It was gorgeous, with huge, expressive brown eyes that held keen intelligence.

"These Vesparan horses are famous for their stamina, you know. They're good long distance riders," Aldric said proudly, patting the horse on the neck. I glanced around.

"Where's my horse?" I asked. There couldn't just be one. It would be harder on the horse to have two riders for long distances.

"Oh, it's not what you think. Your horse is over there," Aldric said, pointing over his shoulder. I followed his point to see a servant on their way up the path with a gorgeous, snowy-white horse. It had blue eyes and walked with pride, very regal-looking.

My jaw dropped. "This horse?" I asked incredulously.

"Of course. Only the best for you, Lyra," Aldric said with a wink and a grin. "This is another well-trained horse. I am uncertain how good of a rider you are, so I figured I'd go with one I knew was safe. That it matches your energy is just a bonus."

I couldn't deny being drawn to this horse. It was a lovely mare, very calm. The servant, a young stable boy with golden blonde hair who I was pleased to see was still human and looked unmarked, dropped the lead in my hand. She is gorgeous, I thought with a sigh. And I couldn't wait to go for a ride. I was the most excited I'd been in ages. I hadn't ridden a horse in years, but I'm sure that I would get used to it again easily enough.

Hiking my leg up, I settled myself in the saddle. Immediately, I felt a bit off balance, but quickly adjusted. The horse was very patient with me. "What's her name?" I asked.

"Her name is Lune. I'm sure you can imagine why," he said with an easy smile. "She's been trained with novice riders for a long time, so she should be simple to get used to."

I could tell. She adjusted underneath me to help me balance. I patted her neck gently and tied the lead rope into a loop on the halter, tucking it in so I wouldn't have to worry about removing it while riding.

"Lead the way, Lyra," Aldric said gallantly, as though we were two knights about to embark on a journey. In some ways, it felt that way. With a gentle nudge, I pushed Lune into a trot and we began our trek back to Sylvan Reach.

It was a few hours later when we took our first break. There was a brook heading down away from Vespara, and it was a good time to give the horses a quick break to take a drink and graze.

I also needed to stretch my legs as they ached from riding. I was very out of practice, it seemed. Chewing on a bit of bread I'd packed into my bag, I sat down near the edge of the brook. I felt Aldric's presence behind me before he said anything.

"Are you holding up alright?" he asked. He sat down next to me, his movements silent and graceful. The sun still had a couple of hours left before it would rise. Luckily, the moon was full and bright and lit our way enough to make a decent pace. It would still be at least a week-long journey, but better than the pace I'd had to take to get to Vespara to begin with.

"I'm okay. Just been a while since I'd gone riding," I said. I stretched my legs out in front of me and sighed, taking another bite of bread. Aldric didn't pack any food it looked like. I had to wonder what he was going to eat. I took a sidelong glance at him. He was looking at the horses grazing and drinking from the brook, his expression still holding that melancholy expression he held whenever he wasn't joking around and being a flirt.

Despite myself, I had to wonder why he wore that expression. He seemed to have it all. He was royalty, he was powerful, incredibly good looking, I admitted begrudgingly to myself. What would make him look so... sad? I didn't give into my curiosity though. There was no reason for me to get any closer to him than I had already.

Instead, I turned my thoughts to Griffin. It had been a month since I'd left Sylvan Reach. Was he still okay? How were things going? I had to wonder. The chain at my neck warmed up, and I jolted. I'd forgotten that I was even wearing it. It kept getting hotter and hotter until I feared it would burn my skin. I quickly unclasped it from around my neck and looked at the chain. The locket had tiny words scrawled on it in messy script. I brought it closer to my face and saw that it said 'open me'.

I stood abruptly and strode off. I called over my shoulder, "I'll be right back. Need to step away for a minute," and started heading off the path without waiting for a response. Once I was sure I was far enough away, I opened the locket. There was a tiny image of Thorne on the opposite side of where the tiny vial lay. My mouth gaped open. What magic was this?

"Lyra, thank goodness. How are things going there?" Thorne asked urgently.

"I am on my way back to Sylvan Reach now. How are you doing this?" I asked.

"Never mind that, Lyra. Things have gotten worse. It's your parents and… Griffin," he said, his voice heavy.

My heart nearly stopped. I felt like I couldn't catch my breath and that the world had spun off-kilter around me. I gripped the locket tightly in my fist until it cut into my hands.

"What do you mean? What's going on with them?" I asked, my voice raw.

"I think you know, Lyra. It's the plague. It's gotten to them," Thorne said. An image of my parents sick in bed, their eyes wide yet unseeing the world around them flashed up on the tiny locket. My eyes immediately stung and panic gripped me.

"How long have they been afflicted?" I asked harshly. "Why is this the first I'm hearing of it?"

Thorne looked apologetic in the tiny image as he said, "They've been sick for a couple of weeks. I've been doing my best to manage them because I didn't want to distract you from your journey. Hurry back to Sylvan Reach."

"Where is Griffin?" I asked. "You said he was affected, too."

Thorne cringed as he said, "Griffin left. He departed from Sylvan Reach before the sickness got too bad. Said he had someplace else he needed to be."

My jaw dropped and I shouted, "What do you mean he left? Where could he possibly have to go?" I was enraged. How could he have left? Who would provide better treatment than Thorne? I needed to get back to Sylvan Reach, and fast.

"I don't know, Lyra. But you need to hurry."

"I will," I said with a snap, closing the locket and re-clasping it onto my neck. I needed to keep going. Now wasn't the time to break down.

I made my way back to the path near where Aldric still sat, waiting for me. My heart felt like it was being squeezed in a vice and it must have showed on my face, because Aldric sat up ramrod straight when he took a look at my face, his eyes wide with concern.

"Everything okay, Lyra?" he asked, climbing to his feet. He whistled, and the horses made their way back over.

"We need to get back to Sylvan Reach as soon as we can. I don't want to stress the horses any more than we need to, but we need to take as few breaks as possible," I said, wringing my hands. Lune came over to me and I clamored back on top of her. She patiently waited for me to get adjusted. Meanwhile, Aldric gracefully climbed into the saddle, looking as though he was born to ride.

He took his long, raven-black hair and tied it up high into a knot on top of his head. Aldric looked at me once more before urging his horse into a canter. I did the same, nudging Lune into a trot, then a canter, speeding up until I overtook Aldric. They had to be okay. They just had to be.

Another four hours and we took a quick break to give the horses time to recoup. Aldric said that a rest every three to four hours was needed to ensure the horses had enough stamina to get us all the way to Sylvan Reach. Luckily, there were streams and creeks all around this area of Aethralis, giving the horses plenty to drink and eat. I paced, my anxiety rising. We were making excellent time, but it would still be another few days at a minimum before we would make it to Sylvan Reach.

Aldric watched my pacing with concern on his face. Eventually, he wandered in front of me and reached out, grasping my shoulders in his hands. "Lyra, stop. What in the world is going on?" he asked, surprisingly gently. "You're acting strangely."

"Just because I'm not blushing like a thirteen-year-old with their first crush every time you look at me doesn't mean there's something wrong," I snapped, my anxiety coming out as anger.

Aldric was unphased and pulled me close until we were standing flush with each other. My breath hitched, but I didn't immediately pull myself back. "But there is something wrong. I can sense it. Plus, your heart rate has been high ever since you left me earlier," he said, grasping my jaw and tipping my chin up to look at him. The swirling depths of his eyes drew me in, like molten metal and moonlight, and I took a shuddering breath.

"My parents have become sick," I finally muttered, slowly extricating myself from his embrace. Or I tried, but for once, he didn't release me. His grip tightened, and he stroked my hair, breathing in my scent. "The healer was able to contact me out here."

"We will be there soon and you can take all the blood you need once we're there," he said reassuringly. And strangely, his words actually were reassuring. I found myself circling my arms around his waist, holding us tighter. I needed the physical contact. His voice was soft and husky as he said, "You are truly beautiful, you know." He lifted a hand and stroked it softly down my cheek. "I've never seen another who looked like you."

"Yeah, it's been a great help to me thus far as I've hidden myself away," I said bitterly, releasing my hold on him and trying to part from his warmth yet again. This time, he let me go and I took a couple of steps back, wrapping my arms around myself.

"Why do you keep pulling yourself away from me? It really does hurt my feelings, you know," Aldric said, but he had a faint smile on his lips.

"I have feelings for someone else," I said flatly. "He's another reason we need to hurry back."

I could have sworn I saw a flash of hurt in Aldric's eyes, but it was so quick I must have imagined it. "I see," he murmured. "Well, I don't mind some competition."

"There's no competition, Aldric. It's just me and him," I said firmly. I resolved to distance myself from Aldric before we made it to Sylvan Reach. Once we got there, I could leave and he could go wherever he wanted to go, once Thorne got the blood he needed.

"We'll see," Aldric said with a wink. "I've been told I'm fairly irresistible." Despite his playful words, he looked a little reserved. I had to wonder why.

After the horses had a bit of time to cool off and eat and drink, we started off yet again. I noticed we seemed to avoid paths that would lead to towns and villages nearby. I tried to lead us down those paths several times, but Aldric would always direct us elsewhere. Was he hiding something? Did these people know him?

I slowed Lune down until we rode next to Aldric. He glanced over at me and flashed me a sunny smile. "To what do I owe the pleasure?" he asked.

"Why don't you want to go to any towns?" I asked bluntly.

Clearly he wasn't expecting that question, because his smile faded. "Ah. I wondered when you might bring this up." Aldric sighed and scrubbed a hand over his face. "The villages this close to Vespara know who I am. And I don't want to deal with that," he said. "As we get further from Vespara, it won't be as big of an issue."

"Ah," I said. "That makes sense, I guess. What does it matter if they know who you are though?"

"As you may have noticed during our little nibble session, vampire saliva can feel pretty... pleasurable," he said with a smirk. "It's more potent the older and more powerful you are," he explained. "A lot of vampires have made forays out into the villages this far and let's just say our reputation proceeds us. I'd rather not have humans begging for me to bite them or bed them."

I scowled. Of course, that would be the reason. I could imagine why he would want to avoid being around humans who knew who he was then. And to bed them? Did he have a reputation for just… being with whomever he bit? I muttered a curse and refused to think about that anymore.

"What's with that expression, Lyra? Are you… *jealous?*" he asked, waggling his brows at me.

"Oh, shut up. I am not jealous," I muttered, though my mind whispered that I was a liar.

"You know, that sounds exactly like something a jealous person would say," Aldric said with a laugh. I glared at him, a blush creeping up my cheeks. I refused to entertain this conversation any longer and pushed Lune into a canter, overtaking Aldric yet again.

His guffaw of laughter followed me and I couldn't help thinking, yet again, about how annoying he was.

CHAPTER 19

We finally stopped to sleep when the sun crested over the horizon. Much like Aldric said before, he didn't burn up in the sun or really seem bothered by it at all, which explained his complexion. He was the only vampire I'd seen with any kind of tan on his skin. It was faint, but still there. Despite that, I figured it would be good to stop for now.

The horses were tired, I was tired, and we needed to rest in order to push further along on our journey. No matter how much I wanted to just keep going, I couldn't do that to Lune. She was a sweet girl.

As I laid out a small bedroll, I turned to Aldric. "You never said what your horse's name is, by the way."

He glanced over at the ebony horse, who looked as gorgeous as ever as he stood in a nearby stream, drinking the clear water. "His name is Nocturne."

I mulled over the name. It seemed to fit. I nodded an

affirmative. "I like it. It suits him. And our horses look good together. Are they a pair?" I asked.

"They do look good together. So do their riders," he said with a grin.

"Not going to happen, unfortunately for you," I said, sticking my tongue out at him. I didn't care if it was juvenile. He pulled out that side of me. He laughed in response, shaking his head. "So are they?"

"Yes, actually. I figured they got along well enough and they're both from good bloodlines. They've had some handsome babes," he said, eyes on the two horses as they stood near each other, Nocturne grooming Lune. They seemed to be glad for the break.

I checked under my bedroll for rocks—not doing that again—and settled myself inside. I had to sleep while I could and then we had to get going. The horses also seemed to feel the same, finding a soft patch of ground to settle themselves on. They had dozed standing throughout the night when we'd taken breaks, so I supposed they were due for a lie-down.

I was surprised that Aldric didn't feel the need to tie the horses somewhere, but evidently he had trained them for recall as they came back any time he whistled. It was good for them to have more space for grazing. The area we were in was becoming less mountainous and more plain-like. Much more flat, solid ground. Hopefully, within a couple of days, we would hit Sylvan Reach. As long as nothing came up, which I desperately hoped nothing did.

"I am going to go for a hunt," Aldric said abruptly.

My spine went ram-rod straight. "What do you mean you're going for a hunt?"

"It's exactly what I said, my dear," Aldric said. Then, when I gave him a dirty look, he amended, "Sorry, I mean *Lyra*. I need to feed. Unless you're offering?" he asked hopefully, his pewter eyes alight with anticipation.

I glared at him and said flatly, "Absolutely not."

"Oh, how you wound me," he said dramatically, but flashed me a smile. "If you will not provide me with any blood, then I'll have to go get some now, won't I?" he said, standing and stretching his arms over his head as though limbering up.

"Where are you going to go? There aren't any woods around here for hunting," I said.

"Yes, well. There is a town nearby a few miles away. I'll be quick," he said. When I scowled at him, he smirked. "What? I have to get blood from somewhere."

I didn't know what to say that wouldn't sound ridiculous, but all I could imagine was him between the legs of some random woman and felt the burn of jealousy deep within me. What was wrong with me? I had Griffin to worry about and here I was getting all bothered by Aldric needing to feed. I just waved him off instead, though my mind screamed at me to ask him to stay.

"Just hurry back. We'll need to start traveling again soon," I said, though the words tasted sour on my tongue. I laid down on my bedroll and quickly covered up, turning away from him. I was being childish, and I knew it, but I couldn't help feeling betrayed somehow. It was ridiculous. I had feelings for Griffin. He was sick, and yet I was acting like a possessive wife over Aldric.

I sensed Aldric's eyes on me before I heard a whisper of fabric, and suddenly he was gone. Glancing over my shoulder confirmed he had left me. It hurt my feelings somehow, though I refused to consider why. Instead, I just took deep breaths, focusing on sleep until it finally, fitfully took me.

I awoke a few hours later, exhausted still but needing to press on. The horses had shifted to sleeping standing up and Aldric was nearby in his own, much more comfortable-looking bedroll, snoring gently. His cheeks were flush after a new feed and I felt a white-hot spike of envy at the person who he had drank from. The idea of him drinking blood from someone and *not* having sex with them was ludicrous. I almost stepped over that line myself and I had someone waiting for me.

Packing up my bedroll, I made my way over to Lune and gently pat her on the neck to help her wake. She stirred, and I stroked down her neck, murmuring sweet-sounding words at her. I would be so sad when I could no longer ride her. She was one of the best horses I'd had the pleasure of working with. She whinnied softly and Nocturne also woke up, shifting and stretching.

Finally, after hanging my pack from the saddle, I begrudgingly made my way over to where Aldric still lay sleeping. I poked at him with my foot. He didn't wake, nor did he even shift around. So I poked him harder. With that, he muttered something nonsensical, and I had to wonder just how much he fed to be in this deep of a sleep. At that, I got a little frustrated and reached down, slapping Aldric's cheek hard enough to sting. That one roused him and he reached up, his hand circling my wrist in an iron grip.

"Now whatever was that for?" he murmured, his voice husky from sleep. His brows were furrowed, whether in annoyance or from being abruptly awoken.

"You wouldn't wake up, so I decided to take more drastic measures," I said, not even a little bit sorry about it.

A smile slowly spread across his face, and he laughed, the sound low. "Jealousy looks good on you, Lyra."

"For the last time, I'm not jealous," I snapped. "We just need to get up and going. I got Lune and Nocturne ready to go. We're all just waiting for you." I crossed my arms and huffed. Aldric's smile never wavered, though he crawled out of his bedroll and packed it up, loading his own backpack onto Nocturne.

I couldn't help but blurt, "I hope your meal was ever-so-tasty."

Aldric chuckled before stretching, his shirt lifting high enough to almost show a sliver of skin. I looked away, striding over to Lune and climbing back up. Once I was settled, my eyes fell on Aldric yet again. He re-tied his hair back and I couldn't help but notice how well the light from the setting sun played off of his body.

Liquid pooled low in my belly and I fisted my hands, aghast at myself. Why did I feel so drawn to him? There was just something there that I couldn't figure out. It was just getting increasingly frustrating being near him.

Without waiting for Aldric, I nudged Lune into a walk. I heard Aldric murmur something to Nocturne, and then he was following behind. Aldric quickly made his way up next to Lune and reached out to me with a paper-wrapped package. I hesitantly reached out and took it from him.

"What is this?" I asked.

"It's a gift for you," he said. "I thought you might be hungry, too. Didn't think bread would be enough."

With his words, I glanced at the little package. It looked like a bakery box. I kept one hand on the reins and sat the box between my legs, using my thighs to keep the package braced while I unwrapped and opened it. It looked like a couple of pork rolls. My mouth immediately watered from the smell wafting up and teasing my nose. I whipped my gaze over to Aldric.

"Why did you get this for me?" I asked, though I immediately picked up a pork roll and bit into it. It was glorious, savoury, and buttery. A moan of delight slipped through my lips.

"Well, now I'll have to get more just to hear that sound again," he said with a flirtatious smile. "But I got it for you to keep your strength up. If we're going to keep up the pace you want, we can't afford to have you going weak from hunger."

I couldn't help but be touched by his gesture. He didn't even know me, and yet here he was, being concerned for my wellbeing and my needs. "Thank you, Aldric. It means a lot," I admitted. "I'm not used to people looking out for me."

"Well, you'd better get used to it. As long as I'm around, you won't have to worry about anything," he said earnestly.

"How can you say that?" I asked, genuinely curious. Lune side-stepped a stick and brought me and Aldric closer, close enough that I could see the swirling molten depths of his eyes.

"I'm drawn to you, Lyra. I won't lie and say I'm not furious that you're with another man," he admitted. "But I'll wait. You can't resist me forever." He chuckled as though he had full confidence that was true. He stroked his chin, now dusted with stubble from our travel, then pushed Nocturne into a trot. I followed quickly.

He might just be right, some traitorous side of me whispered.

It was pitch-black when a scream pierced the night, high and inhuman. Aldric's head snapped up across the dying embers of our campfire, his eyes gleaming in the darkness like a cat's.

Adrenaline sparked through me like a lightning strike, burning away any vestiges of sleep. Before I could even move, Aldric was suddenly in front of me, tucking me behind him. "Fae beast," he breathed, the words barely audible. The undergrowth rustled softly, something massive moving in the shadows. My power stirred and Aldric's hand snatched my wrist—his grip as strong as a manacle. "Don't," he murmured. "It will sense your power."

Instead, we stood frozen as what lurked unseen stalked ever closer. The horses were nearby, and I could only hope that this monster would leave them be or that they would wise up and run. Mana poured from the direction of the beast, causing flowers and grass to bloom where it lingered. It would have been beautiful, if not for the sense of impending doom. This magic felt ancient, deadly, unlike anything I'd ever experienced outside of these creatures.

Was this the same one I had encountered with Griffin? Had it lived?.

Aldric slowly pulled me to my feet, careful to make as little noise as possible. The last time, this creature was silent like death. Why announce itself? Unless…

Was it calling to something?

The thought hit like a punch in the gut, and I gripped Aldric's sleeve urgently. "We need to get out of here. Like, now."

Aldric wasted no time, clutching me to his chest as easily as if he were holding nothing more than a knapsack, and took off running at preternatural speed in the opposite direction of the hulking shape. The world sped by in a blur and it took my breath away. I couldn't keep my eyes open and instead turned my face inward to Aldric, the scent of thunderstorms and night filling my nose.

He loosed a high whistle, and despite our incredible speed, within moments, I heard galloping. How were the horses able to keep up?

Another terrible screech sounded from somewhere behind us, closer than I would have liked. Aldric's head dipped close to my ear.

"I want you to wrap your legs around my waist and your arms tightly around my neck," he said, shouting to be heard over the sound of the wind passing us.

The unearthly feeling of the ancient magic tingled across my skin and I didn't hesitate, shuffling around in Aldric's arms until I was gripping him tightly with all of my limbs. We careened to the right until the sound of hooves pounding the dirt was louder than ever before, then I felt Aldric reach up and next thing I knew, we were in the air. He swung himself onto Nocturne's back, his free hand holding me tightly against him as we landed hard in the saddle.

But the horse didn't even flinch, instead taking off at breakneck speed away from the beast. My heart was in my throat as I peeked over Aldric's shoulder, barely able to open my eyes against the wind whipping against us. I saw a flash of too-bright green eyes fading in the distance much faster than I would have thought possible.

We were safe. For now.

CHAPTER 20

Much later, when the imminent danger was gone, and the sun was high overhead, Aldric and I found an open field to take a break in. The horses were sweating, especially noticeable on Nocturne, where it was white against his dark coat. He had thrown his head in frustration, and we knew it was time to let the horses cool off. My body was so stiff. I began doing stretches as soon as my feet hit the ground, groaning as my too-tight muscles loosened.

"How can the horses *move* like that?" I asked when I found my voice again.

"They're special. If they weren't able to keep up with our speed and faster, why use a horse when you could just run?" Aldric asked, his gaze sliding over my body before quickly glancing away.

"Yeah, but how is that actually possible?" I asked, incredulous.

"We have our own kind of magic, too, you know," Aldric said with a wink. "We may have imbued them with power thousands of years ago until we ended up with what we have now, some of the fastest and most intelligent horses in the world. It's not my area of expertise, so unfortunately, darling, I can't tell you for sure."

I nodded. It made sense. Once my body no longer felt like a wound spring, I sat on the ground in a huff, drawing my knees up to my chest. That stupid Fae beast. Why did it have to show up at all? All our supplies had been left behind. What were we going to do now?

"I know what you're thinking," Aldric said, a smile in his voice. "We'll be fine. You're with me, remember?"

I leveled a glare at him, refusing to be charmed by his perfect smile and his too-white teeth. "What does that have to do with anything?"

"There's a village not too far from here. I'll be back before dark." He stood and turned towards the nearest path, and my chest seized in panic.

"No, don't!" I shouted before I could stop myself. "Don't leave."

Aldric immediately turned and knelt next to me. "It's okay, love. I won't be gone long at all, I promise." He reached out and gently cupped my cheek, running his thumb over the curve there. I jerked my chin away from his grip and he stood, a now-familiar hurt flashing across his features. "If anything happens, I'll know. I'll be back in a flash. Unless you'd rather join me?" he asked cautiously.

Scrubbing a hand over my face, I sighed and crossed my arms over my knees, putting my head down. "No, I don't want to go," I mumbled into the crook of my arm. "It'll be fine. I'll be here when you get back."

There was a tense silence before I felt Aldric leave. It left me bereft in the same way it always did, my stomach hollow. Why did I feel this way about him? And why did he treat me like I mattered? A frustrated sound escaped me and I stood, making my way over to the horses where they lay in the dew-covered grass, cooling off. Lune raised her head and whinnied at me. I cautiously approached and sat next to her. She craned her neck over to me and bumped me with her cheek until I came closer, nestling against her side.

That is where Aldric found me hours later, sleeping. He carried two new packs of supplies, though it was more meager than what we started with. It would do. With a little rest and with the horses cooled off, we started back on the path to Sylvan Reach, and to Griffin.

A couple of days have gone by since we saw the Fae beast. It seems to have given up on the chase, although I'm not complaining. What are the chances that I would see the same Fae beast twice? Although I couldn't say for sure if it was the same, I just had a feeling deep in my gut. But now, after all of this travel, we're almost to Sylvan Reach. We would finally be safe there. The terrain we'd been going through has luckily been easy on the horses, mostly flat land. We'd continued to avoid towns and villages as much as possible, with few exceptions.

We'd camp near enough to a place with humans living in it so that Aldric could slip off while I was asleep. And I was totally fine with that. It didn't bother me in the least. Or at least, that's what I told myself, though I would be irrationally angry with him every time he came back. I also felt guilty about that, because if I was refusing to feed Aldric myself, he couldn't just starve until we got to Sylvan Reach. But it didn't stop that sense of betrayal I felt every time. A sigh escaped my lips and Lune whinnied softly in response, nodding her head. I reached down and brushed my hand along her neck.

Lune was the one good thing that I had going for me right now. She and I had truly bonded. She was more likely to approach me when I called than she was to go to Aldric. It felt like a small victory every time. After all, she wasn't my horse. Every part of me wishes she were, though. I hadn't felt this kind of bond with an animal before. But that was just another sacrifice I was going to have to take.

Maybe I could steal her while Aldric was distracted, I thought with a snicker, though I dismissed the thought almost immediately. He was doing me a favor, after all. My gaze slid over to him, riding next to me. Nocturne was a tireless horse. He rarely showed signs of tiredness even on days we pushed our travel for longer. As though sensing that I was thinking about him, Nocturne nodded his head at me. Aldric murmured something soft and sweet to Nocturne, and my eyes fell on him instead.

They traced up the line of his boots, his thighs straining against the fabric of his pants, then up his muscled torso draped in linen, to his strong neck, and finally the curve of his jaw, dusted with dark stubble. His lips curved up and our eyes met, and I found he was already watching me in return. His eyes, as always, drew me in, like molten silver swirling in a cauldron.

"Do you like what you see?" he asked, laughter in his voice.

A blush immediately crept up my cheeks, and I looked away. "Nope. Absolutely not," I lied.

Aldric scoffed, offended. "You sure seem to look this way a lot for not enjoying the view," he said, leading Nocturne to walk closer to Lune and I. Once we were within arm's length away, he reached out and traced a line down my arm with his fingertip. It sent a shiver through my body and I glared at him.

"Quit doing that."

"Oh love, when will you stop denying your destiny? You and I met for a reason, you know," he said, his voice rumbling through me.

"Yes, we did," I acknowledged. "We met for you to help me with this gods-awful plague."

Aldric looked curious, cocking his head to the side as he thought. "You know, I never really asked you about that plague, did I?" he asked.

My jaw dropped before I caught myself, snapping it closed with a *click*. "You promised to come with me, to give your blood, for a plague you didn't even think to ask about?" I was incredulous.

"Well, sweetheart, I had other things on my mind at the time," he said with a wink. Then his face grew more serious. "When I was called from the castle to go to Caelius's estate, they made it sound as though it wasn't very serious. And honestly, being in the castle gets ever-so-boring, so I thought it would be a pleasant change of pace, even if I'm just entertaining someone who doesn't have a serious issue." His honesty rocked me and offended me in equal parts.

"The plague *is* serious," I bit out. "It's a wasting disease. The people who are afflicted become mentally addled, their senses going out of control, and they end up catatonic. Unable to respond to the outside world. Who knows what is going on in their heads or whether they're aware of this happening and feeling their bodies waste away?"

The thought of this happening to my parents made my throat seize up, and I felt the prick of tears. Not to mention this happening to Griffin. Did he even make it out of Sylvan Reach? Where would he have gone? He couldn't make it back to Haleshade before the sickness took him.

I couldn't bear continuing that line of thought and shoved all the thoughts into a mental box to deal with later. I didn't want Aldric to see me this way. Instead, I looked back at the path we were riding on and choked back the tears before they could fall.

But it seems he knew, anyway. Nocturne sidled up to Lune, and I felt Aldric's hand trace my back in a reassuring touch. Though I would curse myself about it later, I didn't shy away. I felt so close to breaking apart, the stress of everything shattering me. And yet, Aldric never seemed to mind. It was like he always knew exactly what I needed, even in a way Griffin never did.

That thought rocked me to my core. How could Aldric, who I barely knew, understand me in a way Griffin never did, even after months of living together? I quickly admonished myself. I didn't give Griffin the chance to. Fear of letting someone in always held me back. But then, how did Aldric know?

Maybe it was sharing blood with him, I reassured myself. After all, there was no way he would just *know* without another explanation. Guilt still pricked at me, regardless. I couldn't think of Aldric this way. My heart belonged to Griffin. No matter how Aldric stirred my feelings and my body.

The time I spent thinking about this, Aldric never stopped lightly tracing his hand up and down my spine in reassuring brushes. I felt shame for this, too. Like I was leading him on somehow, even though I kept telling him that there was no way we could be together. Even though I felt drawn to him like a moth to a flame. And like a flame, he would burn my fragile wings and leave me smoldering. A shuttering sigh escaped me and I straightened my spine, leading Lune to go ahead of Nocturne.

"We're almost there," I said, more firmly than I felt. "Maybe another day's travel at this pace." I gestured at the hills far off in the distance, the trees dotting along them.

I heard Aldric mutter an affirmative, though I felt waves of disappointment and… sadness rolling off of him. My heart gave a painful squeeze, as though his sadness was mine, too. The feeling was strange, and I only seemed to be more attuned to him the closer I stayed in his proximity. Getting to Sylvan Reach and separating was for the best.

It was, I told myself firmly, though I knew the words were a lie.

CHAPTER 21

We finally broached the forest. It welcomed me in like an old friend and I immediately felt my magic respond to the energy within Sylvan Reach. It was like a breath of fresh air after being smothered. Even Aldric seemed to respond, his shoulders stiffening and then relaxing once he got used to the feeling of being in this place.

"It's nice, isn't it?" I murmured, looking around at the tall, majestic trees.

"Yes, it is. It's unexpected," he admitted, his eyes holding a certain wonder to them. "I've never been to this place before. Vampires and mages haven't exactly had a good rapport over the last few thousand years."

At that, my gaze snapped to him. Varen had said something along the lines of the last mage who came to Vespara, but he didn't expand on it and then there was so much going on I'd forgotten to ask.

"Why is that?" I asked, feigning innocence.

Aldric looked back at me, surprised. "I can't imagine that you wouldn't know this story. But, essentially, the last mage who came to Vespara had a power similar to yours. They used their ability to transform into one of the royal family who ruled over the kingdom at that time, the Casperians. Using that disguise, they absolutely obliterated that family and no one knew who it was until there was no Casperian left standing except for the mage."

I was enraptured by the story. I'd never heard it before. Though I had heard that the last transformation mage was just absolutely awful, no one had mentioned anything about the vampires and how it affected them. Although knowing that mage blood is a hot commodity to them, I can't blame the elders of Sylvan Reach for not knowing themselves.

Seeing the keen interest in my eyes, Aldric continued, "The Casperian family was another group of living vampires. We used to be more numerous back in the day," he said with a wave of his hand. "I have to wonder why that mage did what they did, although from what I've heard, they just wanted to incite violence wherever they went and killing off the royal family was one hell of a way to do it," he said, his voice dripping with malice.

His rumbling words sent goosebumps erupting across my skin and I shivered. Part of me wondered if he had been there. He seemed to be too angry not to. But before I could ask, he continued telling me the story.

"Once the Casperians were well and truly gone, the mage just disappeared. No one knows where they went off to. It was like they were gone in a puff of smoke. They should be damn glad I never caught them," he muttered darkly. "With the royal family dead, all the clans of living vampires immediately began a bloody war. It lasted longer than it ever should have, but you know how vampires are. We have a reputation for having a lust for power."

"That's horrible," I said, my voice shaking. "Why would they do that?"

"Who knows? But, my family came out on top. We eliminated every other living vampire clan who opposed us. And now, we've been the ruling family for the last two thousand years. House Winters."

"Were you alive when this all happened? I don't know how long living vampire's life spans are," I said.

Aldric barked out a humorless laugh. "Longer than you'd ever want it to be, love. Yes, I was alive then, though I was but a young boy. I saw all the bloodshed with my own eyes. That was also when the caste system was implemented, and I don't agree with that either," he said, his tone bitter. "Without the ruling family to enforce rules, lesser vampires were just going out in droves and turning whatever humans they could to try to gain some power for themselves. You see how that turned out."

I nodded, the memory of the vampire who confronted Caelius flashing through my mind. "It was awful. They're treated like animals."

A wry smile twisted Aldric's face, and I saw a rage simmering there. "That's why they don't want me on the throne," he said. "I would eliminate the caste system so all vampires are treated the same and we would enforce laws regarding the turning of humans. It's a dangerous game they played, turning them to begin with. Most die. And for what?" he asked, his voice dripping with disdain.

"What power could they hope to gain? It seems—," I started to ask, before being cut off. Lune nickered and nodded her head, so I slid a reassuring pat down to her. My gaze turned to our surroundings for the first time in a while. I'd been so enraptured by the story, I didn't realize just how deep we'd gone into Sylvan Reach. In front of us was the very circle of stones that I crossed all of those years ago. Panic gripped me and my breathing became harsh. This was where it all began. Where my life had changed for the worse. Sensing my distress, Lune started dancing around, shaking her head from side to side. Aldric immediately slid off of Nocturne and came to Lune, whispering to her.

Concern etched itself into his face as he glanced up at me, soothing Lune. He wordlessly came to my side and helped me to slide off of Lune. She immediately wandered away from the circle and went to stand by Nocturne instead. My entire body was shaking violently as flashbacks of when I first received my power burst through my mind. I had felt so free, only for everything to come crashing and burning down on me.

How had we ended up here? Why? And why with *him*? I didn't want him to see me like this. But I couldn't bring myself to speak, my throat practically collapsing in on itself as I tried to hold back the tears and failed. Deep, racking sobs took me and my knees buckled, sending me to the ground. Aldric was immediately pulling me onto his lap and wrapping me in an embrace. He tucked my head under his chin and just stroked my back while I lost myself in grief.

Grief for myself, for the little girl I was who had so much hope for her future. Who just wanted to make her parents proud. Who just wanted to fit in with the rest of the kids in her village. And who had that taken away by the 'gift' bestowed upon her by the magic of the forest. It was a curse. Transformation was a *curse*. I felt like I couldn't breathe, and Aldric tightened his grip on me. I felt a wave of calm come over me and realized that he was using his magic to help regulate my emotions. My sobs slowly subsided, though my breath kept hitching.

I felt so distant from my body right now, watching it from above. Aldric looked so concerned and just gently stroked my hair and back, helping me come back to myself.

When I found my voice again, I rasped, "Can you please take me away from here?" My eyes slipped closed. I didn't even want to see those stones. I didn't want to think.

Wordlessly, Aldric picked me up as though I weighed nothing and strode deeper into the forest. He whistled, and the horses followed us, Lune whinnying as though concerned. I tucked my face into the side of Aldric's neck, taking whatever comfort I could from his stormy scent. My body slowly relaxed the further we got from the glade, and after a few minutes, Aldric slowed, and I felt the vibrations going through my body as he spoke.

"Are you okay, love? You seemed really shook up back there," his voice was so gentle. "I'm here."

It took a minute for me to find my voice, but I said, "Yes, I'm okay. I'm sorry. I know that came out of nowhere." Shame colored my cheeks a bright red, and Aldric's grip tightened on me.

"Don't worry about it. I am here, darling," he said again, nuzzling his cheek into my hair. I closed my eyes and let myself take the comfort he was offering for another few seconds.

But then it had to end, just like everything else. "Can you put me down, please?" I asked reluctantly. Things had changed between us in some way because of this. I didn't know how to deal with it and I chose to ignore how bereft I felt once his hands slipped away from my body. I had enough going on as it is.

"Of course, Lyra. Are you okay?" he asked again.

I nodded hesitantly. The panic had released its hold on me and I felt like I could breathe again. "Thank you, Aldric. For taking me away."

"Do you want to talk about what happened?" he asked, his head turning slightly to the side as though trying to figure me out.

I loosed a shaky sigh and wrapped my arms around my middle. "I guess so. That place is where young mages go to be gifted with their power. In the old days, it would be a trek to make their way here, but nowadays it's less of a big deal because we already live in the forest." I said, babbling. "I was gifted true transformation right there. And nothing has gone right since." My voice broke and I fought to choke back more tears.

Aldric looked like he wanted to embrace me again, so I took a step back, shaking my head. "I just hate to be reminded of that place. And I never wanted to go there again, so the fact that we just ended up there while talking about the last transformation mage is ridiculous."

"That sounds like it was a really painful time for you," he said, his voice achingly soft. I wanted nothing more than to be back in his arms, but I couldn't do it. I needed to do better for Griffin. This wasn't the time for a mental breakdown just because of some stupid circle of stones. We needed to get back to Thorne fast.

I made my way back over to Lune and put my hand on her neck. She wrapped me up in her own version of a hug and pressed herself against me. Tears again pricked my eyes, but I forced them back. "I'm okay, Lune. Thank you, girl." I lovingly stroked down her muzzle. She lifted her lip playfully at me and it startled a laugh out of me, though it was weak. It was just what I needed, and I steeled my resolve, climbing back up into the saddle.

It's time to get to the village. I urged Lune forward and we made quick work of the rest of the distance until the familiar houses came into view. I braced myself for the worst. For good or bad, we were here.

CHAPTER 22

Before entering Sylvan Reach, I briefed Aldric on the disguise I would be taking. Despite the warning, I heard a sharp intake of breath when I resumed Louise's form. My body ached and I felt tired almost immediately. I forgot how awful I felt in this form. I had to wonder if Louise took any potions or medicines to help with these aches and pains.

"You have to look like this the whole time we're there?" Aldric asked curiously.

"Yes. Other mages don't exactly like me," I said bitterly. "I have to disguise myself so they don't attack me, or the people I may be with." I gave him a pointed look, and he nodded.

"That must be incredibly lonely," he murmured. The words sliced right through me, because they were true. It *was* incredibly lonely. But now I had Griffin to get me through and I could always rely on him. My chest got tight at the reminder. I had to hurry so that we could cure him. I could only hope he hadn't…

I refused to finish the thought and grabbed Lune's lead, walking her into Sylvan Reach.

Once we stepped into town, I realized just how quiet it was. Even more so than the last time I was here. It was broad daylight and yet there were no villagers hurrying about the streets. All the windows were closed. I gasped, shock clear on my face. How could this have happened so fast?

I tied Lune to a nearby post, and Aldric did the same with Nocturne. Once the horses were secure, I grabbed Aldric's hand and rushed to Thorne's house towards the edge of town. His long legs had no trouble keeping up with my stride and he wisely didn't question where we were going, reading my urgency.

Before long, we stood in front of Thorne's home. I knocked hard on the door and only a few seconds later, Thorne opened the door, looking frazzled. His hair was unkept, and he smelled as though he could really use a bath. But I understood, he's probably been all over town helping sick villagers.

"Lyra! You're back," Thorne said, then glanced to Aldric behind me. "And who is this?"

"This is Aldric, the vampire prince. He wants to help with the plague and opted to come with me to ensure it is taken care of." I said. Aldric inclined his head in agreement.

"Aldric. I understand you need some of my blood to formulate a cure," he said, holding his hand out to Thorne, surprisingly aloof and very unlike his normal self.

"Yes, yes. Come in, Highness. Come in," Thorne said. And

with that, he dragged Aldric through the door. Aldric glanced over his shoulder at me and we made eye contact before the door was slammed closed. I was shocked, having expected more of a discussion between Thorne, Aldric and I. But I didn't have time to deal with that, anyway. I needed to find Griffin. Thorne said he was sick. I couldn't cope if something happened to him.

I began racing through the streets, Louise's older body aching fiercely, though I barely felt it. Maybe he was still here somewhere. I went to the makeshift hospital where we saw Elder Brynn, but he wasn't there. Panting, I put my hands on my knees. This would be so much easier if I didn't have to wear this awful form! I pulled my hood down tightly over my face. The villagers weren't out and about, and I didn't have time to waste.

I released the form and took a deep breath of relief as the pain faded away and my stamina returned. I went around the perimeter of the village, and when I didn't catch sight of Griffin, I started down the path that we had taken from Haleshade. That's the only other place I could think of that he could have gone.

I was only a few minutes out of the village when I spotted a large, chocolate-furred wolf in the foliage. My heart almost stopped right there and my knees went weak when it turned its sunshine-colored eyes on me, full of keen intelligence. I just knew it was him. And I laughed through tears when its tail wagged and he bounded over to me. Mid-run he began to Shift back into his normal form, which sounded incredibly painful, but he didn't seem to care. He stopped in front of me and scooped me up, crushing his mouth to mine.

I was pressed fully against his hard, naked body, and I inhaled his woodsy, citrusy scent. My arms and legs wrapped around him and relief flooded me. When we came up for air, I was crying all over again.

"Griffin! I thought you were sick," I sobbed. "I was so worried you would die."

"Lyra," he rasped, his voice husky and rough from the change. "I was, but it wasn't like it is for the mages and the humans. I got over it within a few days. It was disorienting, but I wasn't in any danger," he murmured, burying his face in the crook of my neck. "I missed you."

"I missed you, too," I said, kissing his forehead. Then it hit me. I was pressed up against his *very* naked body. The evidence of his excitement at my return was currently pressed firmly against my core. I shifted slightly and heard a breath hiss from between his lips as I rubbed against him. Smiling devilishly, I leaned back in his arms to look at him.

I definitely had missed him.

But before we could do anything else, someone cleared their throat behind us, sounding incredibly pissed off.

I recognized that voice and my heart dropped into the soles of my feet. I quickly disentangled myself from Griffin, standing in front of him so that his nudity wasn't exposed, and turned back to see Aldric, his face dark with anger.

"And who is this, Lyra?" Aldric said, his voice low and dangerous.

Glancing between Aldric and Griffin, I cleared my throat. "Aldric, this is Griffin. I told you about him."

"Ah, yes. Your current beau," he said, looking Griffin up and down. His voice dripped with disdain.

Griffin put a hand on my shoulder as though to move me behind him, but I didn't budge. "Aldric? As in, the vampire prince you were supposed to go see? Why is he here?" Griffin shot out question after question without giving me a chance to respond.

I shifted uncomfortably on my feet. This was *so* awkward. "He came to help with the sickness. He offered to come and give blood to Thorne directly."

Aldric's mouth twisted into a wry smile as he looked at Griffin. There was none of the familiar warmth he had whenever he looked at me, just cold steel in his eyes as he said, "Yes, it was part of our bargain. Remember, Lyra?"

Panic gripped me as soon as he said the words and I swallowed hard, my throat suddenly dry. Griffin looked between Aldric and I, concern etched on his brow. "What bargain?"

"Just a little taste between us," Aldric said with a wink. "How do you think I found you two out here? Now that I've had a bit of a nibble, I can follow her scent anywhere."

My heart nearly stopped right then and there and I closed my eyes, turning away from the both of them. I *just* got back to Griffin and now Aldric has to ruin it over some petty jealousy? *Why did this type of thing always have to happen to me?* I thought bitterly.

Griffin turned me towards him and captured my jaw in his

hand, tipping my head back to look up into his golden eyes. I begrudgingly opened my eyes and saw that there was hurt was clear in those sunshine depths. I felt the hot lick of shame set my cheeks ablaze. "What is he talking about, Lyra?"

"I did what I had to do to get his blood, Griffin," I said, my voice soft. "He required some of my blood in order to get him to agree to come here. But that was all! Nothing else."

Griffin released my chin and backed up. "You gave your blood to him? To this *monster?*"

"I had to. You know as well as I do that we needed his blood for the cure," I said, though my voice cracked.

Aldric huffed behind me, but I ignored him. Griffin took another step back. "And you traveled back with him? Alone? Did you give him blood the entire time?" he asked, his voice harsh.

"No, of course not! It was a one-time deal, and he knows it. I wouldn't do that to you, Griffin. I just wanted to get back to you," I insisted, tears pricking my eyes.

Griffin was shaking his head, and he wouldn't look at me. "I need some time. Wait for me and I will come and find you," he said and within moments he had Shifted back into a chocolate-furred wolf, bounding off into the forest as I cried his name.

My heart was shattering and my legs gave out. I collapsed to the ground and just sobbed. Who knows if Griffin would forgive me for this? And what if he didn't? I'd have no one. I'd be alone again. Aldric approached from behind me and he got onto his knees next to me, stroking a hand over my back. I reached back and slapped at his hand, my magic surging forth and making the strike that much stronger.

"Don't touch me! Why would you tell him like that? I had planned to—to…" The words wouldn't come out. I *was* going to tell Griffin. I was.

"I'm sorry, love. It just came out of me. Please, forgive me," he murmured, though he inched away.

"Just leave. I need to be alone," I rasped, my voice broken. Just as I was broken.

CHAPTER 23

I don't know how long I stayed there on the forest floor before my tears dried and I picked myself up from the hard, cold ground. At some point, Aldric had indeed left. I didn't know where he went, nor did I care right now. Slowly, numbly, I made my way to what was my parent's home in Sylvan Reach. I didn't know if they were even there, or, hell, if they even still *lived* there.

It was a modest cottage, just enough rooms for a family of three. It looked just like it had the day I was chased out. My cloak hood was low over my face, just on the off-chance I ran into any of the other villagers. I knocked on the door, the sound as hollow as I felt. No answer. I tried the handle and found the door unlocked.

I slowly trudged through the front door, making my way towards my parent's bedroom. I pulled my hood back and found myself looking upon their two still forms. They were tucked into bed next to each other, and to my immense relief, they were still breathing. They just looked asleep, but I could tell based on the potions all over the bedside tables that it wasn't as simple as it appeared.

I pulled a chair up to my mother's side of the bed and clasped her clammy hand in mine. I gently stroked her fingers and when I spoke, my voice was a bare whisper. "Hello, mother. I came back. I know you never wanted me to, but I'm here trying to help."

I told her all about my escapades so far since leaving Sylvan Reach, from my adventures wandering Aethralis aimlessly, to finding Haleshade and Griffin, though speaking about him made my voice crack in anguish. Then I told her about working with Thorne and making my way to Vespara to meet with the living vampire prince, bringing him back, and finding my way to them now.

I leaned over her unmoving form and just cried. She smelled the same way she did when I was a little girl, like green tea and honey. I only wished that she could comfort me the way she used to when I was a child.

I pulled myself together and padded over to my father's side of the bed, brushing aside his blonde hair and planting a kiss on his forehead. Then, I made my way to my childhood bedroom. I wondered what they had turned it into.

To my surprise, the room looked exactly the same as I had left it, down to the unmade bed from when I got up that morning. Realization hit me like a gut punch. They never changed it. Why didn't they? I knew I was a disappointment to them. They never wanted a child cursed with my power. But they must have missed me. Otherwise, why not change this room into an alchemical laboratory for Mother's potion making? Or a study for Father?

Because they didn't want to forget me. A gentle smile traced my lips as I ran my fingertips over my old desk. I spent many nights awake reading here, or waiting for Mother to finish cooking supper. At least, before the night I was thrown out.

With that thought, I turned on my heel and left the room. I didn't want to think about that now. Nostalgia only got you so far when most of your memories of a place were awful. Gently closing the door, I glanced one last time towards my parent's bedroom, then turned towards the door. Just before I went through the front door, I saw a picture hanging up on the wall. It was my parents and I, and to my surprise, Thorne was there, standing behind me and ruffling my hair. Did I know him as a child? I couldn't remember. Regardless, I needed to find Thorne.

I slowly made my way back to Thorne's home. I didn't bother with disguising myself. It felt like the entire village was gone. *Or dead,* I thought darkly. Walking through the streets was like walking through a ghost town. The only thing missing were a couple of tumbleweeds. I couldn't believe just how bad it had gotten since I was here last.

And what had Griffin been doing when I found him earlier? Why was he roaming the forest in his wolf form? Had something happened? A pit opened up in my stomach at the thought of him. I had to hope he would stay true to his word and find me later. I wanted to explain myself to him and beg for his forgiveness.

My chest was tight, but I refused to give into despair right now, not when we were so close to figuring out what was causing this sickness. The sight of Thorne's house came into view, and I released a small sigh of relief. I know it hadn't been long since I was here last, but I wanted to see if any progress had been made. Magic could be wondrous, and who knows how fast he could create a cure or an aide to help with the symptoms?

I knocked on the door and waited. In a couple of minutes, I heard a clinking of bottles and the door cracked open. Thorne released a sigh of relief when he saw it was me, and he pushed his hair back out of his face.

"Lyra! Come to see me, have you?" he asked, cheerful as I'd ever seen him.

"Yes. I wanted to see how things have gone since you got the blood from Aldric," I said. With his jovial demeanor, I hoped that meant it was good news.

"Oh yes, I'm making progress! I'm using various methods to isolate different aspects of the vampire blood to test which part of it is immune. That way I can synthesize a cure from it," he said, the words escaping him in a rush. His eyes were bright with excitement.

"Well, that sounds promising," I said, softly. "Good to know that it wasn't all a waste."

"Do you want to come in, Lyra?" Thorne asked, with a sweeping gesture behind him. Even from outside, I could see the room was a mess of potion bottles, bunsen burners and papers scattered all over every surface.

My brows rose, and I said, as gently as possible, "I would love to, but I can't stay. It's been a long, long journey. I am going to go rest at the inn."

Thorne was already nodding before I'd even finished what I was saying. "Once I have made good progress, I will come for you. I want you to be there when your parents wake up."

At that thought, it reminded me. "What happened to all the villagers? This place is like a ghost town."

Thorne frowned, and his excitement dimmed. I almost felt bad for bringing it up, but he said, "The plague spread faster than we anticipated. So everyone is in isolation who is not already ill. Luckily, it doesn't seem to have a one hundred percent rate of contagion. So some villagers have remained healthy this entire time. But in case of mutations, I do not want that to change."

It made complete sense to me, so I nodded along. "Well, with that in mind, I will see you when you make more progress. Thank you for all of your work in this, Thorne. We couldn't do it without you."

Thorne smiled warmly at me and reached out to clap me on the shoulder. "Of course! It's nice to be needed, though I wish it were under better circumstances," he said. His hand dropped to his side. "Now, go and get some rest. I've got to get back to work."

"Yeah, you're right. I will talk to you soon," I said, and turned towards the inn, shifting my form into Louise on the way. Part of me wondered where Aldric went off to, despite my resolve not to think about him.

I managed to get into the same room that I had used the last time that I was here. Hopefully that was a good sign and that it would be easy for Griffin to find me. I collapsed onto the bed with a huff. The room was small and dingy, but at least there was a bed. It wasn't the most comfortable, but there were no rocks digging into my back, so that was a plus.

I sighed, the stress of the last few days bearing down on me. Between feeling like I betrayed Griffin to finding out about my parent's illness, to the long journey with Aldric, it just felt non-stop. The world kept spinning despite how much I wished it would stop and give me a chance to catch my breath.

Begrudgingly, I went for a quick shower, then after toweling off and throwing the towel aside, I peeled back the thin covers and threw them over my head. I just needed to sleep. Some actual, decent sleep. I closed my eyes and tried to rest.

CHAPTER 24

I don't know how long I laid there before I finally fell asleep, but when I awoke, the room was dark except for a hint of moonlight filtering through the curtains. Immediately, I was straining my ears to see what had awoken me and heard a faint tapping on the door.

My senses were on high alert and I crept over to the door, still wearing Louise's form. Carefully cracking the door open, my knees went weak with relief when I saw the hint of a glowing amber eye.

I flung the door open and stepped back, wordlessly inviting Griffin in. I released Louise's form immediately once the door was closed. Tension filled my body. Was he here to tell me he was leaving? That had to be it. I steeled myself for whatever he had to say.

"Lyra," he said, his voice little more than a growl. "Did you do anything else with that vampire?"

My hands clasped in front of me, I shook my head. "No. I told him absolutely not, nothing more than a single drink of my blood for his own to go to Thorne," I said.

Griffin nodded, as though that's what he expected me to say. "I believe you. I'm sorry I ran off earlier. It was just shocking to hear. I've heard plenty of stories about vampire bites and how they can… affect the person being bitten. Jealousy had me not thinking straight." He looked away, clearly uncomfortable.

Without thinking, I walked over and reached a hand up, cupping his cheek. The stubble there prickled at my palm and I smiled. "I just want you, Griffin. No one else," I said firmly. I determinedly pushed Aldric from my mind.

Griffin leaned into my touch and his eyes slid closed. "I know we started off a little rocky, but having you around… It was awful when you were gone. I want to be with you, Lyra. Don't leave me again, please."

Hearing his admission, heat bloomed in my chest. A huge smile broke out on my face and I grasped his shoulders, going on my tiptoes to gently press my lips to his. His lips were surprisingly soft, and he smelled of the woods. His hand slid into my hair and he cupped the back of my head. My arms slid around his waist and Griffin pressed tightly against me.

A short gasp escaped my lips, and Griffin took the opportunity to brush his tongue against mine. It was tentative at first, but before long the kiss deepened, his mouth slanting over mine. He tasted of mint and citrus, and a moan slipped from my lips.

Soon we were mindlessly pulling each other's clothes off, a fever-like heat growing between us. Griffin growled as we parted so that he could take his shirt off, and I quickly did the same.

His eyes roved over my bare chest and my nipples pebbled under his gaze. Warmth suffused my cheeks, and he brought a hand up, cupping my breast in his palm. His calluses were rough on the delicate skin there and a breathy sound escaped me.

Griffin's eyes darkened, and he quickly got to work removing the rest of my clothes. I fought the urge to cover myself. Griffin's eyes were like a flame over my skin, burning a path across the sensitive flesh. I felt exposed in a way I had never had before. Reaching for his pants, he caught my hands gently.

"Just let me look at you," he murmured, his voice husky and dark.

He slowly pushed me back onto the bed and knelt in front of me, my legs draped on either side of his shoulders. And then he paused, just watching me. I bit my lip, nervousness rising. What if he didn't like what he saw? What if I was bad at… being intimate? I had never been in a situation like this.

"Have you done this before, Lyra?" Griffin asked, his voice soft. He must have noticed my nervousness.

I paused, unsure of what to say. "N-no, I haven't," I replied softly, looking away. It felt strange to admit. Admitting that I've never been close to someone in this way before.

He grinned wolfishly, saying, "Good. I'll be gentle."

With those words, he leaned up and captured a rosy nipple in his mouth, using just enough teeth that it elicited a cry from me, pleasure spearing through my core. His hand plucked and pinched the other breast, and I squirmed, arching under his touch.

A growl of approval escaped his lips and his other hand

dropped lower, tracing a line down my stomach. His mouth released my breast with a *pop* and followed the same path as his fingers, making his way down my abdomen. He laid kisses along the skin there and when he reached the apex of my thighs he paused, giving my thighs a squeeze and nipping the sensitive flesh there. I jumped and tried to close my legs.

"Don't hide yourself from me, Lyra," Griffin said, the words causing a shiver to trace up my spine. His hands were heavy on my thighs, keeping them open. I sat up on my elbows, watching him. He looked at me from beneath his lashes as one hand went exactly where I needed him.

At the first touch against the sensitive bundle of nerves there, a throaty moan escaped me, my back arching and pushing me more into his touch.

A deep, rumbling chuckle reached my ears as Griffin said, "You're so sensitive, Lyra. I'm going to imprint myself on your body so you'll never think of anyone else."

Despite his words, a flash of raven-black hair and silver eyes sparked in my mind. I viciously shoved the thought away. What was wrong with me? Determined to forget Aldric, I moaned, "yes, Griffin. Please."

His answering growl rumbled through me, drawing me back into the moment. He swiped his finger through my slick folds, circling the most sensitive part of me until I felt like a spring wound tight, just waiting for release. But before I could get it, his ministrations stopped, and he put his hand on my thigh, massaging the muscle. I groaned in frustration and tilted my head back.

"Patience, Lyra," he said. I could hear the smile in his voice. But before I could respond, I felt his hot breath replacing his fingers, then he slowly dragged a tongue up my core, ending in a light nip. My eyes shot open with surprise and I shattered, moaning his name. He hummed his approval against me, lapping at the sensitive bud.

His tongue was rough, yet silky and I couldn't help reaching a hand down and fisting them in his chestnut waves, riding his face with wanton abandon. I'd never felt pleasure like this before and I wanted—needed—more. An ache was building inside of me and only he could fill it.

"Griffin," I moaned, frustrated. "Please." I didn't even know what I was asking. My mind was completely empty except for the sensations he was pulling from my body.

He pulled back just enough to blow air on my core, the sensation startling. A shudder racked me, and he grinned. "Yes, Lyra?"

"Please," I repeated, writhing before him.

"I want you to say it," he murmured, his voice low and sensuous. "Tell me what you want."

"I want you," I said, blushing furiously. "I *need* you."

"What do you need from me?" he asked, a feral smile on his face. His thumb swirled around the sensitive bud, eliciting a sharp intake of breath from me.

"I want you inside of me," I said, though I felt embarrassed to say it aloud. It felt so dirty. My cheeks burned. "Please. I need it."

He hummed, and as he did, he slowly slid one finger inside of me, right where I needed it. But it wasn't enough, and I groaned, grinding myself against his hand.

"Griffin, please," I breathed, even that small stretching sensation easing a little of the ache.

He withdrew and stood, finally pulling his pants down. His length sprang free from his pants and my mouth went dry. It was a dark pink, tapering into his normal tanned skin, with a short nest of dark hair at the base. I held my arms out to him and he slowly lowered himself on top of me.

"I'm going to take you, Lyra. You are mine," Griffin growled against my neck. As if to erase the bite from Aldric, Griffin's mouth sealed against the delicate flesh there, biting down hard enough that I knew it would leave a bruise, eliciting a gasp from me.

For a moment, I was back in another place, with another mouth there, my hands fisted in raven-black hair while I writhed against a hard thigh. I groaned, frustrated. Why did I keep thinking of Aldric right now?

I gave a small shake of my head to dislodge the thought before I ruined this moment with Griffin. I was here with him, giving myself to him. This wasn't the time to think about another man. What the hell?

Determinedly, I wrapped my legs around Griffin's waist, guiding him to the apex of my thighs. Or I tried, but he didn't budge. Griffin kissed his way up my jaw and looked me in the eyes as he said again, "You are mine."

As though to punctuate his words, he bucked his hips and slid his length against my core, the friction enough to draw out a long moan from the both of us. I felt like I was on the edge of a precipice, just waiting to throw myself off.

I cupped his jaw in my hand and said, "I am yours, Griffin." I drowned out every thought of moon-bright platinum eyes, focusing instead on the way my body felt right now, so sensitive and yet so ready for more. With my words, he groaned and positioned himself at my entrance, the pressure intense.

"Say it again," he rasped, his body trembling.

"I am yours," I murmured.

Slowly, he pushed his hips forward until I loosed a hiss of pain.

"Are you okay, Lyra?" Griffin asked, concern etched into his expression despite the sweat on his brow from holding himself back.

"I am. Take me, Griffin," I said, peppering his jaw with kisses.

He growled and began to move inside of me. The pain quickly subsided, and I was left with a pleasure I wasn't expecting. I felt like my body was going to combust and I reached up, digging my nails into Griffin's back. An animalistic sound came out of Griffin's throat as he pumped harder, our skin slapping together.

He reached a hand between us to rub that sensitive bundle of nerves and finally, the tension snapped and I cried out his name, my core milking him for all it's worth. He growled, his hand roughly grabbing a breast and toying with my tight nipple, eliciting a sharp gasp from me.

Before the movements became too much, he slowed his pace. His thrusts became more slow and sensual, almost pulling out before seating himself completely within me. My grip on his back lightened, becoming more of a caress. He reached up, grasping my chin in his hand, and gave me a languid kiss, his tongue tracing my lips until I opened for him.

He slanted his mouth over mine, and his hand slid to cup the back of my head, tilting it back. It was loving, the way he kissed me. Like he didn't want to let me go. And yet, there was some traitorous part of my mind that was thinking about eyes of liquid mercury, wondering if he would have kissed me the same way.

I buried that part of myself before it could take hold. Why couldn't I just focus on the here and now instead of wondering about *him*?

I reached up and tangled my fingers in Griffin's hair, gripping the chestnut waves. Griffin rumbled in approval, his pace becoming more forceful. With each stroke, it felt like I was being stretched to the limit. I tilted my head back a little to break our kiss and instead, I bit his lower lip hard enough to sting.

He laughed, the sound like velvet. He braced himself above me, readjusting his body for better leverage. I moved my hips with him, meeting him thrust for thrust. Finally, I could just lose myself in the moment, our bodies working together for our shared pleasure.

Griffin sat up, his hands grasping my hips hard enough that I would probably have bruises. He guided us into an ever-faster pace, the tension swirling higher and higher between us. His hoarse groan filled the room, our sweat-slicked bodies reaching a fever pitch as I reached one last release, crying out his name.

He pulled me tightly to his body, losing a bit of rhythm until finally he pulled out, his voice rough with desire as he said my name, spurting hot waves of seed all over my thighs and belly.

My legs were shaking like crazy, and my skin was flush. Griffin leaned over me, kissing every part of my face. My lips, cheeks, forehead, eyelids. My body felt loose and languid, not to mention *sore*.

"I feel like I am made of jelly," I murmured and Griffin rasped out a laugh, shakily standing to find a towel in the bathroom. He came back and gently wiped away the evidence of our tryst, tossing the towel aside before we scoot across the bed. He tucked me back against the warmth of his body and draped an arm over my waist.

"Thank you, Lyra," he murmured against the shell of my ear.

"For what? The best lay of your life?" I asked, teasing.

"Yes. But also, thank you for coming back to me," he said seriously. His hand stroked an idle pattern over my stomach, comforting me.

"Of course, Griffin. I thought of returning to you every day I was gone," I said, snuggling back against him.

"I thought of you every day, too. Afraid I may not see you again. Don't leave me again," he whispered, nuzzling against my neck.

"I won't," I promised, despite lingering uncertainty. If I ever had to return to Vespara... Aldric's name whispered unbidden through my mind and I willed the thought away, burying it deep within myself.

Despite my inner turmoil, a wave of drowsiness took me and I fought to keep my eyes open before finally succumbing. My last thoughts were about how familiar and yet different this felt to the last time I laid with someone this way.

CHAPTER 25

The next morning, I awoke feeling both refreshed and gods-damned sore. I stretched, feeling like I had run a marathon. I absently wondered if it would be a bad idea to put some ice between my legs.

A heavy arm laid across my waist, tucking me back against a warm, hard body. I glanced over my shoulder and Griffin chuckled, nuzzling into my neck.

His voice was husky with sleep as he murmured, "Good morning, Lyra." His hand caressed my hip gently.

"Good morning, Griffin," I murmured in response, warm and cozy. I wasn't quite sure what to say the day after… something like that. So I stayed quiet, just enjoying the physical contact.

"Are you feeling okay?" Griffin asked, as though sensing my awkwardness.

"Yeah," I said with a small laugh. "Just sore. Slept like the dead, though."

"Did I go too hard on you?" he asked, his voice rumbling against my shoulder.

"I mean, if you're asking if I had fun and would do it again, then yes. After some recoup time," I added hastily, eliciting a laugh from Griffin. It was earthy and deep, and incredibly comforting.

"Okay, good," he said once his laughter subsided. "I just know it was your first time and all."

"Ah, yes. Sorry if I wasn't, you know… good at it," I said, suddenly embarrassed. My cheeks heated.

Griffin tugged me until I flipped onto my back, looking at me seriously. "You were just fine, Lyra. I don't expect you to be some kind of sex goddess," he said, his brows lowering. "It'll take time to learn each other's bodies and what we both like."

"You seemed to figure mine out just fine," I said with a hint of a frown. I felt like I didn't get to touch him at all. How would I learn what he liked if he didn't give me a chance? It was my first time, though. Maybe he was just trying to make sure I had fun, I reasoned with myself.

Griffin cupped my cheek, stroking it with his thumb. "Don't worry, Lyra. We have plenty of time to figure this stuff out. I just have more experience, is all. I still had fun," he said, giving me a feather-light kiss. "On another note, I am *starving*. Are you hungry?"

I hadn't thought about it until he asked, but at just that moment my stomach decided to loose an audible growl. I looked away, embarrassed. "You could say that," I muttered.

Griffin snickered, then crawled out of bed, dragging on his pants. "I'll go see what I can get us for breakfast," he said. "I'll be back in just a bit."

Nodding, I sat up, the blankets pooling around my waist. Griffin's gaze dropped to my chest before making their way back up to my face. He smirked. "I could get used to this view."

I immediately drew the blankets back up over my chest, sticking my tongue out at him. "Well, that won't be today," I said, giggling at his disappointed face. "I'll see you when you get back. I'm going to hop in a bath. See if that helps the soreness."

"I'll see if I can get you some medicine to help with that, too. I'll be back soon," he said again. With one last, lingering look, he left the room. A pang of disappointment speared through me, as I wished he would've given me a kiss before he left.

After soaking in the bath for about half an hour, I felt immensely better. It helped with my muscle soreness, at least. I slowly dressed and walked to the bed. A blush crept up my cheeks at the rumpled state of the bed and got to work on straightening things out.

However, I found once I started moving the blankets around that I had apparently bled during our… foray last night. I quickly stripped the bed, leaving the soiled sheets in a bundle in the corner, and headed out to ask the person manning the desk for a new set of bedding. Before I forgot, I grabbed my cloak, slinging it over my shoulders and shifting my form to Louise.

Once I got to the lobby, I found there was no one there. I looked around the small inn and rang the bell that was sitting on the edge of the desk in case maybe someone was in the back. No one came out. I frowned. Where was everyone? Surely they didn't just leave the inn entirely.

I waited for a while, sitting on one of the uncomfortable over-stuffed armchairs sat facing each other in the lobby with a squat, oval-shaped coffee table between them. As the time passed by, I got more and more impatient. Just what was going on?

I ran up to the room and scribbled a note to Griffin, letting him know I was going to head to Thorne's. I figured I could come back later to get the bedding. Outside, it was just as quiet as it had been before, the streets empty.

I know Thorne said that he would send for me when he made some progress with the cure, but I supposed I could go to him instead and see how things were going. *Worse comes to worse, he just won't have anything interesting to share with me*, I thought.

With that thought, I strode off in the direction of his house, the hood of my cloak pulled low over my face, just in case.

Before long, I was standing in front of his door. It looked like he hadn't watered his plants outside for a while. The leaves were wilting and there was debris around some of them. There was a watering can sitting on a pedestal near the door, so I opted to water the plants before knocking on the door. He was working tirelessly on this cure. The least I could do was help him out.

As I watered the plants, I noticed a silhouette in the window. I jolted, before realizing that it was just Thorne. He gave me a small wave before wandering over to the door and opening it. He popped his head out with a smile.

"Hey, Lyra! What brings you here?" he asked, his head cocked in curiosity. I noted that his blonde hair was clean, tied high on his head. He looked more rested than I'd seen him before.

"Hey, Thorne. I just thought I'd come by and see how things were going. Then I noticed your plants looked a little thirsty," I said, gesturing at the pots scattered about with foliage in various states of life. It was too late for some of them, I was sad to notice.

"Thank you. I suppose I'd forgotten about them with everything else going on," he said, rubbing his neck as though embarrassed. "Would you like to come inside for a cup of tea in return for your help?"

I thought about that for a few seconds. I'd initially just wanted an update, but what could a cup of tea hurt? Maybe I could ask him about that photo I saw at my parents' house. I nodded. "Why not? I'll just finish up out here and then I'll come in for some tea."

He clapped his hands together with a grin. "Marvelous! We can discuss this business with the cure as well," he offered.

I nodded again. "That would be great, Thorne."

And with that, I set to work on watering the rest of the plants, refilling the watering can and returning it to the pedestal I found it. Thorne had already gone inside, and I followed him now that I was done.

Thorne's house was much cleaner than the last time I'd been here. There were still bottles and vials all over, along with papers scattered here and there, but they were at least in neat piles instead of filling every square inch of space.

"Have you seen Aldric since I brought him here?" I found myself asking.

Thorne's pale brows rose. "Not since you brought him, no. He let me take a few vials of blood, which is more than I needed. He said he would stay nearby for a few days, though, just in case it wasn't sufficient. Said he had to fulfill his side of a bargain. I assume you had something to do with that?" He went to the same chair he sat in last time I was here, the simple wooden chair creaking as he leaned back and crossed his legs.

I nodded hesitantly, a blush creeping up my cheeks. "Yes. He and I struck a bargain. I took care of my side, so him coming here to help find a cure was his."

Thorne shrugged as though unconcerned and gestured to one of the other remaining chairs. "Please, take a seat. The tea should be ready in a few minutes," he said, hiking a thumb over his shoulder. I assumed the kitchen must be in another room.

Wordlessly, I sank down into a chair. Silence lapsed between us, and I shifted uncomfortably.

"So, did you know my parents when I was young?" I asked, thinking of the photo from my parents' wall.

A warm smile spread across Thorne's face as he said, "Yes, yes, I did. I've actually always worked with your mother. She learned how to properly use her healing ability while working with me as an apprentice. Virtually all the healers from Sylvan Reach have worked with me at one point or another. Why do you ask?" he asked.

I nodded. "That explains a lot. I found a picture of you and my family. I was just a little kid in the photo. To be honest, I don't remember seeing you, though," I said.

"Ah, yes, that's because more often than not, I was at the Arcane Order as you started getting older," he said. "I had a lot of work to do, training new healing mages, traveling, things like that." He gestured vaguely.

A crease formed between my brows as I mulled over his words. Before I could say anything else, though, a whistle sliced through the air and Thorne hopped up with a broad smile. "Tea's just about ready. I'll be back in a minute," he said.

I nodded, and he left the room through a side door. Once he was gone, I found myself looking around. Most of the jars of dried herbs had been returned to metal racks lining the walls, and there were medical instruments were neatly lined up in rows beneath them.

He must have done a lot of cleaning in the last day or so. Even coming here with Aldric, Thorne had looked a mess and so had his house. Maybe he felt some relief from finally having the chance to cure this illness and that's how everything ended up getting straightened out. Or maybe he needed the room for something.

I shrugged my shoulders to myself. It didn't really matter why he cleaned up in here. But he seemed quite a bit different, too. Happier. I wonder if he was making some good headway.

I could only hope that was the case. That way, my parents could finally wake up. I wondered who was taking care of them, since I had seen none of the healing mages in any of the streets. The thought of what would happen when my parents woke up flit across my mind. Would I show myself to them? Could I trust them not to tell the Arcane Order that I had returned?

But then I thought about my untouched room. I don't think they would want to wish me harm. I think I would take the chance. After all, I only have one life to live and I was tired of being constantly in hiding, even from the people I cared about. When it came down to it, it wasn't my parents' fault I was found out. They told me to hide my abilities, and I chose to practice in secret. Maybe if I hadn't, I never would have had to leave.

But then you wouldn't have met Griffin… and Aldric, my mind whispered, unbidden. I shook my head, shoving those thoughts down deep. Now was not the time to think about Aldric. And yet, despite myself, I felt a pang of guilt at the thought of him. I had been cruel to him when we last saw each other.

Before I could continue that train of thought, Thorne came back into the room carrying a tray with a tea set and a second tray with some finger sandwiches.

I immediately stood and held my hands out. "Let me help you. That looks like a lot to carry," I said. He slid the sandwich tray into my hands and I sat it in the middle of the table. Last time we were here, it had been covered with a large map and various other papers. Now it had been completely cleared. Thorne deftly sat the tea tray down and began pouring a cup for each of us.

"Please, help yourself," he said, gesturing to the sandwich tray. "Two sugars, right?"

"Yes, how did you know?" I asked, puzzled.

"You can't forget, I was fairly close to your mother. We talked about you all the time!" he said with a chuckle.

"Still, I'm surprised you would remember a small detail like that. I haven't been back in Sylvan Reach for ten years," I said.

He tapped a finger on his temple. "This old brain never forgets. After all, if I didn't remember small stuff like that, how would I remember all the various remedies and potions for different illnesses? The seemingly insignificant differences between poisonous and non-poisonous plants? Don't stress yourself too much about it," he said with a wave of his hand, throwing a couple of sugar cubes into my steaming cup of tea and giving them a stir before passing it along to me.

He filled his own cup as well and sat back, his posture relaxed. The tea was fragrant and a deep ruby color. I'd never seen one like this before, but it had been a long time since I'd been back. Who knows what kinds of imports we'd had since then.

He was right. *I am being silly*, I thought. Of course, he'd have a good mind. He'd probably know all the best herbs to take for improved memory, even if he didn't have a penchant for it. Then, a thought occurred to me. "How have my parents been since I was, you know…" I couldn't finish the sentence, my gaze downcast.

"They've lost their sun. Honestly, they're pretty gloomy people nowadays," he said, rubbing his chin. "I think it destroyed them when you were forced out, and I don't know that they've ever recovered."

"…Oh." My heart broke to hear this. Despite everything that happened to me, my parents were good people. *They didn't deserve a daughter like me*, I thought with a heaviness in my heart.

"Don't feel too bad, Lyra. It's not like you had a choice," he said, picking up his own teacup and taking a sip. I leaned forward and looked in my cup, seeing the sugar had completely dissolved. I gave the cup one last stir and picked it up, inhaling deep of the floral scent.

"What kind of tea is this?" I asked, curious.

"Ah, it's an import from Cairnard," he said, beaming.

I sat up straight. "The human kingdom?" I was surprised. The mages and humans hadn't had good relations since the last Transformation mage had wreaked havoc across Aethralis.

"Yes. I had to travel there and was able to heal a member of the royal court with one of my poultices. In return, we have established a small trade between Sylvan Reach and Cairnard," he said, clearly proud.

I smiled, glad things were finally turning around a little for Sylvan Reach. Even if I wasn't a part of it. Sitting with Thorne was getting to be pretty awkward. I was running out of things to say.

"How are things going with the cure?" I asked, taking a sip of tea. It was fruity and floral. Delicious, actually. A comforting warmth spread through my body, my nerve endings tingling. Absently, I wondered what went into this tea. Maybe some kind of strange flower or herb caused this sensation.

"Oh, wonderful! I was actually going to send for you later today. I've made significant progress," he said, a wide grin on his face. He began to tap his foot repeatedly on the floor. "I'm actually pretty excited to begin implementing it."

"That's great to hear," I said, relief flooding me. My parents would be okay. Not to mention all the other people who are afflicted by this plague. I took another sip of tea and the warmth spread even further. It was pleasant, so I dismissed it, focusing on Thorne's words.

"And it's all thanks to you, Lyra. If you hadn't gone to Vespara and risked your life, we never would have gotten this close. To you," he said, tipping his tea cup back and finishing it in two long swallows.

I followed suit, draining the rest of my tea. However, when I went to put my teacup back on the table, my hands trembled. I dropped the cup onto the tray with a clatter and brought my hands up to my face. What was going on?

My limbs felt heavy and weak and my head was spinning. Startled, I looked to Thorne, and he was standing, pushing his sleeves up.

"Yes, yes… it's all thanks to you, Lyra," he murmured before everything went black. "Everything."

CHAPTER 26

I woke slowly, feeling as though I had been trampled by a herd of horses. My entire body ached and burned, and my head felt like it was underwater. I opened my eyes just a slit and everything was blurry and too bright, like I had too many glasses of wine the night before.

As my eyes adjusted, I shook my head slightly to try to clear it. What happened? I couldn't remember. My head felt like it was filled with cotton and I was just trying to slog through to find complete thoughts. I got to Thorne's house and then what? Only bits and pieces returned to me. As my mind cleared, I became aware of a dull throb that bloomed in my left arm and I hissed out a breath. I tried to sit up, only to find that I was restrained. By what?

I opened my eyes further to find that I was strapped to a wooden table of some sort. It looked similar to something that you might find for surgery. Looking blearily around, I saw a needle and hose sticking out of my left arm, draining blood into a large glass jar. Immediately, I felt horrendously nauseated and dry heaved at the sight. I swallowed back bile and tried to focus.

It looked like I had already lost around a liter of blood. If I lost another liter, I would probably die. I looked desperately around the room. It looked like a basement of some kind. There were cobblestone walls, and the floor was packed dirt. The air was heavy with the scent of damp earth and mildew, each breath feeling thick in my lungs. There were various alchemical implements and jars filled with various herbs and liquids placed on racks lined up against the far wall.

The room was dimly illuminated by a single grime-covered window set high in the wall, and there were unlit torches mounted in various places around the room. There was a single table nearby with a setup of bunsen burners, test tubes and empty bottles and vials of various sizes.

A wave of dizziness hit me suddenly, and I had to close my eyes against the room, spinning around me. I needed to get out of this. I tried to pull my magic and felt not even a flutter. I must be too weak right now. My heart sank and tears pricked my eyes. Was I going to die here? After everything?

I refused. I fisted my hands and pulled against the restraints. They didn't even budge, and my anxiety rose. My breaths started coming faster and faster until I was borderline hyperventilating. I bit my lip, hard, and dug my nails into my palms hard enough to draw blood. The pain gave me a path through the panic. If I broke down, if I raised my heart rate, I would just lose blood faster.

I slowed my breathing, trying to calm my heart rate. What was happening? How did I get here? My memory was spotty. Desperately,

I tried to see if there was anything I could use to free myself. There was a covered bundle against the wall, and any sharp instruments were well out of my reach. I continued to pull against the restraints, even though I knew it was fruitless. I had to do *something*.

As I continued to struggle, a door opened at the top of the stairs on the far side of the room and Thorne descended, a frown pulling the corners of his mouth down when he noticed I was awake. I froze, eyes round with shock.

"Lyra! I had hoped you would sleep through this process," he murmured, as if to himself. "Maybe I can give some more sedative." He paced across the room to the shelf of jars, shuffling them around and filling the air with the sound of clinking glass.

"What the hell, Thorne? What is this?" I spat, fury overriding my common sense. "Why am I strapped to this table? Why are you draining my blood? What is *wrong* with you?"

He strode over to me, cupping my cheek. He looked apologetic, his dark eyes like the deepest ocean at midnight. Vast, yet empty. "I know you won't believe me, darling, but this isn't what I wanted," he said, his voice gentle, like poison wrapped in honey. His eyes gleamed with dark conviction. "But I have to do this for the greater good. You won't use your power like I will. The right way." Each word dripped with obsessive energy, and I knew in my heart he truly believed what he said.

If glares could kill, Thorne would combust right where he stood. "What do you mean, this isn't what you wanted? What is this?"

Thorne crossed his arms and leaned against the table, the glass vials gently clinking together as the table shifted under his weight. He spoke so softly I had to strain my ears to hear the words. "You wouldn't know this, but I've actually been studying transformation magic for decades. And when you were born, I just had a feeling that you were special."

A growing horror bloomed in my chest at his words, but before I could say anything, he pushed off of the table, the implements rattling, and began to pace in front of me. "When your mother told me about your power, well… I never meant things to turn out like this," he said, looking away with shame written across his face.

"She told you?" I gasped out, shocked. I couldn't even process what he was saying. Betrayal flared anew. How could she? *Why* would she? He worked for the Arcane Order! I didn't, couldn't understand what would bring my mother to do this.

"Of course she did! I told you, your mother and I were always very close, after all. Or…we used to be." He looked sad, lost. For a split second, I almost felt bad for him.

"She wanted to know if there was anything we could do to seal your power away so you would be safe," he scoffed, running his hands through his hair. The hay-colored strands fell across his face, throwing it partially in shadow. "She *trusted* me, you know. Your mother told no one else."

My heart sank. "What happened after she told you?"

He huffed out a laugh. He wrung his hands together, muttering. I could only make out some of the words. "I never should've… When you got sick, they all left me. And I couldn't even clean up the mess."

I didn't understand what was happening. I was never sick. But I thought back to the photo from my parent's house. Thorne with my parents and me as a child. Why didn't I remember him?

"What do you mean? Clean up the mess? When I was sick?" Thorne was practically speaking riddles with all the sense he was making. The ache in my arm was getting worse, and I looked down at the jar. It was filling more and more, pulling my life away with it. I had to see if I could get through to him. He didn't seem like this is what he *wanted*, more like what he felt he had to do?

He looked up sharply as though he had forgotten I was there, his eyes piercing through me as easily as a blade. "Yes, yes. But none of that matters now. All that matters is that I'm going to fix it. Everything leading up to now won't matter in the end. I'll heal the sick."

"Thorne," I said, my voice pleading. "Just let me go. We can figure out whatever it is together."

He turned, slamming his hands on the table. A vial fell to the ground, shattering. He turned to me, his face a mask of pain. "You think I haven't tried? I've spent countless hours, *years* of my life, trying to solve this plague! And nothing has come of it. *Nothing*! I never meant for this to happen, I only wanted to help your mother. To show her I could do what no one else could." His voice sounded raw, the words broken. His eyes shone, and I was startled to see that they had welled up with tears.

How could I reconcile the Thorne that I thought I knew with… whoever this was? Just what had happened to him to make him this way? My thoughts were becoming muddied. I was losing too much blood. This couldn't go on much longer.

What could I say? How could I get him to let me go? I had to try a different approach. "It's not your fault, Thorne. This plague, its magic—," I said before being interrupted by Thorne.

"I know all about its magic." His face contorted into an expression of rage. "I was just trying to give you a normal life!" he shouted. This wasn't good. He was so volatile, swapping through emotions between one breath and the next. My heart raced, and I tried desperately to calm it, to give myself more time.

"Give me a normal life?" I murmured, fighting off the dizziness. I closed my eyes to stave off the nausea.

"Lyra, I was just trying to lock your powers away. Your mother, she gave me a small sample of blood. I thought that by infusing it with some of my own magic, I could put a damper on it. Suppress your magic somehow. But it reacted almost like an immune system and caused you to become very ill," Thorne said, running his hands through his hair again. He was filled with nervous energy.

My eyes popped back open, his words opening a pit in my stomach. "I became ill? Ill how?" I couldn't remember any type of sickness, but if I was bad off, maybe I just didn't recall?

"It became the plague," he said, his tone mournful. "I was just trying to make your life easier. Your parents' lives easier. But, it's too late for all of that now. To turn into any person and immediately be able to diagnose them? To feel their aches and pains as though they were yours? It sounds so insignificant, but you don't know how to use the power. And you brought exactly what I needed for me to have it," he said, picking up a vial of swirling red liquid. Aldric's blood?

"What do you mean?" I asked. I was losing too much blood. The world was getting dark at the edges. I fought to stay conscious.

"The vampires. They can absorb some of our magic temporarily when they ingest our blood. They can't wield it. It's too different from their own vampiric magic. But they can draw it in. That's what makes them thirst after mage blood so much. But thanks to you, I could identify the compound that allowed for them to absorb the power and amplify it. And now, I just have to distill your blood down so it is more potent and I will be able to transform, too," he said, absently holding the vial up as though inspecting it against the dim lighting.

It was getting harder to concentrate, Thorne's words buzzing in my ears.

"You would never use your power in a way that matters. But I can. And I will. I'll finally be able to cure this damnable plague and remove this stain from my soul. I'm going to drain every last drop of your blood, combine it with the compound from the vampire blood, and I will become another transformation mage. A better one. One that will use the power as it should be wielded. To help the world and to heal the impossible," he said, his voice holding a tone of reverence.

He was truly insane.

Thorne straightened and flung his arms wide. "Don't you see, Lyra? Your sacrifice will usher in a new age. I will be more powerful than any other mage in history, and I will use it for the greater good! Everyone suffering from the plague will be healed! It will all be worth it for the pursuit of progress."

I heard footsteps and jolted when I felt his hand trace my cheek. His voice was soft, almost tender. "I am sorry that it had to be you, Lyra. This was never what I wanted, but your sacrifice will not be forgotten. Not by me, at least."

Weakness was spreading through all of my limbs. I was getting so cold, ice spreading through my veins. Was this what dying felt like?

I heard a soft groan to my right and fought to focus. Thorne stiffened, striding over to the covered bundle. He pulled it back to reveal… Griffin? He was tied up, unconscious, but alive.

"This is your friend, isn't it?" Thorne said, his voice quiet, regretful. "I found him wandering around outside. He said he was looking for you, and when I told him you'd never made it to my home, he refused to leave. But I had just the thing for him. I couldn't let him find you, to try and stop me. This is for all of Aethralis, after all."

"Griffin!" I cried weakly. This couldn't be happening. He didn't stir.

"He's not going to wake up, Lyra. The potion I slipped him is a powerful tranquilizer. It'll be ages before he can even open his eyes," he said, though he sounded tired himself. He stood, turning away from Griffin. "I hope to be out of here before he does."

I was becoming too weak to form words. Fighting through the haze encroaching over my vision, panic set in when Thorne made his way back to the table, picking up a wicked-looking knife.

"This is just in case. I won't hurt more people than I have to," he said, his finger tracing the curve of the blade as he softly spoke.

Darkness was blooming over my vision, and my chest was beginning to feel so heavy. I was tired. Thorne seemed to be debating something, but his face became resolute.

Tears pricked my eyes and fell as Thorne walked over to Griffin and hauled him to sit up against the wall. "I'm so close to this plan coming together, Lyra. I can't afford any mistakes. He means a lot to you, I know. And if this was any other world, if you weren't the one with this power, I would never do something like this. But this is for the greater good," he said, and without hesitating, he drove his blade deep into Griffin's abdomen with a sickening thud.

Griffin's eyes immediately shot open, and he started to Shift, instinct driving him before he was even really aware. Thorne loosed a string of curses, gripping the blade tightly with both hands as he fought against Griffin's changing body. Griffin's half-formed snout tore into Thorne's left forearm, blood spraying in a wash of crimson over Griffin's face. He reached up with a clawed hand and dug it into Thorne's arms, his preternatural strength able to pull them apart despite being drugged. The blade fell to the ground in a wash of blood, skittering across the floor.

The sight was horrendous. A half-formed beast and a crazed man, locked in a dance of life and death. Thorne's arms were becoming mangled, the force of Griffin's blows powerful. However, he was slower than he should have been. And it was that slowness that allowed Thorne time to grab the blade, though his grip was loose.

Despite the exhaustion tugging on my being, I tried so hard to pull my magic, and all I could feel was a gaping maw inside of me, bereft of any power. I could only look on in terror, not for myself, but for Griffin. Thorne was hacking and slashing at him, the blade wickedly sharp. But it didn't even seem to phase Griffin, who kept coming despite the dark puddle spreading across the ground.

"Thorne, you don't have to do this. Let him go!" I cried. But Thorne didn't even look back. Griffin was becoming sluggish, weak. Despite his initial vigor, the blood loss was getting to him.

His hands, caught between man and wolf, reached for his abdomen in a futile attempt to stem the flow of his life's energy leaving him. His eyes rolled around in his head until they finally found me—the gold contained within, dimming like the last rays of the sun, dulled with pain and fury. Griffin took a heavy, staggering step towards me and my arms strained against the restraints, fighting to catch him. To hold him. To heal him somehow. His arm reached out, grasping at nothing to reach me. My heart shattered in that moment as I screamed his name and he crumpled like a puppet with strings that had been cut. His hand twitched, still outstretched towards the table where I lay, unable to reach him.

His gaze remained on me, the warmth fading until there was nothing left but emptiness. I couldn't look away, my mouth working soundlessly until finally a harsh, keening wail sounded in the room. Eventually, I realized the sound was coming from me. My stomach roiled, my entire being rejecting this reality.

I screamed, my voice raw. "Stop, stop! You can't!" I didn't even know who I was talking to, Griffin or Thorne. I kept screaming until my voice was gone and my throat felt bloody. More than anything, I just wanted to tell him how much he had meant to me—he was the first person who made me feel safe, how his acceptance made me feel like an actual person again, and not just someone cursed with a power I never wanted. But all I could do was watch as the person who'd first shown me I deserved more from life slipped away into nothingness.

Thorne looked remorseful as he looked at me, pulling his blade from Griffin, who laid unmoving on the floor in a dark puddle. The sound the blade made as it pulled from his flesh made me retch, nausea roiling within me. That darkness beneath him was spreading impossibly fast, and it felt like my heart was going to stop. This couldn't be happening. It couldn't be happening. The words repeated in my mind like a mantra. I had to be dreaming. My heart cracked, crumbling into thousands of pieces.

My gaze was trained on Griffin, forever caught between man and wolf. His face was still turned towards me, his golden eyes staring sightlessly ahead, and yet it felt like they were piercing right through me, straight into my blackened soul. This was all my fault. He was only targeted because of me. And now, he was going to be lost to me forever. A sob wracked my body. Why? Why, why, *why*? I couldn't *do* this anymore. Something in me broke, watching him lie there. I couldn't even tell him goodbye.

Thorne came over to me with what looked like pity in his eyes despite the carnage and swiped the tears from my cheeks with his bloodied, trembling fingers, leaving smears of red behind. The touch was tender, and it filled me with disgust. He said nothing and strode over to the racks on the wall. I couldn't even bring myself to care what he was doing. My world is shattered.

There's no way Griffin could survive this. And I couldn't help him at all. I was useless. Completely, entirely useless. My life is truly cursed. I finally find one ray of sunshine and it has to be snuffed right in front of me, leaving me in the darkness, completely alone yet again.

I had to be going into shock. But it didn't really matter. It's just what I deserved. My breathing became shallow and my chest ached fiercely. Would my heart just stop? Sweat broke out over my skin and I strained against the restraints. But soon, I was too weak to move.

Distantly, I heard a crash. But it was so far away, I barely registered it. A muffled shout rang out, along with the sound of splintering wood. But I didn't have the energy to see what it was. Something registered distantly in my fading consciousness, maybe a certain noise or scent, but I couldn't focus. My eyelids were so, so heavy. I could barely keep them open.

This was it. The world began to blend together in swirls of color before bleeding into gray. The scent of copper was fading, along with everything else. I felt as though I were floating, disconnected from my body. Is this what dying felt like? Is this what Griffin felt at that last moment? Or was he in pain all the way until the end? As my eyes slipped closed, hot tears fell from my cheeks, and then I felt nothing.

At least we would be together in death, I thought, falling into the void.

CHAPTER 27

I was adrift. Was I alive? I couldn't open my eyes or move my body.

Something was dripping into my mouth. It made me think of drinking liquid starlight. Somehow both cool and warm, it tasted like berries and honey, bright and impossibly sweet. A warmth bloomed in my body like a comforting blanket. A soft sigh escaped me.

I fell back into unconsciousness.

My body was gently swaying, and I was pressed tight against something firm. The motion was rhythmic and there was a subtle vibration every few seconds. A crease formed between my brows. What in the world was happening? Where am I?

My head was pounding and my body felt like lead. A flash of Griffin laying on the ground in a puddle of red surged in my mind and my eyes popped open with a gasp. I immediately groaned and pressed a hand to my forehead, the sudden brightness causing pain to surge behind my eyes.

"Easy, love. You very nearly died," Aldric's smooth voice said from behind me. When did he get here? How did he find me?

"I had been looking for you to apologize," he said, and I realized I must have spoken aloud. "And I scented your blood. A lot of it. You were… almost lost when I arrived," he murmured, his voice cracking with some unnamed emotion. He cleared his throat, but his arm around my waist tightened.

I realized I was sitting on a horse, cradled in Aldric's arms. I looked around. We were on a road… but where? I don't think I'd ever been here before. I glanced down at the horse. It was Nocturne, Aldric's Vesparan horse. Dark as midnight and incredibly majestic. I glanced over Aldric's shoulder to see Lune trailing behind us. She nickered as she saw my head pop up.

"W-what happened to Griffin? Thorne?" I asked, my voice hoarse. I had to wonder how long I had been unconscious. My entire body felt like a bruise.

"Is Griffin the man I saw you with?" Aldric asked carefully.

I nodded, looking up at him through watery eyes. "T-Thorne, he… he…" I couldn't get the words out.

Aldric looked truly remorseful as he shook his head. "It was all I could do to get you out of there. As it is, Thorne somehow transformed into a monster and I was forced to retreat with you, so I wasn't able to see what happened to Thorne. He was injured when I arrived, so I'm not sure how far he could have gone. But Griffin… looked as though he was already gone when I arrived."

A deep sob wracked my body. I knew it, I did, but I still

hoped that Aldric would have somehow been able to save Griffin, too. I felt like I couldn't breathe through the pain, and Aldric pulled Nocturne's reins, so he slowed to a stop.

He turned me around in his arms and cradled me against his chest. His stormy scent surrounded me and I was surprised to find that I could *feel* a deep sadness emanating from him, the similar-yet-not emotion swirling through my own. I felt almost as though I had another heartbeat behind my ribs.

"What is this?" I asked through my sobs.

"You couldn't die. I had to save you," Aldric hesitantly said by way of explanation.

I looked up at him, tears streaming down my cheeks. "What do you mean? What did you have to do?"

He took a deep breath, nuzzling the top of my head. "I had to give you some of my blood. Please don't be angry with me. I had to save you. I had to," he said, his voice rough.

"Aldric, you barely know me," I said, my tears slowly drying as his words sank in. What did that mean for me? What would drinking vampire blood do to a mage?

"I do know you, Lyra. I know enough. The rest will come with time," Aldric said, as though trying to convince us both. A feeling of desperate hope crept through, taking my breath away. And beneath it all, a crushing loneliness. What is this? My already beaten and bruised heart broke yet again.

"Aldric…" I didn't know what to say. I was incredibly grateful that he had saved me, but I couldn't understand why he would do it. Why would he risk his life like that?

"Yes, love?" he asked.

"What does drinking your blood mean?" I asked, wiping away the last traces of tears on my cheeks.

"We've got a bond, Lyra. I can feel some of what you feel, and you can feel some of what I feel. But it's not solid. It's been too long since I've taken any blood from you," he said, having the grace to look embarrassed.

"A bond?" I asked, shock written plainly on my face.

Aldric looked away from me for the first time, his eyes darkening to steel. "Yes. Normally, this is something that is mutually agreed upon. It's a big deal in Vespara. Reserved for mating pairs of vampires," he explained.

It felt like my heart was going to stop. "M-mating pairs?" Why was this happening to me? *I just lost Griffin*, I thought, my throat painfully tight. *And now I'm in a bond with a vampire?*

Aldric nodded, his mood incredibly subdued compared to the easy flirtation I usually saw from him. "I'm sorry. I didn't want to force this upon you, but I just couldn't let you die. If we don't share blood for a few months, it will probably fade away."

I couldn't believe what I was hearing. "Probably? You don't know for sure?"

"Like I said, love, this is usually done with the consent of both parties. So an incomplete bond is fairly unheard of. It'll also fade once we're apart from each other again," he said, though his voice was uncertain.

I felt like I was getting more of my wits about me and

straightened in his arms. Nocturne was dancing impatiently underneath us. "I want to ride Lune. Alone," I said, a whirlwind of emotions all fighting for dominance inside of me. Disgust, fear, sadness, grief. I didn't know how to feel and I would need time to work through these feelings.

"Listen, darling, you've only barely recovered—," Aldric began, but I held up a hand.

"Don't call me that. I want to ride Lune," I said firmly. "You'll be nearby if something happens, I assume."

He nodded, though it was clear he didn't want to let me go. I planted a hand in the middle of his chest and pushed, trying to extricate myself from his grip. He didn't let go, however, keeping me gently cradled against his chest.

Some hidden part of me wanted to stay there and sink into the warmth and comfort Aldric offered. But it felt like a betrayal and I couldn't bring myself to do that to Griffin.

"Lyra, you must be careful. You're probably still going to be fairly weak. Let me help you."

I stubbornly refused to listen and slowly, carefully slid out of his arms and out of Nocturne's saddle. I landed hard on the ground, my knees giving out. Lune threw her head and whinnied, coming to stand next to me.

She seemed to sense that I was weak, because she laid down next to me, making it easier for me to climb into the saddle. It felt like I was moving through water, my limbs shaking.

Once I settled in the saddle and picked up the reins, Lune carefully got back to her feet. I glanced at Aldric. His expression was pained, concern rolling off of him in waves. He looked disheveled, and I realized he had a healing wound on his shoulder that I couldn't see before.

"What happened to you?" I asked, unable to help myself.

"It was the fight with Thorne. It's like I told you, he became some sort of beast I'd never seen before. I barely got out of there with you," he admitted, embarrassed. "He caught me off guard, because I thought you were the only transformation mage."

The thought of Thorne using my magic against Aldric left a bitter taste in my mouth and my stomach roiled with nausea. "I am. He used your blood to steal some of my power through my blood."

Aldric's expression became murderous. "He used my blood for *that*? To steal power from my—from you? How?"

What had he almost said? Carefully filing that thought away for later, I explained everything I remembered from my conversation with Thorne. "I was so certain that I would die, but it felt peaceful, at the end," I admitted. "Even if I lost Griffin, I thought I'd see him again."

There was the pained expression again. I didn't understand. Why was he hurt by this? He and I barely knew each other.

"I know that you have some kind of crush on me, Aldric, but... It is—was different with Griffin," I said softly. "Are you... are you certain that he..." I couldn't bring myself to say the words.

"I know he meant a lot to you," he murmured. "But yes, I am sure. There is nothing that could have saved him at that point."

I felt a profound sense of loss, like a part of me had been ripped away. I had never even told him I cared about him, I realized, a pang ripping its way through me.

Aldric's face fell, and I realized he could probably feel some of this anguish within me. I choked the emotion back. I needed privacy to work through this grief. And, I had to admit, guilt whispered through my mind that I was forcing him to feel these feelings, too.

I resolved to change the subject, to get my mind off of these depressing thoughts. "Do you know many vampires who have bonded?" I asked.

Aldric seemed surprised by the question. "Honestly, no. A lot of vampires are selfish. And tying yourself to someone else for eternity, well, it's not everyone's cup of tea."

"I see. What happens if a vampire bonds itself to someone that *isn't* another vampire?" I asked, urging Lune to walk.

He did the same with Nocturne, and the sound of gently clopping hooves filled the air. It was a welcome distraction from the silence as he considered his words. "I'm not sure. I would assume you would get some benefit from having my blood, but I can't say. We'll just have to find out, won't we?"

CHAPTER 28

After riding Lune for a few minutes, lost in my thoughts, it finally occurred to me to ask, "Where are we?" If I had to guess, we'd gone to the East, closer to the human territories. The sun was high overhead, and the land was dotted with hills and valleys.

The mages had a fairly tumultuous relationship with the human kingdom of Cairnard, so I'd never ventured near it. It was because of the last transformation mage that we'd been ousted from the human kingdoms to begin with, so if I was found out, it was basically a death sentence.

"Oh, love. No idea! But we had to get out of Sylvan Reach. I didn't want to risk that man coming after you. I wanted to give you time to recover," Aldric said easily, riding next to me.

There was a niggling thought that was bothering me. "We need to go back," I said immediately.

Aldric ran a hand through his raven-black hair, exasperation emanating from him. "What do you mean? We *just* got out of there. You're barely even conscious! Don't think I haven't noticed how you're struggling to ride Lune."

I grit my teeth. He was right. I hadn't pushed Lune past anything but a slow walk because I didn't think I could keep myself upright. But that wasn't the point. "If you won't go with me, I'll go myself. I need to check on my parents." The thought of going back to see them turned my stomach, but I couldn't just leave them with no one to check on them.

I turned Lune around, and Aldric swore viciously. "You don't even know where you're going," he ground out. "What if Thorne is still there? What will you do?"

"I don't know, dammit! But I can't leave them there. I can't. So you either show me the way back or I'll try to make my way there on my own," I said stubbornly.

Aldric scrubbed a hand over his face. "It'll take half a day to get back to Sylvan Reach, you know."

A spark of hope fluttered to life in my chest. It would be much easier if Aldric traveled with me instead of having to travel on my own. I didn't know if I could make it alone. Plus, he was right. I had no idea where I was going. I'd never been here before.

With a sigh of resignation, Aldric turned Nocturne around, and we started back the way we came.

After a few hours, the sun sank low on the horizon and we were back in the forest. I wasn't concerned with the forest magic anymore. If something were to come for me, it would be exactly what I deserved. And I figured Aldric could care for himself. The eerie sense of the forest wasn't lost on him, however, and he rode with his back ramrod straight, his head on a swivel.

"Is it always so… strange in here? I don't remember the last time we traveled in the forest being like this," Aldric said. "And that was only a few days ago."

"The last time we traveled in here, it was daytime," I said. "The energy in the forest is only wild at night. It's still there during the day, just more of a pleasant hum."

"Should we stop for the night and resume travel tomorrow?" Aldric asked. I could tell that he really wanted me to say yes, but I shook my head.

"We don't have time to waste. I don't even know if any of the other villagers are alive. I don't want to risk leaving my parents there to die. Time is of the essence," I said.

As we rode through the forest, a breeze carried with it the scent of damp earth and rain. Suddenly, a vivid image of Griffin clutching his abdomen as we locked eyes flashed in my mind, and I squeezed my eyes shut tight, wrapping my arms around myself. Why was I thinking about that? My heart pumped fast in my chest and I curled in on myself. I felt like I couldn't breathe, my breaths coming faster and faster.

Aldric was suddenly there, Nocturne and Lune side by side. He rubbed my back in soothing circles.

"I'm here, love," he murmured. He said nothing else, but he didn't have to. The simple act of being in his presence helped to bring me back to reality slowly. I don't know how long we stayed like that, but eventually the vice around my chest slowly loosened until I felt like I could breathe and my adrenaline started to leave me.

Lune responded to my emotional state and came to a slow stop, Nocturne mirroring her movements. She nickered softly and bobbed her head to get my attention, and I reached up to gently stroke her neck. The feel of her soft white fur helped me to snap out of... whatever that was. Eventually, my heart rate slowed, and I straightened. Shame warmed my cheeks. I should be stronger than this.

"I'm okay," I whispered. Even if it wasn't really true, at least I felt like I could breathe again.

"Listen, darling. Even though I wasn't there, you can still talk to me, you know," Aldric said softly, dragging his hand away from me. Immediately, I missed the warmth of his touch and I wordlessly reached out to him. He wrapped my fingers in his, the small touch meaning more than words could express.

Against Aldric's advice, we continued to make our way towards Sylvan Reach even during the night. The moon was barely there and the darkness was thick. I had no doubt that Aldric could still see just fine, being a vampire, however I was struggling and my magic... I couldn't bring myself to use it. Not now. Honestly, I wasn't even sure that I could. My body was still recovering, despite whatever healing Aldric's blood had given me.

Thinking about his blood... I was reminded of the taste, like the sweetest wine. If my blood tasted as good to him as his did to me, I could see what he meant when he said he could become addicted. But at the same time, the thought repulsed me. How could I think that blood tasted *good*?

There were a lot of things about Aldric that I didn't understand. His motivations, the draw that I felt towards him. And how that draw made me feel so incredibly broken. I felt like Griffin's body hadn't even cooled yet and here I was feeling an attraction to another man. Self-loathing filled me, turning my blood to acid. How could I even be near Aldric right now? I knew he had to feel some type of way about me, in that he was willing to risk his life to save me.

But why? As a prince of Vespara, he could have anyone, and I mean *anyone*, and yet he's here with me. I sighed, exhausted. I didn't have the energy to think about the meanings of these things right now. As it is, I could barely stay awake feeling the rhythmic motion of Lune walking beneath me. The fear that I felt before when traveling through this same forest with Griffin had withered and died, leaving apathy in its place.

I couldn't help but feel immensely disappointed that I didn't die too. Griffin suffered in death and for what? Because he traveled with me? Cared about me? I wasn't worth it. Not worth anything, really. That's how it's always been. I dug my fingernails into my palms, hard enough to draw blood. Worthless. I was worthless.

My life had no meaning. The moment I thought I found something, *someone* to care about, it's ripped away from me. I should have died, I thought darkly.

Aldric cleared his throat next to me, and I glanced up, startled out of my thoughts.

"Listen, love. You were meant to live. I know how you must feel, but… you weren't supposed to die there. You weren't.

Otherwise, fate never would have brought me to find you there," he said earnestly, his hands holding Nocturne's reins with a white-knuckled grip.

"If the fates are real, they have a twisted sense of humor," I said bitterly. "My entire life has just been full of pain and disappointment. My parents had to deal with rumors going around about me from the time I was born. I was cursed with this gods-damned power I never even wanted, and I just want to find a *home*." My voice broke on the last word, and I looked away, my vision watery.

I was bone-tired. Tired of everything. Aldric must be feeling more of my emotions than he let on because he was unusually somber. Guilt spiked through me at the thought.

"You'll have one," Aldric murmured. "You could always stay with me."

For a moment, the only sound was the horses navigating the underbrush of the forest. Then, Aldric's words sank in.

"I can't, Aldric. It wouldn't be right. Griffin and I… We were together. I can't just give up on that, even though he's gone," I said.

Aldric was quiet for a moment. A wave of emotions whispered across our bond—sadness, and something else I couldn't quite place. Grief? When he spoke next, his voice was so gentle, as though he was afraid of spooking me.

"You're not obligated to be with me romantically. I know you're grieving. But I'm offering a safe place for you to be yourself, to heal and to figure out what you're going to do next. No strings attached."

Surprised, my gaze shot to his face. His eyes glowed with the reflection of the moonlight, the swirling depths pulling me in.

"I know you may think that I wouldn't understand, but I do. I know what it's like to feel lost, to not have a place you feel you belong. Remember, I've lived for thousands of years. There were plenty of times that I felt just as adrift as you do now. Let me be your sanctuary," he said, his words resonating deep within me.

Sanctuary, I thought. Aldric would accept me, broken pieces and all. Some part of me knew this. And yet, I couldn't help but feel doubt.

"Why would you do that for me? You'd be putting yourself at risk," I said, my voice barely above a whisper. That's what Griffin did, and look at what happened to him, I thought, sadness permeating my soul.

Aldric huffed out a laugh, but the sound was sad. "I know enough. I told you that before. You're brave, resilient, caring. You've faced more than anyone should have to, and yet here you are. And not only that, but I know that you're still fighting to do the right thing." He paused, then added with a wry smile. "Besides, maybe I'm being selfish."

"Selfish?" I asked, my head cocking slightly to the side as I thought about what he could mean by that.

"I told you before. There's something about you I want to figure out. And I can't exactly do that if we're not together, you see. So maybe I'm not being entirely selfless with my offer," he said with his first genuine smile since he rescued me.

I considered his words. "Aldric, I just... I don't know. I'll think about it. But first, we need to get to Sylvan Reach. We need to check things out there, and I need to see if my parents are still alive," I said the last in a whisper, the words choking me.

He nodded, understanding and a flicker of... hope passed through the bond. I didn't think I'd ever get used to that. The feelings were the same, yet not. Muted.

"The offer still stands, Lyra. Whenever you're ready. If you're ever ready. I will be there," he said with a wink.

Despite myself, a small smile bloomed on my face. He just had that effect on me.

CHAPTER 29

I had the same feeling I had the last time I traveled through Sylvan Reach at night. That there was something just out of view, watching. However, I found I didn't feel the same lingering fear. The only concern I had was for Aldric. If we were to get attacked, I didn't know if he'd be able to protect himself.

We were close to the village by now. The hair on the back of my neck had stood on end, and Aldric had kept his head on a swivel. I wondered if he could sense the same thing, but then I realized his senses were likely better than mine. I kept my shoulders loose and just focused on staying balanced on top of Lune. Content to ignore the thing following us, I was surprised when Aldric spoke.

"You know there's something out there, right?" he murmured. His eyes glowed like drops of moonlight, slicing through the dim of the forest.

"I do, but I'm not sensing any malice," I whispered back. "It seems to be waiting for something. Not sure what."

I saw the tops of the buildings on the outskirts of Sylvan Reach. Given that Elder Brynn had said she hadn't heard of anyone seeing the Fey beast, I felt pretty confident that it wouldn't cross the threshold into the village. With a last glance around, I urged Lune into a canter. There was nothing racing to attack us, so I figured my hunch was correct. If this was a Fey beast, it was keeping to the background for now.

Aldric was just behind me, the hoofbeats pounding a powerful rhythm on the path. Once we got to the village square, I dismounted carefully from Lune. Stayed on my feet this time, which was a win. But I was still incredibly weak. My body felt bruised and battered. Aldric was quick to my side, bracing me with an arm around my waist. I ignored the soft flutter the sensation caused, guilt crashing into me like a ton of bricks.

I just needed to see my parents. Nothing else mattered right now. I slowly made my way to their home, Aldric helping me every slow step of the way.

Once their cottage came into view, my stomach churned. Would Thorne have left them there, unable to fend for themselves? And where were the rest of the villagers? Even now, I looked along each road and found them to be completely empty. Surely he didn't allow everyone to die? Regardless of how crazy Thorne is, he wouldn't do that, would he?

"Is this the place?" Aldric asked me softly. His touch was tender, and no more than what I could handle. He was easy company to keep. He seemed to anticipate every need before I could even bring myself to voice a want for help. I hated how that made me feel. Relying on someone… all it did was cause death. The memory of sunshine eyes growing dim haunted me, tormenting me.

I knew that after this, there was one more stop I'd have to take, no matter the risk to myself. Aldric traced a soft line up and down my back as though sensing my distress, his long, slender fingers soothing me with their gentle touch.

"Do you want me to check?" he asked, his dark brows furrowed.

"No, they're my parents. I need to be the one to help them," I said, my voice more firm than I intended. I cleared my throat and said a little softer, "I will be back in a few minutes. Please wait out here."

Aldric hesitated, but slowly withdrew his arm from around me. I immediately missed his support, but I shoved that feeling down deep. I didn't have room for another person anymore. With that depressing thought, I looked up at the simple cottage and made my way to the door. It was still unlocked. A sense of foreboding chilled my spine.

I cautiously opened the door and glanced back to where Aldric stood waiting. Concern was plainly written across his face, but he made no move to follow. I felt a lot of gratitude for that, because I didn't know if I'd have it in me to send him away if he tried. Strengthening my resolve, I turned my gaze forward and made my way into the house, checking around every corner.

After I was satisfied that there were no hidden boogeymen, I made my way to my parents' bedroom. A smell hit me before I opened the door and my heart sank to my feet. Not them too. Please. Not them. Gently pushing the door, horror slammed into me like a physical blow, my meager rations making their way to the floor in front of me as my body violently rejected the reality of what was before me.

The scent of sickness and waste was strong, so thick in the air that I could taste it, wafting out into the hall where I stood. I covered my nose and made my way inside the room, my eyes watering. Both of my parents lay there as though asleep, unmoving. No one had come to attend them in who knows how long. They were laying in their own waste, pallid and sweaty. But breathing, I realized with a sigh of relief, which I quickly regretted. How was I going to get them out of here? I couldn't leave them to waste away.

Where were the rest of the villagers? Maybe I could find Elder Brynn and she could help. The thought made a spark of hope ignite. She could help and keep them safe. I brushed the sweaty hair from my parents' foreheads and whispered that I would be back, rushing with a renewed vigor. I needed to make it to the makeshift hospital.

Aldric looked surprised when I returned so quickly, but his nose wrinkled. I could only imagine how bad I smelled even from the short time in there, but I paid it no mind. There were more important things to worry about right now.

"We need to make it to the college. They were using it as a

hospital to care for the afflicted. They're alive, but in rough shape," I said, forcing the words out around the lump in my throat.

"Just tell me where to go, love," Aldric said easily, scooping me up in his arms despite my protests. "It'll be quicker if I take you. You aren't exactly a distance runner right now, no offense," he said with a hint of a smile.

I knew he was right, but it still burned me up. "It's midway to Thorne's house from here."

Aldric barely let me finish speaking before he moved with preternatural speed, carrying me as though I weighed no more than a handkerchief in his hands. The world blurred by us so quickly that my stomach revolted and I fought not to get sick again.

"If you can run this fast, why do you have a horse?" I said, but the words were whipped away by the wind.

He seemed to hear me anyway, because he glanced down at me with a grin, though he didn't answer me until we came to a stop in front of a large building. "Is this it?" he asked.

When I nodded, he said, "I have Nocturne because I enjoy him, and it's less conspicuous of me to be riding a horse."

I waited for him to put me down, but when he didn't, I pointedly shifted around in his arms. Aldric glanced down at me and his arms tightened around me briefly before he reluctantly placed me on my feet.

"Thank you for, uh… for the ride," I said. Warmth bloomed on my cheeks and I wrung my hands together. I didn't wait for a response before I strode towards the large academic building, stopping just shy of entering. Now that I had a proper look at it, it was a bright, cheery building. It had stained glass windows and was made of bright stone. It could almost be interpreted as a church if you didn't know better. Atop the building was the symbol of the Arcane Order. An eight-pointed star encircled by runes with an open book at the center.

The sight put me on edge, but I shook it off. I instinctively tried to pull Louise's visage over my own, but I couldn't muster the magic. The well within me was still completely dry, and my stomach sank. What could I do?

I grit my teeth. I would just have to try, anyway. Shoving all of my hair back into my cloak, I drew it down over my face. Hopefully, they wouldn't look close enough to realize it was me.

It was too still, too quiet. I made my way towards the area Griffin and I saw Elder Brynn last. The thought of Griffin sent a pang of sadness through me and I sucked in a breath, but I shoved the feeling away for later. I couldn't break down right now. There were other pressing things I had to focus on. No matter how hard I wanted to.

A sense of foreboding tingled my spine as a scent hit me. Death, decay. Surely, surely they were okay. Or maybe they had left? Slowly, I turned the corner into the large room that had once been filled with those afflicted by the plague. The sight that I was met with froze the blood in my veins. Bloated, black bodies, some covered with stained sheets and others just laying on the floor like toys tossed aside. How long had they been dead here? Did Griffin know?

He didn't. He couldn't, I reasoned with myself. Griffin

would have told me. But as I looked on in horror, I realized I didn't see Brynn. She wasn't amongst those who had died. And there weren't enough bodies to account for all the villagers here. She must have taken the remaining villagers and left.

Aldric sucked in a sharp breath beside me as the room came into view. "What happened here?" He held a hand over his nose and mouth to try to block out the smell, but we both knew it was fruitless. I steeled myself and took a cursory walk through the room, weaving through the bodies. I just wanted to know if I recognized anyone.

Some of these bodies… some of them were too small. Too fragile. Bile rose in my throat, but I swallowed it down with some effort. How could I bury all of these bodies? I didn't want to just leave these villagers here to… to rot. They may not have treated me like a human being, but they deserved some decency in death. I was more than what they thought of me.

Aldric wordlessly followed me, breathing shallowly. I made my way over to the cabinets at the far end of the room and took out as many sheets as I could carry. I took time to carefully cover each body. This may be the best that I could do for right now, but I refused to just leave them to lie here. As I kept going, I was saddened to see Marla and her husband amongst the dead. She was always kind to me, even when I was a child.

"I knew her," I said, sorrow in my voice.

Aldric dropped a hand on my shoulder, his touch warm even through my cloak. Sometimes it was hard to remember that he was a vampire. He never had the chill that you expected when you thought about being touched by a vampire. Brushing those thoughts away, I moved away. His hand fell to his side, and I sensed disappointment coming through the bond. But I didn't have time to worry about him right now.

I couldn't stay here for long. I needed to get back to my parents. Maybe Aldric could help me bring them… somewhere. There was no plan, I realized. What could I even do? I didn't have a healing ability. My heart rate picked up, beating hard in my chest. How could I help them? I didn't want… didn't want them to die, too. They were all I had left.

You have Aldric, the dark parts of my mind whispered. But I refused to listen to that train of thought. Aldric walked with me side-by-side, covering each body. From the elderly to those who had barely begun to live, no one was missed. Looking out at the sea of white, I felt some small part of my soul ease. It was all I could do for now, but I felt as though I'd returned some small measure of dignity to these people.

Going back to the cabinets, I rifled through them to see if there were any healing potions, any tinctures, anything that could possibly help my parents. Then, I had an idea. An awful idea, but an idea nonetheless.

I strode towards the exit of the makeshift hospital. There was no point in me staying any longer. I didn't know what could help my parents, but I knew where I could find information about it. Aldric was right behind me, and he grasped my arm, stopping me in my tracks and turning me back towards him.

"Lyra, what are you doing? Where are you rushing off to?"

he asked, his brows furrowed. I fought the urge to smooth the line between his eyes, instead fisting my hands.

"I need to go back to Thorne's house," I bit out, trying to pull my arm from his grip. Aldric just held me tighter, not budging an inch.

"Lyra, you must be insane. You almost *died* and you want to go back to the site of your torture?" Aldric asked incredulously. His eyes grew dark, steely. A wave of goosebumps rose on my skin. He was angry. His aura was completely different, dark like a cloudless night sky.

Aldric must have felt my fear because he dropped my arm as though I had burned him. "Lyra, you can't."

"I have to. I have to see if he has any information that can help my parents. They can't die, Aldric. They can't," I said, choking back sudden tears. Knowing that they were probably okay had gotten me through the years, but now being faced with their death was rocking my entire world. I had to do everything in my power to help them.

"Would your blood help them?" I asked in desperation.

Aldric took a deep breath and loosed it. It looked like he was trying hard to calm himself, but his jaw was still set on edge. "I don't know, Lyra. But for you, I can try if you cannot find any other option."

Wringing my hands, I nodded. "I am going to go to Thorne's house. Can you… can you watch them for me? I don't have anyone else and I trust you with them," I said, shocked to find that the words were true. I did trust Aldric. He'd never given me a reason to think otherwise.

"Lyra, I can't let you go alone. What if Thorne is still there?" he asked.

I knew he was right. I knew it, but it didn't stop me from grinding out, "I don't care if he is! It's the only choice I have. And I need you to do this. For me. Please." I would beg if I had to. Aldric could give them his blood if they were going to die while I tried to find something to help them.

Aldric scrubbed his hand over his face before pinching the bridge of his nose. I so desperately wanted to go to him, to ease his frustrations, but guilt froze me in place. I couldn't do that to Griffin.

Griffin.

I wondered if he was… if he was still there. At Thorne's house. Would Thorne have left him behind? Left him… like that?

All the more reason to go, I told myself angrily. "I'm going. Please. Go to my parents' and keep an eye on them for me. Don't let them die," I whispered, my voice cracking.

Aldric still looked as though he wanted to protest, but he must have sensed that I would not back down and instead, he nodded. Gratitude made my knees weak, but I steeled myself. Resolve pushing me, I straightened my spine and walked out the door, turning towards the road that would lead to Thorne's house. I was still weak, but dammit, I was determined to make it there. I would make this right.

Aldric's eyes were burning a hole in my back as I walked away, but I didn't turn back.

CHAPTER 30

The door to Thorne's house was open, the blackness of the interior like the maw of a dungeon beast. I slowly crept towards the entrance, my head on a swivel. I couldn't be caught unawares. Especially now that I knew just how twisted he was. Gently nudging the door further open with my foot, I silently padded inside.

All the lights were off, and it was like a pit of night. I wandered to where I recalled a gas lamp and turned the handle to spark the light. The blaze of the small lantern cast a strange, cheery light around the room that didn't seem to fit the mood in the least. There were papers strewn about and bottles lying everywhere, some broken, some still filled.

It looked as though Thorne had left in a hurry. Was he concerned that Aldric would return? That people would come after him? Why would he think that? Unless… maybe he didn't know the other mages had left? He seemed to spend most of his time here at his house, judging by the clutter.

I stood in the middle of the floor, listening intently for any sounds of life. But there were none. He seemed to be well and truly gone. Where could he have gone? I didn't know, but I would try to find out. Resolute, I rifled through the papers left scattered about. Most were from various medical journals and made little to no sense to me. However, some of these looked like… journal entries?

I picked one up and began to read.

Selene brought her daughter to me again today. She had been crying, her eyes red and puffy. I wanted to help her. Seeing her in pain was worse than being in pain myself. So I told Selene that I would try. I took blood from the girl. Time to experiment.

My gaze roved over the page, enraptured. I didn't remember this at all. My mother had brought me here to see Thorne? This would have been after I had gained my abilities. I would have been twelve—I should remember this. I continued to search through the scraps of paper on every surface, desperate to find more information. Hands trembling, I picked up a different page, this one yellowed with age.

Selene had never realized my feelings. Instead, she fell for Gregor. He's not right for her. That's probably what caused their daughter to gain such a cursed power. I was older than her, yes, but I could have taught her so much more. Been so much more.

Reading those words turned my stomach. Thorne seemed so bitter. I wasn't sure what to think. His messy scrawl caught my eye on another page. This one was another medical page, but it had Thorne's words on it.

Use Cairnard Emberleaf tea to lower fever.

Silvermint to ease breathing and help with pain.

I turned the page from front to back, desperately trying to find any other herbs that may help to ease the symptoms, but there were none. I shoved the parchment into the pocket of my cloak and resumed my search.

It was fruitless. There was nothing else. I swallowed hard and made my way through the house. I knew where I'd be most likely to find the information I needed. And before long, I found it. A heavy wooden door that had been smashed against the wall. A sound flashed through my mind, the sound of wood splintering and shouts.

I put my head into my hands, trying to breathe through the vision. My heart was racing and before I knew it, I was on my knees, curling into myself. I couldn't breathe. Rocking back and forth, darkness swirled in my vision. Fisting my hands, my nails cut into the flesh, and the pain gave me a small sliver of clarity. My parents couldn't want for me to have a full mental breakdown. They were relying on me, I told myself.

I sat there on the floor for what could have been minutes or hours before I got myself together enough to stand. My heart sank as I looked down towards the dark abyss that was the basement. An awful smell wafted up from the opening and my stomach twisted itself into knots. Surely—surely he won't be there, I told myself vehemently.

Even if he is, can you afford to wait? My mind whispered to me. And I knew I couldn't, no matter how desperately I wanted to. Taking a deep breath, I descended the stairs.

The smell grew stronger as I made my way towards the bottom of the stairs. My legs trembled like a newborn deer and I desperately kept hold of the bannister as I made my way down. I brought my cloak up to cover my nose, breathing shallowly. As I finally stopped on the dirt floor, I glanced around the room. It looked different from this angle. There was no jar of blood, just a few droplets where it had been. The needle and tubing were gone. However, I saw with rising horror that there were dark stains all over the ground. The fight between Griffin and Thorne had been even bloodier than I thought.

A metallic scent mixed with the odor of decay and mildew. Nausea roiled within me. There were splatters across the table, a handprint next to the implements, a smear on the wall there, and…

I had avoided looking long enough. Slowly, my gaze fell to the body lying on the floor a few feet away. A pit opened up in my stomach and I almost fell into the void, holding on by sheer will alone.

He was a mangled mess of wolf and human. Fur had sprouted in places, and his face had a half-formed snout. His skin had become discolored and mottled. I crouched in front of him and every sane part of me rebelled at what I was seeing. His eyes had glazed, the sunshine contained within forever dimmed by the haze of death.

Tears sprang to my eyes and I couldn't stop the harsh, racking sob that escaped me.

"I'm so sorry," I whispered between gasping breaths. "So, so sorry. I—I love you," I blurted. I couldn't tell him in life, but

I could tell him now. And I had. In some way, I had loved him. And it could have grown between us, had it not been prematurely snuffed out like a match flame.

"You deserved better than me," I murmured, tracing a hand lightly over his face, careful not to disturb him. "And because of me, you—," I couldn't bring myself to say the words, my throat too tight.

My world broke and me with it. I felt so lost. Everything I had envisioned for my life died with Griffin. And I had nothing left. What could I do without him? I was pathetic. If I had been stronger, if I hadn't been cursed with this power, I thought bitterly, he wouldn't have died. He had made me feel so safe, and yet when he needed me, I couldn't provide that same safety in return. I didn't deserve him—I never did.

Tracing the lines of his face, it was so different from how I remembered him. My mind refused to reconcile the two, the version of Griffin I had grown to care for and this version that was so twisted. But his eyes were the same. They'd lost their luster in death, but they were the same.

Curling over on myself, I broke down.

Eventually, I managed to pull myself together. My eyes were red-rimmed and my throat was raw. The odor of rot was becoming too much, bile burning in my throat. I swallowed thickly, determined not to get sick. It felt disrespectful to him, somehow. I felt so exhausted, but I could rest soon enough.

After tearing the basement apart, I shoved the table in

frustration, only to hear the faintest *clink* sound. Crouching down, I looked underneath the table and couldn't see anything, so I strained every muscle to slowly flip the table onto its side. There, I saw an indentation in the wood. Cautiously pressing my fingers against it, I found another stash of papers, along with some vials hidden in a compartment underneath the table. Unlocked, but I assumed that was just because he never thought people would actually come down here without him. Either that, or Thorne had been in too much of a rush to care. The papers had brown stains—blood, I realized.

He must have hidden these after Aldric rescued me. My gaze kept trying to slide towards Griffin, but I forced myself to stay on task. I needed to bury him, to put him to rest. It was disrespectful to leave him in—in this place. Shuffling through the papers, I found more journal entries and medical documents.

I picked up a vial and held it up until it caught the small amount of light filtering in through the dirty window. It was black as night, with some type of sediment at the bottom. It had a label—*attempt 1*. There were a few others, all with varying numbers on them, until finally there was a bottle tucked under some papers with a heavy-handed, excited scrawl. *My first success!*

I set the small ampoules aside and turned my attention to the sheafs of paper instead. Picking one at random, I started to read.

The girl's blood seems to react well enough to a little of my magic. I think my magic is strong enough to quell her ability and to cause it to become dormant. And my power is relatively harmless, so I don't see it causing any long-term effects to the girl. Selene was lucky that I cared enough not to betray her trust. Anyone else would have told the Order for sure.

After all, to have a power like hers is to introduce chaos. The last mage to have that power, well… The Order wouldn't take any chances. We barely survived the last time when all the Otherkind turned on us.

I'm going to tell Selene to bring the girl so I can try to give her some of my magic directly through an infusion. If all goes well, Selene will be so grateful to me, and maybe she'll finally realize that I would be good for her. Even if Gregor had her first.

The way Thorne spoke about my mother, as though she were a piece of meat to be passed around, it made me sick. And I don't think he even realized how disgusting he was being. There was a strange reverence to the way he spoke about her. Like despite how 'sullied' he may have thought she was, he wanted her all the same.

The medical documents were next. There were just lists of symptoms, some underlined or scratched out, but nothing of note. I shoved them into my pocket anyway, just in case it could be useful later.

At the bottom of the stack was an especially darkened page, smeared with old blood. Some words were smudged and hard to read.

…sickness. Selene was so upset with me—but how could I know?

—ings hadn't gone to plan.

Spreading slowly to—her magic and mine fought—almost like an immune system reaction.

Getting—survived, but barely. It was all I could do to keep her alive. I don't know how to help the others, but hopefully it will die out.

Most of the words were intelligible, but it looks like this is where he detailed my sickness. It was spreading, even back then? How was it I didn't know? I felt like this would have been hard to suppress. But then it occurred to me. The Order probably knew that there was a mysterious magical illness going around, and the last thing they wanted was to have it come out that it originated within Sylvan Reach. When I found out, it was just that it had spread too far for them to contain. The thought soured my stomach. They would rather risk their own people dying than to ask for help? The Order was full of awful people.

Taking all the papers I could possibly manage, I filled my pockets and carried the rest. I stopped at the racks on the walls and took any potions or vials that had names that were listed in the notes. I was going to have to walk carefully, but anything that would help, I would find a way to carry back. Taking one last look at Griffin's still form, I promised him he would be put to rest soon.

And with that, I made my way back to my parents' house.

CHAPTER 31

It took me a long, grueling couple of hours to make it back to my parents' house. The sun was setting, painting the skies in crimson and violet. I had to walk slowly, carefully, to avoid dropping any of the glass jars and vials I carried. But eventually, I made it to find Aldric pacing, practically wearing a hole in the carpet in the living room.

"Lyra, oh thank the gods," he said, moving with preternatural speed to stand in front of me, brushing his hands over my hair, my face, my neck, checking me for any injuries. I shook my head and stepped back.

"Aldric, not now. I'm fine. I'm carrying a lot of stuff," I said, shrugging my shoulders for emphasis and causing the glasses to clank against each other. Aldric quickly helped me to offload my arms, and I stretched, trying to ease the tension in my body. I'd been carrying it for so long, my body was a mess of tight muscle.

Aldric hovered as though worried I would break.

"Listen, I am fine. How have my parents been?" I asked pointedly, trying to get Aldric back on track.

"They are... the same. Not well. But alive," he reassured me. "I cleaned them up. Changed their bedding out."

Immediately, I was touched. I hadn't expected Aldric to do something like that for them. Especially since he didn't even know my parents. "Thank you. Truly," I said earnestly. "That is more than I could possibly have asked of you."

"I would do anything for you, love," Aldric said, his eyes luminescent in the dim of the house. He said it so straightforwardly, it was hard not to believe him.

Before I could respond, there was a crash outside. Aldric immediately rushed to my side, shoving me behind him. I stumbled back into the coffee table and the impact caused the glasses to rattle. My heart jumped into my throat as I whipped around to make sure none of them fell. I didn't know how much of these things I would need, or what I would have to use.

"Aldric, what was that?" I asked, adrenaline coursing through my body. I felt the first stirrings of magic returning to me, and it simmered under my skin.

He didn't answer, instead suddenly he was gone. There was a small *whoosh* and my hair whipped in front of my face as he left. I didn't think I could ever get used to him moving like that. I glanced back at the documents and bottles, then dashed out the front door after him.

I looked desperately around, trying to find where Aldric went. But he was just... gone. There was no trace of him outside.

A whisper of sound behind me sent chills up my back and I whipped around, my hair standing on edge. And to my horror, I saw a pair of glowing green eyes. The world shifted, ebbing and flowing around them. The Fae beast?

My mouth opened and closed soundlessly and I stumbled back, landing hard on my backside. A jolt of pain traveled up my spine and I sucked in a breath before scrambling to my feet. I tried to pull my magic, and I was surprised to find myself transforming into a beast so similar to the one in front of me. The world became a kaleidoscope of colors and I was disoriented. But before I could think about it, I lunged forward, claws extended and ready to rip and tear into this thing.

"Koto! Come here," a melodic female voice drifted on the wind. I whipped my head towards the sound and missed the Fae beast, crashing into the wall instead. I shook my head, trying to gain my bearings. But before I could do anything else, my beast form melted away like snow in the summer heat, and I was left trembling. I looked desperately at my hands. How could my magic fail me now?

I was going to die, I realized. After all of this.

"Hey, you!" the voice called. My gaze snapped up, and I was met with eyes as green as a spring meadow. I took in the rest of her appearance and froze. She had tanned skin, blue-black hair pulled tight on top of her head, but what drew my attention the most were her ears. Pointed. Surely this couldn't be…

"Are you one of the Fae?" I blurted. Great. Now she would definitely kill me.

"Was it the beast that gave me away or my jabby ears?" she said easily with a smoky chuckle. She wore combat leathers that clung to her curves. She wasn't what I'd expected of a Fey.

Instead of being ethereal and waif-like, she was short and curvaceous with a wry smile and a commanding aura. Although I supposed you would need it to bond with a Fey beast.

"Is—Is that your Fae beast?" I asked hesitantly.

"You bet. Her name is Koto," the Fey said, giving the beast a hefty pat on the head. It was hard to see, but it turned its head in towards her, giving her an affectionate bump.

"What are you doing here?" I asked, looking around. "The Fae aren't usually found in this area."

"Yeah, you'd figure that. But there are Fae all over the place. We just aren't out in droves, like other species of Otherkind. And we have a glamour, which is convenient. You can see me as myself because I allow you to," she said, her head cocked. Koto rubbed her side against the Fae. It was strangely like a large house cat when around its handler. I didn't know what to make of it.

"What are you and—and your creature doing here?"

Her expression hardened. "Her name is Koto. And she's not a creature. She's a Feralumin. They help us protect the Starfall Veil from… things like you," she said, looking me up and down. "And I am here to investigate. There have been some instances of sickness occurring within the Starfall Veil. Koto was able to trace the scent of the magic back here."

My mouth was agape, and I snapped it shut with a click. It could smell magic? And not just that, it could smell magic well enough to follow it across the Veil? That was hard for me to wrap my head around.

"You're a transformation mage," the Fey said flatly. "And Koto has attributed at least part of the sickness to your magic. What have you done?" she asked, a sneer on her face. "Are you trying to follow your predecessor and ruin all of Aethralis and the Veil?"

"No, no!" I insisted, holding my hands up. "It wasn't me! Or it wasn't directly me, at least," I said, stumbling over my words. "The sickness is because of another mage. His name is Thorne. He was trying to seal my power away, and the combination of his magic and mine did… something. I don't understand how, but the sickness came from that," I said.

The Fey looked skeptical, and panic spread through me. Fey were known for being incredibly powerful magical beings. They had magic long before the mage race. It was a combination of Fey and humans that had let to mages' existence. So there's no way I could be a match for her if she decided I was the source and wanted to eliminate me.

"I have proof," I said quickly, gesturing back towards the house. "I have his notes. He talks about it in his journal entries."

The Fey turned her eyes towards the house behind me before training her gaze back on me. "You know if you're lying, you know what will happen, right?"

I nodded and backed up towards the door. Koto sniffed around, sliding in the door behind me before I could pass the threshold. I heard a grunt and a hum from behind me.

"It sounds like Koto thinks you may be telling the truth.

She tells me that the scent on the parchment within ties with your own and is similar to the scent of the sickness." Despite her words, the Fae still looked skeptical.

"You need to come with me. You can join your lover while we figure this out," she said easily, as if everything were already decided. But I couldn't go anywhere.

"Wait, no!" I shouted, before I could stop myself. "My parents, they—they're sick and everyone left." I said desperately.

The Fae looked me up and down as though unimpressed. "And why should I care about that?"

"Because why would I have created this damnable plague and afflict my own parents with it? Why wouldn't I just cure them?" I asked furiously, my temper escaping me.

The Fae cocked her head as though considering my answer. She mulled the words over for so long that I began to feel antsy, shifting on my feet and glancing back to the Fae beast behind me. I had to hope that it wouldn't go to my parents.

"I can help you, if you want," she finally said. "Your words taste like the truth."

"What does that even mean?" I asked before I could stop myself.

"Let's just say that I have a penchant for knowing when I'm in the presence of liars. It doesn't mean I trust you, not in the least. But I at least believe that you're telling me the truth about this. My name is Seren," she said, striding up to me and holding her hand out expectantly. I wasn't sure what to do and held my hand out as well, and she clasped my forearm.

An eerie feeling spread from our contact, as though she

was rifling through my mind like pages in a book. I jerked my arm back, but her grip was like steel. She looked at a spot over my shoulder, and after a few moments, she let go. The scent of flowers and freshly cut grass was strong now that I was close to her. Was this the scent of her magic?

"Lyra, is it?" Seren asked, though the way she phrased it, she seemed to know the answer.

"Y-yes. How do you know?" I felt uncomfortable, exposed. Had she somehow read my mind?

"It's my specialty. I can delve into thoughts," Seren said easily, as though it wasn't anything to be worried about. But my mouth was agape. She didn't even ask, she just jumped into my mind without consideration at all.

"Before you complain, from experience, if I ask, most people freak out. It's just easier to do it and get it over with, then ask for forgiveness later," Seren said with an easy smile. I didn't know what to make of her.

Suddenly, something she said earlier snapped into place. "Wait a minute. Earlier you said you had my lover? What—how? And where is he?" I sputtered. Aldric was incredibly powerful. How had she taken him captive? I refused to think about why she would call him my lover, choosing to ignore that little tidbit.

"Ah, as a beast master, I have a bit of a special ability," she said by way of explanation.

"But I thought you just said your speciality was delving into thoughts?" I was confused. This entire situation was so surreal, I was having difficulty keeping up.

"Fae have more than one specialty. It's not like mages where we only get one ability for our whole lives. We're the original magic users, you recall. And I just used another ability to transport your lover across the Veil. No harm will have come to him," she said, holding her hands up to placate me.

I shook my head. This was a lot to take in. "How can you help me with my parents?" I asked. "I—I can't leave them behind. Everyone else is gone," I said, my voice tight with emotion.

"It's simple. The Fae have the best healers in all of Aethralis. If nothing else, they could stabilize your kin," Seren said, waving her hand as though the information was obvious.

"And why would you do that? You don't know me," I said, wrapping my arms around myself as though it would stop me from falling apart.

"We could use an original case of this sickness, anyway. Consider it a boon for the both of us," she said, shrugging. Looking over my shoulder, she called, "Koto! Grab the two older mages in there, if they're still alive."

Immediately, my hackles rose at the thought of the Feralumin getting close to my parents, who were completely helpless. "Wait! How is it going to get them?" I started after the beast regardless of how weak I still felt, but Seren's hand dropped on my shoulder like an immovable vice. I strained against her touch, trying to pry her fingers off, but I couldn't dislodge her. Just what were the Fae made of? Stone? Slowly, she pulled me back, so that I was out of the way of the door. "What the hell? Let me go! They're helpless!"

"Calm yourself, young one. Koto won't hurt them. She's

much more intelligent than your species gives credit for. Besides, don't forget. She's also a magical being," Seren said. As if to prove her point, within moments, Koto returned with my parents laid over her back like a couple of sacks of potatoes. They were still breathing and seemed unharmed. I couldn't fathom how this beast moved them on its own, but Seren was right. Koto was a magical being and likely had its own ways of doing things.

I stroked my mother's hair away from her face, her skin clammy. "We need to hurry if they're going to stay alive," I said urgently, glancing over my shoulder at Seren. She snapped her fingers and in a flash, my world twisted in on itself and my vision went black.

CHAPTER 32

My stomach violently rebelled when the world re-formed around me. I stumbled forward and fell to my knees, bile burning my throat. After I got that out of my system, I wiped my mouth and shakily got to my feet. Everything was spinning around me, and I heard a tinkling laugh. Slowly, the world righted itself. This place reminded me of the glade where I was gifted my power when I was a child. This is what the Fae lived with all the time? It's no wonder they were such powerful, magical beings.

"First time, eh? I don't blame you, it takes a while to get used to," Seren said, amusement in her voice.

"Yeah, no, I've never done anything like that before. What in the world happened?" I asked, struggling to stay on my feet despite my trembling muscles.

"I just shifted you to Starfall Veil," Seren said casually, as though she was telling me what she had for breakfast.

"It's that easy for you?" I gasped out, my mouth watering as nausea roiled yet again in my stomach. I closed my eyes and took some deep breaths, trying to calm my body.

"It takes some power, mind you. But yeah, it's pretty much that easy," Seren said with another laugh. Glad I was so funny to her, I thought with a scowl.

Finally, my equilibrium returned, and I slowly opened my eyes. Looking at the world around me, my eyes went round and my mouth dropped open in awe. The sky stretched above us, the color of the deepest sapphire, the stars bright and twinkling even in the daylight hours. There were massive trees all around us in varying hues of pastel rainbow, all reaching their branches high as though trying to grasp the atmosphere itself. The earth beneath us was saturated in color too, an unnatural-looking emerald hue. It was as though someone had taken the saturation of the world and turned it all the way up. It was almost painful to look at for too long.

Slowly, I turned in a circle, feeling the mana calling to me. It pulsed beneath my feet like a living, breathing entity. I'd never felt anything like this before. Sylvan Reach paled in comparison to the majesty of this place. Large, crystalline spires jut up from the ground in the distance, light refracting from them in mesmerizing patterns. Mist clung to the hills and valleys surrounding them, slowly making its way towards us. The very air was cleaner, more pure, scented like fresh grass.

There were strange little floating orbs of light that danced through the air like butterflies, drifting lazily about. I couldn't believe that something like this existed in Aethralis.

"Are those things… living?" I asked, watching one of the

lights as it drifted close enough for me to see the patterns swirling within it, like galaxies trapped within a bubble.

Seren smiled indulgently. "In its own way, yes. They're called Stardrops. Pieces of ancient magic that never quite settled into the earth here. They're quite beautiful, mostly harmless. As long as you don't touch them, at least." She walked over and blew a breath of air against the Stardrop. It drifted helplessly away, spinning delicately through the trees. I felt almost sad as it fell out of view.

"What—how—what?" I sputtered uselessly. I didn't even know what to say, blinded by the beauty of this place as I was.

"Yeah, I know. It's pretty, huh?" Seren said before grabbing my arm and leading me towards the crystal spires. "We need to go there so you can reunite with your boy toy," she said with a wry smile. "Your parents are already there, likely being attended to by Willow."

"What is that place?" I said after I could formulate proper sentences.

"It's Everall. The royal city," she explained. "Luckily for you, your new friend is a member of the royal guard. Or unluckily, I suppose, depending on how you look at it," she said with another broad smile. She seemed way too easy-going for this type of job.

"What friend? Why the royal city?" I asked, my palms starting to sweat.

"Why, me, of course," she said with another musical laugh. "It's like I said. We need to figure out what's causing this sickness, so the royal family is involved. And I think it would be good to bring you to them," she said, continuing to drag me along. I started to follow behind her, and she released her heavy grip on my arm.

"Whatever it will take," I murmured. "Thank you, Seren."

"For what? You can't leave Starfall Veil without me, so I've basically taken you prisoner, you know," Seren said, her vibrant green eyes landing on me with a skeptical look.

"For helping my parents. For believing me, not attacking me, a lot of things," I said, returning her gaze earnestly. "Although you should know, Aldric—the man who was with me—isn't my lover." I don't know why I felt the need to correct her, but I did.

That took her by surprise. "Really? But you're bonded," she said incredulously.

"Yeah, he had to do that to save my life," I said, shrugging my shoulders. "The mage who did this—," I started, but she cut me off.

"No, not like a paltry blood bond. You're *bonded*," she said, putting strange emphasis on the word. Something about the way she said it had my stomach twisting itself in knots. What wasn't she saying?

"Yes, I know, Aldric told me. It's from him having my blood and me having some of his," I said warily. Why was she acting strange about this?

Seren grasped her chin in one hand, tapping her cheek with her index finger. She opened her mouth, then closed it again as if she thought better of it and shook her head. Her expression closed off as effectively as shutting a door. "I'm not worried about that right now. We'll see what comes of it," she said cryptically. "We have to get to Everall."

My feet were aching when I finally decided to ask, "Can't you just, you know, magic us there somehow?" I was so tired of walking.

"No. I can magic us across the Veil, but not to the royal city. That wouldn't exactly be very secure," she said with a chuckle. She was strangely cheery for a guard. "The city is warded. I won't explain further. You don't need to know."

I nodded. That did make sense. But at the same time, this was awful. Irritation and anxiety flared within me in equal parts. I didn't know what was happening with Aldric. I didn't know what was happening with my parents. There was just too much I didn't understand.

"Aldric is there, right?" I asked. I wasn't sure if she would answer, but I needed to know.

"Yes, bitey boy is there," Seren said, rolling her eyes. She tucked a loose strand of hair behind her ear.

"Bitey boy?" I asked, caught by surprise. A giggle escaped me despite myself.

"Yes. You should have seen the way he charged at me. He was like a demon," she said seriously. "If I'd been any slower moving him across the Veil, I'd have died. But luckily, I wasn't unprepared. I had a team waiting for me on the other side who captured him and brought him to Everall."

My heart constricted painfully. "Did they—is he hurt?" I asked. The thought of him being in pain caused me more distress than I wanted to admit.

Seren shrugged, trudging through the brush to another path.

I refused to let this die, though. "Is he? Tell me. I need to know," I insisted.

Rolling her eyes, Seren sighed as though this was the most ridiculous question to ask. "He's only as injured as he needed to be to be captured. My team wouldn't hurt him needlessly, despite what you may think of us."

For whatever reason, that made me feel strangely guilty, but I kept my mouth shut. I wasn't about to apologize.

The silence between us grew heavier with each step we took towards Everall, broken only by the strange calls of the creatures found in the Veil. Every once in a while, I glimpsed movement in the shadows between the trees—fleeting forms that may have been animals or something else entirely. There was no way to know, and I wasn't going to ask. There was a strange, dreamlike quality to this realm. But was it really a dream, or a nightmare? I would soon find out.

We were making good time. The spires were climbing towards the sky, impossibly high and borderline painful to look at with the way they caught the sunlight. Suddenly, Seren blurted, "I can't say if the vampire is seriously hurt. But I think I did a pretty good job sending him right into their trap, so hopefully they just caught him by surprise."

I said nothing. My hands shook with anxiety and I wrung them together, gripping my fingers tight. I clumsily drew on the bond. It was harder to do it on purpose, and especially with us being so far apart, but I vaguely felt a sense of anger and… fear.

What could he be afraid of? I tried to send reassurance through the bond, and it was almost like he was calling out to me from across the ocean. Just a hint of a thought that seemed to say my name.

The feeling was disorienting, but a sense of relief filled me. I wasn't sure if it was mine or Aldric's or both, but at least he was alive. I didn't want to admit how much comfort that brought me. The now-familiar pang of guilt stabbed me at the thought, and I shoved those feelings down. Now was not the time.

Seren was watching me curiously, as though she knew what was going through my mind. And gods, maybe she did? I had no idea how her power worked. Could she feel the bond with Aldric if we were to touch? She must, because she knew it existed. That made me feel... strangely violated. The bond I shared with Aldric was private. The thought of her feeling it, maybe feeling the emotions through it, felt too raw. Too naked. But I didn't have the nerve to ask. We continued our trek in silence.

Eventually, we crossed from dirt path to road. It was made of a nice, white cobblestone. We were almost in the city. Silence had fallen between us, neither of us deigning to break it. I didn't know what to say, and Seren just seemed bored trekking with me across the valley. I glanced back at where we'd come. The forest was beautiful, all-encompassing. It went as far as the eye could see, except within the city walls. There was a wall of trees surrounding it, and then just more of those crystalline structures.

I was surprised to see that it looked like those were the buildings used in the city. They had been carved into houses, apartments, rooms. I'd never seen anything like it. The city itself seemed carved of nature. It resonated with something deep inside of me. The entire walk, I'd felt the earth humming beneath our feet, the magic barely contained within it. And this is where mages had originated. How did the first humans come here? Or were they brought here against their will? I wondered absently.

They couldn't cross the Starfall Veil on their own. Or maybe the worlds were one back then? I resolved to learn more about this place. Did true transformation originate here? Or was it some kind of magical mutation over time? Did they have any information about what my powers could do? What my limits are? How I can learn to better control it?

"Prepare yourself," Seren commanded suddenly, breaking me away from my thoughts. I immediately steeled myself, caught by surprise. We passed some invisible threshold, and it felt as though I was being skinned alive. The force of the barrier was insane. My own magic blustered in response, stretching my muscles and ligaments from the inside until I felt like I was being ripped apart.

A scream dimly came into focus and I realized it was coming from me. Seren was pulling me along quickly because I couldn't bring myself to keep walking. After making it further inside the city, the feeling dissipated enough to let me breathe.

"I'm surprised you felt that so strongly," Seren said, giving me a moment to compose myself. "Most people find it very uncomfortable, but not painful."

"I—I felt like I was coming apart," I ground out while trying to shove my magic back down into a box inside of me so that I could keep going.

"Strange," Seren murmured thoughtfully, but she said nothing else.

After a couple of minutes, I straightened my spine and loosed a deep breath. I had to keep going. "Can you take me to Aldric?" I said.

"After we meet with the royal family, you will be reunited with your… friend," she said.

"Why are you saying it like that?" I asked, scowling.

"No reason. Let's go," she said, starting to reach for me again before I danced out of her reach and followed where she pointed. She let her arm drop with a grin, and I resolved to keep out of her hands as much as possible. I didn't trust anyone that could read my thoughts.

My gaze tracked with her point, and my mouth fell open. It was a huge, crystalline castle that looked as though it had been carved from an enormous diamond. I couldn't look at it for long, the sun glinting off of the facets of the structure blinding. How could they live in places like these? How comfortable could it really be? Is this what all the Fae cities were like?

As we got closer, the hair on my neck stood up. We were slowly being surrounded by Fae in different armor, from plate armor to leather. They carried a variety of weapons as well. Some had no weapon at all, but I knew better than to underestimate them. Who knows what types of magic they could wield? Even Mages who went unarmed could be formidable if they were an elemental specialist.

The Fae glanced amongst each other as they approached me and I heard murmuring, their faces a mixture of fear and disgust. What did they think they knew about me? What did they know about transformation magic? I had to wonder what stories had been told here. There was no mention in the tales told of the last transformation mage about Starfall Veil. Did they do something here too? Something that we didn't know?

I kept my gaze trained forward, determined not to show any weakness. The Fae had a completely different culture than I was accustomed to, and I was afraid of saying or doing the wrong thing. Seren was proof enough of the difference between mages and Fae.

Before long, we were at the bottom of a flight of sparkling steps. Slowly looking up, my calves balked at the thought of climbing that many stairs, but I was determined not to falter.

The sound of my boots on the gemstones was soon overshadowed by the many footsteps of those surrounding Seren and I. Why were there so many? I had to wonder. But then again, if they thought I was the mastermind behind some horrible plague, it made sense. Who knows what kind of magic I could unleash on them? What kind of horrible malady or illness? Honestly, it was almost flattering how much caution they were using.

My power continued to simmer just below the surface despite my attempts to tamp it down. Almost like it sensed that there was something strange, but that's odd because it almost makes it sound alive. In a way, I supposed it was. All magic drew from the earth. And the earth was a living thing. That made the Fae so incredibly powerful. They were bonded to the world around them more than the rest of the Otherkind.

Finally, we reached the top of the stairs and my muscles were screaming, but I didn't let it show. I squinted against the brightness of the castle, and Seren again gripped my upper arm and dragged me inside.

Time to enter the belly of the beast and hope for the best.

CHAPTER 33

The inside of the castle was surprisingly welcoming, despite the intensity of the power within. There were plants everywhere, the scent of growth and freshly turned earth filling the air. The furniture was understated, with tones of green and brown. The rooms were large, but despite that, they felt somehow cozy.

It truly felt like a place that would be lovely to take a book and curl up to read on one of the many plush chairs that dotted the rooms we passed. I had little time to admire the decor as Seren continued to drag me along, down hallways, up a flight of stairs, down more hallways, until finally stopping before a large set of double doors.

The doors were ornate, heavy black oak doors with carvings of vines intertwining from top to bottom. There were jeweled flowers blooming on each of the vines in a myriad of colors. It looked like the entrance to a throne room befitting of spring.

Here, more than anywhere, the walls sang with ancient magicks. It wasn't a gentle hum like the power of Sylvan Reach.

This was something wild, something untamed and immense. Each facet of the walls showed a different scene as the light shone through. Some were spring meadows, flowers of all colors and types blooming brightly. Others were emanating with a winter chill, the ground covered in snow and the trees barren. And in yet another still, the summer sun blazed in the sky, the plants growing wild and untamed. How could a place this beautiful and terrifying exist?

Despite myself, I stood to admire this place and just what it meant, taking a deep breath and steeling myself for what was to come. Above us, the ceiling opened to a sky of impossible stars. We were inside of a huge chunk of crystal, and yet it was like the brightest night. The constellations swirled in mesmerizing patterns I'd never seen. Seren surprisingly gave me a moment to collect myself. Within a minute, though, she nodded to the guards at either side of the doors and, with barely a whisper, the doors slowly opened. My heart felt like it was in a vice.

Meeting with Fae royalty would either help to save Aethralis—or doom it.

As I stepped over the threshold, I could faintly feel Aldric's presence somewhere within these walls. There was the barest hint of his emotions coming through, and I swallowed hard. Was he okay? What were they doing to him? My magic crawled beneath my skin as if in rebellion of the mana that surrounded us in this place. This castle was saturated with powerful energy. No wonder the Fae royals opted to make this their home.

As Seren led me along, I was taken aback by the sight that

greeted me. There were two beautiful thrones sat upon a dais that both looked as though they were growing out of the ground itself. They were made of interweaving gray branches, and on the larger of the two, lovely pink flowers bloomed. The seat was so tightly woven that there were no gaps, but there was also a cushion of leaves and flower petals that looked surprisingly soft.

The smaller of the two thrones had maple leaves in a wash of autumn colors growing from it, a pleasant contrast to the other seat. Seated upon these two thrones were a couple so heart-achingly beautiful that it was uncomfortable to look at them for too long. They both had white-blonde hair. The King looked to be sculpted by the gods themselves with aristocratic features, clean-shaven and tall. He had bright blue eyes and his skin was lightly tanned, the same as Seren's. He wore a pair of white fitted pants and a surprisingly simple white linen shirt. Sat upon his head was a crown of interweaving branches and a round ruby at the center.

Power radiated from the King in waves, the very air around him seeming to bend towards him like a black hole. It felt as ancient as the world itself, as immovable as a mountain. Just how old was he? Or was this the power that came with being a royal? It was no wonder that any mention of the Fae royalty was spoken with an undercurrent of fear and reverence.

The Queen looked somewhat similar to him, also tall and lithe with angelic features. She had chocolaty brown eyes that looked warm and inviting. She wore a mint colored goddess gown with a golden braided belt around her waist. Atop her head was a matching crown to the King's. They were an incredibly attractive couple. Her power whispered along my skin like an autumn breeze, the bite of winter's chill just beneath. Once I could pry my eyes away from those two, I quickly glanced around the room.

Arranged artfully around the room were rows of chairs upon which were seated various types of Fae. Nobility, I had to assume, given their opulent garb. There were a myriad of expressions playing across their faces, from sneers to open curiosity.

I was surprised at how different the Fae could look. Some were short and stout, others long and lithe. Their features were also heavily different from one another, some with white, milky eyes that looked as though they were blind, others with eyes black as night and dotted with stars. Some had wings, some fins. I didn't know there were so many types of Fae. Murmurs spread through the crowd. I only caught bits and pieces, but it was enough to twist my stomach into knots.

"Is it true? A transformation mage?"

"The vampire's pet."

"A horrible omen…"

Seren stopped just behind me and when I looked over my shoulder at her, she gave me a gentle shove towards the dais. I lowered my head respectfully, but my mind was racing. What did I say? What did I do? How could I help them understand that I wasn't behind this? I stood paralyzed, but before I could word vomit an excuse, the King's voice rang out.

"You are a transformation mage," he said, his voice deep and melodic. It was not a question. The timbre of his voice sent a wave of goosebumps pebbling up on my flesh. I could definitely tell he was royalty. The way he spoke brokered no arguments.

I nodded silently.

"Am I to understand that your magic is the cause of this sickness spreading across the Starfall Veil and Aethralis?" he asked, his head cocked. The Queen strode over to him and placed her hand on his arm. He looked at her and they seemed to communicate something wordlessly between them. Was this her ability, or was it some bond between them?

The Queen's voice was soft, seductive. "Seren has told me that it is not you, but your magic combined with another." How had they communicated this? I was with Seren this entire time. The Fae must be more powerful than I realized. Would I be able to escape if I had to? Could I do anything against beings like this?

I nodded again, waves of my hair falling in front of my face. I hurriedly tucked it behind an ear. "Yes. I was recently captured by this other mage. He said he was trying to cause my ability to become dormant when I was a child, but it failed. The sickness was a result." I realized how crazy that sounded as soon as the words left my mouth, but it was the truth, so I had to hope they believed it.

"And where is this other mage?" the King asked. He casually slid an arm around the Queen's waist. They were a united front, but I refused to cow beneath them as they looked down at me.

"I'm not sure, Highness. He almost drained me of all of my blood and I was rescued by… my friend," I said hesitantly. Yes, Aldric was my friend. He could be nothing more, no matter how he made me feel. I couldn't…I couldn't lose someone else. Griffin's glazed-over eyes flashed across my mind, and I viciously shoved the image away. I had to focus.

"Ah, yes. The vampire," the King said, his nose wrinkled in distaste. Irritation flared in me, unbidden. What did he have against Aldric? "Tell me more about this other mage," he commanded.

Despite my anger, I did. I told as much information as I knew. Everything about him knowing my parents and studying my ability, to what I knew of the plague and how he had attempted to cure it unsuccessfully thus far. Then I told them about how he stole my blood, but I omitted Griffin. It just… it felt too raw to talk about.

Seren came to stand next to me at the end of my story when I described going back to help my parents. "In this, she tells the truth," Seren said. She held several sheafs of paper. "These were in the home of her kin, along with several bottles and vials that were scented with the magic of the other mage, Thorne."

"How did you get those? I don't recall you going in the house," I blurted. Embarrassment colored my cheeks when she just winked at me and murmured, "I've more abilities than you realize." I should have known. She transported me across the Veil like it was nothing. How much more difficult could it be for her to do the same with some pieces of paper?

The King beckoned Seren forward, and she handed him the parchment. The room was tense and silent as his eyes roved over the words written there. He was quiet for several long moments as he glanced between the pages and my face. I clenched and unclenched my hands over and over under my cloak.

The King handed the documents over to the Queen, who did the same, silently reading. She again touched his arm once she finished, and they had more of that strange wordless communication. The King nodded suddenly, and they both turned in unison towards me.

"We will need to study your power. Until we can determine how this plague has come into being, you will stay here at the castle. We will reunite you with your bonded one in the keep until we determine you are not a threat," the King said, his voice booming.

The words had barely left his mouth when the guards converged on me, painfully wrenching my arms behind my back. Before I knew it, my cloak was wrenched from my body, my arms were manacled with heavy chains, and there was a collar around my neck connecting to the weight around my wrists.

A chill spread across my body at the points that the metal touched my skin. They were almost black, with white etching all along the length of the chain in a language I didn't understand. The language of the Fae? Were these manacles enchanted somehow? I'd never felt anything like this. My magic dulled to the barest whisper within me, and I had to fight to feel it at all. It felt as though ethereal fingers of frost were grasping it away from me.

Through our bond, I felt a tug. Aldric must have sensed my distress even through the weak connection. I tried to reach out to him, but the connection felt as though it was withering away. Panic seized me.

A shocked gasp escaped my lips, and instinctively I tried to pull my wrists apart, causing painful pressure at my throat as the metal bit into my skin. Looking around in desperation, I found no allies. A few of the Fae had a delighted smile, but most seemed bored and uninterested. My gaze fell on Seren, who had a pitying look on her face, but carefully masked that expression as she turned to the royal Fae and held a fist over her heart in salute.

"As you wish, Highnesses. I will escort the prisoner myself," she said, her voice resolute.

"Wait!" I cried. "Where are my parents? Are they okay?"

But no one responded. It was like I had said nothing at all. A wrinkle appeared between Seren's eyes at my words, but she kept her mouth shut. The King waved his hand in dismissal, and Seren took my elbow, dragging me behind her despite my struggling. Tears pricked my eyes, but I refused to let them fall. I could not show weakness here. Before long, we were descending into the bowels of the castle. I'd survived so much so far, I wouldn't let this break me. Aldric had to be waiting below. Whatever came next, I wouldn't face it alone.

CHAPTER 34

We descended lower and lower, the crystals of the wall giving way to stone. The temperature dropped until I could see my breath puff out in front of me. I had thought it would be warm underground, but evidently not here. I glanced at Seren, but she kept her eyes trained forward. There were many footsteps echoing out behind us as well, so it wasn't a good time to ask her questions despite how the words itched at the back of my throat.

Eventually, we reached what appeared to be the very bottom keep of the castle. The rocks making up the floor and walls were rough and covered in moss. Water leaked through in some intersections of stone, making the halls smell of stale water and mold. This did not seem befitting of royalty, but maybe that was the point. You knew better than to cross them or risk becoming ill in a dungeon like this.

I shuddered as the chill descended over my skin, and I immediately missed my cloak. Seren took a deep breath and continued to drag me down hallway after hallway, the walls giving way to cells. Some had heavy wood doors with slits and food pass boxes, others were more like what I had expected: reinforced iron bars. The scent of waste and sweat filled the air, and I wrinkled my nose in distaste.

As we navigated through what seemed like a maze of hallways, I slowly felt a bit more emotion through the bond. Was I getting closer to Aldric? I felt—pain. Regret. Fear. I was on edge. What had they done to him? Why was he down here? Seren looked almost apologetic as we stopped beneath one of the reinforced iron doors.

"This will be your home for the next little while," she said softly. Her voice was tinged with… regret? Why? "I'll ensure that you get fed on time, at least."

With those words, she opened the door with an awful screech of metal on metal and led me inside. There was a bare cot with a thin brown blanket, a sink on the far wall, and a small toilet. No door or walls for the bathroom. My cheeks heated at the thought of having no privacy at all in this place.

That was a form of torture in itself, I thought. I turned back towards Seren, pleading with my eyes. It wasn't likely that she could help me, but she *knew* I was being honest. That it wasn't my fault. But she deliberately avoided eye contact and backed out of the cell, the door clanging shut with finality. I looked on in horror as all the guards and Seren left without saying another word. Then it was just the sound of my blood ringing in my ears and a gentle dripping sound.

I turned to watch them walk away, but something else caught my gaze and I sucked in a shocked breath. In the cell across from mine was Aldric. He was manacled to the wall, a collar and chain around his neck. Blood seeped from beneath the metal and his head lolled.

"Aldric!" I screamed before I could stop myself, pressing myself against the bars. But I couldn't move my hands, the chains straining painfully against my body. I tried to call my magic, but the white writing on the manacles pulsed, repelling my ability to draw on my abilities. Instead, the power painfully stretched beneath my skin and it felt as though my body was being pulled apart from the inside. An agonized cry escaped me and I fell to my knees, shoving my magic back down deep.

Just what the hell was *that*? At the sound of my voice, Aldric's head snapped up, and I was heartbroken to see a scabbed, split lip and a black eye that was swollen almost completely shut. "Fan— fancy meeting you here," Aldric murmured, his throat sounding impossibly dry and his voice cracked. He cleared his throat. Then he looked at me seriously, a silver of moonlight showing between his swollen lids. His voice was raspy and thin as he said, "I was so worried, love. I am glad to see you."

Relief made my body weak and if I wasn't already on the ground, I would have been just then. "I was scared for a moment that you were—that they had—," I couldn't bring myself to say it.

A wry smile twisted Aldric's lips, and I was saddened to see it open the cut on his lip, blood dribbling down his chin. His tongue darted out to catch it, leaving a smear of red. "I'm happy that you care," he said with a hint of teasing. Despite his attempt at being light-hearted, he looked awful. Leaning against the cold metal of the cell wall, I got to my feet. An ache grew in my chest and I began to pace, trying to work out this anxious energy that had me wrapped in its fist.

"Of course I care! How could I not?" I retorted, incensed. This whole situation had me pissed off. I'm in some ridiculous Fae realm that I can't leave on my own. Aldric was hurt to some unknown degree, and my magic was bound somehow and unusable.

"What happened to you?" I asked, my eyes roving over his body. His shirt had been removed or cut off, and bloody cuts marred his skin. He still wore his black fitted pants, so it was hard to tell if he'd been injured on his legs at all. His boots were gone, his feet bare and dirty.

"Let's just say I didn't go willingly and paid the price," he murmured with a hoarse chuckle. The sound trailed off into nothing, leaving us in silence.

His gaze was trained on me with an almost unnerving intensity, and I felt a whisper of hunger through the bond. Dread filled me as I realized I didn't know the last time that Aldric had fed. And it's not like I could feed him, unable to reach him or to use my magic to transform into something small enough to fit through the bars.

What were we going to do?

Aldric's eyes gleamed in the dim light. As I focused on the

sensations coming through our bond, I realized it was worse than I thought. A mix of need and weakness flowed between us, and it hit me. Aldric needed blood—and soon.

"Lyra," he whispered, his voice raw, guttural. "I don't know how long I can—" The words never left his mouth, but his eyes told me all I needed to know. A shadow I'd never seen before lurked in his gaze, swirling in their depths.

Hunger rolled off him in waves, dark and primal, ancient and all-encompassing. Would it consume him entirely until nothing of Aldric was left but a mindless beast? I felt powerless to help, and I stopped my pacing, pressing my body against the bars as though I could phase through them and reach him, feed him as much life-sustaining blood as he needed.

Slowly, I sank down to my knees in the dank cell, the trauma of the last few days wearing on my body. Aldric strained against his bonds. "Lyra, are you okay?" he asked, panic clear in his tone. "Gods damn these bonds," he snarled.

"I'm okay," I murmured, trying to sound reassuring. "Just tired."

As the weight of the chains pulled me down, I heard footsteps approaching. It felt as though there were a tug inside of me, and my magic responded. Pain sang through my body, and I fought to breathe through it. Was there a threshold I could reach? Surpass? As my power pulsed within, slowly, a bright glow appeared on the manacles chaining me. It appeared to respond to my mana.

"Interesting, isn't it?" Seren asked from outside my cell, startling me. The glow slowly subsided, leaving us back in the dim lighting of the keep.

Aldric hissed, pulling heavily on his restraints and filling the air with the sound of metal on metal as he pulled the chains against the anchor. "Let her go!" he roared, his eyes wild, shining like liquid mercury. Hunger was already loosening his restraint. I'd never seen him act like this before.

Seren ignored him, instead turning to face me. "Your magic… we've only seen something like it once before, thousands of years ago. And as I'm sure you know, the other… well, they weren't exactly a good person. The Fae put a stop to it before Aethralis could fall completely to ruin. Let's hope this isn't a repeat of past events," she murmured.

I sent reassurance through our bond and Aldric quieted, exhaustion flowing back to me. Maybe if I could convince Seren to help us… we would have a chance.

"What does it mean?" I asked, my voice barely above a whisper.

Seren's eyes met mine, bright with curiosity. "It means, Lyra, that you may just be more important to the fate of both of our realms than anyone realized." She then paused, pursing her lips and glancing over her shoulder at Aldric. I wondered if she could sense the state he was in. Her expression grew grave. "The King and Queen will soon request your presence. They've found something in Thorne's journal. I just wanted to let you know. Prepare yourself." And with those cryptic words, she turned on her heel and left, leaving just Aldric and I once again.

An emotion I couldn't name—or one I didn't dare to—surged through our bond, and I turned to meet Aldric's gaze. It was heady with unspoken words, the silver of his eyes glowing like moonlight itself was contained within, illuminating the darkness between us. At that moment, I made a silent vow. I would find a way to get both of us out of this. Aldric would not die here. I would not allow it. I would uncover the truth of my magic, stop Thorne, and save Aethralis.

And gods help anyone who dared to try to stop me.

S.D. GREDELL